The Reclaimer

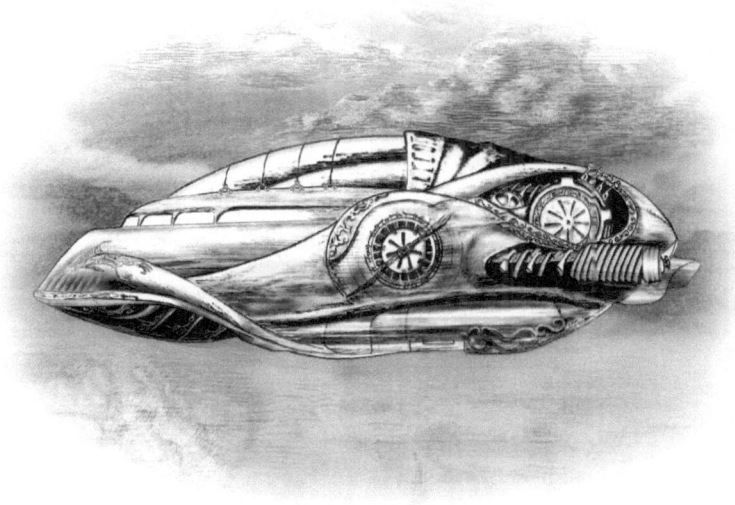

Ryan Dunlap

First Printing, December 2014
Copyright © 2014 by Ryan Dunlap
All rights reserved.
ISBN-10: 0-9859976-2-1
ISBN-13: 978-0-9859976-2-5

First Edition.

Printed in the United States of America

Front cover art by Grant Cooley (www.GrantCooley.com)
Illustration & back cover art by Marisa Draeger (mgdportraits.com)
Cover design by Phil Earnest (www.PhilEarnest.com)

www.TheWindMerchant.com

The text type was set in Adobe Caslon Pro

For Mom and Dad, because you taught me what is possible with enough hard work and dedication.

ACKNOWLEDGEMENTS

There are so many people I'd like to thank for helping continue the story of Ras Veir and Callie Tourbillon. My wife is always an inspiration, and my character banter would be terribly dull if she didn't keep me on my toes. Sarah, I love you. Life changed forever during the writing of this book (*for the better*), and keeping up the energy to stay creative wouldn't happen without your help.

David Cole has been an incredible editor. Patient and steadfast, he will someday educate me on the proper usage of gerunds and the pitfalls of dangling participles. The fact that he is one of the smartest and most loyal men I know makes me feel lucky to have him in my corner.

Grant Cooley created an original piece of art for the cover. Last time I wrote a scene in *The Wind Merchant* inspired by his artwork, this time I got the distinct honor of having an established scene come to life with his brush. Marisa Draeger brought the illustration of The Kingfisher to life in a fun way, giving it detail that inspired some story elements. Phil Earnest is a Photoshop master. I never dare question what he's doing, I just wait a few moments for him to make things even more awesome.

Amber Hezlep spent almost a year of her life working with me on the accompanying children's book, *The Littlest Clockwork*, and for that I am grateful. Chuck Beard got my books on real shelf space, and if you're in Nashville, you should check out East Side Story.

I want to thank my alpha and beta readers for spending so much time in a world that sometimes feels larger than what can fit inside my head. Getting feedback at such an early stage helps me stay on track, and I'm incredibly grateful to the following readers and friends: Lory Dunlap, Sarah Dunlap, Mark Gullickson, Amber Hezlep, Ola Jordan, Rachel Long, and Stan Meador.

To everyone who made *The Wind Merchant* a reality by supporting its creation, I can't thank all of you enough. Everyone who backed the original campaign made an investment in my creative endeavors, and every time I put pen to page I'm happy to know that I'm writing for you. I'm excited to round out this trilogy with *The Elsewhere Knight*, and can't wait to share the full story with everyone.

The cast and crew of *Greyscale* informed much of this book for me. Knowing what it's like to have a group of amazing people to work with brought me to the heart of this tale. I am honored to have worked with you all.

Once more, at the risk of sounding cliche, I must chiefly give thanks to the Originator of Creativity and Story, who I am daily inspired by. Without Christ, I am nothing.

Sincerely,
Ryan Dunlap

The Reclaimer

Prologue

At best, the plan was ill-advised, hastily crafted, and short sighted.

It had to work.

The twisting knot in Dayus Ofanim's stomach overwhelmed any solace he might have gleaned from the field of glinting stars above. As of late, their promise of something grander than the day's troubles had faded to a whisper. He clasped the tip of his wide-brimmed hat, focusing his attention on the world below.

The city of Bogues had been abuzz with activity since Dayus' arrival just before sundown. Aside from the initial Illorian assault three years prior, the city-turned-war camp had remained mercifully intact throughout The Clockwork War.

From the former mayor's balcony, Dayus watched the subjugated men and women haul Elder supplies beneath the streetlights. Despite the powered suits the Illorians wore, the natives bore the brunt of the preparation work.

Dayus sighed. No amount of preparation would suffice for what hung on the horizon. The war across Imago had taken its toll, and pushing the Elders back into a retreat came with a price. The war was merely a piece of a larger picture, one which would accrue a debt he wished he could ignore.

Only several days prior Halcyon Napier had effectively routed the Illorians at the Battle of Treding. Bogues remained the Elders' final stronghold, but that would soon change.

Ornate chandeliers chimed out a faint tune on the breeze. Light bounced from the crystal in odd reflections, piercing most of the shadows on the third-story patio. A glance to the left at the two men in mechanical Elder-suits standing guard at the mansion's entrance reminded Dayus that this was in fact his open-air prison. He reached up and adjusted the thin chain around his neck out of habit, seeking from its familiar braided texture the comfort that he hadn't been able to find in the stars above.

"Do you miss Illoria, turncoat?" A filtered voice from behind Dayus disturbed the peace of the crisp night. Whirring clicks and huffs of steam preceded heavy footfalls that shook the balcony.

"I cannot say it ever felt like home," Dayus said, paying more attention to the damage the Elder suit did to the marble flooring than the hulking machine itself coming to rest beside him.

Silence hung for a moment. "You do not know what you threaten by helping these people."

"You are all sons of Imago," Dayus said. "You would do well to remember this before the war ends tonight, General."

The Elder chuffed. "This war is far from over."

"In some ways." Dayus doubted the General knew the half of it, fighting a war for reasons only those at the top of the Illorian Council knew. It was a shame so many had to find themselves in the crossfire. "You operate on too many assumptions."

"Enlighten me, traitor," the Elder said, canting his helmeted head.

"I never left Illoria's service—"

"I'd say giving the Outsiders our technology falls well outside the call of duty," the General said.

"I can see how it might appear as such," Dayus said. "But my captain is not my commander."

"Are you telling me that you're a spy?" The General leaned forward, inducing Dayus to turn away from the glowing eyes.

"Sometimes one has to play the long odds. Plain speech is not always becoming," Dayus said, feeling the cool iron railing beneath his grip. He glanced at the ground thirty feet below, then began walking along the edge of the balcony away from the General.

"You are in no position to dance with subtlety." The mechanical voice took a hard edge of distortion as the suit failed to properly process the increased volume. "Why are you here?"

"I came to deliver a message."

"I didn't take you for a pawn."

Dayus turned to face the General. "I have come to inform you that in less than one hour's time, Halcyon Napier will lead the First Airship Brigade in an attack on Bogues."

"And you volunteered to be here when it happens?"

Dayus shook his head. "I don't believe you understand my meaning," he said, walking back toward the General until the two stood toe to toe. He adjusted his hat so the glow of the machine's eyes met his. "No, I'm telling you that if you want to survive this war, you and your men will leave before they arrive. You weren't at the battle over Treding. I was."

A low, rhythmic sound akin to a chuckle filled the open air. "Whose side are you on?"

Dayus stared into the glow of the Elder's eyes, his expression blank. "Hope's."

In the distance, a green flare illuminated the edge of the city. The unmistakable sound of a fleet's worth of Windstrider engines reverberated throughout Bogues, followed by several faint pops of cannon fire.

The howl of incoming ballistics pierced the night, their growing shrieks faint at first. Dayus took a deep breath, bracing himself for impact. An instant later, something smashed into the mansion's wall next to the balcony. The building shook, prompting Dayus to tighten his grasp on the handrail. Airship engines faded into the distance, their black silhouettes shrinking in the night's sky. The barrage ended as quickly as it had begun, harming the city little but leaving the people on the street in shock and confusion.

The damage from the strike was minimal, but out of the scar in the wall, a small, green ember of light flitted onto the wind. The flicker of light cast unnatural shadows as it floated away, lazily making its way toward one of the balcony guards. The ember danced about the Elder's head, ignoring the man's best attempts to swat it away. With a swirl, it slipped into the neck joint of the metal suit.

"Get it out!" the guard screamed as the white lights inside his helmet flashed green.

With an unholy sound, the guard's suit of armor bulged outward, retaining most of a concussive blast that still managed to knock

Dayus onto his back. The balcony shuddered. Dayus lifted his head and saw a gaping hole in the mansion's wall where the guard once stood, a haphazard pile of Illorian machinery now his memorial.

The ember emerged from the destroyed Elder suit twice as large, danced with its shadow counterpart across the open entrance of the mansion, then found its way into the armor of the other guard. Shouts of panic competed with this grotesque display for Dayus' attention; he looked out at the terrified citizens of Bogues through the balcony railing.

Explosions rocked through the city square below in a ripple effect of devastation. One by one, flittering lights shot through the men and women in the streets, erupting them in washes of green.

As one man detonated from his proximity to the small orb, a half dozen men nearby rocketed away from him. Some bowled into other groups of men and women while others were thrown into buildings, sending the structures crumbling in their wake; yet others hurtled into balls of green Energy and themselves erupted, their essence immediately feeding into the convergence of destruction.

The balcony shook again, then lurched as the remaining Elder guard evaporated with a screech. Dayus' ears rang loudly, mercifully numbing him to the screams of terror below. He felt large metal hands grasp him roughly by the shoulders as the structure attached to the mansion began to collapse.

"What have you done? You're killing both sides," the General shouted, wrapping his free arm around the metal railing, crumpling it in his grasp. His helmet swiveled as the ball of Energy exited the empty shell of the guard's armor. With his free hand, he hoisted Dayus up as a shield between himself and the small orb.

The light flew toward Dayus, who clutched at the chain around his neck, but the Convergence stopped mere inches from his face, pausing almost as if to consider the being before it. Dayus blinked to clear his head, but before he could reconcile the moment, the sphere whipped around him and into the General's mechanical suit.

Losing his grip on Dayus, the General ripped off his helmet, treating Dayus to a full view of the frightened man awash in green. The man erupted with a blast of Energy, throwing Dayus back into the mayor's mansion just as the balcony crumbled.

The ever growing orb hung in the air, now as large as a man's head, then bobbed gently in the breeze as though nothing were out of the ordinary.

"Aether preserve us," Dayus said softly, the words distorted to his own ears.

The city square lay dormant aside from the crackling fires, devoid of targets for the newborn Convergences to feed upon. All around, dark smoke did its best to choke out the starry night's sky as it joined in with newly formed roiling clouds.

Muffled screams and explosions added to the rising horror of the night. The orb flitted away to join its brethren in chasing down every man, woman, and child in their attempts to escape the city as it burned to the ground.

This was only the beginning. One of many. Too many. The fires would consume their way around the world, as was their nature. *Hopefully*, Dayus thought, *hopefully history will forget who held the match this time.*

At best, the plan was ill-advised, hastily crafted, and short sighted.

It had to work.

CHAPTER ONE
The Gatekeeper

ONE HUNDRED YEARS LATER.

THE HUM OF *VERDANT*'S ENGINES BENEATH RAS VEIR'S FEET WAS the only thing providing him comfort.

For three months he had dreaded this day, and as soon as his leg had healed enough after the fall from *The Winnower*, the thought of spending any amount of time in Mr. Tourbillon's office had set him to pacing.

"I'm going to keep her safe, sir," Ras said, the picture of a cautionary tale in heavy bandages from head to toe covering his otherwise loose fitting brown jumpsuit. Having his right arm in a sling at least helped him fight the urge to scratch the lingering itch beneath his leg brace. Not wincing at any given point was a struggle.

Callie's father stared up at Ras from across his office desk; he had yet to offer his guest a seat. His upper lip twitched, causing the well-groomed mustache to dance a bit. A long silence settled in the dark room. The only light peeked in through the blinded window behind him, backlighting the man and causing Ras to perpetually squint.

"Did 'keep her safe' not work last time because you didn't promise or because you hadn't learned things the hard way yet?" Mr. Tourbillon asked.

"I did what I set out to do, sir. I'm a man of my word."

"*Man,*" Mr. Tourbillon said with a faint smirk. "How old are you, Erasmus? Twenty?"

Ras gritted his teeth. His age didn't exactly stack up with his accomplishments. Stopping The Collective from ripping the world apart seemed to matter less to Mr. Tourbillon than his inability to legally consider himself an adult. "Almost twenty-one," he said. "Sir."

"Men aren't *almost* anything. They are what they are," Mr. Tourbillon said, pointing at Ras. "And what you are is unprepared."

Ras' eyes moved from Mr. Tourbillon's finger to the side, noticing the wall-sized map of The Atmo Project. Seven of the twenty-one floating cities were marked through with a dark X, indicating they had been destroyed by either sky pirates or some mechanical failure since the Great Overload. If anything, the wounds he and Callie had incurred three months ago were proof they were directly responsible for keeping *Verdant* from earning its own X. "I…*we* saved this city," Ras said.

"I don't know why you expect to be thanked for that. You cleaned up your mess, is all," the older man said, holding up his hand. "I'm sorry, *my daughter* helped you clean up your mess. And what did that get her?"

"Freedom from her headaches and a lifetime of wasting away in your basement," Ras said. This wasn't going as well as he would have liked. Those hopes had been far too high to begin with, but after Callie left *Verdant* without a proper goodbye to her parents, this talk was inevitable. He knew antagonizing Mr. Tourbillon wouldn't gain him any ground, but he felt the points were at least worth addressing.

"It got her shot," Mr. Tourbillon said, placing an uncomfortable amount of stress on the last word. "Does your word stop bullets, Erasmus?"

Ras inhaled sharply, ready to begin pointing out that it was technically an Energy beam his daughter had been shot with trying to save his life, but he caught himself. "All we have to do this time is fly around in *The Kingfisher* and destroy Convergences."

Mr. Tourbillon raised his eyebrows. "Excuse me?"

"From two-miles away," Ras amended, holding his good arm out in defense, which still tugged painfully at the healing stitches across his chest where Foster had slashed him. "It's…safe. With *The Winnower* gone, the Origin is still pumping out too much Energy to make surviving beneath the clouds possible. Destroying the Convergences should allow Atmo to land safely and then everything can go back to the way it used to be." *More or less.*

"What research have you conducted to ensure a city could land safely? And why would my daughter want to chase Convergences instead of finishing her time at the University?" Mr. Tourbillon asked, adjusting a picture frame on his desk.

Ras sighed at the obvious trap. "I thought you two had spoken since we came back." Ever since *The Kingfisher* had made port at *Verdant* a week ago, Callie had spent her time with her parents while Ras stayed onboard the ship, planning out this interaction.

Mr. Tourbillon glared. "We have. I just want you to hear how the answer sounds with your own voice," he said. "Neither of us expects you to win this argument, but it might as well play its course."

Ras reminded himself that the point of this meeting wasn't to come out with an unbruised ego, so he walked willingly into the setup. "She can't finish her time at the University because…"

"Go on."

"Because she bought me a ship," Ras finished.

"And where is that ship?"

Thinking about *The Brass Fox* was a bittersweet pastime. Half of it lay at the foot of the Time Origin while the other half was just… gone, thanks to a lucky Energy beam from *The Winnower*. "I'd like to think I've upgraded—"

"Then you can sell it and put Callie through graduate school as repayment," Mr. Tourbillon said.

"She doesn't want to go back," Ras said, more forcefully than he had intended. "She wants to see the world."

"I'm sure with you by her side, there won't be much left of it to see by the time you're finished with it."

Ras felt stupid for hoping everything would be different once he returned home. The fact that he had bought peace for everyone in his home city had been logged away as a footnote to the return of the true hero of *Verdant*, Elias Veir, in the legendary ghost ship, *The Kingfisher*.

The clock on the wall chimed.

"Erasmus, I'm saying these things for your own good. I hope you know that," Mr. Tourbillon said, his expression softening discernibly. "You mean well, but you wreck things, and I don't want my daughter around something like that." He nodded toward the typewriter key bracelet on Ras' wrist, which read D-O-N-'-T-G-I-V-E-U-P. "The thing my daughter, and you, don't understand is that never giving up is only worth something if you aren't making things worse." The clock chimed again. "I'm late for the meeting you caused."

Ras did his best to let the verbal barbs roll off his back, but the effort wasn't enough. He knew every word would revisit him verbatim on nights when sleep would be elusive. He took a deep breath. "What meeting is that?"

Mr. Tourbillon stood and stepped around his desk to open the door. Offering a palm to the hallway, he waited for Ras to move. "We're voting on zoning for the arriving refugees."

"Refugees? From where?" Ras asked. *Verdant* still felt overcrowded after the Merronians arrived years back when India Bravo had destroyed their city, and that situation was still being sorted out. Ras took the cue and gingerly took a step with his bad leg toward the doorway.

"All over," Mr. Tourbillon said, his imposing form pressing forward until Ras realized that he'd been backed out of the room entirely. "*Nalon, Kenus, Worick*...even some from *Derailleur*, I'm told." Mr. Tourbillon shut the door behind himself, locking the deadbolt with a heavy key. "With The Collective in its current state, sky pirates have nobody to keep them in check. Thanks to you."

Ras looked over the crowd in the high-ceilinged hallway. Men in *Verdant*'s official garb darted through the clog of people in well-worn traveler's clothing. The stench of men, women, and children who had only had time to flee with the clothes on their back overpowered the corridor.

It made sense why they'd come to *Verdant*: no other city had the reputation for repelling pirate attacks, which had become an especially appealing virtue now that the city's staunchest defender was rumored to have returned.

"Did Callie tell you my father is on my crew?" Ras asked. "He doesn't cause damage." The bargaining chip was a weak one, and based off a lie even his own mother hadn't been set straight on yet. Nobody knew Elias had set out to cause the collapse of The Collective when he left ten years ago, and now Ras wondered if Elias giving him credit for Foster Helios III's fall was an act of humility or self-preservation.

"She did not," Mr. Tourbillon said. His eyes narrowed as he escorted Ras toward the end of the hallway. "Perhaps this would be an excellent opportunity for you to learn from his example."

Ras stopped, backing up traffic. A burly man swiped his right shoulder, flaring pain through his recovering arm. He gritted his teeth. "With all due respect, sir, Atmo is going to fall."

A passing woman stopped next to him with a look of horror on her face.

"Eventually. Someday," Ras amended in the most placating tone he knew. He turned back to Mr. Tourbillon, speaking softly, "If Atmo is going to survive, it needs your daughter, and she can't save it without me by her side. That's just the mechanics of it. I'm not being unnecessarily dramatic, here." Ras searched for something besides the obvious disbelief and contempt in Mr. Tourbillon's eyes. "She's old enough to make her own decisions, sir. I just thought it was the honorable thing to come here and ask your permission. I didn't have to."

Mr. Tourbillon took a long, measured breath and let it out steadily through his nostrils. "I can appreciate the bravery it took to come to me, but that's where it ends," he said. "You are a young man of diminishing returns, is what you are. To fix *Verdant*, you sacrificed the safety of Atmo." He looked around at the crowd, then his pocket watch. "When I say no, I want you to understand that the answer is qualified in every displaced man, woman, and child's face you see. My answer is permanent, resolute, and I will think you a fool even more so than I already do if you ever come to me asking for my daughter's hand in marriage again." He stared at Ras as if to let the finality seep in. "I'm late for my meeting." With that, he spun on his heel, leaving Ras with the throng queued in the long hallway.

It took nearly twenty minutes for Ras to hobble his way out of *Verdant*'s Capitol building and down its steps. The pain from his wounds still lingered, despite Dayus' constant remarking on how quickly Ras had managed to heal.

The injuries didn't bother him nearly as much as seeing the state of Atmo. Waiting three months and relying mostly on his father to work with *Verdant*'s City Council on developing a plan for Atmo had been far more difficult than he had expected.

Delegations had been sent to the other thirteen floating cities of Atmo in an attempt to find a solution to the fuel shortage created by the collapse of The Collective. Retrofitting the engines to once again accept raw Energy seemed the best proposition. None of the ships had yet to return to *Verdant*, and with the refugees pouring in, Ras now had a clue as to why.

Dixie Piper, out of sheer boredom, had volunteered to head up the delegation for the floating city of *Nalon*. If sky pirates were attempting a coup, she was likely busy starting a counter-revolution.

"Mister?" a young voice called out. Ras' attention snapped to the fact that he had shuffled his way into *Verdant* Park, attracting looks from some of the families enjoying a meal outside.

A boy, likely five or six years old, scampered away from his picnicking parents and made an awkward dash toward Ras. "Are you him?" he asked breathlessly.

"Milo!" the boy's father called out from his family's picnic blanket. He waved apologetically to Ras. "Don't mind him."

Ras waved back. "It's fine," he said, then looked down at Milo. "Who do you think I am?"

Milo shrugged, his shaggy brown hair dancing with a gust of wind. "The hero guy that saved *Verdant*."

"You're probably thinking about Elias, my dad," Ras said. "We kind of look alike. My name is Ras."

"Yeah, Ras," the boy said emphatically. "Ras Veir. You fought with the Elders, The Collective, and saved a princess."

Ras pursed his lips, then with great effort, crouched down to the boy's height. "Did a pretty girl with red hair pay you to say that?"

Milo shook his head back and forth. "Nu-uh. My neighbor told me. He said you'd be easy to spot."

"Oh?"

"Yeah, he said you'd look like you got run over by a skiff."

Ras chuckled despite himself. "I suppose I do, don't I?"

"How do I get brave?" The boy blurted, then looked down at his shoes.

"That's a big question, Milo," Ras said.

"I need to know." The boy looked back at his parents, then turned back to Ras, his voice barely a whisper. "My parents are really scared of sky pirates. They don't think I know, but I do. I thought if you told me how to be brave, they would see I wasn't scared, and maybe they wouldn't be scared anymore either."

A faint smile tugged at the corners of Ras' lips. "I'll tell you a secret, all right?" He paused until Milo met his eyes. "I really, really don't like heights."

"But you're a wind merchant."

Ras nodded. "Being brave doesn't mean you can't get scared. Being brave means looking at something terrifying and telling it you're not giving up." He wasn't certain if that was the definition of courage, but it sounded about right. Ras lifted up his wrist, jangling the typewriter-key bracelet from Callie. "But even 'hero guys' still need to be reminded from time to time."

Milo nodded, staring up as Ras stood with a grunt.

Fishing into his left pocket, Ras produced a small brass compass, then offered it to Milo. "Keep it. In case you ever need a reminder."

"Does it have any special powers?" Milo asked, eyes wide as he took the compass gingerly in his hands.

"Um, it always points north?" Ras guessed. "Unless you shake it hard, but it'll get back to where it needs to be eventually."

"Don't you need it?"

"Used to," Ras said. "Then I found a really great navigator."

"Thanks!" Milo said, then turned and dashed back toward his parents with his new treasure outstretched for show-and-tell.

Ras watched for a moment as the boy rejoined his family, then walked to the edge of the park, where a skiff waited for him. He opened the passenger door and eased his way into the seat.

"Do you remember when your dad and I would take you out here between his collection runs?" Emma Veir asked. Her genuine smile had taken a little bit of time to get used to. She had rarely not been smiling ever since her husband returned. She wore her hair down now instead of in the pulled-back style she had worn for almost a decade, giving her a younger look. Ras wondered if she did it in an attempt to compensate for her husband's not having aged for ten years, but since Elias had already had a five-year head start on her, neither of the two looked out of place with each other.

"Barely. Did I run up to strangers like that?" Ras asked, nodding back toward the family.

"You were far too shy," Emma said. "You liked kites, but you'd only fly them with your father, though. You said it was a boy thing."

Ras smiled a bit at that.

"So, how did it go?" Emma asked, nodding toward the Capitol building.

Ras looked over to the driver's side of the skiff at his mother's hopeful face. "He said no."

"Just 'no'?" she asked.

"You know Mr. Tourbillon has a way with words," Ras said. "I'm being selective in my memory for the sake of my self-worth."

"Did you at least show him the ring?"

Ras carefully began to pull a box out of his pocket. "I think I've got enough red in my ledger with him that I doubt a little ingenuity would make a difference."

Emma reached a hand over as soon as Ras freed the case. With a fluid motion, she carefully lifted the makeshift box from Orville's Clockworks and inspected its contents. "Every bit helps."

Ras looked at his own handiwork. Without the means to procure a more traditional ring, he had disassembled the pocket watch his father had left for him at Orville's on *Derailleur* and used the parts to craft the piece of jewelry. It had been difficult to casually explain for three months why he would steal away periodically from the rest of the crew on *The Kingfisher*, but the result was worthwhile.

The ring itself was the fob circle where the watch formerly attached to the chain. A series of impossibly tiny gears adorned the top, all arrayed to showcase the largest red jewel the pocket watch used to contain.

"I love how the gears still move," Emma said, placing a finger on one of them. "But I'll let Callie have the first spin." She closed the box with a clap and returned it to her son. "Well, it's a shame old fuddy-duddy said no, but it's not like he's the only father you can ask."

"Mom," Ras protested, laughing. The levity felt nice. "It's not like I'm going to unfreeze a bloodthirsty Illorian army with a century-old grudge just to ask a stranger for his daughter's hand."

"I'm just saying you have options."

THE AIR SMELLED SWEET, stopping Callie Tourbillon in her tracks. This elicited protests from other shoppers in the crowded market-place as they narrowly avoided running into her. She sniffed the air a few more times and wrinkled her nose. The scent was fainter now, and one of the men passing by was certainly not the source of the pleasantness.

Her mission to find suitable supplies for a sub-Atmo journey had been hijacked by a lovely detour, and she redoubled her efforts to discover which booth in the street bazaar provided such a sweet scent.

She absentmindedly twirled her floral-patterned parasol, surveying the overly crowded marketplace. The covering provided little relief from the harsh sunlight, but it was the best she could do to emulate the last few months spent beneath the constant cloud cover. While Ras repeatedly told her she looked just as beautiful sun-kissed, she was less than enthralled with the advancing army of freckles she had accumulated over her formerly porcelain skin.

Simply being able to exist outside of her parents' basement was an upgrade. The annoyance of an occasional sunburn was well worth the trade of not suffering from the crippling headaches she used to endure.

That pain seemed like something from a semi-forgotten nightmare. The monster lurking in the recesses of her mind had been slain after Dr. Lupava had injected her with his Lack serum back on *The Winnower* to dull her sensitivity. It was just about the only thing she could find herself thankful for from The Collective.

And Ras. If anything, he was just as responsible for freeing her from that prison. She would still be in a basement if it weren't for him, and now she got to see the world she had always read about.

Her eyes darted about, taking in the different wares for sale. Men, women, and children crowded at the fronts of every stand, making it difficult to see what each vendor sold.

She chalked the long lines up to the influx of refugees. They needed to stock up, and it wouldn't be long before *Verdant* began to feel the strain of the added hungry mouths.

The scent taunted her again. She spun, and the loose material of her white sundress swished with her. Although it was a reminder of her former captivity, there was something to be said for not having to wear clothes designed for running away and narrowly avoiding danger.

Pushing her way through the crowd, she instinctively held her left arm over her tender mid-section. Dayus had been diligently tracking the healing process after her foolhardy mission to retrieve Ras from the Time Origin and acted the part of the overprotective mother more than anyone else on *The Kingfisher*. She wouldn't have been terribly surprised if he was somewhere nearby.

The last of the crowd in front of the vendor parted, and Callie stood before a table with orange spheres stacked in a rapidly deteriorating pyramid. Two young men worked to unload a new crate from the back of the booth.

Callie picked one of the dimpled spheres up and smelled deeply. Case closed.

"Hey lady, you smellin' or buyin'?" a middle-aged man with thick glasses asked. "These applefruits aren't gonna last forever."

"A what now?" Callie asked. "Applefruit?"

"Yeah, applefruit," the man said. "First time we've had 'em on *Verdant*, as far as I know. One of the refugee ships from out east brought a whole shipload."

"I believe they're called oranges," Callie said. "Apples are a different kind of fruit."

The man laughed, turning to his business partner who was busy collecting money. "Hey Kev, the girl here says these are called oranges. Who calls something by its color, huh?" The shopkeeper elbowed his partner, then turned back to Callie. "How dumb do you think I am, huh?"

Callie pursed her lips. "Not dumb, just ignorant, and there's nothing wrong with that as long as you're willing to learn," she said, mostly ignoring the reddening face of the store owner. "They don't grow on the mountains, so somebody out east must have found a way to harvest them from beneath the clouds." She blinked, snapping herself out of her thoughts. "Sailors used to eat them to prevent scurvy." She smiled, holding the orange to her nose again.

"Right. Well, whatever," the clerk said, then turned his attention to the customer behind Callie.

"How long do these keep?" Callie asked.

"Why ask me? I don't even know what they're called "

"I'll take a case," Callie said. "No, two. Have your boys set them aside and one of my crew will come by soon from *The Kingfisher*." She tossed the orange up a few inches and it smacked pleasantly in her palm upon its landing. "I'll just hold onto this one for safe keeping."

With a price finally agreed upon after a bit of haggling and a 'historian tax' added atop it all, Callie made her way back to the main avenue of the market. She took in the vibrant colors, the sounds of life, and the overwhelming citrus smell and smiled.

This was freedom.

Several hours of checking off items on her long shopping list passed, and she began her walk back to the docks to report which vendors held goods to collect. She was lost in another series of thoughts on wondering what Hal was up to back in Illoria when she noticed a familiar locksmith's shop. She imagined being an outside observer to the moment she had surprised Ras with the set of keys to *The Brass Fox*.

Reaching up, she felt the chop of her hair and wondered if she would ever grow it out again. If she was honest with herself, she missed brushing it; and moreover, she missed how her mother brushed it ever so gently.

Callie dreaded the inevitable discussion over her heritage. With everything that had transpired in the previous months, she hadn't really had the time to prioritize working through the information that she was Illorian, and beyond that, that she was born before The Clockwork War over a century ago.

Her life had been on pause for so long that it didn't seem real that she finally had some say in which direction it went. She wasn't entirely certain she knew all of the options. She wanted to be with Ras on *The Kingfisher* so Atmo could be saved, but anything beyond then didn't seem like it could be real.

Passing beneath a familiar sign, Callie realized she was still standing in front of the locksmith's shop with orange in hand, staring off in the distance. She glanced around to see if anyone had noticed.

Someone had.

"How long have you been back there, Dayus?" Callie asked the man with the wide-brimmed hat who stood in plain sight on the sidewalk a good twenty paces behind her. Even having just one holdover crew member from Hal's days as captain of *The Kingfisher* ensured a degree of continuity on the ship. She guessed Dayus had also been tasked to make sure the new captain didn't do anything too rash with *The Kingfisher*, like naming the legendary vessel *The Platinum Fox* or something of the sort.

Dayus shrugged as he closed the distance between them. As he approached, he removed his hat out of what Callie assumed to be respect. The new light caused him to squint, forcing something that almost looked like a smile. Callie knew better than to expect such expressions.

"I see you've taken an interest in exotic fruit," Dayus said.

"It smells nice. Again, how long have you been following me?"

"I have several pithy responses that I've been developing in the time I've been watching over you," Dayus said. "Each took several rounds of revision, but I believe any of them are worthy of garnering a smirk."

"Sounds like you've been mostly practicing that one," Callie said. "Have you dispatched any would be assassins I should know about?"

"My goal is to keep you safe, Miss Calista. If you are in any amount of substantial danger, I will be certain to inform you," Dayus said with all seriousness. "And while this falls well below the definition of substantial, I would like to save you from the unpleasant experience of biting into your orange with the peel still attached."

"Oh, right." Callie hefted the orange. "I knew that," she lied.

"Of course," Dayus said unquestioningly.

"So why didn't you just do the shopping yourself if you were going to follow me all day?" Callie asked.

Dayus glanced over her shoulder. "There's something to be said for autonomy," he said, then returned his gaze to her. "Also, I find haggling distasteful."

"Well, they say something is only worth what someone is willing to pay for it," Callie said, then turned and glanced at what had captured Dayus' attention. Ahead, the docks were bustling with activity. Ships jockeyed for open ports and faint shouts of arguments carried on the wind. "Busy day."

"Quite," Dayus said, stepping around her and taking the lead. "We should get back to *The Kingfisher*. I fear all of these new eyes bring more curiosity than is healthy."

Callie let Dayus put a short distance between them, then broke into a half jog, half skip that tested the strength of the bandages around her stomach.

"The wound is doing better," she said, arriving next to Dayus.

He nodded, eyes still focused on the docks ahead.

Callie dug a thumb into the peel of the orange, spurting juice onto her arms and white dress. She frowned, examining her front, then absentmindedly placed her thumb in her mouth to clean off the juice. The sweet tang of flavor danced across her tongue and her eyes shot wide open. "It tastes better than it smells!" She placed the puncture of the orange to her mouth, then drank away the excess liquid. She giggled, then sighed as she began ripping away the outer layer.

"Are you pleased with your purchase?" Dayus asked.

"Mmm-hmm."

"Are you going to share the rest with the crew?" he asked, lifting an eyebrow.

"Of course," Callie said defensively. "I hope we'll find more below Atmo when we hunt Convergences…I wonder what other delicacies we'll find."

"I have always been fond of pineapples," Dayus said.

As they reached the docks, Callie struggled to remember what she had read about pineapples. The only thing that came to her was an illustration of a spiked object that looked more suitable for primitive warfare than it did for eating.

Another transport airship pulled into a nearby slip. The frazzled looking men of *Verdant's* Port Authority worked to secure the airship to the dock. A young man caught a rope tossed by a gaunt man at the bow of the vessel.

"If you're looking for immigration—" the young dockhand began.

"Tourism," the gaunt man said hastily. "We're all here for tourism." He disappeared back to the deck and became lost in the long line of haggard looking men exiting onto the dock.

"Let us move quickly," Dayus whispered.

"Pirates?" Callie whispered back, her heart quickening.

Dayus narrowed his eyes, then faintly shook his head. His arm rested protectively across her shoulders as they walked past the group of men.

"Hey gramps," one of the disembarking men called out.

Dayus acknowledged his presence with a slight turn of the head.

"Any truth to the rumor that Eli Veir is back?" the man asked. He appeared to be in his mid-thirties, formerly in good shape aside from looking like he and all the men surrounding him had forgone attention to hygiene for the past month.

"Did you come all this way just to find out?" Dayus asked.

The downtrodden man refused to meet Dayus' eye as he nodded. "Things are getting rough out there. We could use a little hope."

Dayus patted Callie on the shoulder, then gave her a gentle nudge forward. "Why don't you make your way back to the ship? I'll see what I can do for these men."

Callie looked at the men, wondered where their families were, then wondered what scurvy looked like. She turned and handed the orange to Dayus with a shrug. "Maybe you can see if any of them need this."

"Certainly," Dayus said with a wink. It was more of a reaction than Callie had ever been able to get out of him previously, and it caused her to smile.

Callie continued down the busy docks, idly taking in the various shapes and sizes of the vessels presumably from all corners of Atmo. Some had brightly painted balloons while others looked ready to fall apart at the seams if they were to meet more than a light gust.

To her left, *Verdant* looked different somehow. It wasn't the damaged skyline still under repair ever since India Bravo had attacked months back. It felt smaller somehow. *No, not smaller. . .just contextualized after a trip to Illoria and back*, she thought.

The Kingfisher was moored a dozen ships down the dock, and she quickened her pace. The ship had taken on a worn look under its newest Captain, shifting from a gleaming silvery white to an oxidized patina that caused Ras a good deal of grief. Whatever metals comprised the hull obviously weren't designed to weather the rainstorms beneath the clouds.

The usual crowd camped around it, perhaps hopeful to see Halcyon Napier pop his head out to wave or maybe sign a few old propaganda posters from The Clockwork War.

With Hal being clear across Atmo, Dayus would be the closest thing the crowd could get to seeing a relic of the old war. But without the context of Napier, Dayus just looked like any other old man in his seventies.

The crowd ahead shuffled, parting at the order of a couple Port Authority workers as a skiff arrived. From only twenty feet away, Callie could easily pick out the heavily bandaged form of Ras exiting the vehicle next to his mother. His half-white shape had become easy to spot from a distance, and before long, Callie found herself pressed into the growing crowd as newcomers added themselves to the back ranks.

"Is that Elias?" one crowd member asked.

"Elias! Elias!" a short woman next to Callie shouted, obviously unable to see over the heads of the crowd.

The crowd fell in step with the impromptu chant, and Callie saw Ras's smile fall a little before he turned and began walking toward the ship's extending gangplank.

"I don't think that's Elias," someone said.

"Are you sure? I heard he came back looking younger after he found the fountain of youth in The Wild!" a teenager said excitedly.

"Ras!" Callie shouted, struggling to squeeze through the clump of men and women crowded together in front of her. She reached her arm high, extending her parasol and waving it wildly. "Ras!"

Ras spun on his heel, searching through the crowd turned mob. "Callie?" he shouted. He hobbled down the gangplank, eyes searching until they locked with Callie's and only darting away to get the Port Authority workers to spot her.

Before too long, a path cleared, and Callie walked through the parted corridor of people to Ras. She wanted to hug him, but refrained for the sake of both his healing torso and what might happen to *Verdant* if they were to touch and overload within the Energy-dependent city.

The last time they had touched after Dr. Lupava's serum had made her a Lack like Ras, they had accidentally knocked *The Winnower*'s fuel supplies out. Spending time together on the ground was one thing, but touching near anything that needed to remain in the sky was another prospect.

"Hi," Callie said, folding her hands in front of her, resisting the urge to embrace him.

"Are you all right?" Ras asked, showing considerable restraint himself.

"Yeah," she said, nodding. "Just got lost in a sea of admirers."

Ras choked back a laugh. "I think they showed up for someone else."

"Not all of them," Callie said, then walked past Ras with a smile and headed up the gangplank to *The Kingfisher*. Once inside, Callie walked the familiar white hallway lined with paintings of the world beneath the clouds until she reached Hal's study. *Well, Ras' study now,* she supposed, even though she had trouble imagining him studying anything.

"There she is!" A welcoming voice came from the door leading to the galley. Callie leaned over, spotting Elias Veir setting down the bowl he had been cleaning at the sink, taking up his crutches, and mobilizing his singular leg to head toward the study. He looked more like Ras' older brother now that he had spent the previous ten years frozen in time, but seeing him like this made Callie feel like she was nine years old again.

She remembered seeing him for the first time after Ras had saved her from the Illorian weapon and thinking she had to have either died or been dreaming for what she saw to be remotely possible.

Callie stepped forward, meeting him halfway and accepting his warm embrace.

"How'd we do?" Elias asked. He sniffed at the air. "I don't mean to be rude, but is that you?" He shifted his position, stabilizing himself with an arm over her shoulders.

Callie laughed. "If it's a good, sweet smell, then yes." She held the front of her sundress forward, displaying the stain. "I got a crate of oranges for us."

"Excellent!" Elias said. "What are oranges?"

"They had oranges in the market?" Emma asked, distracted from fussing over her son's array of bandages. "I haven't had one of those since I was a little girl at the Caretaker Festival. I wonder how they got up here."

The intercom system crackled to life. "Dayus to *Kingfisher*. Dayus to *Kingfisher*. Scramble the ship. I repeat, scramble the ship. I just received word that India Bravo is threatening to drop a floating city unless Ras is brought to her. I'll rejoin you with the shuttle."

"What?" Ras asked, rushing over to the comm unit. "Where did you hear that?"

"The refugees," Dayus said. "They're not here to live on *Verdant*. They're here to find you."

CHAPTER TWO
The Recruitment

PACING HURT, BUT IT HELPED RAS THINK. IT HADN'T TAKEN LONG to launch *The Kingfisher* straight up above *Verdant*, and as soon as Elias leveled the pitch of the ship, the pacing resumed inside the well-lit study.

"Ras, stop," Elias said. "It's painful just watching you." He eased into a padded leather chair with the aid of Emma, who pulled a second chair close enough that she could hold his hand.

"I just want to know how India even got out of Illoria," Ras said. Last he remembered, the sky pirates' of Bravo Company teaming up with The Collective meant the vast majority of either force was left frozen after their skirmish with the Elder fleet. Odds had been high that India was still aboard her frozen flagship, *The Dauntless.*

"Maybe she didn't," Callie said, leaning her elbows on Hal's old desk. "Does anyone have actual proof she's back? Maybe it's just someone wanting to take advantage of a power vacuum."

"Assuming it is her," Emma spoke up, "why would her one demand be you?"

"Because I killed her business partner?" Ras asked. "I helped start a war that got most of her fleet frozen?"

"I think your dad got the ball rolling on that last one if people want to point fingers," Callie said, then looked up at Elias. "No offense."

Elias shook his head. "I've only left this ship a few times since we got back. India would have plenty of motive to do some horrible things in retaliation because of me, but I don't think she'd threaten to sink a city based on the rumor that I'm alive."

"Maybe she's trying to find out if the rumor is true by bringing me in," Ras said. He stopped pacing and looked out the window at the tiny *Verdant* below. "Mom, how many Convergences do you think are on the ground?"

Emma turned her attention from Elias to her son. "Oh, I don't know, it's been so long since I've been down there. A lot could have changed."

"Like Collective diver teams scooping them up to put in *The Winnower*," Callie offered. "That takes care of at least eight Convergences. Plus the one Ras originally found in Framer's Valley, and the one under *The Halifax*. So we've already taken care of ten of them. I mean, we have no clue what capabilities The Collective had for in capturing and storing them. For all we know, they could have caught them all by now."

Callie's mention of the Framer's incident still brought back a twinge of guilt in Ras, but he knew she meant no malice by it. Looking into her beautiful blue eyes brought some level of solace even amidst the turmoil, the way it always had. "Dad, how big are Collective fueling stations?"

Elias blinked, pulling himself out of some thought. "Oh, ah, they might be big enough to house one Convergence each."

"All right, so that's another thirteen," Ras said. He watched his father once more drift off in thought. *Was this how he acted before coming up with plans to fight India Bravo?* "So, with ten destroyed and thirteen above the clouds, twenty-three Convergences aren't on the ground, but out of how many?"

"Right," Callie said hesitantly. "But…"

"But?" Ras asked.

"What if she attacks the city's engines instead of choking their fuel supply?" Callie asked.

Ras took a deep breath. Just when he had a plan to save Atmo by destroying Convergences, something had to go wrong. Again. "Well, a head on confrontation is suicide. We have one ship without a full crew," he said. "Dad, how did you beat Bravo Company in the past?"

"*Verdant* had a fleet," Elias said.

"But not at *New Crispin*, you didn't," Ras said.

A distracted grin played over Elias' mouth. "How do you know about *New Crispin*?"

"We stopped by on the way to Illoria," Callie said.

"That was dumb luck that I survived that one," Elias said. "How was everybody? Pop? Krantz?"

"Foster Helios led sky pirates to it," Callie said, mercifully omitting that Helios' looking for him was the reason the pirates had arrived in the first place. "But Pop and Krantz and everyone else were getting to their ships last we saw. I'm hoping *The Halifax* was enough of a distraction that the sky pirates didn't notice them escaping."

Ras had assumed they stayed and fought for their makeshift city, but he liked Callie's hope-laced theory better. "Well, you fought her fleet off with Energy," Ras said. "Why not do it again?"

"With what Energy?" Emma asked.

"The Convergence at the fueling station of the city she attacks," Callie said, understanding dawning on her face.

Ras pointed his finger excitedly at Callie. "Exactly. Unhook the poor Knack from the Convergence on the station and start pumping out raw Energy instead of the fuel. It'll tank Bravo Company's Helios engines and they'll be dead in the sky. That might buy us enough time to kill all of the Convergences and let Atmo land."

"Except she'll probably have Energy beam weapons from The Collective," Elias said. "If she'd had those at *New Crispin*, none of us would have survived." He looked down at his wife's hand within his own. "I'm not sure there's a perfect solution to this, Ras. Usually, you just have to go with the plan that causes the least amount of damage to the fewest people."

"Like letting one city fall so I can clear the ground for the rest?" Ras asked, voice rising. "Are you honestly suggesting that?"

"We haven't thought through everything yet," Emma said.

"Right, like India not stopping after she sinks the first city," Ras said. "I can't have that blood on my hands."

Elias struggled to stand with Emma's help. "I'm not suggesting letting any city drop, son," he said. "I...*we* all need you to understand what's at stake for all of Atmo if we lose either you *or* Callie, so I'm going to be hesitant with any course of action that puts you two directly in harm's way."

The ship's intercom buzzed to life with Dayus' voice. "Shuttle is on approach. I've brought a guest."

Ras furrowed his brow, then realized he was still looking at his father and probably had given him a dirty look. "I'm sorry, I didn't mean to snap," he said. "I just wish Hal had shared everything with me before asking for 'a tank of air.'"

Elias nodded. "You're not the only one."

The Kingfisher shook slightly at the shuttle's arrival. With a pressurized snap-hiss, a door in the hallway opened and Dayus walked through, escorting into the room a man unfamiliar to Ras. The malnourished newcomer's ragged clothes matched his hollow, haunted eyes.

"This," Dayus said, "is Lev. He is the one who told me of Bravo Company's plans and the search for Ras Veir." He shot a stern look to Ras. "I told him I knew some people that would be quite interested in what he had to say."

"If you have any leads…" Lev said, trailing off.

"You're the man from the transport," Callie said.

Lev nodded quickly, stealing only a glance at Callie. "Yes, and thank you for your kindness. My friends are in your debt."

"For the orange?" Callie asked.

"For the cases of them," Lev said, missing a shrug from Dayus. "Some of us hadn't eaten for…a while. *Verdant* was further than we'd thought and we weren't given provisions."

"You're…you're welcome," Callie said. Ras knew her voice of hidden disappointment.

"So is this…*The Kingfisher?*" Lev asked.

"It is," Ras said, despite a glare from Dayus.

"So does that mean you're Hal Napier?" Lev asked, looking Dayus over.

"The ship is under new management," Dayus said quickly. "I'm afraid we're short on time…"

"Oh," Lev said. "The long and short of it is that ever since most of The Collective up and left to go east, nobody seems to know what happened to them. It's like they completely forgot they were fighting a war against sky pirates." He shifted his weight as he spoke. "I guess word hasn't made it back this far west, but one might say Atmo is also under new management."

"How?" Elias asked. "There aren't enough sky pirates to manage that."

"That's what everyone thought until they just kept coming," Lev said. "Nobody knows where they're from, but all they had to do was hijack each city's fuel supply and threaten to let 'em fall if demands weren't met."

"And this happened to your city?" Ras asked.

"No, a faction of The Collective is still holding onto *Nalon*, but it's one of the three India is threatening to blow out of the sky if Ras Veir isn't at her doorstep by the end of this week," Lev said.

Ras did a quick mental check. They had four days left on the deadline, and *Nalon* was somewhere between a one and two day trip with a ship like *The Brass Fox*. He didn't know how quickly *The Kingfisher* could get there, but it was obvious they didn't have much time. "What about the *Verdant* delegation to retrofit the city's engines? If sky pirates aren't controlling the city, then Dixie should have made it back by now."

"I hadn't heard of anybody from *Verdant* coming to *Nalon*," Lev said.

"Dixie's kind of hard to miss," Callie said. "White hair, disproportionately loud…"

"Sorry," Lev said. "We've been more focused on finding Ras."

"What makes you think Ras is on *Verdant*?" Callie asked.

"News traveled when *Verdant* was on the verge of sinking, then again when…" Lev trailed off.

"Out with it," Dayus said.

"When he kidnapped Miss Tourbillon," Lev said, pulling out a heavily creased wanted poster with sketches of Callie and Ras' faces. "So when we heard later that India Bravo was looking for a kid with the same name…" He gave Ras an apologetic shrug.

Ras sighed, recognizing the wanted poster from the library back on *Derailleur*. "Why tell us all this?" he asked. "Wouldn't that make me harder to find? Obviously this ship can out-climb any transport."

Lev sighed. "I'm not the type to force anyone to do what should be their call, but I thought you should know that every man on those transports has a wife and kids back at home. The Collective threatened to fire on our ships if we come back without you."

"That's horrible!" Callie exclaimed.

"They didn't tell us the last part until we shoved off. One of the ships turned around, then was shot down by our own city's defenses," Lev said. "Please, Mr. Veir…we're in something of a tight spot."

Ras hobbled over to the bookshelf behind Callie, careful to not stand too close lest he start her overloading process. "Thank you for your honesty, Lev."

"If your father were still around, I would have asked him instead," Lev said apologetically. "Atmo knows you didn't cross Eli Veir."

"Do they, now?" Elias asked.

"Yeah…" Lev said, stopping himself before squinting at Elias. He looked to Ras, then back to Elias. "No." His eyes widened. "That's not right. You're barely older than me and I was still a boy when he saved *Verdant* the first time."

"Spending a decade in The Wild does funny things to a man," Elias said.

Lev snorted and blinked hard as though it might realign reality with his sight. "Well, I hope it doesn't take the fight out of him."

A faint smile came to Elias as he made eye contact with Ras. "I'm not exactly a one-man army," he said.

Lev took a hesitant step forward. "Ras…I have a selfish request."

"Yes?"

"If you choose not to go to India Bravo before the deadline…is there any way you could find it in your heart to take me to *Nalon* so I can save my wife and kid?"

The request broke Ras' heart. The earnest plea seemed honest enough, but too much was happening too quickly. "I'll have to give it some thought, Lev."

Night fell and Ras looked down at the sparkling gem of *Verdant* from the main parlor window. Little flecks of light danced to and from the city. It was good to see The Bowl alive again, but quickly he realized the vast majority of the traffic was arriving rather than leaving the city.

"Dayus should be back soon after dropping Lev off," Elias said, his reflection growing in the glass as he hobbled toward his son. "I had him tell Harley to move tomorrow's crew recruitment meeting to tonight, and to only have the people he absolutely trusted know about the change."

It had been a couple months since Ras had seen Old Harley. Aside from Callie, the aging dockhand had been the most excited about the prospect of going out and seeing the world. *Wonder who actually would want to be on my crew*, he thought. He looked over his shoulder as Elias approached. "Do requests like that happen often? Lev, I mean."

Elias stood next to his son and focused on the city below. "Once people see you for what you can do, they can be quick to put their needs before yours." He shook his head. "It's never easy saying no, but sometimes you have to do it so you can say yes to better things." He handed Ras a mug of some warm, sweet smelling liquid, then leaned in and whispered, "How'd the meeting with old Mr. T go?"

Ras almost spilled his drink looking back down the hallway to see if Callie was anywhere within earshot. "I did what I could," he whispered back.

"Well, that's all anyone can ask."

Ras took a sip of the sweet drink. It was a new, rich flavor that tugged on the taste-buds in the back of his mouth. "What is this?"

"Dayus calls it 'cider.' He taught your mother how to make it."

"Dad, I know you promised to take her back to her hometown. I didn't mean to postpone the family reunion—"

Elias laughed heartily. "Don't worry about that. Her family hates me. *Skyfolk* are always up to no good," he said in an unfamiliar accent. "I hope they like you better."

The idea of finally seeing people living beneath the clouds excited Ras. He had actually looked forward to meeting his mother's side of the family, but it seemed once more that what he wanted to do and what was required of him were at odds with one another. A long pause. Another sip. Finally, "Why aren't you leading this mission? This is more your area of expertise, isn't it?"

Elias scratched at his stubble for a moment. "I know you'll never have to experience this firsthand, but when Foster blasted off my leg and the Energy caused me to start overloading, I knew...I *knew* I was gone. I had used up all my luck waiting a decade for you to snatch me out of the air."

"But you're fine. You're home," Ras said. "We have each others' back."

"Ras, if you get used to me always leading, to me always being there with the decision when things get tough..." Elias trailed off. "What I'm trying to say is that I'm not always going to be around, and if you haven't had to learn things the hard way by that point, then I'm afraid I've failed you."

Ras sighed slightly, then pressed his lips into a thin line. "I think I've done plenty of figuring out how to get by without you here," he said softly. "I wouldn't mind getting to know what it feels like having you around, if that isn't too much to ask."

"Fair enough," Elias said, placing a hand on Ras' shoulder. "I won't go anywhere. Not if I can help it."

"Thank you."

"Did I hear the cue word?" Emma called out from the galley.

"No," Elias called back, "but you might as well come out now."

"Not without a cue word," Callie's voice joined.

Elias shot Ras a grin. "Fine. *Captain.*"

Emma immediately rounded the corner with a small cake propped up under both hands. Atop it, the letters C-A-P were written in blue icing. "Did somebody say *Captain?*"

"I think he just did," Ras said, pointing to Elias and playing along.

As Emma placed the cake onto Hal's desk, Callie entered with a couple of plain brown boxes. "Which one should he open first?"

"It isn't my birthday, guys," Ras said. "And technically I've been a Captain before..."

"Let's let your mother celebrate, huh?" Elias whispered.

Emma grabbed the smaller of the two boxes, thin and rectangular, then handed it to Ras. "This one is from me." Her eyes danced between the box and Ras' face. "Go on, open, open."

He obliged, lifting the top off of the box, revealing folded brown cloth with stripes and brass buttons lining the front. Upon extraction the item unfolded, revealing itself to be a well-tailored vest.

"Ooh, I like it," Callie said.

"You helped pick it out," Emma said.

"Reinforcing that I like it."

Emma quickly moved to unbutton the front and begin dressing Ras.

"I can do it, mom. I hear Captains dress themselves..." He gave her a wink, then winced as he gently removed his sling. The gunshot wound in his shoulder still ached, but it wasn't much compared to his leg. "So, a wind merchant jumpsuit doesn't look *Captain-ish* enough?"

"I just want you to make a good first impression with your new crew," Emma said.

Ras was certain he'd already made an impression on everybody in *Verdant*, but he let the point pass. He slid his arms through the holes, then pulled on both lapels. "Buttoned or unbuttoned?"

"Buttoned," Elias said, "if you want to look like a banker."

"I think buttoned looks dapper," Emma said.

"Callie with the tie-breaker?" Ras asked.

"Unbuttoned looks rakish," Callie said. "Might make at least one woman I can think of swoon."

Unbuttoned it is, he thought. He leaned in to give his mother a hug. "Thanks, mom. You didn't have to do this."

"All right," Elias said. "Mine won't come as much of a surprise." He leaned over and patted the long wooden rectangle of a box. The top slid off, revealing a disjointed looking metal brace that shined in the dim light of the room.

"Your grapple gun?" Ras asked. "I thought I lost that back on *The Winnower.*"

"You did," Elias admitted, "but I can't have you going out and about wearing Foster Helios III's grapple gun, now can I?" He crutched over to inspect the device. "Had the same craftsman who built mine make one for you. Top of the line machining. Look, even had your name engraved on the side."

Ras stepped over and ran his hand over the ornate script. *Erasmus Lionel Veir.* He had never owned anything so nice before. "I don't know what to say."

"Say you won't have to use it often," his mother replied.

"Put it on," Callie said. "I want to see what the new Captain Ras looks like. Oh! Just a moment," she said, stepping out of the room and quickly returning with his wrench holster. "We should complete the outfit."

"I'm starting to feel like I'm wearing a costume," Ras said. He dropped the KnackVision goggles he usually kept perched atop his head down over his eyes. "Is this what a Reclaimer is supposed to look like?"

"You'll have to ask Dayus," Elias said. "Look, you're responsible for stopping The Collective from repressing all of Atmo. While your outfit doesn't define you, I think you've earned the license to have others look at you and see a leader."

In the window, the dark form of the shuttle grew as it approached *The Kingfisher.* "Looks like our ride is here."

"I'll wrap up your cake for the trip," Emma said.

"Ras?" Elias said.

"Yeah, dad?"

"You're going to do great things, buddy," Elias said, clapping a hand on his son's good shoulder. "Now, let's find you a crew."

THE SHUTTLE RIDE BACK TO *VERDANT* was largely uneventful aside from Dayus' taking the time to swap out Ras' bandages, allowing Elias to pilot the shuttle. After each new wrap was applied, Dayus would hold his hands over the wound for what felt like an awkwardly long time. Every prior mention of this had been met by chastisement on the lack of wisdom in interrupting Illorian healing practices, so Ras held his tongue.

Elias eased the shuttle in for a landing. The deployment of the landing gear jerked the vessel slightly; a moment later, it made contact along a sparsely populated street and rolled to a stop. He climbed out of the pilot's seat. "This isn't exactly a parking spot, so you might want to launch as soon as we get out."

"Where are we?" Ras asked.

"Blocking one of the entrances to The Engine," Elias said. "Where did you drop Lev off?"

"On the other side of *Verdant*," Dayus said, opening the shuttle door. "Hurry. You're already late for your meeting."

"*Hurry* might be a stretch," Ras said, placing more weight on his leg brace, causing shooting pains to course throughout his body. "Too bad a crutch just doesn't go with the whole fearless leader image."

"A little fear is good for a leader," Elias said. "Keeps him from letting everyone around him follow along to certain death." Before they could tug open one of the large double doors, the shuttle launched from behind them with a blast of steam.

Ras pulled on one of the doors to The Engine and eased himself through the narrow opening. The loud droning of the machinery and the overwhelming scents of engine grease and sweat brought him back to a time when *Verdant* had less than a month left to stay in the sky. Now it was all of Atmo, but at least this time he had his own plan and more allies.

As they approached the main office, he could imagine Billie sitting at her old desk, a fist clenching some of her curly hair. He still felt responsible for her death, even though there was little he could have done.

"Dad, did you know many people from The Engine?" Ras asked, surprised by the tinge of nostalgia he felt as he took in the engineering marvel that was a floating city's innards.

"Some," Elias said. "Never had much reason to come down here. From what I understand, they like to keep to themselves. Why do you ask?"

"I was just curious if you get as turned around down here as I do."

"Nope," Elias said, tapping one of the many pipes running along the wall. "The Energy gives me a nice compass. Your mother used to tell me how she'd grown up next to a set of mountains. Seeing which direction they were always let her know which way she was heading. Same idea."

The occasional Engine worker only gave a lingering glance to the Veir men as they passed. Ras thought he recognized a few of them, and one of them even used a bit of sign language to greet Ras briefly.

"Well, that was rude," Elias said.

"He was just saying hello," Ras replied. "Trust me, it's better than shouting over the engine noise."

Elias' crutches clanked onward down the metal grating. "Dayus said Harley moved the meeting to one of these rooms." He pointed to a series of doors down the hallway. One of them had a piece of paper tacked up on the door; upon reading it, Elias let out a laugh.

Ras leaned in to look at the sign. *Emergency: Sewage Leak. Appropriate personnel only.* "Not the most clever ruse," he said, cracking open the door. A rank smell filled the hallway, causing both men to choke on the air.

Elias lunged for the door, closing it immediately. "That would definitely thin a crowd if he held it in there." He looked around. "We're on Sub-Level One, right?"

Ras shook his head, still with a hand cupped over his nose and mouth. "Level Zero. We'll have to go down one floor."

"Looks like we'll be fashionably late, then."

One rickety elevator ride later, Sub-Level One welcomed Ras in much the same ruined state it had previously.

"What blew up down here?" Elias asked.

"I keep forgetting it hasn't been all that long since Bravo Company attacked," Ras said, navigating a segment of corridor pinched in by bulging bulkhead.

"It's a wonder she still flies with all the abuse she's taken," Elias said, searching the doorways along the hall.

The sound of muted hubbub came from behind the second door on the right. A heavily recycled piece of blue paper boldly marked in ink with the letter "H" hung on the door.

Elias took a deep breath, then let it out quickly. "You ready for this?"

"Saving Atmo? Sure. Public speaking…" Ras lifted a flat hand and waved it back and forth.

"After you," Elias said, opening the door. Old Harley's excited voice spilled into the hallway, and Ras stepped past his father into a dark, crowded room with rows of chairs holding at least twenty people. The only light in the room hung just above Old Harley, turning his wispy white hair into a halo and making it difficult to see the perimeter of the room.

From where Ras stood, he could see maybe another thirty men lining the walls. Standing room only. *Old Harley must have a lot of friends,* he thought. Everyone stared at the man under the light, ignoring the newcomers. A faint, familiar smell hit him, but he couldn't quite place it.

"—surprising number of you showed," Old Harley continued. "I know I said to only tell those you absolutely would entrust with the lives of your family, but I guess that's *Verdant* for you. Tight knit."

Ras glanced through the ranks of men and women, mostly men, who had shown up for the opportunity to be on his crew. A few of the faces along the wall to his right seemed familiar, and he chalked it up to remembering them from back in the mess hall.

A man with a shock of red hair sat in the front row, close enough to Old Harley's light that the fiery coloration practically glowed. *Finn. It would be good to have a friend aboard,* Ras thought. *And a medic that didn't lay his hands on you for longer than necessary…* He looked back around the room for anyone wearing an eyepatch, and his pulse quickened until he was able to reasonably rule out Guy's presence. *I bet he and dad would get into it on a regular basis. Or just once.*

It only then occurred to Ras that as Captain, he chose who would come along on this trip with him and had final say. He decided to tune back in to what Old Harley was saying.

"—can't really divulge what all this mission entails due to the level of secrecy needed for it to succeed, but I *can* say that, theatrics aside, the crew will be called on to save all of Atmo from plummeting to its own demise," Old Harley said gravely, gesturing to the crowd with his cane in a wide sweeping arc.

"Who's the captain?" one man shouted from the back.

Old Harley shielded his eyes from the light to survey the crowd. "Please hold your questions for later. This is a monologue, friend, and I've worked very hard to do it justice." He scratched at his gray scruff. "Where was I?" A pause. "Oh, yes, Atmo falling. Well, almost all of Atmo falling. Due to the extraordinary lengths and the wise idea not to jump on The Collective's Helios engine bandwagon, *Verdant* is safe from the menace that threatens the other cities."

A murmur arose in the crowd until Old Harley raised his hands to quiet the room.

"The time commitment is indefinite. We don't know how long this will take, so favor will be with those not leaving behind family or important duties to the city." Old Harley shielded his eyes once more. "Anyone out?"

Nobody moved.

Ras' nose twitched. The offensive odor had lingered since he entered the room, but he just assumed the scent from the sewage leak room had just stuck with him.

"Would the Captain like to say a few words?" Old Harley asked, making eye contact with Ras. He raised his cane and used it to swivel the spotlight until it pointed directly at Ras, who instinctively shielded his eyes.

The room burst into more murmurs and Ras surveyed what little of the group he could see with the light pouring in on him. Half were referencing their tattered copies of the same wanted poster Lev had.

Finn waved exuberantly.

"Get 'im!" someone yelled. The sounds of shouts and chairs being upended filled the room.

Ras bolted for the door, slamming back into his father. With a loud clang accompanied by the sound of a shattering lightbulb, the room dropped into blackness.

Hands groped at Ras, ripping at his clothes and bandages.

Donning his KnackVision goggles provided a map of the city's Energy piping, allowing Ras to gain his bearings. He noticed something new when he looked back at the rest of the room. Fifty faint green lights glowed as the men bobbed about.

Ras' hands found the knob as he struggled against being pulled back into the crowd. He yanked the door open, and light spilled in from the hall.

Elias tumbled into corridor first, followed by Ras, who spun and fired his grapple gun charge at the metal door. It stuck with a clang, starting the game of tug-of-war.

"Dad! Pull me back!"

Elias threw his arms around Ras in a hug-turned-tackle. Both men fell, pulling the cable taut and snapping the door shut. "Fire the other magnet!"

"How long will that last?" Ras asked, launching the other side of the magnetic grapple to the wall opposite the door, keeping the cable taut as he did so.

"Let's not find out," Elias said.

Ras stood despite the protest of his healing leg, then grimaced as he pulled his father from the ground. After retrieving Elias' crutches, they began their father/son three-legged race back to the elevator.

Ahead, a chime indicated the arrival of the elevator car to Sub-Level One. "That's lucky," Ras said.

The doors opened. A dozen men in ratty clothes spilled out into the hallway and fixed their eyes on the Veir men.

Elias tugged on Ras' arm, leading them down a side corridor. Ahead, a couple of engineers on ladders worked on pipe repairs. The dank scent of sewage filled the hall.

The Veirs hobbled toward the ladders as the refugees rounded the corner. "Once we clear the ladders, grapple the pipe!" Elias shouted.

The two Engine workers attempted to climb down their ladders before the mob could knock them over.

"Sorry!" Ras shouted as they passed beneath one of the ladders. He aimed the grapple gun and struck the fresh patch of pipe. At a hard yank, the pipe gave, and sewage cascaded onto the pursuing mob.

Cries of protests and iterations of swears new to Ras echoed down the hall as they continued onward.

"What else is on this level?" Elias asked, his crutch-work barely faster than a jog.

Ras remembered well what they were approaching, and the idea of leading a dozen men covered in fecal matter through the sterile medical station made him cringe. "Finn forgive me…"

"What?"

As they hobbled toward the double doors of the medical ward, Ras shouted, "Injured men, incoming! Open the doors, it's an emergency!" The statements were *technically* true. The sewage drenched dozen were gaining and would be on them in seconds.

One of the doors opened and a nurse stepped out to see the horde charging toward him as Ras and Elias shoved past her and into the medical wing.

"Lock the doors! Lock the doors!" Ras shouted. "Fecal matter," he said, panting and pointing to the door. "Keep them out."

Orderlies rushed to the door to help lock it. The doctors looked at Ras and Elias. "Are they hurt?"

Ras shook his head. "No. Just disgusting."

"Are you hurt?" one of the doctors asked, taking in the heavily bandaged Ras.

"All over," Ras said, catching his breath. He surveyed the room. There were too many entrances to the medical center and he would need to find a way out before the makeshift bounty hunters found any of the ways in. *At least we'd smell them approaching.*

From the other side of the ward, doors flew open. Men and women in grease stained green jumpsuits with patches embroidered with the number "8" filed into the room. At the group's front stood a man with malice in his eye.

"Guy!" Ras shouted. "Thank Atmo you're here."

"You know," Guy began, his gruff voice sending a shiver down Ras' spine, "I heard a rumor you came back. I also heard about the bounty Bravo has on your head."

"Hey," Ras said, "I made good on my promise to save *Verdant*."

"Seems I recall you promised you'd die trying, like your father…" Guy's eye flicked over to Elias, then narrowed. "On behalf of every Merronian alive and dead I think I just became a bounty hunter."

CHAPTER THREE
The Barricade

RAS PUSHED AS HARD AS HIS PAIN TOLERANCE WOULD ALLOW against the stack of gurneys barricading an entrance to the medical unit. The slightly emaciated state of the refugees thankfully worked to his favor, but the strength of their assault showed they obviously had a numbers advantage.

Guy stood in the middle of the room with his arms folded as the crew from Engine 8 scattered across the various blocked entrances. "Seriously? I gave an order," he said with a growl. "Back off the doors."

"He's one of us," one of the younger engineers called back.

"He got Billie killed," Guy said, "and now he let the sky pirates take over." He turned his attention to Ras. "Which, I forgot to say thanks for that."

"Don't bother with him," Elias said, pushing against the gurneys alongside Ras. The little bit he contributed against the oncoming rush didn't help nearly as much as the emotional bolster he provided. "Focus on how we can get out of here."

"Dad, what if they took me?" Ras asked. "Their city would be safe and we can figure out a way to get me out later."

Elias shook his head. "There's no telling what that mob would do to you before they delivered you."

"I kind of wish there was an easy way to let them all know I'm trying to save their city," Ras said.

"Saving another city? You really need a new hobby," Guy said.

"What's his issue?" Elias asked.

"He's Merronian," Ras replied.

"Being Merronian is *not* an issue," Guy shot back, stepping up to Ras with fists clenched. "In fact, it gives me a special bond with these people, knowing there's a Veir who is capable of saving his city, like he did *Verdant*, and choosing not to."

Elias turned to face Guy, but still held on next to Ras. "Do you think anyone offered to help *Verdant* when Bravo Company arrived?" He asked, voice clear and strong. "We watched half of our military fall in the opening attack. Where was *Merron*? Where was *Derailleur*? Where was The Collective, huh?" The bucking doors shoved him forward and he fought back. "Nobody came to help us. We had to rise up and fight, every single one of us, either until we pushed India Bravo back or she inherited an empty city.

"We lost too many good men and women to keep what was ours, but we kept at it until we couldn't last any longer and then some," Elias said. "Which is why we failed to push India away from *Merron* when we attacked her."

"You're lying," Guy said.

"I bet when you moved to *Verdant* you were put in a fully furnished house," Elias said. "Seemed a little too generous, right?"

"I…" Guy began.

"Oh, we had plenty of room here on *Verdant* after we lost dozens, if not hundreds more Verdantians when *Merron* fell…we just had the decency to not bring it up to the surviving refugees who lost *everything*."

Guy's arms uncrossed, his defenses battered.

"I don't blame you," Elias said. "How could you have known? You never bothered to ask. No place in your heart with all that bitterness, and now you're wanting to turn in the one person India Bravo fears so much she's willing to threaten entire cities to have. You want to give her what she wants. You're giving in. Do I understand that clearly?"

Elias looked around the room and raised his voice. "Letting Ras fall to these refugees will only make things worse for them and you if he can't complete his mission. So, push with everything you've got."

Guy looked down at the floor for a moment, then joined the other engine workers as they redoubled their efforts.

Ras looked over at his father in awe.

Elias just winked. "We may just get out of this yet."

"Thank you, dad," Ras said quietly.

"Just stating facts," Elias said. "Arguments tend to go better when you have the truth at your back."

STANDING BEFORE HER FATHER in his Energy-lit office, Callie could feel the beginnings of tears stinging her eyes. She was thankful she had never turned on the waterworks to get her way when she was younger, which meant if something upset her, her father knew the gravity of the situation instantly.

"I am not sending the Sheriff's office to deal with your boyfriend's mess," Mr. Tourbillon said, reclining in his chair. It wasn't unusual for him to spend late nights at the office, and the story told by the bags under his eyes was corroborated by the large stacks of paperwork strewn about his desk. "Not if you're just going to run away with him again. You broke your mother's heart, and mine, last time."

"He is in this mess because he saved this city," Callie said, "which includes you." Her eyes darted to a picture hanging on the wall of her family, posed for the portrait. Her parents looked so happy. That reality had become relegated to the past, only visible in glimpses. She had to get him to realize what was at stake.

"And according to you, now there's an even bigger mess for any city with Helios engines," he said.

Callie took a deep breath. She could feel her self-control chipping away. Why did he really hate Ras so much? "The Collective dug that hole for themselves. Their whole Helios engine system was...*is* fueled by the suffering of others and they failed to share that information. We're lucky *Verdant* was too poor to buy those engines, and we never would have found out about it if wasn't for Ras.

"I've seen what those systems do to people, firsthand." She jutted a hand out toward his window. She had intentionally left the more gruesome details of the previous journey out of her original report, but since he couldn't be bothered to listen to her, she would *make* him listen. She took a deep breath. "I've *been* in one of these machines," she said. She watched her father's jaw drop. "I've had the needle plunged in my arm and I've begged for death. Begged. And that's what's happening to people *right now* on every other Atmo city. And as far as we know, Ras and I are the only people in Atmo that can stop all of this by destroying the Convergences," she said. It was time to pull out every stop. "I also know that you chose not to tell me I was adopted."

Mr. Tourbillon opened his mouth to speak, but nothing came.

"Daddy, I saw the train where Dayus found me," Callie said, "and as hard as it is for me to say this, I also know how long ago I was born."

"What are you talking about?"

Callie took a deep breath. This had to be the least favorite discovery of her lifetime. "I was born one-hundred and three years ago."

"How could that even be possible? You're nineteen going on twenty, not one-hundred and four."

"What did Dayus tell you when you adopted me?" Callie asked. Her father wasn't one to flat-out lie to her, but she hadn't before thought that her parents might not have had all the information. *Then again, who would believe a man offering an octogenarian in a three-year old's body?*

"He said you were very sick, but that his benefactor would pay for any bills," Mr. Tourbillon said. "Your mother and I tried for years to have a child, and with adoption being hard enough as it is in Atmo… when he paid for us to have a house and a little girl to call our own on *Verdant*, of course we took the opportunity."

"Daddy, I was sick because I was stuck for over eighty years on a train out of Illoria…or The Wild. Dayus just wanted me to be as far away from there as he could get me so I might survive, but the only reason I did was because we lived next to the Veirs. While that deserves its own explanation I really, really need you to call in a favor with Sheriff Pauling to get Ras out of the The Engine so he and I can save Atmo." She gave a faint smile as the tension from her shoulders eased. "You're still my daddy. I understand and respect how much you want to protect me, but I'm not a sick little girl anymore. I just need your help. Atmo needs your help."

Mr. Tourbillon sighed, absentmindedly rubbing a spot on his desk with his thumb, then picked up the phone on his desk. "I'm only doing this for you. Not *him*. Not even for Atmo. Just you."

"So, HOW MANY PEOPLE in that meeting do you think actually wanted to be on my crew?" Ras asked behind gritted teeth as he pushed against the bucking barricade. He didn't know how much longer he could hold.

"I'd say all of them, given the right circumstances," Elias said.

"Do you think Lev tipped them off?"

"Don't know," Elias said. "He didn't seem the type to—"

Something hit the door with such force that it threw both men back. The faces of several refugees peered through the cracked open doors before two orderlies ran over, staving off the breach. Another slam against the door threw everyone back, and this time a long, thick pipe poked through, wedging itself between the doors. A thin refugee attempted to slip through the gap unsuccessfully as one of the orderlies threw a bedpan, pegging the man in the forehead.

Cries escaped from one of the other entrances as a pipe wedged through those double doors as well, then another.

Suddenly, all shoving against the doors ceased.

"They're leaving!" Ras said.

"No, they're consolidating," Elias said. "They're going to focus on overpowering just one entrance."

A hand grabbed Ras' collar, jerking him backward. He almost lost his footing completely when he saw the source.

"Everyone protect the kid," Guy said. "They're getting in here sooner or later, so where can we hide him?"

Ras righted himself, stumbling slightly. "If they're all consolidating, then they're leaving other entrances open."

"Or they want us to think that and open a door for them."

The entrance on the opposite side of the room burst open in a flood of refugees, easily overpowering the Engine workers.

"To Ras!" Guy called out. The outnumbered Engine workers and orderlies did their best to intercept the invaders as Guy pulled Ras toward the nearest entrance.

"I can walk!" Ras protested as he began pulling at the gurneys to free up the doors before the throng could overtake him. He glanced over his shoulder. His allies were being pushed back and trampled. Every fiber of him wanted to stop the chaos and the pain. He'd never outrun the mob, even if he made it out of the medical unit. There were too many of them. He heard the entrance open behind him, but he had made up his mind.

Ras turned on his heel and faced the onrushing crowd. With arm outstretched he shouted, "Stop!"

The crowd halted. *That worked?*

A deafening musket shot blasted next to Ras' left ear. Smoke filled the vicinity as the mob backpedalled merely ten feet away. He looked behind him to see the sharp features of Sheriff Pauling. In the doorway, a dozen men aimed guns at the mob in a stacked formation.

"Now, I know what you're thinking," Sheriff Pauling said. "You're thinking, there are more of us than he's got guns…and I'm afraid you'd be quite incorrect." He held his rifle up. Someone behind him grabbed the musket and replaced it with a new, loaded one. "I understand you're hunting Mr. Veir for your wives and children. And while I can sympathize, I can't have this going on in my city."

Looking back through the haze, Ras could barely make out the excited form of Callie down the hallway, waving emphatically at him. Once she had his attention, she pointed to all the armed men, then jutted a thumb back at herself with a huge smile.

"So, listen up," Pauling said. "This is how we're going to play it: I'm going to take Mr. Veir here, and I'm going to hold onto him until tomorrow morning. As soon as the sun crests the clouds, I'll release him on the Eastern docks and you can resume your hunt. Sound fair?" He chuckled. "I know it doesn't, but guns create an unfair disadvantage against the have-nots."

Several deputies grabbed Ras, pulling him behind the line of muskets and into the hallway. Elias and Guy fell in behind him.

"Sunrise! Eastern docks! Be there!" Pauling shouted as he turned and began walking down the corridor.

"You can't be serious," Elias said. "James—"

"Eli, I'm acting under orders," Sheriff Pauling said. "With the number of *tourists* on *Verdant* only looking to see the one sight that interests them, this was the City Council's solution."

"You're going to give us a head start, right?" Ras asked. He glanced over to Callie, whose smile had completely evaporated.

"Son, you're going to be lucky if they don't find you before the morning," Pauling said.

"Why not just let me leave now?" Ras asked.

Pauling shook his head. "Word needs to spread so every refugee leaves with you tomorrow morning. If you disappear, they're going to keep looking around here for you. I can't have that."

"Whose idea was this?" Ras asked.

"That's an excellent question, Ras," Pauling said, keeping his eyes forward. "Might ask your girlfriend."

"Callie? Did your dad come up with this?" Ras asked.

She drew her lips into a thin line, looked down, and nodded. "It made the most sense." She paused, keeping her eye on Pauling. As soon as the Sheriff looked back to bark orders at his deputies, she shot a wink to Ras. The beginnings of a smirk tugged at the corners of her mouth, accentuating her cheekbones.

The entirety of the Sheriff's department escorted Ras, Elias, and Callie down one of the corridors. "I had daddy clear a transport for all of us."

"On the surface?" Ras asked.

"No," Pauling said with a huff. "Now that Verdant's got wind of the price on your head, the sight of you is enough to whip anyone into a bounty hunter."

"What's the bounty?" Elias asked. "Out of curiosity."

"Not dropping a city, for one," Pauling said, "and plenty of folk, myself among their number, have relatives on one of those cities. That would be enough for most, but there's a substantial price tag attached to motivate the sky pirates."

Ras shook his head. He had no clue why India Bravo was so bent on his capture. For whatever reason, she had Atmo in her clutches and him in her sights.

He felt reasonably comfortable that Pauling wouldn't just hand him over, mostly out of respect for Elias, but he watched the significant glances traded among the deputies with great interest.

"So, where is this shuttle taking us?" Ras asked.

"It's best if you don't know," Pauling said.

The party reached an elevator and began their descent.

"You're not dumping me in an Energy reservoir, are you?" Ras asked.

"Why would we do that?" Pauling asked, seeming genuinely surprised. "We're not trying to kill you."

"No, just indirectly handing me over to a dread sky pirate," Ras said. "Completely different." The elevator doors closed and Ras realized that Guy stood among their number. "Shouldn't you be making sure your team is all right?" Ras asked. "I think I'm covered in the security department."

"I'm not here for you," Guy said, only glancing at Ras.

In the cramped confines of the elevator, Ras looked over at Callie. She offered a reassuring look. *What are you up to?*

The elevator chimed, stopping on Sub-Level Fifteen. The doors creaked open, revealing a mostly repaired cannon bay. Ras shivered briefly as his eyes immediately traced along the rows of retractable cannons to the spot where Billie had died in Guy's arms. The smell of blood, sweat, and gunpowder returned to him.

"Get the hangar bay opened," Pauling said to a deputy, who broke into a trot down the long room. Once the deputy had reached the controls, the bay door which made up the full end wall shifted, then retracted into the ceiling. A breeze entered the hangar as the dark night sky revealed itself before them.

"Seems like this would be the safest place to keep me," Ras said. "Hard to get to...well-defended..."

"It does have those qualities," Pauling said.

Ras looked at the airship pulling alongside the bay opening. Its armored hull glinted in the light from the makeshift hangar, lined with cannons. "Are we expecting a lot of cannon fire?" Ras asked.

"Can't rule it out," Sheriff Pauling said, not breaking stride.

"We're not staying on *Verdant*, are we?" Ras asked, stopping.

"Observant," Sheriff Pauling said. He waved toward a deputy, who roughly shoved Ras back into a walk. "Only there's no 'we' to it."

"Can I have a moment with Ras to say goodbye?" Callie asked.

"Goodbye?" Ras asked incredulously. "What do you mean?"

"It was part of my deal with daddy," Callie said. "I couldn't find another way to get you off *Verdant* safely." She took a step toward him.

"They might as well just ship me off to Bravo Company in that thing," Ras said.

"That's kind of the idea," one of the deputies said with a dark chuckle.

Callie took another step toward Ras. "You can do this," she said softly. "You'll figure a way out and save the day, because that's what you do." She reached out, grabbing him by the wrist, jangling his type-writer bracelet. She pulled herself close to him. "Trust me." Her blue eyes took on a gray hue until they darkened almost to black.

A buzzing sensation emanated from where Callie held his wrist, then cascaded through the rest of him. Her synthesized Lack nature met his natural resonance. The back and forth feedback buzzed inside of him, facilitating an overload field of Energy-regulation.

The same field that knocked out the engines on *The Winnower*.

Callie threw her arms around him. The faint thrum of the city's engines began to fluctuate in pitch, and the ground shifted underneath with a lurch. *Verdant* began tilting.

Everyone fell in the cannon bay, and members of the Sheriff's department scrambled to get a grasp on anything they could lest they slide down through the open bay doors.

The faltering city collided with the armored airship. The vessel lumbered away to avoid further damage.

Ras struggled to make his way toward one of the cannons, but Callie tapped gently on his back. "No, look!" she said.

The open bay doors dropped, revealing *The Kingfisher* in the place of the gunship. As Ras slid alongside Callie and Elias, he laughed. "Did you plan this?"

He felt her head nuzzle an affirmative nod against his chest.

The bay of *The Kingfisher* opened, ready to swallow him, Callie, Elias, and Guy.

"Guy! What are you—" Ras' inquisition was cut short as they reached the end of the metal floor and collectively fell the two-foot drop into *The Kingfisher's* bay.

Emma reached down and helped Callie while Dayus picked up Ras with more strength than a seventy-something year-old man should have possessed.

"Guy?" Finn asked. "What are you doing here?"

"Putting in my application."

Ras looked up to see Old Harley and a couple faces he didn't recognize.

"Gents, may I introduce you to your Captain," Old Harley said.

RAS WATCHED AS *VERDANT* SHRUNK. In the dark, it was difficult to tell, but it seemed like the city had righted itself, so, no permanent damage had been done to its engines.

He turned to survey the study of *The Kingfisher*, taking in new and familiar faces alike. "Harley, is this everyone you hoped for?" he asked, leaning in slightly to the old dockhand, then began counting the number of heads in the room. *Callie, mom, Guy, Finn, Lev, Old Harley, and two guys I think I recognize from Port Authority.* Nine, including himself. Eleven, if he counted his father and Dayus on the bridge.

"Everyone and then some," Old Harley said. "I don't know the gentleman in the eyepatch, the redhead, or the skinny one, but everyone else I can vouch for."

"Who are the two guys—"

"Shane Hollister and Caedmon Patrick," Old Harley said. "Shane is my great-nephew. Caedmon is his second-cousin or some-such. Figured you'd need some good Port Authority muscle." He looked Ras over, then tapped the wrench holster. "Careful, they might mistake you for the ship's mechanic."

"A clumsy one," Ras said, tugging awkwardly at his bandages. The action brought less pain than it had earlier, which came as a surprise after all of the physical exertion back in the medical unit.

Elias crutched his way into the study. "We're clear from *Verdant*. No pursuers," he said. "So, no limitations on movement, if you catch my drift." He nodded to Callie, and Ras felt himself flush slightly.

Yes, the captain with the rosy cheeks. Perfect, Ras thought. He stepped over to Callie, who stood by the bookshelves next to Hal's desk. He placed his arm around her shoulder, not feeling the usual pain from the torso cut. Her eyes turned to a dark blue. "Does overloading bother you?"

"It feels…peaceful, actually," Callie said.

Ras had to agree. There was something *right* about being next to Callie, even if he couldn't find a better way to describe the sensation. Having been starved of it for the past three months was merely difficult. Overloading on *Verdant* had been reckless. They unfortunately had a long way to go before they fully understood how Dr. Lupava's Lack serum worked.

"So, how much of that escape was your plan versus your father's version?" Ras asked.

"They stayed pretty much the same up until the end," Callie said. "I ad-libbed a bit."

"I'd say winding up on *The Kingfisher* versus a transport to India Bravo makes a pretty big difference," Ras said, running a finger through his long hair. *Do proper Captains have short hair?*

"It was an important detail," Callie conceded. "But at least he and I agreed on every point leading up to it."

"Use as much force as possible to get me off *Verdant*?"

Callie pouted. "When you say it that way it makes it sound like he hates you."

"Funny how that works," Ras said, giving her a wink.

"Maybe you should start the meeting," Callie said. "I think we're the only ones talking."

The sentence hung in the room. Ras looked up to see everyone staring at him with anticipation. He let his arm drop from Callie's shoulder. "Ah, right then," he said, raising his voice to a level slightly louder than was needed for the size of the room. Elias winced, discretely holding a hand out, palm down. Ras caught the meaning: *Let's take it down a notch.*

After a stifled cough, Ras took a deep breath and let it out slowly. "Everyone, I'd like to welcome you to *The Kingfisher*," he said. *Good start, now what?* "As you may or may not know—well, you probably do know—well, you wouldn't have joined the crew without knowing…" *Get back on track.*

"Knowing what?" Finn asked with his hand raised.

"Ah, yes. Knowing that this is going to be a dangerous mission," Ras said. "Sorry."

"You don't have to apologize," Callie whispered.

"Right, sorry. I mean, I know," Ras said. "Sorry." He looked back at the crew. "Anyway, Atmo is in trouble, and it is up to you to save it—us. It is up to us to save it. You and me. Saving…Atmo. From danger…ous people. And things." *Nobody said there was going to be so much public speaking. Give me sky pirates and Convergences any day.*

"Like India Bravo?" Lev asked.

"Yes," Ras said, pointing to Lev. "India Bravo, top of the list of dangers to Atmo. Well, second to Convergences. No, third behind an Elder fleet, but they're frozen. Mostly. Still…very dangerous lady." He looked to his father in a half-plea. "Yes, before we can save Atmo, we must deal with India Bravo first."

"Wouldn't dealing with India Bravo save Atmo?" Lev asked.

Ras let an accidental laugh out. "Oh, I wish…No, in order to save Atmo, we have to sink it."

The crowd erupted in a series of overlapping questions in various levels of incredulity. Ras looked to Old Harley. "Was this not covered in the meeting?"

Old Harley shook his head and laughed. "No, boy. My job was to find trustworthy folk, not lead the mission."

Ras felt like a small child as his cheeks flushed again. He raised his arms to quiet his crew. "Hold on now. What everyone needs to know is that The Collective has been using Knacks to make fuel for their Helios engines. It's inhumane, and when everyone finds out, there's going to be a fuel shortage…and it's our job to make it safe for the cities to land by lowering the Energy beneath the clouds. That means clearing out the Convergences."

"But we'll die if we go beneath the clouds," one of the Port Authority workers said. Ras opened his mouth to speak, but was interrupted.

"And if we survive that, Remnants will tear us apart," Guy said.

"We are not going to use that term aboard this ship," Ras said resolutely, then flashed a look over to his mother who gave a slight smile. The epithet for the people left behind after Atmo launched had plenty of misinformation surrounding it. Most people in Atmo assumed if anyone had survived along with Convergences, then some sort of serious mutation had occurred in them. His mother was living, breathing proof to the contrary, but now wasn't the time to bring up such facts.

Ras took a deep breath. "Anyway, we have a safeguard against Convergences." He put a hand on Callie's shoulder. "Two, actually." He looked over to his parents. "No, four. You guys destroyed a Convergence together before I was born, right?"

Elias leaned over to Emma. "I don't remember telling him about that…"

"I told him," Emma said. "Thought it would cheer him up after everyone started hating him when he killed off the only Convergence left in The Bowl."

"Well, not everyone," Ras said.

"The percentage was pretty high," Finn said.

Ras held his hand up in an attempt to regain the floor. "What I'm trying to say is we shouldn't worry about Convergences. I can kill them as has already been mentioned, Callie can too now, and when someone from Atmo and someone from…whatever the ground is called get together—"

"Wait, your mother is a Remnant?" Guy asked.

"What did I just say about using that word?" Ras shouted. He took a deep breath, barely regaining composure. "Destroying all of the Convergences should be the easy part of this mission. All we have to do is survive India Bravo before she sinks a city in four days. So, if anyone has a plan, I'm all ears."

The crew erupted into overlapping questions and comments. Ras sighed, then hung his head and spoke in a low tone. "I'm going to have to get the hang of this, aren't I?"

Callie squeezed his arm. "You'll get there."

"I haven't thought this through," Ras said half to himself. "Everybody!" He raised his hand again to quiet the room. "We can't leave The Bowl. Not yet." Pausing, he waited until the hubbub died. "We have to go back to *Verdant*."

"Wasn't the whole point of breaking you out like that to get you away from those people?" Finn asked, then looked over to Lev. "Sorry, I mean you people. Your people." He cringed, then threw his hands up. "Now I can't open my mouth without my foot finding its way there."

"The Nalonians can't go home without proof they have me," Ras said. "And I want to make sure I have their support by bringing them back to their wives and children."

Lev stood a little taller. "What about the plan to fight India Bravo? I'm not sure our city can—"

"Let me worry about her," Ras said. "I'm not asking you to fight. Not yet." He turned his attention to Elias. "Dad, I hate to ask this of you, but would you be up for a shave and some fake bandages?"

Emma gave Elias a confused look. "Wait, what now?"

"I think I know where Ras is going with this," Elias said, shifting in his seat. "It'll be all right." He nodded to his son. "I'm in."

"Lev, can you convince your fellow Nalonians that my father is me?" Ras asked.

Lev looked at Elias, then Ras. "I guess the resemblance is there. But what happens to him when the city wants to turn him over to Bravo Company?"

"If things go the way I hope, Bravo Company won't even reach the city," Ras said. "Have *Nalon* send a message to *The Kingfisher*, saying you have me. We'll answer the call as Bravo Company, and then demand that my dad...*I* be locked up in *Nalon's* fuel creation station."

"So then we take over the fueling station," Elias said, "tell the real Bravo Company that you're on *Nalon*, and have a Convergence ready to threaten India Bravo with."

"Exactly."

"What are *we* going to do?" Callie asked.

Ras returned a smirk. "We're going to find our favorite white-haired, pint-sized wrecking ball."

CHAPTER FOUR
The Crew

DIXIE PIPER DIDN'T UNDERSTAND WHY THE THOUGHT OF PEOPLE trying to kill her amused her so. Long ago she had decided that if her time had run its course, she might as well leave with a smile. Part of her knew the lack of respect for death meant something wasn't quite right upstairs, but moments of clarity came attached with annoying crises of conscience. She rarely had time for those.

So she awoke with a smile, which quickly faded as the throb pulsing from the back of her head emanated to the rest of her body. Awareness slowly returned to various senses. Touch told her she was facedown on an uncomfortable surface. *How long have I been like this?* Her body lay splayed, her limbs twisted in various angles she would not have chosen herself.

Nalon had been a mess when she arrived a couple of months back. Men parading around in ill-fitting Collective uniforms had taken control of the city. It was hardly the place she had called home for the majority of her life.

Faint screams reached her ears intermittently. Pain. Ugly, ugly pain. She drew her limbs in toward herself, balling up and tried desperately to ignore the angry pounding that her brain seemed to be inflicting on her skull. She barely recalled why she hurt. Someone had betrayed her after she found *Nalon*'s City Council locked up deep in the Engine. Men with clubs came to mind.

Am I in jail?

The scream returned. It didn't sound like a man's scream. *Too young.* The sound echoed in her head, enraging her headache further. Weakly, she pulled herself into a seated position on the floor. She took in her surroundings. The dimly lit prison cells were each filled with small, huddled forms. *A prison for children? Why?*

"Sit down," a sullen looking boy of ten or so said. "Please don't make them come in here."

"Where's here?" Dixie croaked, her eyes slowly focusing on the boy. Her head swam and she raised a hand to steady it.

"The waiting room," he said simply.

"Are we in the Engine?"

He shook his head. "The man said if we're good and wait here for long enough, we'll see our parents again."

"And if you're not good?" Dixie asked. The screaming reverberated down the hallway again, sending a chill down her spine. She had her answer, and the boy seemed to know it.

"Are you the prize?" the boy asked with an uninterested tone. "The men said something about finding a prize."

The prospect didn't sound positive. "I'm nobody's prize. At least to nobody who works in a place like this. What's your name?" Dixie asked. "You can trust me."

The boy stared at her for a moment. "Colin."

"Well, Colin. Are we on *Nalon*?" Dixie asked. She tried to angle her head to see how many cells there were in this corridor. At least fifteen on either side of the walkway.

Colin shook his head. "I don't think so. But they said if we wait and we're good..."

"How long have you been waiting?" Dixie asked. "A week?"

"More," Colin said.

"A month?" The question haunted her as she asked it. It had been over a week since the men of *Nalon* had been shipped off to find Ras, hadn't it? This place could easily have been a holding place for children who lacked a mother to care for them while their fathers were sent off.

"I've probably had two birthdays since I came here," Colin said.

Dixie opened her mouth, then placed a hand over it to hide her horror. "I thought you were waiting for your parents to come back," she said through her fingers.

"No, this is where we wait to go meet them."

"Do you know where your parents are, Colin?"

The boy shook his head, then his eyes went wide as the sound of a deadbolt unlocking clanked from the end of the hall. Soon after, the sound of rusty wheels and heavy footfalls echoed down the hallway.

The children in the cells suddenly leapt to their feet, clamoring for the attention of the newcomers and reaching their arms through the spaces between the bars.

"Pick me! Pick me!" one child shouted.

"I've been here longer!" yelled another.

The sound of the squeaky wheel grew louder; in a few moments, a gurney came into view. Two men in Collective uniforms stopped two cells down from Dixie.

"Hey!" Dixie shouted. "What are you doing?"

The men ignored her. One of them unlocked the cell with a heavy metal key.

In the dim light, Dixie could make out some of the detail on the gurney. Next to the restraints were white tubes. This puzzled her until she recalled Callie's descriptions of the fuel creation spheres back on *The Winnower*.

She didn't know why she didn't put it together sooner. They were on the fueling station.

Rage filled Dixie. "Children?" She screamed. "You're using children?"

One of the men waded into the cell full of kids, then turned his attention to his cohort.

"Shut her up, will you?" he asked before reaching down to pick up the limp form of a young girl, maybe seven years old or so.

The rest of the children cried in anguish, shouting accusations of how unfair it was that one of the newer children got to go next.

"No!" Dixie screamed, grabbing the bars and pushing and pulling wildly against them. "No! You can't have her!"

The man pushed his way to the entrance of the cell with the girl. The door almost caught several small arms as it closed behind him.

"Let me go!" Dixie shouted.

The two men busied themselves with strapping the unfortunate girl to the gurney, then pushed the wheeled slab further along the hallway toward Dixie.

As they approached, she spat her finest curse at the two men.

"Easy lady," the taller of the two men said. "Not in front of the children." He gave a dark chuckle.

"How can you live with yourselves?"

"Lady, you do the math. One kid a month or one-hundred-and-fifty thousand people all at once," he said with a shrug of the shoulders. "I didn't build this system."

"You're worse," Dixie said. "You keep it going. Why don't you hop in that chamber?"

The man stopped the gurney, then took a step toward Dixie's cell. Her eyes flashed from the girl to the heavy key ring on the man's belt. "Not too many people left know how to run this station," he said. "If people like me go in there, everybody loses." He leaned in closer to whisper. "Might as well use the ones who fall through the cracks."

Dixie threw her arm out in a mad grasp for the guard's keys, but he anticipated her play and laughed as he easily stepped out of her reach. "If you weren't worth so much to Ms. Bravo, I'd let you swap spots."

"Why not use sky pirates?" Dixie asked through gritted teeth. "At least punish the ones who deserve it."

"You know what, we tried that at first," the man said, turning back to the gurney. "It didn't work all that great. Go figure."

Dixie watched, speechless for the first time in her life, as they opened the door on the other side of the corridor and exited. She had no bargaining chips. She was utterly helpless.

She felt herself over, wincing with each discovered bruise and cut. Her captors had been thorough, taking every single one of her lock picks. Deprived of her leverage, she fell back on the one behavior that she'd always been able to rely on, shouting until her voice ran hoarse.

The screams outside continued for what seemed to Dixie's tortured mind to be forever; suddenly they were cut short. The thrum of the station changed to a different pitch. *Is this when they swap out the children?* she wondered, then did everything in her power to avoid imagining the anguish that the sweet little girl was about to go through.

The door at the end of the hall where the technician had exited swung open. A lone silhouette stood at the mouth of the entrance, turning its head from side to side as it surveyed the room.

"I'll rip your face off!" Dixie shouted, trying to grab the figure's attention.

"I think I found her," the man spoke into a comm unit in a low, gruff tone. He strode toward Dixie's cell, and she could hear the faint jangle of keys as he walked. "You're certainly a sweet-talker, huh?" As he neared, Dixie could make out his features in the dim light. He rubbed at his scruff, then held a key up to the faint light in the room, studying it with his one good eye. He wore a green jumpsuit, but not a Collective one. It had a patch with an "8" emblazoned in gold on it.

"Who are you?" Dixie croaked.

"Just a guy," he said with a crooked, amused smile that Dixie would have found roguish in almost any other circumstance. He tried the key in her lock, but it didn't work. He moved on to the next one. "If I get you out, will you promise not to rip my face off?"

"Who are you with?" Dixie asked.

"You, soon," the man said. "If I can find the right key. Me and depth perception don't exactly mix."

"That's not what I mean," Dixie said, stomping her foot.

"Well, then I'm with the people about to launch a Convergence straight at Bravo Company."

Dixie's face lit up. "Give me the keys."

THE CITY OF *NALON* SHIMMERED in the orange light from the setting sun, dancing with color as its inhabitants moved about.

Earlier in the day Lev's refugee ship had docked, bringing a throng of people out to see the trophy of 'Ras Veir,' bandaged head to toe, albeit missing a leg. From high above in *The Kingfisher*'s shuttle, details had been difficult to make out, but step one had been accomplished.

Ras' eyes were fixed on the shuttle's comm unit as he placed a call over to *The Kingfisher*'s channel. "Dayus, did you make contact with Bravo Company?"

"I'm sorry, am I supposed to be Bravo Company or *Nalon* right now?" Dayus asked in an amused tone. "I've been practicing voices for either side."

"I like when he tries to be funny," Callie said, leaning forward from the back seat in the shuttle, cautious not to touch Ras lest they accidentally destroy the Convergence. She had changed into what she called her 'adventure outfit' comprised of her tall leather boots, tan corduroy pants, and a white long-sleeved ruffled shirt. He missed the sundress look on her, but knew this outfit was far more practical.

"Bravo Company is well on their way," Dayus said. "They sound quite excited to see you."

"We're in," Guy's voice cut in over the comm. "Elias and the rest of the crew are working on securing the rest of the station. Dixie and I are currently freeing the children."

"Wait, what now?" Ras asked. He hadn't expected to find Dixie just yet. That part of the plan was slated for after Bravo Company had been dealt with. Mixing India Bravo and Dixie was volatile at best.

"Give me that," Dixie's high pitched voice chimed in faintly, gaving way to loud scuffling sounds as Guy handed her the comm. "Erasmus Veir, do you know how many message tubes I've tried to send you?"

"I-"

"Dozens. Do-zens," she said. The garbled sounds of children crying and shouting played in the background. "Where have you been?"

"We didn't get any message tubes," Callie said, leaning in toward the shuttle's dash.

"Great," Dixie said. "Well, Atmo is falling apart, and what's this I hear about us attacking Bravo Company with a Convergence?"

"It's an insurance plan, Dixie," Ras said. "If everything goes wrong."

"I'd say those conditions have been met."

"India is going to sink every Atmo city she can if I don't go to her," Ras said. "Threatening her with a Convergence is the only card up my sleeve keeping me...*us* alive." He looked over to Callie.

"The sooner we sink Atmo, the better," Dixie said.

"Excuse me?"

"Gotta go," Dixie said. "Guards are starting to show up."

"All right, stick with Guy. He knows the plan."

"Got it," Dixie said quickly. A pause. "Thanks, Ras. It's good to hear a friendly voice."

"Good to have you back, Dix," Ras said, then pushed the comm button to end the conversation. He propped up his leg on the dash. He unlatched the brace, then rubbed his knee absentmindedly, massaging away some of the more stubborn tension. "I hope my dad is doing all right."

"I'm more worried about what your mom is going to do to him once he gets back," Callie said.

"Hopefully, we'll be around to see it," Ras said. He sighed. "I'm sorry Callie, I really thought we'd just fly around the surface, pop some Convergences, see the sights, save the day…"

"We are doing that," Callie said sweetly. "Just not in that order. We're saving *Nalon*, and then when we face India, it'll be smooth sailing. Simple as that."

"I'm glad you think it's simple," Ras said, pulling his leg back down to ease himself into a better posture. The ache in his leg had lessened considerably since his time on *Verdant*. His eyes darted about the horizon for Bravo Company. *It shouldn't be long*, he thought. *The Kingfisher* had found the fleet only a few hours outside *Nalon*.

"Do you think we'd see Bravo Company from further away if we gained some altitude?" Callie asked.

Ras thought for a moment. "Probably not. I think we have a pretty good angle on this from where we're sitting."

"Oh," Callie said. "Do you think if I sat next to you we'd be far enough away from *Nalon* that my overload wouldn't hurt it?"

Without a word, Ras re-engaged the engine on the shuttle and pulled back on the controls. The small ship picked up altitude. "On second thought, yes, this is a much better vantage point. The view is much improved."

Callie slid onto the wide, Elder-sized pilot seat next to Ras. He couldn't tell if the buzzing feeling he experienced was from Callie starting the overload process or his just being nervous. The idea of her wanting to be with him almost felt too good for it to be true.

A little part of Ras was convinced it was only a matter of time before the other shoe dropped and he discovered that something tragic had been waiting in the wings.

He clumsily lifted his grapple-gun-burdened left arm and let Callie nestle the side of her head into the crook of his shoulder.

"Are you nervous about meeting India Bravo?" she asked. "Your heart is beating kind of fast."

Ras closed his eyes in embarrassment. Yes, he was nervous, but India Bravo wasn't the only thing on his mind that could make his heart race.

"It's all right," she said. "I'm kind of scared, myself." She shifted her weight gently and lay her cheek lightly on his torso. "Is this all right? I don't want to hurt you."

The slash Foster had given him had been bothersome even on *Verdant*, but at the moment it gave him no issues. "I'm fine, thanks," he said absentmindedly, grateful that the ring box happened to be tucked away in his right pants' pocket instead of his left.

He attempted to casually drop his right hand from the controls and lay it over the outline of the box. He had considered leaving the ring back on *The Kingfisher*, but he just knew he'd somehow find himself in the perfect place to propose without the ring. "Callie, when you look at the future, what do you see?"

"That's a funny question," she said. "Why do you ask?"

"I guess when I look back at being a wind merchant, every day was hand to mouth, and I had to trust that the wind would bring me what I needed to scrape by on," Ras said. "I rarely caught a break, but when I did, I let myself dream about something beyond the worries I had that day. It was nice."

"I guess I've always imagined what life would be like once I got out of that basement," Callie said dreamily. "I don't know. It's funny, because now I find myself appreciating today more. Right now, being with you." She shrugged. "This is nice. I don't want it to end. I'm sure India Bravo will come when India Bravo will come, but she can't steal this moment from me. Worrying lets her do that, and that's a battle I can win."

The advice felt sage. Ras took in a deep breath in an attempt to preserve the moment. Just like on their last outing, they both knew what had to be done, even though every permutation of 'what had to be done' seemed likely to result in sinking Atmo. Mr. Tourbillon's warning of Ras' ruining all he touched played at the back of his mind. He did his best to shut it out.

"I wish you could have stayed safe on *The Kingfisher*," Ras said.

"Well, look at it this way: now you can make sure I'm safe," Callie said, her big eyes looking up at his. "Really, Ras, I'll be all right. I'd rather you not face any of this stuff on your own. You know, you're not the only one who gets to worry about the other's well being." She shifted, leaning up slightly to place a tender kiss on his cheek. "You're sweet."

Ras leaned in to kiss her back, but she fixated on the horizon. He let a slight breath out through his nose in frustration, then a sigh as he noted the specks of Bravo Company slowly encroaching on their moment. "Callie?"

She tore her eyes away from the window and looked at Ras. "Yeah?"

"Before things get too crazy and this plan winds up blowing up in our faces, I just want you to know you're the best thing that's ever happened to me."

A wide smile spread across her lips. She leaned in once more for a long, lingering kiss that made Ras curse India Bravo's presence further. She pulled back, released a contented sigh and said, "I don't plan to let that change."

Ras surveyed the reformed Bravo Company. While it lacked the visual punch it once had due to the notable absence of *The Dauntless*, the fleet had grown by at least one-hundred extra smaller vessels.

A few larger ships were obviously Collective airships, but the insignias were freshly painted over with Bravo Company's colors and images of a red skull with two axes crossed underneath its toothy grin.

"Which one will she be on?" Callie asked.

"There," Ras said, extending a finger toward the vessel sitting in the middle of the fleet. It wasn't the largest, but it brandished a massive flag and it looked newer, like an advanced version of a Collective gunship. He hoped they didn't have The Collective's Energy weapons available to them, but figured he'd be in for less disappointment if he just assumed they did. "At least I hope it's that one."

"If not, this is going to be an awkward meeting," Callie said. "Arr, the warlord be on a different airship," she said, affecting a gruff voice, and held up a crooked finger for a hook.

"I don't think they talk like that," Ras said.

"They do in the books," Callie said with a shrug. "I've always wanted to study their erosion of grammar."

"You can add that to your list of things to do before you die."

"At least I get to cross off 'face down a warlord,'" Callie said with a weak smile.

"You might want to put that last on the list," Ras said.

"The goal is to cross off as many things as you can, not all of them," she said. "I can't imagine not having anything left to do."

"I can't imagine putting 'face down a warlord' on my list."

Callie shrugged. "Sometimes I like to add things I know I'll get to cross off."

"Well, get your pen ready," Ras said as he gripped the controls to move the shuttle forward. "I'd find a place to buckle in." He watched Callie leave and settle into the bench behind him. He already missed her warmth.

The comm crackled to life and the voice of a woman broke through the static. "City of *Nalon*, I applaud you for your valor and tenacity." Her voice held a clarity and a presence to it as though every word were to be studied and understood syllable by syllable. "You have ten minutes to deliver Erasmus Veir, but anything more will result in the slaughter of the delivery crew."

"All right, that's our cue," Ras said. He shoved forward on the controls, dropping the vessel sharply. His stomach lodged firmly in his throat. The speed with which the shuttle could move was a testament to Illorian engineering, and Ras found himself wondering how lopsided The Clockwork War would have been if Hal Napier hadn't jumped sides.

The Bravo Company fleet grew larger in the shuttle's field of view as the vessel roared into a lack of cannon fire or Energy beams. The sound of the engines' repositioning to brake the shuttle filled the cockpit with a rushing whir.

Ras pulled back on the controls, bringing the shuttle to a hover above the bow deck of the flagship. He watched the sky pirates spill out with rifles at the ready from inside the massive vessel.

Flipping the comm to broadcast, Ras picked up the hand unit. "This is Erasmus Veir, announcing my intention to land. Over." At a flick of a switch, the shuttle dropped a couple feet, settling hard on its landing gear. Ras heard Callie's restraints unfasten, prompting him to do the same.

Ras stood and pressed one of the buttons on the wall. The single door of the tiny vessel hissed open, equalizing the pressure in the cabin and causing Ras' ears to pop. Steam emitted from the joints and the door pivoted down to become a set of stairs.

"Fearless leaders first," Callie said, sweeping a hand to the entrance.

Ras stepped through and looked at the firing squad welcoming committee. The goal was to reach India, not pick a fight along the way. As he walked down the steps, he placed both hands high in the sky and looked back to Callie to indicate she should do the same. "I've come to parlay with India Bravo to discuss the terms of survival for Bravo Company," he said as the shuttle's door automatically closed behind them.

The pirates shifted, moving in a surprisingly neat formation, making a third of a circle around the shuttle with guns still at the ready. Ras instinctively took a small step forward and to the left so that he would be eclipsing Callie should the sky pirates open fire.

"I said—" Ras began.

"We heard what you said, you dolt," said a bald sky pirate as he walked out from behind the back line of men. Besides a slight paunch, he had the look of a military commander and wore a long coat with shiny buttons in unnecessary places. "How delusional must you be to think you are in a place to do anything but be told what comes next for you?"

"You underestimate me," Ras said, nervously shifting his weight, but still mindful to cover Callie.

"Yes. I'm sure that will be my fatal mistake," the commander of the troop said. "Is that Miss Dixie Piper there, cowering behind you?"

"Dixie?" Ras asked with genuine surprise. "No."

The firing squad seemed to relax a bit, which irked Ras. "Really? I tell you that your survival is at risk and you ease up because she's not Dixie?"

"If you knew Miss Piper, you'd understand," he said. "As for the terms of our survival, Lady Bravo awaits your presence." The pirate commander gave a calculating grin that lent his lined face the look of a predator. "If you'll please follow me."

Ras took an experimental step forward with hands still raised.

The firing squad stood down, making a narrow gap for Ras and Callie to pass through. Ras lowered his arms slowly, careful to take the path furthest from either side lest the temptation of Callie's proximity be too much for the men to take. A few of them leered in, and one attempted to sniff her hair, which prompted Ras to shove that man into the bulkhead.

Callie threw her arms around Ras, using her momentum to keep them going forward to avoid more of a confrontation. "I'm fine, I'm fine," she said, then quickly released before the overload process could get too far underway.

The pirates laughed at the display, then dispersed into a disorderly set of groupings, casually walking up to inspect the shuttle.

"The name is Graham," the commander said, "I tell you this because it's common courtesy to know the name of the man who will put a bullet in your back if you put one toe out of line." He patted the hilts of the matching pistols holstered to each hip.

"Can't say I knew that custom," Ras said.

Graham motioned to the two sky pirates standing guard at the door from the deck, and they opened the heavy metal door into the belly of the beast. Once through, the two pirates fell in behind Ras and Callie.

The corridor inside was surprisingly well-lit and cleaner than Ras had expected. Along the walls hung paintings that appeared to be centuries old. Callie began to slow down to inspect the art, and Ras put an arm out to touch the small of her back, encouraging her to keep up.

"Impressive, isn't it?" Graham asked, stepping in front of Ras. "If you weren't holding an invisible knife to all of our throats, I might have had time to give you a guided tour."

The fact that nobody had attempted to kill either Callie or him encouraged Ras. Although he felt fairly certain they could be executed at the whim of India Bravo.

"I must say, it was a shame to hear about your father," Graham said, not breaking stride as they turned a corner. Pirates walking down the hallway stood at attention at his passing, which struck Ras as oddly organized. "He always put up such grand fights." Graham sighed contentedly. "Most battles were foregone conclusions before the opening salvo, but not when Elias Veir was around. Sometimes I think Lady Bravo attacked *Verdant* for the sheer sport of it, but such conjecture should be relegated to the mess hall in hushed conversations." He glanced over his shoulder. "I would say you're the next best thing to meeting him, but…"

"So, where's *The Dauntless*?" Ras asked. He knew any information he let Graham know would likely be used against him, so asking questions he already knew the answer to was the best way to pick up information based on how Graham lied to him.

Without looking back, Graham lifted his right hand, and the pirate behind Ras slammed something hard into Ras' back, causing him to stumble forward.

The pain shot from his spine to his extremities. He felt Callie stoop down next to him. "Are you all right?" she whispered, offering a hand to help him back to his feet. He waved her off and forced himself back up.

"We don't suffer mockery, Mr. Veir," Graham said. "Not from the likes of your kind."

My kind? Ras wondered, but the lingering ache in his back pleaded with him to avoid any unnecessary communication.

Graham stopped at an elaborately carved wooden door, obviously not a part of the ship's original design. He knocked three times, then shot a look to Ras. "If I were you, I wouldn't stare at her eye patch." He paused. "Especially if I were you."

The door swung open, revealing an elderly man wearing a fine black suit. The tall butler looked over Ras, then Callie, and turned to Graham. "M'lady instructed me to prepare tea for two, not six."

Graham got a devilish look on his face. "I guess the girl will have to wait with us."

"I'm not thirsty," Ras said. "Tea for two is fine." *Tea?* He attempted to hide his incredulity, and saw the face he wished he could make plastered on Callie's features.

The butler shut the door, and Ras could hear the hard soles of his shoes for a moment as they clapped against the floor in time with purposeful, rhythmic strides.

"Spoilsport," Graham muttered. "You know, I'd rather we just not have found you so we could have sunk a city or two. It would have been like old times." He narrowed his eyes, staring a bit beyond Ras. "Those screams...watching everyone return to the ground where they belong in only a minute." He smiled, lost in some sort of nostalgia. "Those delicious, delicious screams."

The footsteps returned, and the imposing butler opening the door. "Tea for three is served, and may I thank you on behalf of the Lady Bravo for your punctuality," he said with a bow that seemed rather genuine. He held it for a moment until Ras realized he was being ushered inside.

"Remember, the name is Graham," the sky pirate said with a lopsided grin.

Ras let Callie walk in first, entering the opulent quarters, decked ceiling to floor in various hues of red. The door shut behind them, and Ras realized the butler had excused himself into the hallway.

They were alone in the room with India Bravo herself.

CHAPTER FIVE
The Lady Bravo

A HIGH-BACKED CHAIR SAT IN THE CENTER OF THE ROOM, FACING away from the entrance. It held an intricate floral pattern in keeping with the room's red color scheme. Ras' eyes were drawn to artifacts sitting on gray pedestals, contraptions he didn't recognize. The room reminded him of Foster Helios III's office back aboard *The Halifax*, but India's relics looked pre-Atmo.

A manicured hand drummed its well-adorned fingers along the armrest to the rhythm of the somber orchestral music playing from a box next to the chair. It would have been the most beautiful thing Ras had heard were he somewhere else. Anywhere else.

Ras stood at the room's entrance with Callie by his side, not daring to take another step forward until acknowledged. He looked over to his wide-eyed companion and caught her mouthing "wow" as she took in the room.

"You may continue to stand there as long as you are appreciating my treasures and not plotting to kill me," the woman's voice projected from the chair. "Just think on this: I could have had you executed the moment you set foot on my ship, so I expect the same professional courtesy."

A low-muted whistle, barely audible at first, grew steadily in volume into a near scream, overpowering the music from the box. The adorned hand reached forward and collected a metal kettle from a side table, squelching the noise. "Tea's ready. Do join me."

Ras nodded to Callie, then took a step forward down the wooden stairs, then another. *At what point do I tell her about the Convergence?* "It's very kind of you to invite us for tea."

The message of the chair's position was clear. She did not fear her guests. For a moment he wagered whether a spike grapple could shoot through the furniture, then assumed it was probably lined with some sort of metal to prevent assassination attempts during tea.

Ras gave the chair a wide berth. He noticed the table in front of it, set with delicate looking cups and plates. On the opposite end sat two similar chairs, far less throne-like than the one India Bravo occupied.

They approached from the side to get a good look at the woman of legend.

India's black leather boots rose to just above her knee and had no heel to them. Her shirt was composed of heavy black and red lace, mostly covered by a tailored, velvet jacket. The jangle of her layered necklaces announced her movement as she stood, coming to a height of at least a few inches taller than Ras.

Her cherry-red hair had been obviously dyed to hide her age even though her figure had stayed fairly fixed in place throughout the years, it seemed. She looked down at Ras and Callie with her left eye.

Ras worked hard not to focus on the blood-colored eyepatch, and found himself staring into the dark brown eye boring through him with an intense curiosity.

"The resemblance is certainly there," she said, stony gaze fixed on Ras. She offered a hand toward the two chairs. "But does he have the same fight in him?"

Not wishing to interrupt the one-sided conversation, Ras stepped forward, maintaining eye contact until he banged his knee on the edge of the table. The dishes clattered.

India set her well-defined jaw and narrowed her eye, enhancing the wrinkles forming around it. "He seems not to have inherited the grace."

Ras looked to the chair behind him and took his seat, then watched Callie settle in the one next to him.

"You care too much for that one," India said, returning to her throne. "One might consider it unwise to bring something so precious to oneself into the den of the lioness."

Unsure of what a lioness might be, Ras ignored the comment. "I have come to discuss the terms of survival for Bravo Company." He wished his voice matched the strength of the words, but it didn't.

India stared at Ras for a moment; then a thin smile developed, followed by an obvious attempt to suppress a peal of laughter. She took a breath to compose herself. "Threats come after tea," she said, pouring the steaming water from the kettle into the three cups. Adorning the table on a silver platter were various colored spheres that looked like what Callie had previously described as fruit.

"I will say that I am glad you are alive," India said. "I would have had to go on wondering if I had sunk a city because I expected a dead man to arrive." She placed the kettle on a tray. "That could have almost pricked at my conscience."

Ras worked hard at not being obvious as he checked for exits. The peace in the room unnerved him. He had faced full-on battles with less trepidation.

"I heard a rumor that you were in The Wild not too long ago," India said.

"I was," Ras replied.

She raised an eyebrow as she scooped a spoonful of sugar into her tea, then scooped again, gesturing an offer to Ras, who waived it off. She turned to Callie. "My dear, may I suggest the sugar? The tea is somewhat biting without it."

"How do I know it's not poisoned?" Callie asked.

India feigned an indignant look, then smiled wickedly. "Smart girl," she said. "Very wise question. You'll go far in life with a head like that resting on your shoulders."

Callie stared at India for a long moment. "Are you saying the tea is poisoned?"

India gave a Callie a long stare, then sighed. "I suppose I am giving up the game a bit early, but it was obvious you two weren't interested in imbibing, which was wise. My pushing further would have showed my hand." She lifted her ornately decorated cup to her lips and took a sip of what Ras assumed to be non-poisonous tea. "I hate being pedantic. But, I did have to check."

Ras cocked his head slightly. "Check on what?"

"Well, if you are who everyone says you are, you have a lot ahead of you," India said. "And if a bit of arsenic tea could weed you out of the running, then it would stand that you aren't The Reclaimer."

The title caught Ras off guard. "I thought The Reclaimer was just Illorian folklore."

"Evidently they can't claim sole ownership over such a mythic individual," India said. "Which, by the by, who knew they were human?" She laughed heartily, as though life were a game. "You think you have a solid grasp on reality, but reality has too much of a fondness for pulling rugs."

Ras looked over to Callie. "Pulling rugs?" he asked.

"It's short for 'pulling the rug out from underneath you,'" Callie said. "It's not a common expression in Atmo for surprising someone."

"I suppose it isn't," India said, her eye dancing with newfound interest in Callie. "I take it you aren't of Atmo?'

Offering any clues to India felt like an instant liability, but lying could lead to worse circumstances very quickly. "She's not," Ras said.

"Oh," India said in a manner somewhere on the border between keen interest and a command to continue. When Ras remained silent, she pressed further. "I've heard rumors that Veir men prefer their women with at least one foot on the ground."

How would she know about my mother? Ras wondered. As far as he knew, her sub-Atmo origin had remained a mystery to even everyone on *Verdant*.

India shifted her posture, her adornment chiming along as she focused her attention on Callie. "How does it feel to court death?"

"Excuse me?" Ras and Callie said simultaneously.

"Oh, you haven't told her." India broke into a smile featuring most of her teeth. "Would you care to now, or shall I?" she asked. "I'm not much for keeping secrets in a relationship, and I cannot abide it when others do so."

Ras eyed her for a moment. *Are we in couples therapy?* "Be my guest."

"Hmm," India purred. "Well, the common wisdom this side of the Illorian mountains is that The Reclaimer will usher everyone to be with those who died in The Great Overload. He brings death, and one would do well not to stand in his way." She smiled slightly as if a thought had struck her and looked Ras over once more, her eyes finally coming to rest on his bandages. "Although nobody mentioned how easily he could be hurt."

"How come nobody in Atmo has ever talked about a Reclaimer, and you seem rather educated on the subject?" Callie asked.

"Not many self-respecting citizens of Atmo will dive below to collect what was lost once mankind took to the skies," India said.

While the idea of being an agent of death, or death itself, whatever that meant, did not appeal to Ras, he realized the concept could be a useful one. "So it seems finding The Reclaimer was worth threatening to destroy a city."

"The fate of *Nalon* is already decided," India said as her smile faded. "As I understand it, you were not brought to me, which was one part of the terms I was most specific on."

"What exactly were those terms?" Callie asked.

"Whichever of the three remaining Collective-controlled cities that brought you to me *wouldn't* be shot out of the sky," India said. She took another long sip of tea. "Surely you didn't think what you see is all there is to Bravo Company, do you? My ships are waiting for word to strike *Gia* and *Trentin*. Since *Nalon* technically failed to bring you to me as well…"

Ras stared, working hard to contain his astonishment. "You're willing to drop *three* cities? Atmo is crowded enough as it is. What's in any of this for you?"

"I just need to show everyone who is in charge—"

"I am," Ras said before he realized the words had escaped his mouth. "And if you don't want a Convergence ripping through your fleet causing the next Great Overload, I would tell your ships to stand down." *Why am I saying this?* he thought, panicked. *Why isn't anybody stopping me from saying this?*

The toothy grin returned in full force, giving an animalistic hunger to her dark brown eye. "And where would you acquire one of those?"

"Doesn't matter," Ras said. He had already stepped across the line, so the best he could manage was to own the role at this point. "I already have it, and my team is ready to release it if they don't hear from me. Soon." He could feel himself begin to sweat. The moment of unexpected bravado had left as quickly and unexpectedly as it had come.

"And if that doesn't dissuade you," Callie chimed in, "I can freeze this entire fleet."

After a brief moment of shock, Ras picked up and continued the bluff. "She's done it before. In Illoria. I think you remember that, seeing as this isn't *The Dauntless*."

India paused, eyeing Ras. "Oh, this *is* fun." She set her teacup gently onto the table, then leaned forward. "I'm going to assume, based on your threats, and the fact that *Nalon*'s fueling station has been inching its way out toward my fleet, that your trump card is your friends' hijacking and releasing the Convergence if you give the order."

"Or I freeze this fleet," Callie added.

India waved her hand dismissively. "That's not how that works," she said. "My men captured and interrogated an Illorian once. He was most informative between screams. So, really, you've doomed *Nalon* either way. Either you release the thing that makes the fuel to keep the city aloft, or I strike it down," India said, musing. "You'd do that to a city just to strike me down…" She narrowed her eye. "You are a bringer of death, aren't you?"

Ras could feel the nervous chills of adrenaline withdrawal begin to set in. "Why go to all of this trouble? What do you want with me?" Ras stood, gesturing wildly toward the large open window looking over *Nalon*. "You obviously don't think I'm a threat or else you'd have guards—"

"Sit down," India said coldly.

"I struggle to believe that you've somehow rebuilt your fleet to be able to overpower three cities at once when you've yet to successfully take *Verdant*." He eyed the fleet surrounding the flagship.

"Ras, I think maybe you should sit down," Callie said.

"I—" Ras began, but looked down to see India pointing a weapon much like the Energy pistol Foster had onboard *The Winnower*, at Callie. The gesture didn't frighten him, but pulled his emotions in the opposite direction. He managed to speak calmly despite his rage. "When *The Winnower* fell, it was because Foster shot her with a gun exactly like that one." He sat slowly, staring intently at India. "I assume you saw firsthand what happened to it, and if you want to see the engine of every single ship in your fleet fail like *The Winnower*'s did, you can pull that trigger."

Ras hated that he didn't actually know what would happen if Callie overloaded now or whether his bluff was even really a bluff. He especially hated how easily Callie could die if this standoff turned sour.

"But if you want to see how The Reclaimer brings death, by all means keep pointing that gun at her," Ras said with an edge to his voice that scared him.

"You were onboard *The Winnower?*" India asked carefully, lowering her gun.

"I was the last one to leave," Ras said.

Something had engaged her curiosity. "How did you escape?"

Thankful for an opportunity to both tell the truth and sound impressive, Ras grinned. "I jumped off."

"But falling would bring you closer to the Time Origin."

"I'm The Reclaimer," Ras said. "Time doesn't bother me."

India's face relaxed slightly, giving her a more youthful appearance. "I knew it."

"Knew what?" Callie asked. India sat back into perfect posture, resting each hand on the padded armrests, trigger finger no longer a threat. "There is someone I need you to retrieve for me," she said. "If you are able to do so within two weeks, I shall stay my hand from these three cities."

Yet another detour, Ras thought. *A simple grab job shouldn't take too long.* "Who do you need retrieved?"

"My son," India said.

"Your son was on *The Winnower?*" Ras asked, raising an eyebrow. The desperate attempt to reach him suddenly made so much more sense.

"He shouldn't be hard to miss," India said. "I believe you've met him." There weren't too many people Ras had met on *The Winnower,* but—his mind spun. "No…" he said in disbelief.

"What?" Callie asked.

"I need you to bring Foster Helios back to me. Alive."

Ras had difficulty interpreting the placid expression on India's face. In the long, awkward silence that followed, he read in the stark, clean interior of the room a simple truth he had overlooked earlier: This ship wasn't hijacked in the heat of a battle; it had been gifted. Hal had warned in his own cryptic way the two factions were in cahoots. Ras wondered if the old war hero knew the genetic tidbit he had just learned.

"That's going to take a while," Callie said. "Months."

India turned her head toward Callie, but kept her eye on Ras. "I set the deadlines, dear."

"But there's nobody else who can get in there and back but us," Callie said.

"Whether or not that's true, I find that placing time limits on complicated tasks engenders ingenuity," India said, flicking her eye to Callie. "I'll concede the difficulty of this task, so let me offer this compromise. I'll give you three weeks instead of two, but the end of each week, I drop a city."

"A second ago we had two weeks!" Ras exclaimed.

"You wanted more time," India said. "I don't give such things away freely."

Ras gritted his teeth. "And what happens at the end of three weeks?" he asked. "What motivation do you have for us then?"

India gazed out the large bay window to her fleet. "Then I utilize every last resource at my disposal to find you and have my men dissect both of you slowly until we can find out why you're immune to Time."

"Why?" Ras asked.

"Because even the bravest man fears being ripped limb from—"

"That's not what I'm asking," Ras said. "It's obvious you hold all of the cards in Atmo. Even if Foster is your son, why upset the new balance?"

"Would an explanation of my motivations and plans bring him back to me any faster?" India asked. "You have an opportunity to save what I estimate to be a quarter of what remains of Atmo. Let's not muddy the waters with why."

A loud thunk resonated through the walls and as the primary lights flicked off, the red emergency lamps came online, casting a bloody hue on everything inside.

"What's going on?" Callie asked as the doors opened on either side of the room.

Sky pirates armed with rifles flooded inside and lined up neatly beside the tea table. "Lady Bravo," Graham said, "they've released a Convergence."

THERE WAS NO GOING BACK. The release lever had been pulled, and Dixie had never been happier. The room of the fueling platform shook violently, forcing her to hold on tightly to the ball at the end of the lever.

"What are you doing?" Elias bellowed over the warning klaxons. "We didn't receive the signal from Ras!"

"When you can knock India Bravo out of the sky, you don't wait for signals," Dixie said with exuberance. "I am not leaving this station until I know every last child here won't be tortured just so this city can keep flying." She released her grasp on the lever and stepped over to the prone body of the technician in the Collective uniform at her feet. "Either Ras and Callie get the ball rolling by destroying another Convergence or let it rip through Bravo Company. If they're smart, both will happen." She looked over the control room at the aftermath of the brief battle between The Collective and the crew of *The Kingfisher*. One of Ras' men had taken a bullet to the leg, but the redhead was tending to him. "Let's get these kids off this thing, huh?"

"You're not the one in charge, Dixie," Elias protested, crutching his way over to the command station. "You can't just *wing it* against India Bravo."

Dixie fought the urge to kick one of his supports out from underneath him for challenging her. "Then may I wholeheartedly say, 'oops.'"

INDIA BRAVO MOVED with surprising haste for a woman in her fifties as she took the stairs leading to the bridge two at a time. Before Ras could reach the first step, her commanding voice blared throughout the ship's loudspeakers.

"My dearest Bravo Company," she said, a hard edge to her voice. "I would like for you to take this opportunity to observe well the behavior of those entrusted to our care. Before you are the proverbial jaws, sprung to bite the hand that could so easily crush them."

"Should we hold hands?" Callie whispered as she and Ras ascended the stairs with the rest of the armed entourage.

"Not yet," Ras breathed out. They reached the top stair and entered the three-tiered bridge, where sky pirates buzzed about at various command stations. The design of the room reminded Ras of *The Winnower*'s bridge, and he winced slightly at the memory of Foster's shooting Callie.

"Ah, our honored guests," India said, placing a hand over the microphone she held. "Perhaps you would like to witness what poses for a good idea on *Nalon*? I wonder if they realize this is an act of war."

The Convergence looked completely out of place above the clouds, illuminating the darkening sky around it with a brilliant green hue.

"What if we stop it?" Callie asked.

"Callie—" Ras began to protest, but the sky pirate directly behind him slapped the back of his head.

India arched an eyebrow, then raised the microphone to her lips. "'M' squadron, fall back in formation. Everyone else, advance on *Nalon*."

"*Nalon* didn't attack you," Callie said hastily. "It was our crew's backup plan to keep us alive, and we're going to need them if we're going to be able to go find..." she trailed off. "He's The Reclaimer." All of the sky pirates surrounding Callie and Ras drew back. Was that a good sign or a bad sign? It was too late to take it back now. "I'm the...well, I don't know what I am, but together we can destroy that Convergence if we have your word you'll keep your promise and give *Nalon* a week."

The activity on the bridge had dulled to a murmur, and the word 'reclaimer' could be heard intermittently in the pirates' hushed speech.

"Am I the only one who didn't know what a Reclaimer was until I became it—him?" Ras asked, flustered. *How have sky pirates heard of it when nobody on* Verdant *has?*

India Bravo pursed her lips. "You have your assignment, Reclaimer. Just remember, one week per city. The longer you take, the more death you bring." She paused. "Be sure to pass along that any vessel that attempts to escape each city will be shot down."

Ras leaned in toward Callie. "A very large part of me would rather let this thing wreck their fleet," he muttered. "I mean, who is to say they won't just slag *Nalon* as soon as we leave?"

Callie shook her head. "There's been too much bloodshed already." She offered her hand as the faintest sound of the Convergence's unholy chorus reached her ears. "Besides, if you don't want The Reclaimer to bring death, you have a choice right now."

Ras looked at Callie, then her hand, and finally India Bravo. "You're lucky she's here." He grasped Callie's hand, and the tingling sensation returned, clearing his mind of all else but the feeling of peace it brought. For a moment, the world seemed brighter and he couldn't even look at the Convergence itself. A feeling of resistance pressed against his body from the direction of the giant green orb, and the pain in his body receded.

The Convergence began to fluctuate about half a mile away from the front of Bravo Company, then burst into a shockwave that rocked even the large capital ship.

Ras wanted to throw a fist into the air in excitement, but restrained himself. The process worked, which bode well for Atmo in general. He took a deep breath, then let it out slowly. Callie had her jaw clenched in a look of defiance. "Are you all right?" he asked.

Without looking back at him, she nodded.

The two paces of breathing room the sky pirates had given them had increased to ten. Only India Bravo dared to stand near them.

Without a proper escort to shove them in the right direction back to their shuttle, Ras looked around, then pointed. "I guess we just go out the way we came, then?"

India glared.

THE *KINGFISHER* HUNG HIGH ABOVE *NALON*, Bravo Company, and the slowly sinking fuel platform. Evening had given way to night, drawing Callie to the window of Hal's study to observe the stars as they appeared while the rest of the crew bustled about, prepping for departure.

"You know, there's a perfectly good telescope here," Elias said, making his way over to Callie. "I haven't tried it myself, but it's big enough that I doubt it's just decorative."

Callie looked back at the large fixture in the center of the room, then Elias. "I kind of like seeing them all at once," she said. "They give me a sense of scope."

"Like you're tiny and far away from everything?" Elias asked.

She shrugged. "Just that there's a lot more out there." Memories piled atop memories of the nights when she would devote a full hour to peering out her basement window before she allowed herself to fall asleep. Even then, the lights of *Verdant* made it difficult to see many of them. It wasn't until a twelve-year-old Ras took her to the docks that she was able properly to see what she had been missing. "I guess I took them for granted, assuming I'd always see them every night. Now that we're going beneath the clouds…"

The door from the hallway opened up and a burst of noise filled the room as Ras entered, flanked by Dixie, Guy, and Dayus.

"Why are we not diving already?" Dixie demanded, bobbing as she made short strides to keep up with Ras.

"Because the Captain has an important decision to make," Dayus said. "One that would greatly benefit from the wisdom of Mr. Napier."

Dixie took two quick steps and cut off Ras. "Okay, seriously. Helping India Bravo has to be off the table." She looked over to Dayus and pointed a finger at him. "Traipsing back to The Wild is just one stop away from the Time Origin. Don't think I don't know what you're getting at."

"What are you talking about?" Ras asked.

"Sure, it starts with talking to Hal," Dixie began. "Then it's '*Let's attack the sky pirates with Elder ships and take back Atmo.*'" She narrowed her eyes. "Which, while I'm generally pro-attacking sky pirates, we would wind up exactly where we were one hundred years ago."

"Halcyon Napier has absolutely no interest in Illorian dominance, if you'll recall history," Dayus said resolutely. "There's a reason Lady Bravo wants Foster, and Halcyon may have insight."

Dixie gritted her teeth, then held up her index finger. "One, we'd waste time flying into The Wild." Another finger shot up. "Two, we'd just find the mangled remains of Foster in Ras old ship—"

"You saw him?" Ras interjected.

"Yeah," Dixie said, her expression softening. "When I was pulling you and Callie out of the debris. He was kind of hard to miss."

"So he's dead?" Callie asked, stepping away from the window. "You're sure?"

"Well, the half of him I saw that wasn't pinned underneath your jetcycle wasn't breathing, had its eyes wide open, and looked like a pin cushion for glass shards," Dixie said. "I'm sure Mama Bravo would love seeing that."

Dayus gave Dixie a long look. "Did you see anything else?"

"With these two bleeding out, I didn't exactly have time to sight see," Dixie said. "Why?"

The old man shrugged off the question. "No reason."

"Ras," Dixie said, placing a hand on either side of his face and pulling his line of sight down to her. "The Collective is using children as fuel for the Convergences. The ones from *Nalon* are safe, but every second we aren't making the world safer for the cities to land is a second longer those children are being tortured."

"Can we even find all of the Convergences before Bravo drops *Nalon*?" Callie asked.

"*Nalon* may not even have a week now that *someone* released the Convergence to attack Bravo company," Elias said.

"Sure, why don't we just toss the kids back in the furnace," Dixie said.

"If we want to get our bearings, we might consider going down to my hometown," Emma said as she entered the room. "Acerbis used to track Convergences twenty years ago. I assume they still do. If my parents still live there, maybe they could help us find what we need."

Callie walked over to Ras, stepping past Dayus and Dixie. "Hey," she said softly. "Forget what India said about you. I know this is a tough call, but I'm with you wherever you fly."

Ras seemed deep in thought as he nodded. He folded his arms across his chest, placing a hand to his mouth. "We can't fly blind and waste a week," he said. "I think it's time for a family reunion."

CHAPTER SIX
The Descent

CALLIE ADJUSTED THE OVERSIZED PILLOW BETWEEN HER BACK AND the wall as she settled in on her bunk for another reading from *The Demons of Bogues*. The room was suitably small, affording a level of privacy she hadn't known she craved until there were almost a dozen people onboard.

The beginnings of a headache had haunted her ever since the overload on India's ship, but she attributed it to the stress of the day. She couldn't let herself imagine the ramifications of Dr. Lupava's Lack serum's wearing off. Too much of the mission rode on her ability to overload.

She idly flipped a page in her book without reading it. She felt unprepared to interact with people beneath the clouds, and a book of superstitions was as close as she'd get to a cultural guide. Emma had been engaged in passionate discussions with her husband over his role in the prior mission, so Callie would have to make do by herself for now. She still had too many questions.

Bogues is the center of so much. The Illorians had attacked there first to start their war, and it was where The Great Overload had kicked off.

Dayus had rarely offered anything of substance the previous times she had pried for information, citing the excuse of poor timing. The only confirmation she had managed to coax from him was that the white train he had found her on was headed for Bogues.

He's hiding something, she thought. *But why?*

She flipped the page to an illustration of a man-sized creature wrapped head to toe in bandages. It reminded her slightly of Ras. She had no clue how Ras could still stand after all of the abuse he had endured already.

Staring up at her from the next page was a shadowy figure whose only discernible features were the whites of its eyes and pointy teeth shaped into a wicked grin. Underneath the illustration read the caption: *The Thromus*.

"The artist got lazy with you, didn't he?" Callie muttered, skimming the basic information consisting of the same superstitions shared on the other pages. *Don't say his name three times, lurks in shadows, comes for your ember.*

Callie crinkled her nose at the last description in confusion.

A knock came on her door. She checked her watch, noticing it was almost midnight. "It's open."

The metal door creaked on its hinges and Dixie poked in her head. "Sorry, didn't realize this was your room." She ducked out as quickly as she had entered.

"Wait," Callie said, setting the book aside.

Dixie slowly reentered, then shut the door halfway. "Fair warning, I don't do slumber parties."

"I just want to talk," Callie said. "I heard you saw some...*things* on the fueling station."

"Part of me wants to just fall asleep so I can get the nightmares over with already," Dixie said, placing her back firmly on the bulkhead. Her purple leather jacket had seen far better days. One sleeve had been replaced with black leather, and there were dark droplets of what looked like blood stains down the front. "Don't think I'm going to shake that anytime soon."

"Did the children find their parents?"

"I made sure one of them did...I'm sure the others who still had parents probably will," Dixie said, quirking her lips. "Can we be done talking about this? I ask out of politeness, so you can understand how much I'd rather be doing anything else."

"Here, you can have my bed if you want to crash," Callie said, sliding across her bunk and slipping on her shoes. "I was hoping to catch Emma before we land."

"Thanks," Dixie said. She stepped up to the bed and fell forward, face down. She spoke, bedsheets muffling her words: "If you could close the door on the way out."

Callie slipped out of the room and into the dimly lit corridor to peer through the various portholes leading to other rooms. She found Emma sitting alone inside the mess hall.

"She could use a distraction," Ras said from behind her.

"When did you get so sneaky?" Callie asked, smacking his arm without thought. "Sorry!"

Ras winced. "It's all right. It didn't hurt as bad as the bullet that went in there," he said, grinning.

"Have you talked to her yet?" Callie asked, nodding toward the mess hall. She looked into Ras' green eyes. They seemed to sparkle with the reflection of the running lights in the hallway. It was distracting.

"I figured I should go talk to my dad first," Ras said. "Maybe you can give me the highlight of the sub-cloud orientation…what is the world beneath the clouds called, anyway?"

"I'll make that question one," Callie said.

He took a deep breath and let it out slowly. "Sorry it took so long to get beneath the clouds again. I know you've been looking forward to that."

Callie shrugged. "Right now I'm just enjoying seeing the captain at work."

Ras let out a laugh. "Right. I'm a vision of leadership."

"You're going to be the last one to see it." Callie said, leaning in for a peck on his cheek. She felt the rush of the overload begin and suddenly die down as she took a step back. The tinge of a headache continued to play at the back of her mind.

Ras shook his head, his face slightly flushed from the kiss.

"You have a crew, Ras," Callie said. "One that's comprised of more than just me."

"That was a good crew."

"I agree, but without being overly dramatic, these are people following you with the hope of saving the world," Callie said. "That has to be at least a little exciting."

A faint smile grew on Ras' lips. "It kind of is."

"Time for your changing, captain," Finn said as he stepped out from the med unit down the hall, holding up a roll of bandages.

"Can you please start saying that differently?" Ras asked, turning to address him.

"I could, but it's funny every time," Finn said. "Don't be such a baby…sir. Okay, that one went a bit far."

Ras looked back to Callie. "We should land outside of Acerbis in an hour or two. I'll come back here if I can."

"Aye-aye, Captain," Callie said, offering a quick salute before ducking into the mess hall.

The next hour gave Callie the opportunity to drown Emma with a deluge of questions about what ground-living was like. Emma did her best to relay what living on land, called Imago, was like. At several points, she suggested it might be easier to just explain everything insisted of fielding Callie's questions.

If Callie was being perfectly honest with herself, she wanted to also show off how much she already knew. "All right," she said. "The tall pylons outside the cities that keep the Energy from coming into the city; what are those called?"

"You've seen them before?" Emma asked, eyes widening.

"Back when we visited Bogues."

"Oh." Emma gave a slight smirk. "They're called pylons."

"Really? That's it?" Callie asked. "Not *The Great Invisible Walls of Defense* or something?"

"After The Great Overload, we kind of stopped saying 'great,'" Emma said. "It's almost a curse word and the older citizens will get offended."

"If 'great' is bad, is 'bad' good?"

"No, bad is still bad," Emma said. "It's really not all that different from living in Atmo. There's just a general disposition to dislike people who live a lot higher than you."

"Is it true everyone is an artist or has some artistic skill?"

Emma laughed. "Where would you get an idea like that?"

"Well, I heard that Helios picked the most scientifically adept citizens who could manage running a flying city and left the rest on the ground," Callie said.

"That's an interesting theory," Emma said, her eyes flicking toward the door as Dixie, Guy, and Finn entered the room. "But it still requires a lot of mechanical prowess to run a Burrow."

"A borough, like a neighborhood borough?" Callie asked.

Emma made a digging motion with her hands. "Think burrow underground. I'm sure whoever came up with the name thought themselves clever to make it sound like borough," she said. "The giant digging machines that made the underground cities were probably as complex as a floating city."

"Only if it breaks, everyone doesn't fall to his death," Guy said, sitting and propping his boots up on the dining table. He leaned so far back the old wooden chair creaked.

"Well, our digger did actually break when I was a little girl," Emma said. "As the population grew, they would fire the machine back up and drill one more level further down and dig out hovels for homes and shops."

"How deep did it go before it broke?" Callie asked.

"Nineteen levels," Emma said. "People started to live in some of the abandoned buildings topside, but most were so badly damaged from everyone overloading that the common wisdom was to only live there long enough until you could build a home on the outskirts, but that had its own problems..." She trailed off.

"Does anyone have green skin?" Dixie asked.

"Seriously?" Finn asked. "You have a wealth of potential information about the great unknown and that's what you ask?"

"It's better than being caught off-guard by it," Dixie muttered.

"I think it's safe to assume anything you've heard from someone pointing a flashlight at their face late at night shouldn't be taken as truth," Emma said. "Now, spectres on the other hand..."

Callie thought she saw Emma throw a furtive wink her way. "What's a spectre?" she asked, offering Emma a proper set-up to play on Dixie's superstitions, even though she vaguely recalled reading a description of one in *The Demons of Bogues* or something similar.

"There are plenty of theories," Emma said, turning her attention back to Dixie. "Some say they're the ghosts of The Clockwork War, some say they're demons, and some just write them off as figments of tired watchmen's minds who stare out in the night too long."

"Have you seen one?" Dixie asked.

"Twice I've seen the shadows outside of Acerbis move in unnatural ways," Emma said. "But that's all I can really say about it." She waved a hand dismissively. "They're harmless, I think. Just a trick of the light and an excuse to blame bad things on. But if you really want to keep an eye out for them, you'll have to look from the corners of your eyes. As soon as you look directly at them, you can't see them anymore."

Guy let out a deep laugh. "Grinding gears, woman. You almost had me going there for a minute."

Dixie punched him in the arm. "You haven't been down there. You don't know."

Guy snorted. "The late shifters in the Engine say the same thing, only they call them gremlins. Say you can only see them out of the corner of your eye," Guy said, tapping the side of his temple. "Well, I need what I got to not trip over anything. Looking for things that aren't there is a waste of sight."

"Are there any customs we should know about?" Finn asked, raising a hand. The gesture made Callie miss her University classes briefly, but she still considered this mission as a prolonged independent study.

"I would strongly suggest you refrain from letting anyone know you're from Atmo," Emma said.

"She's understating that a bit." Elias' voice filtered into the room just before he and Ras entered. "Being called 'Skyfolk' is about ten times worse than calling someone a Lack in Atmo," he said, then turned to Ras. "No offense."

"None taken," Ras deadpanned, then caught Callie's eye and flashed a smile which faded into a grin.

Elias eased into the chair next to Finn and Ras stood at the head of the table next to Callie.

"If we don't want to get run out of town with pitchforks," Emma said, "we'll need a good cover story."

"I can attest to the pitchforks," Elias said. "I think they're sharpened especially for visitors. I have three scars on my backside to prove—"

"All right," Ras said with an awkward chuckle. "No sense in feeding our imaginations. So, what sort of backstory do you suggest?"

"Expeditionary group," Emma said.

"Where from?" Callie asked.

"Cooke. It's a Burrow just outside of The Bowl," Emma said. "If we say we've traveled from much further away than that, they'll be suspicious."

"How often did you see people from other Burrows?" Callie asked.

Emma looked up as if trying to pull the memory from the ceiling. "I think I remember there being four visitors in the twenty years I lived there," she said. "No, five."

"So it's a big deal to have newcomers," Ras said. He ran a hand through his unkempt hair, beginning to pace. "How long will it take to find out what they know about Convergences?"

"Assuming your grandfather will be willing to help us, less than a day," Emma said.

"And if he isn't?"

"It might be wise to see if Hal left some metal Elder underwear," Elias said.

RAS SHIFTED HIS WEIGHT UNEASILY, pulling at the oversized traveler's cloak. It itched. A lot. Standing at the top of *The Kingfisher's* ramp, he watched Callie thread her way past Dixie, Elias, and Dayus to reach him. He patted his right pocket instinctively for the ring box, and a minor panic washed over him until he remembered stowing it away in his dresser back on the ship. A ruined city didn't seem the most romantic place to propose. "Hey," he said overly casual. "Ready to see the world?"

Callie looked over her shoulder into the black, quiet night outside. The tiny specks of light on the horizon indicated just how far away Acerbis was. "I'd be more ready if I knew what was between here and there."

"Adventure," Ras said playfully. "Or a lot of walking in the dark."

"Or that."

Ras hefted over his shoulder a travel backpack filled with his grapple gun and anything that might give them away as Skyfolk, then extended his right hand for hers.

"But I'll overload," Callie said, surprising him with her hesitance.

"Right, that's the point. We need to keep the rest of the crew safe when we walk," Ras said. "You, me, and my mom aren't enough to cover..." He looked over the away team and softly counted under his breath. "Yeah, there's eight of us with Harley and his two Port Authority guys watching the ship."

Callie took Ras' proffered hand and laced their fingers together. He felt the overload sensation kick in.

"All right," Emma piped up. "Just remember, you've walked a long way, and the less you have to talk about your hometown, the better."

"And let's make sure Emma and I stay at the back of the group," Elias said. "I doubt anyone would remember what I look like after twenty years, but Acerbis is small enough that everyone probably still remembers what happened to Emma."

"Otherwise, pitchforks," Dixie said. "Whatever those are."

Ras led Callie to the front of the group and began their descent into the outskirts of Acerbis.

Before long, the shuffle of feet through knee-high grass accompanied the sounds of nature emanating from the clumps of trees scattered across the landscape. Ras' eyes had begun to accustom themselves to the dark, but without a prominent moon, the clouds above remained a murky black.

"What was that rule we established on *Solaria*?" Ras asked Callie.

"Always bring a flashlight." She reached back with her free hand and pulled a flashlight from underneath her cloak. At the flick of a button, a bright beam shot into the night, almost reaching the clouds.

"If the watchmen see that, they'll come for us," Emma said from the back of the group.

"But we have a cover story," Ras said.

"Not a good one," Emma replied.

"Well, without a light I'm liable to lead us straight into a pit or something," Ras said.

"You won't lead us into a pit," Emma said. "We're coming up on the Fields of Remembrance. From there it's a straight walk to the city's border."

"What are the Fields of Remembrance?" Callie asked as they crested a hill.

Emma didn't have to respond; after a moment more of walking, Callie had her answer.

Ahead lay rows upon densely layered rows of identical white headstones leading all the way to the city lights of Acerbis. The tall grass waved around them, making them seem more alive than thoughts of those whom they memorialized.

"Oh, my," Callie whispered, raising a hand to her mouth. "Are those graves?"

"Not graves," Emma said. "Not exactly." She walked to the first row of headstones and slid her hand over the surface of the nearest marker. "They're here to commemorate everyone lost to The Great Overload."

Ras' eyes went wide as he looked at the rows upon rows disappearing into the darkness in either direction. "Everyone?"

"The ones that lived in The Bowl," Emma said.

"I never realized how many people died," Callie said.

Elias crutched up to Ras, then nodded toward Emma. "Tell them."

Emma sighed. "Each headstone represents one thousand people."

Ras felt a knot build in his stomach. He couldn't fathom the scope of the tragedy. He looked back to Dayus, who stared at the Fields of Remembrance, transfixed with hat in hand over his heart.

"How did this happen, Dayus?"

Lights twinkled on the horizon and the sound of motorized vehicles echoed through the area. A voice half distorted by a loudspeaker barked, "Unidentified party, place your hands in the air and stay exactly where you are."

Hearing no response from Dayus, Ras addressed his crew. "All right, everyone, look hungry and tired." He heard a crunching sound and saw Finn stuffing the last of a large cracker into his mouth. "Seriously?"

"It's hard to look like we're starving when we still have plenty of rations left in our packs," Finn said, crumbs escaping from between his lips.

"Fine, just look tired but well equipped," Ras said quickly.

"We could pretend there were more of us," Dixie said, "but we had to eat them and just took their rations—"

"Dixie!" Ras protested. "Nobody down here is a cannibal." He turned to look at his mother. "Right?"

Emma's mouth fell open.

"Right," Ras said. "Besides, why would we eat our own when we still had rations left? No cannibalism, especially from us." He jutted a finger at Dixie. "And no ad-libbing."

Engines revved as dancing lights darted between the headstones at reckless speeds. Ras counted at least seven, and before he had time to double count, the lights stopped ten yards in front of them. He raised his hand to shield his face from the glare.

"We come in peace!" Callie shouted, then leaned in toward Ras. "I think that's what you're supposed to say."

The engines powered down, the accompanying noise resembling that of an old jetcycle, but the lights continued to blind them.

"Who goes there?" a gruff voice called out.

"We invoke the Sanctuary clause of the Burrow Alliance," Emma shouted from the back of the group.

"All right," Callie whispered. "That sounds a lot more official."

A long pause was broken only by the faint sounds of an argument from the other side of the lights.

"It's been a...difficult trip," Ras called out. He slowly lowered his arms to see if it would earn him any protests from the Acerbis guards. It didn't.

"I can see that," the voice said. "I take it your train broke down?"

"Yes..." Ras said, berating himself silently for his hesitation even as he stammered out the word. "It became...disabled... along the way."

"Where's the rest of your party? Governor Bartleby's missive said there would be twenty-five of you," the voice said with a hint of wariness.

"Eaten," Dixie called out.

"Dixie!" Ras blurted out in frustration.

"We ran afoul of a pack of wolves," Callie covered quickly. "Twice."

Ras left himself a mental note to ask what wolves were later.

"What happened to your suits?" the man asked.

"Wolves," Ras said, then felt Callie squeeze his hand painfully tight.

"It was hard to run away while wearing them," Callie said.

"Is that the ambassador?" the voice asked. Unable to see whom he referred to, Ras looked behind him considering whether one of the crew should play the role or if it was better for the fictional ambassador to have been eaten by wolves. The latter seemed safer.

"I am," Dayus said before Ras could announce the untimely death.

Why does everyone ad-lib? Ras thought.

"Ah, Ambassador Beegle," the voice said, its owner finally stepping in front of the lights. As he entered Ras' view he slung a large crossbow over one of his broad shoulders and sighed audibly. As he sauntered up, a badge became visible on the lapel of his long, dark duster. "My name is Sheriff Prentiss. The mayor will be very pleased to see you." He offered his hand for Ras to shake, then paused to look over the young man. "Are you the leader of this expedition?"

"Our former leader had pressing matters to attend to," Ras said. "He felt this would be good for me."

"And yet he fed you to the wolves," Prentiss said.

"I'm sure it wasn't his intention."

"Do you have a name?"

"Erasmus," Ras said, hoping his full name sounded more like a leader than his nickname.

"Huh," Prentiss said. "That's quite the Acerbian sounding name. Do—"

"Could we please continue on into the city proper?" Dayus asked in a stuffy tone. "Here we are, risking ourselves to the elements while nomenclature is discussed."

"Right," Prentiss said. "Apologies, Ambassador. We have a transport already on its way." He turned to the vehicles behind them and shouted, "Kill the lights!"

Once the afterglow of the retina burn left Ras' eyes, he could barely make out the odd contraptions sitting among the headstones. They looked like large circular rims standing four or five feet tall with an engine and a seat suspended in the middle for the rider. The vehicle seemed as though it needed a great deal of balance to operate, but now that he had seen it, the agile zig-zagging of the lights through the fields earlier made more sense.

"What do you call those things?" Ras asked.

"You don't have Unirotors in Mason?" Prentiss asked, looking surprised.

"We do, of course," Callie said quickly. "He's just curious what people call them outside of Mason." She overemphasized the last word a little too much.

"Well, if the transport gets here in time, you folks should be able to catch the tail end of tonight's festivities," Prentiss said. "We had a big welcome prepared for you all at the first feast of this month, but it's not like we set fire to the banners."

"With all we've been through, a safe, peaceful place to sleep tonight will suffice," Dayus said. "No need for fanfare."

"Come now, we can't send you to bed hungry," Prentiss protested. "The mayor ordered me to bring you straight to him as soon as you arrived, be it day or night, and right now he's presiding over The Caretaker Festival." His tone hardened slightly. "I really must insist."

In a matter of minutes, a boxy six-wheeled transport with "SHERIFF" painted on both sides pulled up. After assurances from Prentiss that no arrests were being made, the crew climbed into the back section onto two wooden benches facing each other. As soon as the back doors closed and the engine started, everyone began asking questions at once.

"You remember your father promised he would end me if he ever saw me again, right?" Elias asked.

"Why is it so improbable that things eat people down here?" Dixie asked.

"What is a Caretaker Festival?" Ras added.

"Can we all just pretend I'm mute?" Guy asked, which suited Ras.

"I still don't know what wolves are," Finn said with a shrug.

"Mom, how big is this festival?" Ras asked.

"The whole town is required to be there," Emma said.

"And what happens if somebody recognizes you, or dad?" Ras glanced over at his father, who looked as though he had swallowed a bug.

"Likely, they'll arrest all of us for being Skyfolk," Elias said. "Well, they'd make an exception for your mother, and likely you, since you're half-Acerbian."

"That mercy may reach as far as a spouse," Dayus offered. "However, barring the bond of matrimony, it is doubtful the Veirs would have any leverage to exploit on behalf of the rest of us."

Ras looked over at Callie, whose mouth sat open as she stared ahead. She looked up, locked eyes with him, then gave an embarrassed half smile. The idea of faking a marriage felt wrong. After waiting for so long to be with Callie, making a ruse of it felt like a mockery of what he wanted most.

"Fine," Dixie said with a sigh. "I'll play the happy little homemaker." With a lopsided grin, she reached over and patted Ras on his knee.

"Dixie, I don't think—" Ras began.

"Oh, c'mon, I wouldn't lay it on *too* thick," Dixie said. "And I'm pretty sure I'm by far the most experienced in busting people out of jail." She lifted an eyebrow and tilted her head toward Guy. "I don't know, though. You look like you might have some stories."

"But if the Sheriff already saw Ras and me holding hands..." Callie said.

"Then you can be his overly affectionate sister," Dixie said, offering Ras a wink.

"Why can't you be the sister?" Ras asked Dixie.

Dixie grabbed a shock of white hair. "Do we *look* like we come from the same family?"

"Now ladies," Finn said. "Don't forget Ras' older and more handsome brother if we're including red hair in the family gene pool."

"No," Ras said.

"But she's got red hair and she's your sister," Finn said, pointing at Callie.

"I am *not* his sister!" Callie shouted, then cringed as the carriage occupants fell silent. "I don't like this plan," she whispered.

"Would they really arrest us for being from Atmo?" Ras asked.

"We've already lied about impersonating an entourage from Mason," Dayus said. "We haven't exactly given them grounds to trust us."

The carriage stopped, halting conversation. As the vehicle was jostled by the dismounting of the driver, Ras pointed to his mother and mimed for her to put the hood of her traveling cloak up. She obliged just before the back doors of the wagon flung open, revealing Prentiss.

"I hope you folk don't mind, but I'd rather you all cross the pylons on foot," Prentiss said. "The field tends to gum up the vehicles if they pass through."

Ras exited and once more felt the breeze tussle his hair. Something savory wafted in on the wind, and faint sounds of music and celebration came from the direction of Azerbis. Lights from the center of the city reflected off the shapes of ruined buildings.

"Have you ever seen a Knack overload by walking through the pylons?" Ras asked, turning from the city to face Prentiss. He could see the hood of his mother shake violently back and forth behind the Sheriff.

Prentiss' expression hardened. "What's a Knack?"

It dawned on Ras that the nickname 'Knack' was likely local to Atmo, as it held a positive connotation for wind merchants. Nobody down below thought Energy sensitivity was an advantage. "Sorry, it's a term we use in Mason."

"We haven't had an overload since the Blessing," Prentiss said cautiously.

"Of course," Ras said with absolutely no understanding.

Prentiss stepped toward the pylon and invited everyone to follow with a gesture.

Ras reached for Callie's hand before Elias could hobble his way to the invisible field that would ignite Energy sensitivity. "Reminds me of Bogues," he said quietly.

"Excuse me," Dayus said, eyeing Prentiss. "I believe you are forgetting something."

Ras turned to look back at Prentiss, whose smile dropped. "Oh, right," he said, then waited for Dayus to announce what exactly the forgotten thing was.

"Yes," Prentiss said with a sigh. "How could I forget?" He looked almost disappointed for some reason. Reaching down for a device on his belt, he pressed a button and spoke. "Drop the field. The Mason entourage has arrived."

Within moments, the hum of the pylons died.

If everyone inside is immune to Energy, why keep these things running? Ras wondered.

Dayus nodded. "Thank you. This trip has been treacherous enough with each new gust of wind." His eyes narrowed, then gestured toward the pylons. "I'm surprised your missive didn't make note of this."

"It did," Prentiss said. "It just slipped my mind. Apologies. And may I congratulate you on your luck of only running afoul of the wildlife."

Ras watched his crew safely cross the pylon threshold. Once his parents made it across, he began walking with Callie, but felt a large hand on his shoulder, halting him.

"A word, Erasmus, if you will," Prentiss said.

Callie nodded to Ras, releasing him. "We'll be waiting."

Once Callie crossed over, Prentiss looked Ras square in the eyes for a moment before speaking. "I'm not the sort of man who makes threats, Erasmus. In fact, my job is considerably easier when everybody gets along nicely," he said, crossing his arms. "But I have a sixth sense, if you will, for when people aren't level with me, and right now I've got all manner of warning signals firing off in my brain."

Ras took a breath to speak, but was quickly cut off.

"Now I don't interfere with ambassador level business," Prentiss said. "We all know there has been a distinct lack of communication among the Burrows. But from what I've heard about Mason, and what I've seen from you and your crew...well let's say I'll be a son of an Elder before I'm made a fool."

"Plainly stated?"

"Plainly stated, I'll be pleasantly surprised if you are who you say you are," Prentiss said in an even tone. "But you need to understand that once you enter into my city, you should abandon all expectation of seeing it from the outside again if I find you're lying to me."

Chapter Seven
The Festival

THE CREW QUEUED UP IN FRONT OF A LARGE, LONG STRUCTURE COVERED with a tarp. At a command from Prentiss, the deputies hauled the covering away to reveal a rusty, dilapidated version of Callie's white train, only this one was a patchwork of dingy metals well past their prime. Aside from the engine, the vehicle held only one passenger car.

"You'll have to excuse the old girl's condition," Prentiss said, placing a hand gently on the train. "Took us months to get her back into working condition after the missive from Governor Bartleby on restoring train routes."

"Where are we going in such luxury?" Dixie asked.

"If you'd rather make the long walk into the heart of the city, be my guest," Prentiss said as he hauled himself onto the first step.

"How does it run if Energy doesn't make it past the Pylons?" Ras asked.

Dayus moved past Ras and onto the train's steps next to Prentiss. "Steam, Erasmus. A technology before your time," he said, then disappeared into the dark cabin of the passenger car.

Once inside, Ras couldn't shake the memory of the Illorian train, and the relatively smaller size and absence of light inflicted a twinge of claustrophobia on him. He sat down with Callie on a backwards facing padded bench, opposite from Dayus. "Was I supposed to know these things didn't run on Energy?" he asked quietly.

Dayus leaned forward. "Mason is far more technologically advanced. Your ignorance is an asset for once."

Ras gave Dayus a sour look. "How do you know so much about Ma—" he cut himself off before Prentiss took the empty seat next to Dayus.

"I hope you don't mind, Ambassador," Prentiss said, reclining. "But it's my duty to ensure your safety." He pulled back his long coat, revealing the glimmer of a holstered pistol.

"Should we expect trouble?" Callie asked.

Prentiss reached forward, pulling something from a pocket; then with a hiss, a match flared to life. He dropped it in a light fixture attached to the wall, warming the area with an orange glow. "I wouldn't expect so, miss, but it's my job to assume otherwise."

A loud chuffing sound shook the entire cabin. The train inched forward.

"Is there—" Ras began, but the train's whistle screamed, forcing him to wait until the piercing sound quieted. "—Anything we should be aware of? You know, to ensure the ambassador's safety."

"Oh, with all of the meetings he's got scheduled with the Mayor, there should be plenty of security available," Prentiss said, leaning back once more.

Ras looked over to Callie, who was completely occupied with the small amount of detail available through the window. The lantern nearby made it difficult for his eyes to adjust to the outside world, but before long he could make out abandoned structures left ravaged by what he assumed were exploding people during The Great Overload.

The occasional building held a faint glow inside a window. As they neared their destination, light shone on the city blocks, gradually making them easier to see. Ras closed his eyes for a moment, allowing himself to pretend the jostle of the train on the tracks was that of *The Brass Fox*'s irregular movement patterns. A surprising pang of homesickness struck him, and he squeezed his eyelids tight until the feeling passed, then opened his eyes to see passing lights strewn between buildings. Large white globes tethered to broken lampposts bounced about on the breeze, lighting the path into town.

With a concussive blast of steam and horrific grinding squeal of what Ras guessed to be brakes, the train began to slow. Callie stood and pushed her face against the window. Ras leaned forward and saw row after row of tables, all populated with people fixated on the new arrival. Many held hands up to their ears to ward off the painful screech, but the excitement in the crowd was palpable.

The men, women, and children were dressed in odd garb. Men wore tall, circular hats and shabby black suits while the women wore dresses which accentuated their hips. He had never seen anything like it above the clouds.

"Looks like the whole city made it out," Callie said, returning a wave to a small child as the train came to a halt.

"It's mandatory here, but at least there's free food," Prentiss said, readying himself for departure. "You act like you've never seen a Caretaker Festival before."

"She hasn't," Dayus said. "Mason doesn't have cause to celebrate such an occasion."

"That so?" Prentiss asked.

Dayus just nodded.

The train released its last huff of steam, drawing gasps from the crowd. One of Prentiss' deputies swung the passenger door open, and Ras craned his neck to watch the man until he disappeared down the steps.

"Can you keep an eye on my mom if I get distracted?" Ras breathed out to Callie. She nodded a reply.

The last of the train's momentum bled away, and without a moment's hesitation, Prentiss sprang to his feet and strode to the doorway. "Looks like you're all clear, Ambassador."

Dayus looked to Ras. "One might consider limiting interactions with the locals wise," he said as he stood, then straightened his clothes.

Finn popped his head up over the seat behind Dayus. "This our stop?"

Ras stood quickly. A slight tinge of pain from his leg reminded him he hadn't fully healed, even if the recent contact with Callie had him feeling otherwise. He headed over to the booth his parents sat in and was mildly surprised to find two hooded figures.

"We're in mourning," Elias said.

"Over what?" Ras asked.

"I should probably come up with a decent reason, huh?" Elias asked, a grin forming underneath the cowl.

"Mom, where are we going after this?" Ras asked.

"To find your Uncle Omri," Emma said. "He'll be the least likely to turn us in."

"It looks like the entire city is out; how—"

"Families are assigned to tables," Emma said. "I'll at least know where to start looking."

"And if he can't get us in to see the Convergence tracking?" Ras asked.

"Then we play the diplomatic inspection card," Elias said. "Assuming 'Ambassador Beegle' is good enough in his role."

Ras nodded, then turned from his parents and walked back toward Dayus, meting up with Callie along the way.

"Ready to see where you came from?" Callie asked.

"I'm ready to see where the Convergences are and then get out of here," Ras replied. "I can have a family reunion after Atmo is safe."

"Well, at least your family isn't frozen until you go and save them," Callie said, a rare note of jealousy on her voice.

"Hey, honey, wait up," Dixie said, bowling in between Ras and Callie from behind. "It's bad enough you made me sit with cyclops and the comedian back there. I'm beginning to think you only married me for my looks."

"I think you're taking the backup plan a little bit too seriously," Callie said quietly.

"*Nalon* filled my quota of jail time for a good, long while," Dixie said. "I think I'll play this one on the safe side. Ain't that right, sweetie?" She placed a hand on Ras' shoulder, so that he had to crouch to her level. "I'm doing you a solid favor. Trust me."

Ras gave a weak smile when he caught Callie's narrowed eyes.

Forming up behind the 'Ambassador,' Ras looked out over the many tables of expectant revelers. The crowd had grown eerily quiet, and only the occasional infant made a noise as the foreigners walked down the short set of stairs.

The feast was set among a grand avenue with ruined storefronts creating its borders. Ahead, an aging wooden stage held a long table full of elderly men and women.

Ras noted the empty plates on the tables. Only small bits of food remained for the feasters. As the crew walked down the center row of tables, the citizens of Acerbis stood, one by one. It was difficult to tell if it was out of a silent respect or if it was because people in the back were wanting a better look at the newcomers.

Regardless, the arrival had been designed as a grand entrance. Having a train arrive in the middle of the town with a dramatic cue would have been quite an exciting event. Ras wondered what happened to the actual party from Mason.

On the stage, a man with salt and peppered hair made a quick motion to the side, prompting a band to rouse to life. The stringed instruments began a melody soft and sweet on the warm evening air. The music grew louder as Ras approached the stage, and soon he was nearly swept away by the piece. The tune held a melancholy intertwined with a slow, deep strength, and Ras wished he knew the song.

There wasn't much in the way of music on *Verdant*, and the only sounds resembling it on this scale were scratchy recordings with the life played out of them or the half-improvised sing-songs of childhood.

As the entourage approached the stage, Prentiss excused himself and made his way up a side set of stairs, meeting privately with the dark-haired middle aged man.

While they spoke, Ras' eye caught a flitter of motion underneath the raised stage. He couldn't quite make out the dark figures, but there was certainly more than one skittering about.

Once Prentiss' private conversation concluded, the dark-haired man rose from his place at the center of the long table and gracefully made his way to what looked like a comm unit standing at the end of a long metal pole reaching up to shoulder height. He tapped it twice, prompting a loud percussive noise from speakers on either end of the stage.

"My dear citizens of Acerbis," the man said with a placating smile. "May I present to you the fashionably late delegation from Mason!" He held up his hands and gave a light clap to lead the crowd in a smattering of applause. "I know we are all very, very eager to hear news from our intrepid adventurers, but I have been informed of recent hardships which deserve the warmest of hospitalities we can offer. So, without further ado, let us see if we can't fill our table of honor with some food, and our very own historian, Artemis Mack, can once more regale us with the tale of The Caretaker!"

The crowd let out something that sounded like a hushed groan. If Ras had to guess, the tale had already been told that night, and the crowd was far more interested in finding their ways back to inviting beds than continuing late into the night for the sake of strangers.

Prentiss caught Ras' attention with a wave, then pointed to Dayus, motioning for the two of them to join him. Other official-looking men ushered the rest of the party to an unoccupied table near the front of the vestibule.

Dayus played the aloof role well, visibly rolling his eyes as though the request was a sincere burden calling him away from some deep and more important thought. Still, he moved with obvious long-suffering, falling in beside Ras as they made their way to Prentiss, who spoke once they had reached him.

"Mister Ambassador, the Mayor has requested you sit next to him for the duration of the night's entertainment. And Erasmus," Prentiss said, pointing a finger to Ras, "the Mayor wishes for an account to be given on behalf of Mason to the citizens of Acerbis—"

"There are things not proper for discussion in public that the Mayor should know about first," Dayus said, giving Prentiss a hard look.

"Then he can make it nice and general," Prentiss said. "These people are starved from outside communication. Perhaps something regarding Governor Bartleby's Unification Initiative?"

It was the perfect trap. A single detail contradictory to what Prentiss already knew would doom the party. *Is there even such a thing as a Unification Initiative, or even a Governor Bartleby?* All he could do was nod an agreement.

Prentiss led Dayus up to the stage while Ras made a direct line toward his crew. The table was less than half-filled with the expectation of the real envoy from Mason. He found an open seat between Dixie and his mother, who still had her hood up. The seat provided an excellent view of the stage, and soon a withered old man inched his way up to the microphone with an ancient-looking, leather-bound book.

A stand for the book was rushed onstage, just in time for Artemis Mack to set the heavy-looking tome upon it. A glance over to Callie affirmed Ras' suspicion that her attention would be locked on the stage for the duration of the story-time, which meant if Ras needed any sort of reference from the evening, all he would need to do was ask her later.

"I take it you've heard this one before?" Ras asked, leaning over to his mother.

The hood bobbed an affirmative. "I just can't believe he's still alive," she said quietly. "He was one of the last two witnesses of the Blessing back when I was your age."

Ras had no idea how one could witness a blessing. "So, can you tell me about Mason while he tells his story?"

Emma turned and Ras caught a look of disbelief from deep within the cowl. "One, it's terribly rude to speak during the story, and two, I know almost nothing about Mason."

"But—" Ras began before he was shushed by the occupants of two nearby tables. Even if they had heard the story once that night, propriety evidently needed to be upheld.

The elderly man cleared his voice into the microphone, then smiled. "Now, as almost all of you well remember, my name is Artemis Mack, and I'm one of the last survivors of those who saw the Caretaker," he said with his raspy voice. "Well, I'll get right to it." He drew a deep breath, then began without opening the book. "Helios had abandoned us," he said gravely. "The cities had launched, and we had been lied to with nothing but holes in the ground to dwell in. Sure, it was better than nothing…but all signs pointed to hope having abandoned us. Those were dark times. Dark times, indeed.

"Until one day, she came. The stranger. She never gave us her name, but when things were at their darkest, she came," Artemis said. "When asked, she said she was simply 'a Caretaker,' but there was nothing simple about devoting your life to the survival of a city and its people. She said there were others like her, traveling to aid the lost and broken, and that it was her duty to watch over us until she could no longer.

"I want you to look at the bulbs above you." Artemis waved a gnarled hand above his head. "Times were, when you saw a Convergence, it could force its way through the city's defenses, and likely it was the last thing you'd see. Acerbis suffered many times over after The Great Overload, and good friends were lost…until the Caretaker came.

"The Convergences listened to her when she told them to go away. She told us that as long as we stayed within the city's limits, she could protect us. And she did.

"We didn't have much, but what we did have we pooled together as a thanks to our benefactor. It took several years of these festivals before we finally got her to partake, but she attended every last one of these dinners until her dying day," Artemis said. Then his expression grew serious.

"Decades passed. She said she had a gift for us, even though she wasn't a woman of many possessions. She said the gift would protect us until one called The Reclaimer came to take us."

Ras perked up at this, suddenly wishing he had a pen and paper.

"One day she grew sick. Sicker than any of us had ever seen her. She had everyone from Acerbis come as close as they could to receive her blessing when it came time for her to pass on."

Behind Artemis, Dayus bowed his head, the brim of his hat covering his face.

"And pass she did. Oh, the light show that played around Acerbis that day. You know what else came? Of course you do. I tell you every year. Convergences came to mock us and sweep us away now that our protector was gone.

"But she wasn't gone. No, not really. She had passed on her protection to each and every one of us within the city. And that is why we are here today. That is why we honor her with this meal, because she is here with each new generation joining us around this bountiful feast, and we need not fear The Convergences any longer. When the skyfolk had abandoned us, we had her." Artemis turned slightly and reached for an old mug sitting on the stool behind him. He hoisted it up. "May The Caretaker protect us," he said along with all of the festival participants, "until The Reclaimer take us...and may he never come!"

The crowd wearily recited the final line and a smattering of unenthusiastic applause and clanking mugs followed before conversation picked up once more.

And may he never come? Ras thought. The Illorians seemed welcoming of the concept of The Reclaimer, but somewhere along the way, everyone else had begun to associate the lore with negativity.

His mind spun considering whom he could safely ask about this. As Artemis descended the stage with the aid of two young women, the mayor approached the microphone in utter silence. He gave a strained smile and put his hands together, prompting patchy clapping from the lethargic crowd.

"And now, a brief report on Mason from one of our esteemed guests!" The Mayor shot an open hand toward Ras' table.

Ras' eyes went wide. He had been so wrapped up in the story of The Caretaker that he had forgotten to use the time to craft the details of his story.

Out of the corner of his eye, he saw someone from his table stand. Callie.

"What are you doing?" Ras asked.

"Giving a report on Mason," she said as though it were obvious, then gave him a quick wink as she continued up to the stage.

Ras knew she'd be better under pressure, and with her general curiosity about the world before The Great Overload, she probably would have at least a cursory historical knowledge of the city. She would probably be fine as long as she didn't go on a wild storytelling streak and do something like telling Hal Napier that *The Brass Fox* was procured as a gift for saving an orphanage. She read enough fiction that feasibility and believability weren't the foremost considerations as she crafted her tales.

Callie ascended the steps, shook the mayor's hand, then walked past Prentiss, who was busy mouthing threats at Ras. She stood with excellent posture as she looked out over the crowd. "First, may I say it is such an honor to be your humble guest this evening. I must confess there was a point in my life I thought I'd never be able to see cities such as yours, but I'm grateful for the opportunity." She casually looked over to Ras and gave a slight smile.

"We've had many difficulties coming to you, but it seems that is the way of things anywhere you go anymore," she said. As she paused, the crowd remained silent, and Ras couldn't tell if it was from being captivated by her as he often was, or out of respect.

More motion underneath the stage again drew Ras' attention. He leaned over to Dixie, casually pointing a finger at the shadows. Dixie shrugged.

"Mason was a great city and still is," Callie continued. "While we no longer truly consider ourselves the capital of our fractured country, we do consider ourselves your brothers and sisters, making our way through the aftermath." She turned to look back at Dayus, who nodded politely, then once more addressed the crowd. "We are working very hard to heal the cracks and fix the divisions created by nearly a century of darkness."

Ras' body tensed. She was beginning to speak about their mission thinly veiled as Mason's plan. He began shaking his head, hoping she would look over to him and somehow understand it meant she was getting too specific, but she was too wrapped up in her story to notice him.

"In our travels we have learned that, in an act we take as goodwill, the structure the Skyfolk had placed over the Energy Origin has been removed," Callie said. The wild gleam in her eye began to show a little. "And in fact, we managed to meet the person directly responsible for its removal, and we have cause to believe that those who took to the sky have an interest in rebuilding what was once lost."

The crowd began murmuring loudly. They didn't sound pleased at the idea of doing anything with the skyfolk.

Callie lifted her arms in an attempt to quell the crowd and bring attention back to her. "And in that spirit of restoration, Mason has begun an investigation on methods of dispelling Convergences. And we think we've developed a solution," she said.

Jeers and cries of "traitor" and "skylover" broke out from the crowd. Ras watched as several people stood, threatening Callie. He began untangling his legs from the bench to intercept anyone who might make an advance.

Beneath the stage, something hissed; a sparkling glow formed there, whipping back and forth. Then a second dancing light joined in, followed by another. Ras stood to get a better look and saw two people underneath the stage, dashing back and forth in the faint glow of the sparks.

Callie's eyes darted back and forth as she took in the agitation of the crowd. "Now, we've been developing this Convergence bursting technology well before we've had any contact with those who…who abandoned us," Callie said, worry plain to hear in her voice. It was obvious the mentioning of *The Winnower* and any positive reference to Atmo was enough to riot a crowd otherwise ready for bed.

It finally dawned on Ras what was going on beneath the stage. "Callie!" he shouted as he scrambled toward the platform. "Look out!" He evaded one young man on security detail, but another guard prevented his ascent up the stairs. "Let me go! Something is going to blow under there!"

Everyone at the long table scurried to their feet, and Callie ran to the side of the structure before Dayus caught her up in a dash toward the steps.

A wailing screech tore through the night, accompanied by a streak of cascading light as a red hue filled the square and washed over everyone. The streak of light exploded high in the air, and shortly another streak launched from just behind the stage, this one a mix of gold and silver. Ras had never seen anything like it aside from emergency flares, but those didn't explode like this.

"What in Atmo…" Ras trailed off.

"You idiots!" one of the security guards shouted, running underneath the stage. "You'll burn the whole town down!" The guard released Ras in order to join his comrade in apprehending the mischief makers.

Ras moved to the side as the elderly men and women descended the steps. He stood by the edge of the stage with arms outstretched toward Callie. "Here! I'll help you down!"

The exploding stars of light left Callie transfixed. "Oh, it's magical."

"We're in the middle of an assault!" Ras shouted over the peals of screeches and blasts.

"Assault? Ras, they're just fireworks!" Callie said, then laughed. She eased out of Dayus' arms. "They're so beautiful…"

The two guards returned from underneath the stage, each doing his best to restrain a struggling teenager.

"We were saving those for the last weekend!" one of the guards said to one of the teenagers, whose dark hair was tied in a long ponytail trailing down her back. She shot a smirk to her accomplice, a young man, skinny and tan with cropped hair.

"They were supposed to go off and give Artemis a big finale, but *someone* forgot to refill his lighter," the young woman said.

The fireworks stopped and Ras could finally hear himself think once more. The crowd hadn't left, but instead stood to appreciate the show.

"What happened to the finale?" the young woman asked. "I thought we lit everything—"

A large concussive blast erupted from underneath the stage, knocking Ras and those around him off their feet as the back half of the stage collapsed.

His hearing immediately replaced by a high-pitched whine, his mind addled by the force of the explosion, it was all Ras could do to run his hands over his prone body to feel for any injuries. His heartbeat sounded loudly in his head as understanding returned to him.

He picked himself up and looked for Callie, who had evidently jumped down from the stage after the blast. She held her hands over her mouth and her eyes were wide as she stared at something behind Ras. He turned to look.

In the blast, his mother's hood had been blown back, and a crowd had begun to form around her.

CHAPTER EIGHT
The Burrow

FROM WHERE THE CREW OF *THE KINGFISHER* STOOD, THEY COULD see all of Acerbis.

"She was right," Dixie said, neck craned back. "Nineteen levels."

"At least it's not a jail cell," Ras said. They stood on the very bottom layer of Acerbis, atop the broken digging machine. The acrid smell of trash that had accumulated from above caused him to blanch. Both of his parents had been taken away from the ceremony in opposite directions, leaving the rest of them to await their judgment at the base of the city.

Thirty foot high walls of sheer stone ran straight up all around them, making it impossible to climb up to the next level without his grapple gun, and if Ras had to guess, one could walk one hundred yards from one end to the other.

"So, brilliant leader, how exactly does this fit into the plan?" Guy asked.

"Oh, come now," Finn said, "I know you love playing devil's advocate and all, but you cut into his planning time every time he has to address one of your attempts at witty banter." He continued to stare upward. "I wonder if the base of *Verdant* could fit in this hole."

"It's a temporary setback," Ras said, giving Guy a hard look. He stepped over to Callie, who stood a good ten feet away from everybody else.

"Hey, are you all right?" Ras asked, stopping just behind her.

She didn't turn to face him. "Guess I got a little carried away."

"I'd blame those light-exploding…things." Ras remembered their name, but the laugh usually accompanying Callie's corrections was well worth the chastisement if it meant cheering her up. No response. "My mom can explain everything. Besides, they won't keep us down here forever. Atmo is at stake, and I'm sure whoever is in charge wouldn't let at least a million people just fall out of the sky and overload."

"Those people did leave millions behind with little more than an invisible fence and a city-building shovel," Dayus said. "You might need to engender goodwill as an ambassador of Atmo."

A spotlight shone on the six prisoners, halting conversation. A loud, distorted voice choked over a speaker. "Erasmus and Calista Veir, approach the wall."

Ras shielded his eyes from the light, then looked over to Callie. "Do you think you're supposed to be my sister or wife?"

"I'll make sure to avoid kissing you," Callie said. "Just to be safe. It's not like you've got a ring on you or anything."

Ras laughed a little too loudly and quickened his stride toward the wall. He looked back at Dixie and mouthed a "sorry."

The rope ladder unfurled and Ras grabbed on, but before he could begin climbing, someone above hoisted him up. The process was repeated for Callie.

Once the spotlight left his eyes, Ras surveyed the half-dozen men surrounding them. Emma stepped out from behind the group, then rushed up to embrace Ras. "I'm so glad you're all right," she whispered.

"What about everyone else?" Ras said, maintaining the hug.

She stepped back, gave a sad smile, then hugged Callie, who wasn't able to hide a perplexed look.

"Follow me," one of the men said in a low voice. As he began to walk, the other five men fell into formation around their prisoners. "Orientation will begin tomorrow morning at precisely at 0800 hours. I recommend you use the remainder of your night for rest."

The large walkway curved in a complete circle. Doors were hewn into the rock walls, and glances down the occasional hallway showed hints of the labyrinthine intricacy of the city.

After a quarter lap around the city's deepest walkway, the group reached an open-aired elevator. As they waited for it to arrive, Ras looked up, wondering if there was any consideration for those too afraid of heights to live on the higher levels.

With the familiar huff of steam, the elevator platform cranked into place. One of the men pulled back the safety grating so everyone

could enter. Once they were all aboard, a middle-aged elevator operator asked which level, but stared at Emma.

"Five," the gruff man said, and with a jerk the platform whisked
them up at a surprisingly quick rate.

"Who built all of this?" Callie asked, taking in her surroundings.

"That will be covered in orientation," the man said.

"Look at the city's floor," Emma whispered, and Callie inched her
way to the edge of the platform.

Ras stole a glance, then instantly regretted it as a wave of nausea
washed over him. Evidently his conquest of his fear of heights didn't
translate as well from cloud-covered Atmo to the solid underground.

What he did see in his glimpse was a very large faded logo.

"Did you catch that?" Callie asked as the platform decelerated.

"Not really," Ras admitted. The platform shook as the elevator
crunched to a halt, and he gripped the guardrail even tighter.

"It said, '*The Helios Foundation*,'" Callie said as they once more
entered lock step with their escort.

The walkway was a good twenty feet across, but the citizens of
Acerbis made sure to give the group a wide berth. The doors and
walls looked older and more worn down than the ones on the
bottom floor.

Between taking in his new surroundings and pondering over why
Helios appeared to have orchestrated both the Atmo project and
the Burrows, Ras only noticed the group had stopped walking by
bumping directly into one of his escorts, who turned and shoved
him back a couple feet.

"This is your stop," the gruff man said. "The Corin family has
agreed to host you tonight. Don't make them regret it."

"Corin," Ras said, "Isn't that—"

The door flung open and seven people stood in a modestly furnished, low-ceilinged room. "Surprise!" a middle aged man said,
arms uplifted. He then looked around the room, frustrated. "You
said we were going to yell 'surprise' when they got here."

A young woman with dark braided hair threw her head back in
a laugh, prompting the two children next to her to follow suit. "And
then I told everybody but you that it'd be funnier if it was just you."

It took Ras a moment to recognize the young woman as the insti-
gator of the firework incident.

"0800 hours," the gruff man reminded. "No leaving until then." He looked pointedly at Ras, then walked off with all but one of his men, who dutifully stood guard outside.

Emma ushered Ras and Callie in through the doorway, then closed the door. "Everyone, I'd like to finally introduce you to my son, Erasmus," Emma said. "And this is Calista, but she goes by Callie."

"Is she your daughter?" the oldest man in the room asked. He definitely shared some of Emma's features, most notably her eyes, which meant Ras saw a bit of himself in the man.

"She practically is," Emma said, prompting Ras to give her a strained look. "Well, I mean that I love her like one of my own. Which means if anyone outside this room asks, then yes, she's my daughter."

"It's all right," Callie said. "I know how to play the adopted card."

"Right, well, this is my family," Emma said, walking into the living room and stopping next to the tall, broad shouldered man with gray hair. "This is my father, Cornelius Corin."

Cornelius stood stalwart in faded blue work clothes, nodding an acknowledgement of Ras' existence.

"And this is my mom, Amelia Corin," Emma said as she stooped down to the couch holding an older woman who wore a home-spun dress. Her bright eyes bored into Ras as the corners of her lips curved, and her white hair bobbed as she bowed her head in greeting.

"It's nice to meet you both," Amelia said. It seemed like she wished she could be more exuberant about the return of her daughter and the news of a grandson, but the patriarch's cool demeanor dampened the occasion.

"And this—" Emma began.

"Omri." The man with thinning hair who shouted "Surprise!" earlier briskly strode up to Ras and Callie, offering his outstretched hand. As Ras reached to take it, Omri used it as leverage, pulling Ras into a tight hug. "Oh, it's so good to meet you!" He released Ras, who stumbled back as air filled his lungs again. "Call me Uncle Omri, okay?" He let out a slight laugh. "I've always wanted to say that, mind you," he said, then snatched a surprised and squeaking Callie up in a brief but vigorous hug.

Omri stepped back and waved a blonde-haired woman forward. "C'mon, Felicia. Skyfolk don't bite." Felicia glanced with annoyance at her husband, then offered her hand to Ras with a polite, if dutiful, expression.

"From how your mother speaks of you, you're quite the ambitious one," Felicia said with a light handshake. "And Calista. It's nice to meet you."

"Now, let's see if I have this right," Emma said, waving a hand toward the three children. "Your youngest is Boscoe." The mention of his name sent the blonde ten-year-old boy ducking behind the couch. "Your middle child is Portia." The blonde girl of fifteen gave a curtsey. "And your oldest…"

The girl sauntered over, tucking her raven hair behind her ear, displaying as a badge of honor the purple bruise lingering on her forehead beside her eyebrow. It was difficult to gauge how old she was. Somewhere between sixteen and eighteen, if Ras had to guess.

She jutted her hand forward for Ras to shake. "I know we didn't officially meet earlier, but I'm A.C." She gave Ras' hand three firm pumps. "Most everybody calls me Ace."

"Most everybody calls her trouble," Portia said.

"Do you *want* me to tell you where I buried your dolls or not?" Ace snapped back.

"Now girls," Omri chided. "Let's not fight in front of our guests. They've come a long, long way."

"Do you all live here together?" Callie asked.

"No," Omri said. "This is mom and dad's place where Emmaline and I grew up. Felicia, me, and the kiddos live quite a bit further down the Burrow."

"We didn't know there would be three of you," Cornelius said. "One of you will have to make do on the floor." He looked to Ras.

"That's fine," Ras said. "My crew has to sleep outside on a metal floor anyway. I'd never hear the end of it if I slept in a bed while they were down there."

Ace shrugged. "Tink has extra pillows in his ground-side loft. I'll throw some down."

"Tell me you're not going into lofts!" Felicia protested. "Those things fall in a strong wind."

"And how do you know how many pillows that boy has?" Omri asked in a stern voice.

Ace sighed, then walked past Ras toward the door. "Good to meet you, cousin." She looked to Callie. "And sort-of cousin." With that, she opened the door and stepped into the night.

Omri took a few moments to wrestle Boscoe down and soon had his son wriggling over his shoulder. "Erasmus, once things settle down—" he paused to readjust Boscoe. "Once things settle, let's have lunch so I can tell you all the embarrassing stories about your mother."

Emma reached over and gave her brother a push. "Go on. I'll see you tomorrow."

It was odd seeing Emma back in her element after all these years. Ras felt a spark of frustration at how joyful she seemed, considering that his father was incarcerated somewhere and the clock was ticking on Atmo.

Felicia and Portia gave their goodbyes, and soon grandma Amelia was searching for an extra pillow and blanket for the floor.

"Emma says you're going to sink Atmo," Cornelius said as he eased into a padded recliner.

Ras could tell his grandfather was addressing him despite a noticeable absence of eye-contact. "That's the plan, sir."

Cornelius nodded. "Well then, I guess you can't be all bad," he said begrudgingly. "Just make sure *Verdant* doesn't fall on us."

Emma gave Ras a sad look with a quick shake of her head. This wasn't a fight he could win.

Amelia poked her head out of a room down the hallway. "Dears, your room is ready."

"Thank you for having us in your home," Callie replied.

Emma walked over and sat down on the arm of her father's recliner. She lovingly ran a hand through his hair and gave him a tight hug. "Daddy, you don't know how much I've missed you." She leaned in and whispered something Ras couldn't hear, eliciting no response. She stood, then walked with Ras and Callie into the bedroom, where Amelia was bustling about, putting the finishing touches on the preparations.

It was easily apparent two very different people had lived in the room. Half of the room was painted a light, sky blue and had pinned up charcoal drawings of flowers, clouds, and various animals, while the other half was painted green and replete with incomplete wooden models and worn out ribbons for some sport.

"Omri insisted we not change anything," Amelia said. "He knew you'd come home someday."

Emma walked over to her bed and picked up a brown stuffed toy, a facsimile of an animal Ras didn't recognize. "Oh, Buster Brown Bear," she said, then clutched the memento to her chest.

"Well, sleep tight," Amelia said, her voice shaky. She sighed. "Emmaline, please tell me if you'll be staying. I don't know if my heart could take getting attached to the idea if it isn't true."

"It depends on what happens with...you know who."

Amelia pursed her lips, nodded, then reached for the door, slowly pulling it shut.

"Mrs. Veir, I didn't know you were an artist," Callie said, inspecting one of the drawings.

Reaching out, Emma plucked one of the paintings of a reddish-orange animal that seemed familiar to Ras. "There weren't exactly a lot of materials to make use of up there."

"So, my grandfather hates me," Ras said. "Can we talk about that?"

"He doesn't hate you," his mother said. "It's just..."

"Just what?"

"You look an awful lot like your father," Emma said, sitting down on her old bed. "And as far as he is concerned, Elias stole me away for the last twenty years."

"And I'm visible proof of that lost time?" Ras asked.

Emma shrugged. "He'll come around."

"Mom, we don't have time for that. *Nalon* has six days left, and I don't know where they're keeping dad, much less how we're going to get access to whatever Convergence information is down here..."

"Your father is working on that," Emma said. "Let's just get some rest and see what tomorrow brings."

"What do you mean he's working on it?" Ras asked, raising his voice.

Emma lifted her hands to quiet him. "He just told me to tell you that you can trust him. He didn't say what he was up to, exactly."

Ras eased himself down onto the floor. "Yeah, well that certainly sounds like him. At least this time he can't start a war between two nations..."

He regretted the words as soon as they left his lips. Emma stood slowly, fixing on Ras the glare that she had always reserved for rebuking his worst behavior. "Show your father some respect. He's in a tough spot, but we both know he's going to act in the best interest of Atmo." She sat down on her old bed, running a hand over the cover. "He always has."

Ras leaned forward, putting his hand on his mother's. She gave a thin smile and squeezed his fingers tightly. It occurred to Ras that she was as much on edge as he was; she just had more reason to hide it—or maybe more experience doing so.

So what if she was happy to be with her family? She hadn't seen them in years, and joy was a fragile thing. He resolved to be less judgmental toward her in the future.

Callie moved over to Omri's side of the room and stretched out on the bed. "Did you paint this?" she asked, pointing to a piece of paper attached to the ceiling. Ras looked up to see a four-legged silver creature with a bushy tail and sharp features.

"Foxes were Omri's favorite," Emma said, half-present, with a gaze reaching beyond the artwork. "He tried to catch a wild one once. I forget how many stitches he had to get."

"Did dad see that?" Ras asked, resting his head on a moldy smelling pillow.

"He did, but didn't know it was a silver fox," Emma said. "He let me name the ship at a point in my life when I was feeling particularly homesick…"

She really missed this place, Ras thought. *Being stuck on a foreign city with a ten-year-old son and no husband for a decade couldn't have helped.* Ras closed his eyes and drifted off, imagining Bravo Company bombarding *Nalon* until it was a smoldering husk plummeting beneath the clouds.

Without sunlight streaming in through windows, Ras had a difficult time telling what time he awoke. The ache in his back from not sleeping on a mattress lingered even after he sat up. Both Callie and his mother slumbered peacefully. By the dim light available in the room, Ras could just see his watch hands. It was only five in the morning.

Sleep wouldn't return for him.

As quietly as he could manage, he stood and collected his goggles from a nearby dresser. The original KnackVisions could provide a crude map to at least show him where Energy *wasn't*, and he needed to find the bathroom in the Corin home.

The door's hinges thankfully made no protest as he eased his way into the hallway. The goggles didn't tell him which of the other two doors led to the facilities, and he certainly didn't want to accidentally wake Cornelius.

"It's the door right in front of you, if you're looking for the head." Cornelius' deep voice came from the dark living room, startling Ras and endangering his need for the bathroom.

"Ah, th-thank you."

After checking off of the first portion of his morning routine, Ras washed his hands and returned to the hallway.

"You drink coffee?" Cornelius asked, still wrapped in darkness.

Ras dropped the KnackVisions over his eyes to see if he could spot his grandfather the way he saw the room full of faint green glowing spots back on *Verdant*, but the whole of Acerbis seemed to be devoid of those soul signatures, or whatever they might be.

"You just going to stand there?" his grandfather asked.

"Sorry," Ras said. "Just getting my bearings. Everything here is so…stable."

Cornelius gave a throaty chuckle. "Still getting your land legs?"

Ras ran his hand along the wall as a guide until it bumped a frame, knocking it free. He scrambled to catch it before it could clatter to the floor. Instead of trying to rehang the frame, he just held onto it.

"Yeah, I guess," Ras said. "Don't waste coffee on me, by the way." He walked timidly toward the living room, stopping at the end of the hall.

"Waste?"

"Most people in Atmo can't afford to drink it," Ras said. "I never acquired the taste." Ras heard the sound of Cornelius rising from his chair. There was a click, and the room filled with a soft orange glow. "Are you up early to make sure I don't run away?"

"Is running away something you tend to do?" Cornelius asked, walking past Ras into the small kitchen.

"Can't say it is."

"Good," Cornelius said, searching the cupboards. "The guard outside would have tackled you." He pulled a mug out, took a step to a silver pitcher, and poured some coffee. "No, Erasmus, I'm up early because the world feels more honest before it's had a chance to wake up properly." He walked out of the kitchen and handed Ras the mug.

The porcelain burned his hand slightly, so he rapidly leaned the picture frame against the side of the recliner, freeing up his other hand to take the mug properly by its handle. "Thank you," Ras said, flexing the feeling back into his fingers.

"Don't mention it," Cornelius said, walking up to a coat rack by the door. "Coffee is cheaper than dirt down here anyway. Hope you take it black." He selected a flat cap and a heavy gray coat.

"Where are you going?" Ras asked as he sniffed at his coffee.

"You mean where are we going."

"I thought I had to show up for some sort of orientation at 0800," Ras said, "and you brought up a very valid point about the tackling guard—"

"I'm giving you your orientation," Cornelius said. "Now finish your coffee and let's go."

Ras took a sip of the liquid, and the bitterness filled his senses until his taste buds burned away. *Why would anyone drink this?*

He set the steaming mug next to the frame holding the picture of a happy family of four. A teenaged Emma looked beautiful with her dark hair up in curls. Omri made a face at the camera from behind his smiling parents. At that moment Ras felt a strong desire to be a part of that family, but knew he was living, breathing testament that a separation had occurred. A separation that Cornelius Corin had had to live with for the last twenty years.

The front door opened, pulling Ras' attention away from the photo. "What about Callie?"

"What about her?" Cornelius asked, turning from the doorway to face Ras.

"Doesn't she need to go through orientation too?"

"No," Cornelius said, then stepped outside.

With a shrug, Ras walked toward his grandfather and closed the door behind him. A guard stood, gave Cornelius a nod, then ambled away with a yawn.

"Erasmus, let me be plain about how this works," Cornelius said, strolling across the walkway to the railing overlooking the layers of Acerbis below.

Ras felt the chill of the morning, its crispness causing his face to tingle as he held his vest tight to his body. Nobody else was out. It would be a perfect opportunity for a fit and muscular man to casually toss his grandson over the railing if he so chose. As he approached, he glanced down, risking vertigo to see if his crew still slept at the bottom of the Burrow. They were either hidden underneath one of the many walkways or had been moved overnight.

"You need sponsorship to be a full citizen of Acerbis," Cornelius said, looking out over the dark cylinder of a city. "A character reference from someone in good standing with the mayor would suffice."

"And what does full citizenship entail?" Ras asked.

"It means you could come and go as you pleased."

For a moment, Ras thought his mother could vouch for him, but it was apparent his grandfather had taken it upon himself to be the arbiter.

"You know, Emmaline was never prone to lying before she met your father," Cornelius said. "Once she stole candy from the local store so she could have something to feed her stuffed animals come tea time. She said it was for one of their birthdays. Otherwise, she dealt straight with everyone."

Ras could imagine his mother furtively placing candy for the toys around the table, and the thought brought him a smile. "She misses this place. I can tell," Ras said. "More than she'll admit to me."

Cornelius stepped away from the railing and motioned for Ras to follow. "Does anybody up there talk about us?"

Ras quickened his pace to keep up. "Most people assume the world below the clouds is unlivable. It's pounded into us that once we drop beneath the clouds, it's a matter of seconds before we overload," he said, snapping his fingers. "It was hard to imagine anyone else being able to live down here."

A grunt of amusement came from Cornelius as they reached the elevator platform. He pressed the button to call for the lift and waited. "So, when did you find out it was all a lie?"

"It's not a lie," Ras said. "We're still prone to overloading. I just had the right genes to survive down here."

The lift arrived. A bleary-eyed operator opened the safety gate, and the two men climbed aboard.

"Nineteen," Cornelius said.

"So, last night was the first time I had heard about The Caretaker," Ras said, bracing himself for the sudden jerk of descent. "Is that why living down here is possible?"

"Some think so."

"Do you?" Ras asked.

Cornelius shrugged. "Some signs point to it. We hadn't left the borders of this city for thirty years before she died. Before that, people didn't come back if they left the gate. Maybe it was genetics, maybe we grew immune, maybe the old woman saved us through some mumbo jumbo."

"And what about The Reclaimer?" Ras asked.

"You ask a lot of questions for an orientation."

"You aren't offering a lot of information."

"You're actually interested in Acerbis?"

Ras nodded.

"The Reclaimer brings death, coming for us all when it's our time," Cornelius said. "Something to get the kids to behave." With a clunk, the lift finished its run to the bottom and the poorly lit section of Acerbis welcomed them with its stale smell.

"So, he's not a person?" Ras asked, curious where Cornelius was leading him.

The older man walked to the edge of the bottom layer, stopping to collect a rope ladder attached to the floor. He tossed it over the ledge. "The Caretaker seemed to think so." He swung a leg over and began climbing down.

After a few moments to let Cornelius get ahead of him, Ras followed suit. "How'd she know all of this?"

"If you don't mind, I'm going to concentrate on not falling," Cornelius said with a strained voice.

Ras followed suit, and within a minute the two men stood atop the metal floor. Cornelius walked purposefully toward the center of the large circle. "Kid, I don't know how she knew all that. As far as I know, she was just some crazy mountain woman smart enough to survive and make it to a city, and then decided it'd be fun to tell people about some guy who is supposed to end the whole world."

Ras stopped walking. "End the whole world?"

"Yeah, but I don't see him anywhere and we're still here," Cornelius said. "Now keep up."

Once Cornelius reached the center of the area, he waited for Ras to arrive. "Stomp your foot three times."

Ras gave a perplexed look, the lifted his undamaged leg and did as instructed. *What sort of test—*

A floor panel to their side opened up and a middle-aged woman in a brown jumpsuit peered at them from below. "This your grandson, Cor?"

"He's Emmaline's," Cornelius said.

The woman squinted at Ras, then waved him closer to the light emanating from the panel. He obliged. "He looks more like the other one."

"Is he up?" Cornelius asked.

"I don't think he slept," the woman said. "He was sitting the exact same way this morning when I got in."

Ras turned to his grandfather. "Is this a prison?"

"At one point," Cornelius said, then walked past Ras and began climbing the ladder down the hatch. When Ras followed, he found himself inside a well-lit corridor that reminded him of *Verdant's* Engine. The similarities made sense if Helios had designed this as well. Pipes ran along the walls down by the grated floors. Ras pulled down his Knack Visions. No Energy here. "What is this place?"

"The Burrower," the woman said. "Helios gave you flying cities while the rest of us got stuck underground."

The idea made sense to Ras. With no guarantee Atmo would stay in the air, humanity in general could survive by not keeping everyone above the clouds, but from the attitudes toward Skyfolk, it seemed as though people down in the Burrows didn't necessarily see it as though they were a part of Plan A.

Ras walked through spiraling corridors, deeper and deeper, until they reached a sub-level with a large, circular door. The woman spun the vault-like door's handle; a loud ratcheting noise echoed down the hallway, until the handle clunked and refused to turn any farther. She tugged on the door and it swung slowly open.

The room inside had a tall ceiling and maps placed along the rounded wall. Tables illuminated from underneath were scattered about the room.

In the back, alone at one of the illuminated workstations sat Elias, focused on the map in front of him.

"Dad!" Ras called out, rushing over.

Elias struggled to lift himself up to a standing position just in time to receive the hug.

"I thought they had you locked away in a cell or something," Ras said, releasing the embrace.

"Initially, they did," Elias said. "But we came to an agreement, and now I'm here." He tapped the translucent map and Ras saw that it said "Imago" in bold, black letters. Many dark dashes ran throughout the parchment. "Decades ago, Mason figured out how to track Convergences, then sent the information to the other Burrows."

"What sort of agreement?" Ras asked.

"Ras, are you listening?" Elias asked, placing the map atop a thick stack of documents. "This shows you the path of every single Convergence," Elias said. "It's as though they move on a yearly cycle like clockwork—"

"Dad," Ras said harshly. "What did you agree to?"

"If you didn't know where the Convergences were, then you couldn't find them in time to—"

"*I* couldn't? You mean *we* couldn't, right?"

Elias sighed. "I have to stay here, Ras. With your mother."

There it was. The continual other shoe's dropping. Nothing good could last. Ras felt his hands shake as he balled them into fists so as not to show his frustration. "I've had you for all of, what, barely three months, and now you tell me I'm never going to get to see you again?" he turned to Cornelius. "What, was this your idea?"

"No," Elias said. "It was mine." He placed a hand on Ras' shoulder. "They might have let you go for being a half-citizen, but the rest of the crew broke their law by coming here. Now they can go free and you can too."

Ras took a deep breath. "I can't do this without you."

"Why not?" Elias asked. "You've fended off India Bravo, exposed The Collective, and taken down the most powerful man in Atmo. You're my son, and I couldn't be more proud of you. You're never going shake the doubt, at least from my experience, but you've got a crew ready to follow you to the ends of Imago on the fastest ship in Atmo."

An emotion burned deep in the pit of Ras' stomach, knotted so tight he couldn't process it all at once. "You really think this is for the best?"

"Ras, once you follow this map, Atmo can land safely and by then Acerbis will just be another city to visit," Elias said. "I just wish I could see the look on Bravo's face when that happens."

"Is this why you suggested we go to Acerbis?"

"To get a map? Yes, we—"

"No," Ras said, holding up a hand. "Putting yourself in this position so mom could finally have you back."

He looked into his father's eyes. Would those be his eyes in a decade? So many choices. So much regret.

"You can do this, Ras," Elias said, avoiding his son's gaze as he reached over and rolled up the map, then collected an assortment of other documents. "Have Callie look these over. At the beginning, they tracked as many as fifty Convergences. Last year's report from Mason says it's down to fifteen. I think *The Kingfisher* can handle that in a week."

Ras clenched his jaw. His father had made a choice, and he couldn't decide if he felt abandoned or empowered. "So, I'll see you again after all this?"

"I'll expect a full report."

CHAPTER NINE
The Origin

RAS' AND CORNELIUS' ELEVATOR STOPPED AT LEVEL 5 TO COLLECT Callie, Emma, and Amelia. Ras clutched the stack of papers to his chest, simply staring straight ahead.

"What's going on?" Callie asked, rubbing her eyes. "Where are we going?"

"Back to the ship," Ras said.

As the elevator reached the top level, Ras caught sight of an orange hue to the ever-present cloud cover, an indication that the sun had risen. Omri stood awaiting their arrival, waving a greeting as the machine ground to a halt.

"Where's your dad?" Callie asked.

"Right where he wants to be," Ras said, garnering a look from his mother.

At the lip of the Burrow, Sheriff Prentiss stood with his crossbow resting on his shoulder. Several deputies standing at his flanks moved to encircle the newcomers, acting as captors as much as escorts.

The sheriff's expression held no joy. "It's not often I'm wrong."

"I think you were pretty spot on that we weren't from Mason," Ras said.

"No," Prentiss said, shaking his head. "You're getting to leave my city after lying to me. But, I can't exactly go against the mayor's wishes, now can I?" He turned on his heel and motioned for the deputies to follow him.

The group began walking toward the ruins of Acerbis. The wrecked stage and scattered benches from the night's festivities had been left untidied after the chaos of Ace and Tink's prank.

To Ras' surprise, many of the townspeople lined the edges of the road. "Looks like we're getting a parade," he said. The people still wore their suits and fancy dresses, although in the light of day, the clothes appeared threadbare. "Is there some kind of dress code for seeing prisoners off?"

"This is how most of us dress, Erasmus," Prentiss said.

"Why?" Callie asked.

Cornelius spoke up. "We're still in mourning."

"I mean no disrespect," Callie said. "But, that was generations ago."

"It's not just for the people," Amelia said. "It's for all of Imago. There are so few of us left. With such little hope, dressing nicely is a small comfort."

"It also didn't hurt that odds were when someone overloaded, they weren't wearing their best outfit," Omri said. "Everyone had an opportunity to dress up if they found a house that hadn't burned to the ground."

They approached the train, but walked beyond it. Evidently non-ambassadors didn't get to ride.

"Where's the rest of my crew?" Ras asked.

"Already back on your ship," Prentiss said. "Where they belong."

Ras leaned toward his mother. "I'm going to miss you."

"Please don't make this harder," Emma said, bringing a hand up to wipe her eyes.

The expressions of the Acerbians ranged from curiosity to utter disgust. Ras decided to keep his eyes forward for the rest of the walk to the pylons. "So, being half-Acerbian…does that mean I can come back when I want?"

"Maybe if you bring back the real Ambassador delegation from Mason," Prentiss said. "Most of us were curious if Governor Bartleby was serious about reuniting Imago." He paused. "Then again, Mason is likely to shoot you out of the sky on approach."

Ras looked over to Omri. "Where's your family?"

Omri gave an apologetic half-smile. "Dealing with Ace after she tossed all of our spare linens to the bottom of the Burrow last night," he said. "Her behavior last night was unacceptable. I feel like she owes you."

"Why's that?" Ras asked.

"Last night's stunt would have probably landed her in much hotter water if everyone wasn't so focused on your arrival," Omri said.

"Ah," Ras said. "Well, thanks for coming to see us off."

"You'll have to invite us to the wedding," Omri said, smiling at his sister. Emma gave him a death glare. He blanched as Callie turned, giving him a puzzled look. "Sorry. I just assumed, what with Emma saying you were practically a daughter and all."

Ras sighed, and Omri mouthed a silent 'sorry.'

They continued to walk in silence to the pylons. The tide of entropy that had washed across the ruins during a century of neglect was evident in the remains of the homes along the cracked street, which were little more than chimneys surrounded by rubble. Ras wondered why there hadn't been an effort to rebuild, but chalked it up to the limitations of a small population whose needs were barely met.

He looked back, barely able to see the Burrow in the ground behind him. *Would landing* Verdant *nearby start a civil war?* he wondered. The old city looked uninhabitable. *Could anybody even make the transition from an Atmo city to what was left down here?*

Just inside the pylons, *The Kingfisher* sat with its hangar bay open. A small crowd had gathered to gawk at the legendary ship which had turned the tide in The Clockwork War.

The rest of the crew stood, waiting for their captain's arrival. Ras felt a hand on his shoulder, and turned to find Cornelius. The two men stopped, which the deputies didn't protest, as the rest of the group walked on to the ship.

"Erasmus was my father's name," Cornelius said. "To his friends, he went by Ras as well." He sniffed at the air. "He survived The Clockwork War, and if he hadn't been airborne when The Great Overload happened, it's likely neither of us would be having this conversation."

Ras nodded, confused as to where his grandfather was headed.

"He chose to stay on the ground when he was offered a ride on *Verdant*," Cornelius said. "He's one of the few who had the option, having been in the military. Felt Atmo was a stopgap."

"He was right," Ras said. "The cities won't last forever up there."

Cornelius nodded. "Sounds like you two might have gotten along." He stuffed his hands deep in his coat pockets. "You might find people from other Burrows are…resistant to help from Skyfolk, even if you mean well."

"Why specifically?"

"When Atmo launched, there were fractures," Cornelius said. "Not just between the land and sky, but among the Burrows too. Visitors only came to steal resources because they didn't know how to manage their own. Food shortages led to war, which led to more death."

"I didn't know," Ras said.

"Well, as far as we knew, Skyfolk were just looking down on us from their fancy escape ships, watching us die."

"But Atmo wasn't...*blessed*, or whatever it is you call it," Ras said. "We couldn't come down."

"Some did anyway," Cornelius said. "To take Convergences, among other things. I'm just trying to say that lifetimes have been spent waiting for help to come from above, so if it finally does, expect Imago to take issue with your timing."

"Well, I came as quick as I could," Ras said. "I'll keep all that in mind."

Cornelius sighed. "I don't hate your father, Ras. I didn't appreciate that he never asked me for your mother's hand, and I didn't have a kind opinion of people living above the clouds to begin with...but I had never met one." He looked Ras directly in the eyes. "I'm hoping to get to know him. Give him a fair shake. He seems to make your mother happy after all these years, so that's something."

"He's a good man," Ras said. "I wouldn't be trying to save the world if it weren't for him." He adjusted his grip on the stack of papers Elias had given him so he could offer his hand.

Cornelius looked at Ras' hand for a few moments, then back up at Ras, who continued to hold it out.

"I hope to get to know you someday, Mr. Corin," Ras said. He wasn't ready to call this man Grandpa yet. "Maybe you could give me a chance too."

Cornelius removed his hands from his pockets, then wrapped his arms around Ras. "You're half Emmaline, so that puts you in better standing than most." He released the embrace. "Good luck, Erasmus. Let me know if you save the world."

Ras took a step back. "Oh, I'm sure you'll find out one way or another." He turned and walked toward *The Kingfisher*, meeting up with Prentiss and his mother.

"I want you to know," Prentiss said, "that if you think about landing *Verdant* anywhere close to here, you will be starting a war."

Ras looked the broad-shouldered man square in the eye. "Good thing *Verdant* shouldn't need to land then."

"You'll be back in a week, right?" Emma asked.

Then or never, Ras thought, but opted to spare his mother's heart. The cracking in her voice was bad enough without him making it worse. "That's the plan," he said, leaning in to hug her. "Take care of dad."

"I will," she said, sniffling.

THE SLOW PULSE of the emerald colored crystal spire jutting out of the ground beckoned with its mesmerizing pulsation like an ancient creature breathing in and out, in and out. This, in conjunction with the Energy Origin's faint hum, was enough to nearly put Ras to sleep. Its unnatural beauty made it difficult to not stare and lose himself in his thoughts.

"Are we sure Convergences are drawn to this?" Ras asked, snapping his stare away from the Energy Origin and rubbing his eyes.

Dayus' silence was likely an answer unto itself. To be fair, Ras had asked the question probably a dozen times throughout the morning, and the older man stood ready at the wheel with perfect posture and only the occasional twitch of his mustache or a quick blink hinted at his not having died from old age or boredom.

Ras turned his attention to the dashboard covered with buttons, toggles, and dials, half of them labeled with Illorian script, half with taped down pieces of papers with the translations written in Callie's penmanship. He lazily traced his finger around a big red button, then felt the raised script of the unfamiliar word under the button forwards and backwards.

He swiveled his chair at the co-pilot's station to look back at Callie in repose. She had fallen asleep in the navigation chair with the freshly bound Convergence report cracked open upon her chest. The book rose and fell gently with each deep, restful breath. Her freckled face looked beautiful, innocent even, which was an attribute not lost by her upon waking.

"Have we learned anything?" Dayus asked, his eyes still fixed to the Energy Origin.

"That's a rather broad question," Ras replied.

"It is," Dayus said. "But an important one."

Ras eased himself off of his seat and placed some weight onto his nearly healed leg. He took the few steps over to Callie's seat, and as he reached the navigation station, Callie took a deep breath, reentering the waking world.

"I think you've exceeded your quota of beauty rest," Ras said, easing himself down onto the large chair arm.

She squinted her eyes against the light spilling into the room from the bridge window. "This is as good as it gets, huh?" she asked, picking up the book and studying the page for a moment before closing it.

"I don't see how you could improve," Ras said. "Looks like the Convergence report is riveting material."

She glanced down, finding her place in the stack of bound pages. "No, it's very interesting. It's just a lot to take in. Most of what we need is on that map," she said, pointing to the unrolled parchment sitting on the table next to her. "According to the report, most of their data came from Mason. I have no clue how they tracked the Convergences, but it's a cyclical thing."

"Maybe the Convergences like to tour Imago," Ras said, glancing at the map.

"They all like to visit the Energy Origin at least once a year."

Ras noted where all of the dotted lines met up, then fanned out to cover the rest of their patterns. "Wonder why." He looked up at Dayus, then back to Callie. "Hey, now might be a good opportunity to talk to…" he trailed off and nodded toward Dayus. "You know?"

Callie pursed her lips, then leaned over to glance past Ras. "I tried asking before," she said softly. "He doesn't like to talk about the…" she puffed out her cheeks and made an expanding sphere with her hands.

"Dayus?" Ras asked at regular volume. Callie's eyes went wide and she mouthed for Ras to stop. "If you knew something important to the success of the mission to destroy every Convergence, you'd tell us, right?"

"I can assure you that I tell you everything you need to know," Dayus said carefully. "Are you concerned regarding my performance?"

"No, no," Ras said as he stood to approach Dayus. He looked back and arched his finger twice for Callie to follow suit. "I just find myself more in the dark about what we're up against…and I'm sure you could practically write a book, or *two*, with all you know on the topic."

Dayus' shoulders dropped slightly as he sighed. "I'm not sure if you're attempting wit or just doing an excellent job of dancing around the concept of being indirect." He turned to look at Ras. "I'm old enough to appreciate brevity."

"All right, direct. I can be direct," Ras said. "I'll have to work on brevity—"

"On *Derailleur* there were two books in the library on the history of The Clockwork War written by a Dayus Ofanim," Callie said, releasing a pent up breath. "Was that you?"

Dayus shifted his gaze from Ras to Callie and the hardness in his expression eased. "I felt there were certain things deserving documentation in case those living in Atmo fell ignorant of the past."

"But the pages on The Great Overload were replaced with blank pages," Callie said. "On *Verdant*, the paper was just ripped out."

Dayus made a thoughtful humming sound for a moment. "At one point in my life I thought I knew the purpose of Convergences."

"And?" Callie said eagerly.

"And redaction is an easier thing than printing a new edition," Dayus said. "My summation lacked an appropriate perspective, and the world didn't need a nonexistent hope written in an obscure text relegated to the dusty bookshelves of woefully underused libraries."

"What did you think they were?" Ras asked.

"Please do not make me rehash this, Erasmus," Dayus said. "Suffice it to say that if you are concerned I am withholding the truth from you, understand that I have devoted myself fully to the cause of eradicating the blight which are Convergences. And if you happen to find an edition of my books unaltered, I would not advise taking in any of the text as useful."

"Maybe now would be a good opportunity to learn something," Ras said, noticing the bright green Convergence flitting about on the far horizon. Its movements seemed sluggish until he realized how far away it was. "That might be the biggest Convergence I've ever seen…"

Dayus pressed a series of buttons, then eased the throttle forward. "I would feel more comfortable if you two could stand a bit further apart," he said, reaching over to pull Callie gently away from Ras before resuming his piloting duties.

"Hold on," Ras said, placing a hand on the main console to steady himself. "I thought the point is that we overload and destroy the Convergence."

"It is," Dayus replied. "But, there are potential dangers to exhibiting your nullifying abilities in the presence of something that arguably gives life to this world," Dayus said, keeping his eye on the Convergence.

"You mean the Energy Origin?" Ras asked.

Dayus nodded. "So, we wait until the Convergence leaves, and then we follow it. May I suggest that everyone return to their seats and utilize their restraints?"

Callie eased her way back to her chair as Ras sat back in the co-pilot's seat and fidgeted with the buckle. He leaned over and pressed a button on the dash to initiate the intercom system. "Crew, this is your captain speaking. Strap yourselves in wherever you can. We're about to begin pursuit of a Convergence."

"We're going to be flying fairly close to the Origin," Dayus said. "Calista, let me know if you start to feel anything odd or think that the serum is failing to do its work."

A look of concern grew on Callie's face. "I...I will. Is there a danger?"

"It seems to be a constant companion," Dayus said.

"Dayus, out of curiosity, were you the one who flew *The Kingfisher* for Hal?" Ras asked.

A sly grin spread across his thin lips. "No, but I always wanted to." He threw the throttle forward, and inertia pinned Ras to the padded co-pilot seat as *The Kingfisher* roared to life toward the Energy Origin.

"Why are we going so fast?" Ras shouted, gripping at his restraints.

"Because we're going to lose the Convergence if we don't," Dayus said calmly.

"It's just fluttering—"

"Energy sources repel one another," Dayus said, "and judging by the size of this one, the reaction might be violent."

"If they repel each other, then why is it approaching the Origin?" Ras asked.

"That is an excellent question," Dayus said. "I would commend you if you could find its answer."

The Convergence bobbled its way toward the Energy Origin, paused for a moment, then dashed forward. Before the Convergence could touch the Origin, a loud crack split the air and the large sphere blasted away at a different angle, seemingly propelled by some unknown defense mechanism borne by the Origin.

"Did that thing just attack it?" Ras asked.

"It almost appears as such," Dayus replied.

"Out of curiosity," Callie said, "what would happen if the Energy Origin..."

"Was destroyed?" Dayus asked. "All life in Imago would likely cease...eventually." He altered course quickly and slammed the throttle forward as far as it would go. He gave a little consideration to the Energy Origin by angling around it, but the ship clipped by with a surprisingly small margin.

Ras then looked back to Callie, whose eyes were wide with excitement. She caught his eye and flashed a big smile.

This was adventure.

A quick shift of The Convergence's path guided *The Kingfisher* to alter its course. They passed over hundreds of small, oddly shaped mirrors that rippled as the Convergence passed over them. *Is that water?* Ahead, mountains climbed on the horizon.

"When is this thing going to slow down?" Ras asked.

Dayus shrugged, still intent on his pursuit.

"It has to, eventually, doesn't it?" Ras looked back to Callie. "That's a science thing, right?"

"It's a mobile, perpetual source of Energy," Callie said. "I think that flies in the face of at least two natural laws."

"Have we gotten far enough away from The Origin yet?" Ras asked, focusing on the approaching mountains. He didn't doubt Dayus' piloting abilities, but he felt safer not needing to test them.

"Now would be a good time to hold hands," Dayus said. "It's going to have the advantage soon."

"Advantage?" Ras asked.

"Convergences don't give much regard to what's in their path," Dayus said, nodding forward. The Convergence reached the first mountain, striking it and effortlessly carving a large hole in its center, leaving only a faint glow in its wake before the top of the mountain crumbled down to fill the gap.

"Won't that slow it down?" Callie asked.

"Oddly enough, no," Dayus said, bringing *The Kingfisher* into a maneuver, skimming the damaged mountain. As the ship began to pass the tall natural structure, he threw it into a quick climb, correctly predicting the rock debris blasting out where the Convergence exited. Despite the expert maneuvering, several chunks of mountains rocketed toward *The Kingfisher*, connecting and shaking the ship violently.

"Damage report?" Ras called out to the comm.

"Minor," Old Harley's voice came through. "What hit us?"

"A mountain," Ras said, then wrestled awkwardly with his restraints for a moment until he felt a hand stop him. Callie had beaten him to the punch and now she was bracing herself against the co-pilot station.

Looking deep into Ras' eyes, she touched his neck lightly with her hand. Her beautiful blue eyes began to shift to an almost black gray. The tingling sensation rushed through Ras from head to toe once more.

Ahead, the Convergence appeared to speed up.

Callie's smile disappeared and she gritted her teeth. "Is it gone yet?"

"You might be pushing it further away," Dayus said. "You should probably stand down and hold onto something."

When Callie moved aside, Ras could see the Convergence still on its haphazard collision course with mountain after mountain. "I thought just being within her overload sphere should destroy it," Ras said.

"Maybe we need to overload with it *inside* our overload sphere to begin with?" Callie asked.

"Perhaps that is a discussion best left for the absence of exploding mountains," Dayus said. "We'll try again when we can get closer."

The Kingfisher wound around another mountain as the momentum from the Convergence finally begin to wane. They left the mountain range behind and soared over a lush field of green that waved gracefully with strong winds that rocked *The Kingfisher*.

Dayus eased off the throttle, bringing the airship to a near stop. The Convergence put a bit of distance between it and the ship before returning to its lazy, bouncing rhythm in the sky. "Let's wait for a moment before you overload, Miss Calista."

Callie turned and gazed out at the Convergence. "To make sure it's within our overload radius?"

"No. To take the rare opportunity to study what we're up against," Dayus said softly.

"Shouldn't we just end it now so it stops putting more Energy out on the wind?" Ras asked. "I've seen these things up close plenty of times. Callie and I went through one once—"

"That's something I'd like to forget," Callie said.

"I'm surprised you remember that," Ras said.

"Falling off an airship has a way of waking up a girl," Callie replied. "Swinging through a sea of screaming green things leaves a mental mark."

"You were right, Erasmus," Dayus said, transfixed. "I do believe this is the largest Convergence I've ever seen."

"How many have you seen?"

"All of them," Dayus replied.

"How did this one get so big?" Callie asked. "The report said they grew when absorbing the Energy from overloading Knacks. Did it find more people to overload since you last saw it?"

"Must have…" Ras said, realizing that it had to be at least ten times the size of the previous Convergences he had come across. "At least this should be a good step toward dropping the Energy levels." He watched the swirling orb of Energy. Tendrils danced along its surface, almost crackling like lightning. "Okay, are we studied up?"

"Not really," Dayus said.

"How much more time do you need?" Ras asked.

"Decades."

"Well, hopefully we'll find another one for you to look at," Ras said, reaching his hand out for Callie, who took it without hesitation.

The buzzing feeling returned as Callie's eyes darkened. Ras turned his head to watch the Convergence in the distance. In that moment, he could *feel* its presence and the resistance of the sphere in his mind. It didn't want to leave.

Ras placed his KnackVision goggles over his eyes, nearly blinding himself. "Dayus, could you fly us closer?" he asked, only half aware he was even speaking through the force that the Convergence was exerting on him.

As *The Kingfisher* moved closer, the resistance grew like a pressure against the front of him. He squeezed Callie's hand gently. "Are you all right?"

"I think so," she whispered. "I know this is an odd time, but could you remind me what the three things you promised me back on *Verdant* were?"

"Right before you gave me the keys to *The Brass Fox*?"

"Yeah," Callie said. "It's okay if you don't remember them."

"Of course I do," Ras said. The pressure decreased slightly. "How could I forget? One, I solemnly swore that I would do everything within my means to save *Verdant*."

"Right."

"Two, that if I saw you in danger," Ras said, "I would save you from whatever it was."

"As long as it didn't kill you first," Callie amended with a small tug at the corner of her mouth.

"I did say that, didn't I?" Ras asked. "Three, that I had to take you with me, and I couldn't say no to that."

"You couldn't because I wouldn't let you?" she asked.

"No, I could have, but at the same time I couldn't."

Ahead, the perfectly spherical emerald shape began to warp ever so slightly. The haunting sounds of screams enveloped *The Kingfisher* before The Convergence erupted into a shockwave rippling through the sky.

The KnackVisions showed the dispersal of Energy onto the wind. It didn't dissipate evenly, but broke apart into a dozen currents racing off in every direction.

The Kingfisher shuddered for a moment as one of the waves of wind and Energy reached the vessel. Ras braced himself, holding Callie tightly until the moment passed.

"Are we clear?" Callie asked.

"I think so."

"One down, fourteen to go," Callie said, awkwardly pulling away from his embrace and stepping over to collect the map. She picked it up and settled it atop the main dash. Tracing a finger from the Energy Origin, she ran it across the dotted line marked across the mountain range to the east.

Shouldn't she be more excited about popping the Convergence? Ras wondered. "What was the three promises thing about?" he asked, unbuckling himself.

"Just testing a theory," she said.

"Which was?"

"I'm still working it out," Callie said. "I think there might be a correlation between an emotional state and the ability to destroy Convergences."

"Oh, well, let me know when the results are conclusive," Ras said. "Where are we now?" He walked over to examine the map.

Callie stepped away as he approached, then settled into the navigation chair and picked up the Convergence report. She flipped to a page near the back. "There's a timetable here," she said. "It logs where each Convergence should be at any given time." She flipped one more page, then held a very complex looking chart up close to her face.

"Huh," she said.

"Is 'huh' a good or a bad thing?" Ras asked.

"From where we are now, the closest interception point is…Treding."

"Remind me where I know that name from?"

Dayus sighed. "It's where Halcyon routed the majority of the Illorian military," he said. "It was the bloodiest battle of The Clockwork War."

"Well, I did promise I'd show you all the sights," Ras said. Something felt off about Callie's mannerisms. He decided he would ask her about it when they had a moment alone together.

"Sir?" a voice came from the back of the bridge. Old Harley. He leaned against the doorframe, using the hand holding his crutch to wipe his brow. "Permission to approach the bridge?"

"Harley, you don't have to—" Ras began.

"I'm afraid we have a problem, sir."

Ras paused to let Old Harley deliver the news. Nothing. "Out with it—"

"We have a stowaway, sir."

CHAPTER TEN
The Battlefield

"How did you even find this ship?" Ras shouted at Ace, who reclined in the back seat of the shuttle. Next to her sat the young man who had acted as her accomplice during the firework prank.

"Tink found it after he left the Caretaker Festival," Ace said, jutting a thumb over her shoulder. "He was hoping to see the Mason train so we could glide behind it when it headed out, but this was way better."

"And you just thought you'd hop a ride?" Ras asked, swinging an arm as though he were inviting her aboard.

"Well—"

"Do you even know how dangerous it is to be here?"

"Did you know you have a vein that pops out from your neck when you're angry?" Ace asked. "Wait, why is it dangerous?"

"What's all this shouting about?" Dixie asked, joining the crowded area in the hallway outside the shuttle.

"Stowaways," Guy said.

"Who? Them? Nah, I let them in," Dixie said, then turned on her heel toward the main lounge.

"We'll talk. Don't go anywhere," Ras said, pointing a finger at Ace.

"Where am I going to go?" Ace asked.

Ras stomped down the hall after Dixie. "Why didn't you tell me you let them on?" he called as she disappeared into the lounge.

When Ras rounded the doorway, Dixie was already reclining on the fainting couch, her legs crossed at the ankles. "Technically, I didn't let them in...I just didn't kick them off when I found them."

"Dixie, she's my cousin—"

"Which is why I didn't think you'd mind so much," Dixie said, rubbing her temples. "Besides, she reminds me a lot of me."

"One of you is enough," Ras muttered.

Dixie gave a genuine smile. "That is so sweet of you to say." She sat up and hunched forward. "Not that I expect you to know, but it is incredibly difficult to be a stowaway, and I can't even imagine how rare an opportunity it is for a Remnant—sorry, Imago…an—or whatever they call themselves—to go off and see the world."

"This isn't a cruise ship," Ras said, "and we're turning back around as soon as we finish off these Convergences."

"Great, then their parents will barely know they've left," Dixie said. "Aren't you happy to have some family back on board?"

"That," Ras said, pointing, "hardly equals losing my parents. Which, to the point, those two are directly responsible for that happening after the whole 'blowing up the Caretaker Festival' thing. I barely know her, and if the trend continues, those two are going to cause more trouble than they're worth."

"She tossed me a pillow last night," Dixie offered.

Ras took a deep breath, then let it out slowly before storming off toward his quarters. He passed by the mess hall where Caedmon and Shane were playing cards and almost stopped to yell at them for the security breach, but he had grown tired of shouting.

Approaching his room, he heard a faint, low whistle coming from behind the door. He sighed, then worked the latch to slide the door open. Wind whipped wildly at his hair and clothes as daylight poured in through a hole about the size of his fist at the base of the wall. At present, his bed sheet was attempting escape through the opening.

A chunk of mountain debris had impacted on the fine Illorian bureau. He didn't have many possessions, but he had stored the trinkets he had amassed he stored in there. Items lay scattered on the floor, and he stooped to collect them, mentally taking inventory.

Cold sweat crawled across his forehead and down the back of his neck when he noticed the top drawer lying upside down on the floor next to his bed. He looked around the room for his ring box, and with every trinket that his eyes passed over, every knick-knack that wasn't the box, his panicked heart beat faster.

Ras positioned himself between the hole in the wall and the inverted dresser drawer. He lifted it up cautiously, trying to still the trembling in his hands, and immediately the photo of him and his father on *The Silver Fox*'s bridge slipped out from beneath it, flittering about the room like a feather in a windstorm. He grasped wildly for it but came up empty; the picture danced its way past the bed sheet and out into Atmo.

The only photo he had left of his father was gone.

A knock came on the door, and Ras slammed the drawer back down to the floor. "What?" he shouted over the deafening moan from the bulkhead breach.

The door slid open, revealing Guy. Ras couldn't think of anyone on the crew he'd rather see less.

"What do you want?" Ras shouted.

Guy simply held up a square of metal and a welding torch. He stepped over behind Ras and tried to pull at the bed sheet. Unsuccessful, he flicked on the torch and burned the fabric until half of it fluttered away on the wind, then he placed the thick metal over the hole. The sound in the room subsided, replaced by the cracklings of the metal being welded to the wall.

Ras lifted the drawer once more, hastily tossing its upended contents inside and placed them on his bed.

The ring box was nowhere to be found.

Guy finished his patch job as Ras just sat, shell shocked.

"Hey, it could have been worse," Guy said.

"How's that?" Ras asked.

Guy fished into his pocket, then tossed the ring box onto Ras' lap. "She could have already said 'no.'"

Ras stared, flabbergasted. "But—I—uh, how?"

"I was making repairs, saw the hole, saw the ring, figured you didn't want it blowing out to Atmo, then got distracted by your cousin," Guy said. "Didn't have time to save everything, so I put it all under that box." He looked over at the burned bed sheet. "Hope you sleep in pajamas." He slid open the door to leave.

"Guy?" Ras managed to croak out.

"Yeah?"

Ras held up the ring box. "Don't...tell Callie. Please?"

"Since I don't like being owed favors, at some point you can tell me about that Dixie girl," Guy said, then left the room.

As the shock wore off, Guy's words sank in. *An on-ship romance, that won't complicate anything,* Ras thought. Being captain felt different without his father around. Part of him wished Elias was there to be his safety net, but it wasn't like his dad had the safety net of his grandfather when he went out to save *Verdant. And it got him frozen in Illoria for a decade.*

"There's no time to feel sorry for ourselves," Ras muttered, then fought to remember where he had heard that before. *Billie.* It was pretty much the last thing she had said to him before Bravo Company attacked *Verdant.*

Mostly though, he missed having a confidant. Someone to check in with to see if things were normal, not that any of the last few months had resembled normal...or even the last century, come to think of it.

Ras stuffed the wedding ring box back in his pocket and listened to the relative silence after the chaos of the vacuum leak. There was calm, for the moment, and it would have to be enough to last him the inevitable drama of acclimating to two new crew members.

Ras heard muffled shouts from outside his room. Happy shouts. He went into the hallway to investigate. The voices came from the hangar bay door, and as he approached, he saw Dixie furtively looking through the porthole into the hallway. She jerked back in surprise when Ras appeared in front of her.

Behind Dixie, Ras could see Ace standing dangerously close to the edge of the open hangar bay. Attached to the wall, feeding out to the open sky, was a thin cable that looked familiar.

Ras tried the handle. Locked. "Open up! That's an order!"

Dixie's shoulders fell. "They're just having fun!"

Ras pointed emphatically, and in response the deadbolt thunked loudly. He opened the door, compromising the vacuum seal, and entered the hangar. "Remind me to never let you babysit!"

"Are you saying what I think you're saying?" Dixie asked excitedly.

"What?" Ras asked, confused. "No! Callie's not pregnant. That's not even possible."

The shouting alerted Ace, who looked back with a manic expression as she waved emphatically to Ras. "You've got to see this!"

Ras slowly made his way across the hangar along the wall, reached the taut cable, then walked his way along it to Ace. He peered over the edge to see Tink bobbing about on the wind behind the ship, gaining and losing altitude in wild maneuvers. Some sort of metal glider appeared to be attached to his feet, and he stayed connected to the ship by way of Ras' grapple gun on his arm.

Despite the pang of vertigo that washed over Ras, it looked like a blast.

Remembering he was currently not in control of his crew, the smile on Ras' face vanished. He waved his arms to catch Tink's attention.

"We worked out a system," Ace said. She picked up a wrench and struck the cable three times. Tink looked up, and soon began respooling the cable back into the grapple gun.

As soon as Tink reeled fully in, Ras mashed down on the red button, initializing the closing of the horizontal bay door.

Tink had a wide grin. "Works," he said, holding his palm up for Ace to slap, which she did. He held up his hand to Ras.

"I told you to stay put," Ras said, ignoring the celebratory gesture. He hated how in less than an hour, he had already turned from captain into a sour disciplinarian.

"Well, we didn't know if you were going to drop us off or turn the ship around," Ace said with a shrug. "It was kind of our only shot to see if Tink's glider was going to work."

"Sorry," Tink said, offering the crescent moon shaped device to Ras.

Ras took the glider in his hands and found it surprisingly light. Flipping it over, he saw that the leather foot straps went through to the bottom. "What's this made from?"

"Scraps," Tink said.

"Would you call yourself more terse or laconic?" Dixie asked.

Tink shrugged.

"Did you want a turn?" Ace asked, lifting her eyebrows in an obvious sales pitch geared toward getting herself out of trouble.

Ras walked over to the comm unit on the wall, pressing its button. "Dayus, what's our ETA on Treding?"

"A good forty minutes yet," Dayus said. "Might I inquire as to why the cargo bay was opened?"

Ras looked back to Ace and Tink. "We're just testing out a new tool."

It only took two minutes to step into the rig, and only five more for word to have spread among the crew until everyone but Dayus had crowded into the bay to watch their leader embark on the foolhardy endeavor.

"So who gets to be Captain if the cable breaks?" Guy asked, arms crossed.

"Callie," Ras said without missing a beat. "Besides, I have this thing." He patted the grapple gun. "If something happens, have Dayus slow down and I'll reattach." He double-checked his restraints. "You know, this thing could come in handy when—"

Dixie slammed her palm on the button to open the hanger door and Ras was sucked out of the room.

He watched *The Kingfisher* rocket away from him, and he quickly worked the grapple gun's controls to spool out some extra cable. He added tension to the line so he wouldn't dislocate his shoulder again with a sudden snap.

The wind whipped hard against the flat sheet of metal attached to his feet, pulling him horizontal. He dug his heels down and tucked his knees in to angle the glider forward.

Ras quickly dove as he struggled to bring the glider perpendicular to the ground rushing beneath him. Convergence hunting meant flying beneath the clouds, but it also meant less room for error if he were to fall.

He forced his attention away from the deadly drop beneath him and pushed his heels into the resisting wind current. The rush carried him higher. Soon he had risen enough to once more be in view of everyone in the hanger.

Adjusting altitude took a little bit of work, but after a few accidental plummets due to not holding the right amount of tension in his calves, he started to get the hang of the glider's operation. Next, he tried shifting his weight from side to side, moving him in the direction he leaned.

The sudden lifts were his favorite part. If falling was terrifying for him, then its antitheses was exhilarating, all the more so because at the apex of the climb came a momentary sensation of weightlessness. Soon he was repeatedly dipping up and down, riding the wind currents. Eventually, however, he glanced at the hangar and saw everyone but Callie had grown tired of his flying session.

Checking his watch, Ras realized he had been joyriding for nearly half an hour. He pressed the button, retracting the cable.

Once safely inside, Ras motioned for Callie to close the bay door while he extracted himself from the glider rig.

His ears rang in a way that reminded him of his time on open-aired ships. If anything, it was a familiar sort of deafness that brought him a bit of nostalgia. He pulled off his KnackVisions and smiled broadly as Callie approached.

"Looks like you were having some fun out there, flyboy," Callie said with a grin mirroring his. "It's good to see you smiling like that."

Ras undid the first strap of the grapple gun around his waist, then moved on to untying his feet. "What? Do I not smile?"

"I think it's the first time I've seen you play in almost a decade."

She was right. There had not been much cause for celebration or the usual childhood playtime after his father had ventured off to The Wild. Of course, Mr. Tourbillon had also cracked down on their interaction not too long thereafter.

"You know, fun and responsibility don't have to be mutually exclusive," she said.

"I kind of figured this fun would come after the world had been saved," Ras said. "Then again, there wasn't exactly a parade in our honor when we got back from saving *Verdant*." He leaned over to collect Tink's invention, tucking it underneath his arm. "For all I know, letting Atmo land might spark a civil war, thanks to me." Tapping the glider, he said, "Guess I might as well have some fun while I can."

"You think too much."

"I need to," Ras said.

"Have you thought of any scenarios where we win and people realize everybody else should have a shot at surviving peacefully?" Callie asked.

"Sometimes I worry 'Happily ever after' only happens in books because they get to end and we don't see what happens afterward," Ras said. He knew what he said would hurt Callie, and he regretted it, but he couldn't lie to her. Not to the woman he loved.

"Take that back," Callie said sternly.

"I want to be optimistic," Ras said. "I really do. But I set out to fix a problem I caused, and things just got worse. And now I'm hoping I don't wind up literally killing everyone with kindness." He walked past Callie and opened the door to the hallway. "I don't want to be

The Reclaimer if it means I'm going to wind up ending the world."

"Does that mean you're going to quit?"

"No, I—"

"Because that's not the Ras Veir I know," Callie said, "and better we go out with a bang because we were trying to help everyone than be the death of everyone because it was easier to give up and just watch Atmo crash. Neither of us could live with that." She walked purposefully up to Ras. "Maybe you're taking too much stock in what old men who looked for everything to end after The Great Overload have to say."

"Maybe," Ras said. "That's not what I want to be."

"I know," Callie said. "Then offer hope of things continuing. Reclaim that, because Atmo knows we could all use a little 'happily ever after.'"

The comm unit on the wall gave a faint hiss. "If I'm not interrupting," Dayus' voice said. "We're approaching Treding."

"Thank you, Dayus," Ras said to the comm.

"And might I say I personally support your stance on staying on the side of hope," Dayus said. "I've seen men try to move forward without it, and I've yet to note a successful life lived. And whether or not that hope is you, people will latch on to those moving forward."

"Thank you, Dayus," Ras said once more.

"You're welcome, sir," Dayus said, and the comm unit clicked off.

"I think that's the first time he's called me 'sir,'" Ras said.

Callie nodded, a sad expression still on her face.

"I'm not giving up, Callie," Ras said. "At least not when I have you."

"Promise me something," Callie said.

"Anything."

"Don't stop with me," she said. "I don't want Atmo to fall if something were to happen to me. That's a lot of pressure."

"Just don't go making me have to fulfill that promise, all right?"

She nodded.

"All right," Ras said. "Now, let's see if the bloodiest battlefield of The Clockwork War can't cheer us up."

LITTLE DARK MARKS POCKED THE SKY as far as the eye could see.

"Funny," Dayus said, "I didn't figure the sky mines would have stayed up this long." He pulled back on the throttle, slowing the ship.

Ras looked out at the spots with a new clarity. He donned his KnackVisions. The Convergence in the center of the mine field held his attention. He turned back to address the entire crew on the bridge, but was distracted when a tendril of Energy passed from directly behind *The Kingfisher*, racing toward Treding.

He watched the wave of Energy deftly maneuver through the mines, eventually striking the large green sphere. The wave added itself to its mass, growing the Convergence. The difference wasn't easily discernible, but it was there.

"Did anybody else notice that?" Ras asked, pointing ahead. "It grew."

"Maybe it just moved closer," Dixie said.

"No, a piece from the last one we popped just joined up with it. Then it grew."

"Look!" Ace cried, entering the bridge and nearly bowling over Ras to get a good look out of the window. "I've never seen a real Convergence."

"Erasmus, it's your call," Dayus said. "We can go above or around, but we can't go through."

Ras surveyed the field. There were plenty of gaps where *The Kingfisher* could easily chart a course. "Why not—"

"They're magnetized," Callie said. "Assuming Dayus' book on the history of the war is accurate."

"Foster Helios designed them himself," Dayus said. "The metal hulls of the Illorian vessels would attract them, but they would ignore wooden bodies."

"Smart," Ras said. "You'd think they would have drifted into one another by now and blown themselves up."

Dayus nodded toward Callie, and she picked up on the cue.

"Their magnets repel one another to keep stasis," she said, then looked around. "See the edges of the battlefield?" She pointed at the structures that looked like the pylons outside of all of the cities. "Those things keep the whole field from drifting off."

"Why don't we just go around the minefield?" Ras asked.

"Because the Convergence...stopped," Old Harley said, pointing to the middle of the field.

"Convergences don't stop," Callie said, bringing the map to Ras. "Not if they're supposed to stay on this schedule."

"This doesn't make sense," Ras said, lifting the KnackVisions. "I thought they went wherever the wind took them. What would make them follow a distinct pattern, and why would it stop?"

"Maybe they're sentient," Finn suggested. "That Convergence is just making its rounds, and then along comes a piece of another broken Convergence to come warn it about a new predator."

"I would be scared if I were a Convergence," Callie said. "It would finally have something to be afraid of after a century."

If the Convergences could think, Ras wondered what the one stuck alone in Framer's Valley had been doing. He scanned the battlefield ahead. Wrecked carcasses of airships lay strewn about, discarded hulks of machined death. "Are those Elder suits?" Ras asked. It didn't make sense why the secret of the Illorians' being human rather than Clockwork men had never been revealed. Then again, the concept could have been lost in a generational misunderstanding. A nickname could have been taken literally.

"Is that an order to fly low to investigate?" Dayus asked.

"I suppose so," Ras said. "If you think we can avoid the mines."

Dayus brought the ship into a slow crawl twenty feet above the ground, weaving through an obstacle course of wreckage. Most of the bodies had withered away to nothing after prolonged exposure to the elements, and Ras worked on not letting himself linger on the time-washed carnage.

"So, all of the books say this was the culmination of Hal Napier turning the tide of The Clockwork War," Callie said, "but they never got too specific on how it happened."

"Before Halcyon was elected to the Elder council," Dayus said, threading the ship between two armored tanks that stood several stories tall, "he was a high ranking officer in the Illorian military."

"So, what you're saying is he had the other team's playbook," Ras said.

"He *wrote* the 'other team's' playbook," Dayus replied.

"Hold on," Old Harley chimed in. "You're telling me Napier came from The Wild?"

"As did I," Dayus said, giving Old Harley a look which cut off further questions.

Ras stared at the Convergence. It still hung in the same spot. He looked down at the control panel and looked for the wind monitor.

A strong headwind came from the north, but still the Convergence remained steadfast.

"Has Hal made any communications about what he's doing in Illoria?" Callie asked, her eyes fixed on the battlefield.

"Negotiations. Treaties and the like," Dayus said. "I believe it's his intent to find a peaceful solution for coexistence between the two nations once Atmo is safe."

"Uh, Captain?" Finn asked. "Am I seeing double?"

"What do you mean?" Ras asked, looking back at the red-headed man. He stood back on the side of the bridge and had an angle Ras didn't.

"Another Convergence is on the horizon," Finn said.

"I see it," Dayus said.

Ras craned his neck and spotted the faint glint of green well beyond the battlefield.

"None of the other Convergences are supposed to fly remotely close to Treding," Callie said, consulting the map. "What would it be doing all the way out here?"

Ras dropped the KnackVisions over his eyes and immediately had to squint at how much Energy was being given off on the battlefield. The Convergences ahead of them burned like two suns, growing in intensity as wisps of Energy sought them out and melded with them. He turned to look back at his crew and gasped.

"They're coming," Ras said.

"Who?" Dixie asked.

"Everyone," Ras said, unable to say more as he spun.

Fourteen 'suns' burned brightly from every direction. The Convergences had come to meet in Treding.

"Quick, everyone who is Energy-sensitive, stay close to someone immune," Ras said, then laughed.

"What's so funny?" Ace asked.

"All of the Convergences are coming here," Ras said. "Which means we can take them out all at once."

Callie smiled, offering her hand. "So let's save the world."

Ras hesitated. "I want to knock them all out at once." He looked at Finn. "If it's true these things can communicate, or *something*, I don't want to spook the rest of them by destroying this one."

"Now you're being superstitious," Guy said.

"No, I don't want to blow this opportunity because I couldn't wait five more minutes," Ras said.

The bridge had already begun to warm to an uncomfortable temperature and a trickle of sweat ran down the back of Ras' neck. It was an exciting juxtaposition to the cool days above the clouds, hoping another Convergence would make its way into The Bowl so he could pull a decent wind collection and stay warm while doing so.

Ahead, the Convergence moved slightly over toward a sky mine, detonating it. The concussive force eventually reached *The Kingfisher*, shaking the bridge slightly. The rest of the sky mines rippled away, then returned to their places.

"Was that a warning?" Dixie asked. "That kind of looked like a warning."

"Dayus, set the ship down," Ras said, standing from the co-pilot chair. "Callie, let's take the shuttle and see if we can't get a closer look."

LAUNCHING THE SHUTTLE took little time, and keeping it low to the ground wasn't a hassle. Ras hoped the smaller vessel would be less likely to attract the magnetic mines.

"I'm glad they're all showing up at once," Callie said, slouched in the chair behind Ras.

"Yeah, it's really going to save on time," Ras said, paying attention to piloting toward the center of the minefield. "It'll be nice to not have this whole 'save the world' pressure hanging over our heads."

"That's one way to look at it," Callie said, then paused. "Ras, I have something to confess."

Concern etched onto Ras' face. "What's wrong?"

"I know I should have told you earlier," she said. "But when I overload, I'm starting to get headaches again. I don't know what it means."

What it meant to Ras was that being in physical contact with the woman he loved caused pain. "When did this start?"

"When we were escaping *Verdant*," Callie admitted. "Maybe it's a side effect of whatever Lupava injected me with." She sighed. "Well, at least we can knock all of these out at once."

"So, does being around me hurt?" Ras asked, solemnly.

"No, just the overloading. And it's not that bad," she added quickly. "It's not nearly as severe as the headaches I used to get. Who knows, maybe I'll burn through this serum and wind up back the way I was before."

"But until then I'll make sure not to come too close," Ras said.

"I'm sorry," Callie said. "I know you'd never intentionally hurt me."

As the shuttle neared the center of the battlefield, Ras surveyed the cracked ground. Around the rotted deceased were broken Elder suits, smaller than the ones he saw in Illoria. At first he wondered if they had sent children out into the fray until he saw the pieces of one broken apart, strewn across the floor. "Are those...?"

"Machines," Callie confirmed. "They evidently didn't get it wrong when they called it The Clockwork War."

"I wonder if the Elder suits were modeled after the clockwork or vice versa," Ras said. "Either way it must have been hard to avoid casualties."

"Makes me wonder how many of those are sitting in Illoria, ready to be unfrozen," Callie said.

The Convergence was deceptively large. Flying toward it gave the impression of slow travel until Ras glanced down and saw how quickly they were flying over the ground. He took the opportunity to hand his KnackVisions back to Callie. "Can you check and see how close the other Convergences are? Be careful, it's going to be really, really bright."

"How's it going?" Dixie's voice chimed in over the shuttle's comm.

"We're getting there," Ras said.

"Check your radar," Dixie said. "We're picking up some sort of Energy-based signature running ahead of you."

"So one of these relics is operational?" Ras asked.

"Looks like it. Just didn't want you to be surprised," Dixie said.

Ras looked down at his instruments. The dials were going wild.

"Ras?" Callie asked, offering the KnackVisions forward. "Put those on and tell me if you see something odd up ahead."

Not wanting to be blinded, Ras placed one goggle over his right eye.

In all the Energy there stood a lone black figure, silhouetted against the sea of green.

Ras pulled off the goggles. "What is that?" he asked, not expecting a response but more to share the incredulity. To double check, he

looked back quickly at Callie, then himself. Neither of them registered as a black space in the world of Energy.

"Maybe that's the thing attracting the Convergences?" Callie asked.

"Only one way to find out," Ras said, piloting the shuttle toward
where he saw the dark figure.

Several mines at the corners of the field erupted, beginning a
chain reaction. Ras angled the shuttle to quickly survey the situation.
"The Convergences are coming!" He smacked the comm button.
"Dayus, get *The Kingfisher* out of there!"

In the ripple of explosions, Ras barely had time to think. A ring
of fire began to engulf the battlefield, heading inward for the shuttle.

Racing toward the center, Ras saw a lone man standing directly
underneath the center Convergence, and right next to him, an old
familiar friend: his jetcycle.

"No," Callie said in disbelief.

In the midst of the chaos stood Foster Helios III.

CHAPTER ELEVEN
The Helios

THE WORLD EXPLODED AROUND RAS AND CALLIE AS THE CONVERGENCES encroached from every corner of the minefield. For a moment, the only plan Ras could manage was to run the shuttle straight into the doppelganger of Foster.

Even if the chain reaction had already become unstoppable, at least killing Foster all over again would accomplish something.

The Convergence above the dark figure dropped, smashing into the ground directly in front of the shuttle. The ghostly swirls of Energy within the sphere danced about in a chaotic frenzy.

Ras forced the shuttle down for a crash landing, striking the ground hard just in front of the Convergence. He knew he and Callie could survive being in the Energy, but the shuttle could crumple around them. He wrestled off his restraints, then flung himself to the backseat next to Callie, wrapping her in an embrace.

Once more, the overload sent a tingle throughout his body. "Hold on," he said. "It'll be over soon." *One way or another.* The resistance was back, this time from every direction as though a crushing pressure threatened to cave him in. Ras felt his breath being crushed out of him. He didn't know how to fight back harder.

As the explosions grew progressively louder, mournful shrieks began directly ahead.

"I'm trying," Callie said, her eyes closed and her teeth gritted. "I'm trying so hard." She squeezed Ras' hand until her knuckles were white.

"I love you," Ras said, barely audible over the chaos. If this was to be their last moment together, he thought those words felt the most fitting.

Ras looked to the front of the shuttle. The strongest pressure, presumably from the Convergence directly in front of them, began to let up. The sphere destabilized, warping and becoming translucent. Through the distortion of the Convergence, the man's form danced about, yet he remained in place. Not only was the madman alive, but he wasn't even panicked. A chill of dread raced down Ras' spine, and he looked back at Callie, hoping desperately to find some small bit of comfort in her presence.

She opened her dark eyes, oblivious to the situation outside the shuttle, and her eyebrows twisted together in fear. "I love you too, but I feel like I'm about to break."

One direction at a time the pressure released as the explosions around them subsided. Ras felt like he could breathe again as the world receded back into an eerie peace. He moved away from Callie, ending her overload as she clutched her head in her hands.

He pulled on his goggles and scanned the area for any immediate Convergence threats. Swirls of Energy spun madly on the wind, but no single orb remained. *Where is that all going to go?* Suddenly, a rush of excitement filled him. "Callie," he said, allowing a deep breath. "I think we just saved Atmo."

She rubbed her temples in a circular motion, her eyes squeezed shut. "Yay," she said unenthusiastically. "Let's celebrate after I sleep this off for ten years?"

"That bad, huh?" Ras asked. He looked outside and locked eyes with the man standing amidst the wrecked machinery.

"Let's not focus on the pain," Callie said. "Give me something to think about."

How in Atmo could that be Foster? Ras wondered. "Ah, think about all the children getting to play outside in the grass for the first time after Atmo lands."

A slight grin crept to her lips. "Free to go wherever they want."

"Yeah," Ras said. "Hey, I think I'm going to see what the man outside is doing here."

"I'll come with you," Callie said, unfastening her restraints slowly.

"Maybe it'd be best for you to stay and rest here for a bit," Ras said, stopping himself from placing a comforting hand on her shoulder. He couldn't add to her pain by making her overload again.

"Ras! Callie!" the comm buzzed with Dixie's frantic voice. "Tell me you two are all right! I swear, if something happened to you two, I'd—"

"You'd what?" Ras said, picking up the comm.

"I'd…become Captain," Dixie said, a hint of embarrassment playing on her voice over the outburst. "I'm the original third wheel so that should make me third in command." She sighed. "Did you figure out what the Energy signature was?"

"A jetcycle," Ras said. "From the looks of it, *my* jetcycle."

"How could it possibly be yours?" Dixie asked.

"Because I think Foster is standing in front of it," Ras replied.

A long pause hung on the line. "That's not possible," she said. "No. Not possible."

"I'm about to find out," Ras said. He reached over and worked the latch on the door, letting the bright light into the cockpit. The tang of gunpowder assaulted his nose and made his eyes water as he stepped out of the shuttle.

Ahead, standing between two downed Illorian cruisers which looked like older cousins to *The Kingfisher*, stood a man caked in dirt and dust. His short black hair moved with the strong winds, and he wore what Ras knew to be a once-gray uniform with a bullet hole over his heart.

This is Foster. It has to be, Ras thought. He took a few steps forward, then halted as he noted the Energy pistol strapped in the thigh holster. Thankfully, the weapon would do little more than annoy him, but it had the capacity to severely wound Callie again.

Aside from Foster's unexplainable presence, the thing that bothered Ras the most was how Foster looked at him. With head turned slightly, Foster stared at Ras from the corners of his eyes, as though he was incapable of looking his rival straight on.

Ras wished he had some sort of weapon on him, even just a grapple gun or a wrench.

"Hello," Ras said cautiously, raising his voice to bridge the twenty foot distance.

"Hello," Foster responded casually. "I know you, yes?"

The question took Ras aback. *How could he forget a man with whom he fought to the death—well, supposed death—with? Did the fall break his mind? How did he escape being frozen by the Time Origin?*

Too many questions. He hesitated. If Foster truly had gaps in his memory, would it be better if he didn't remember Ras?

"Did you have something to do with the Convergences?" Ras asked.

Foster cocked his head the other direction, still eyeing Ras. "Why did they go away?"

So, he doesn't remember what happened on The Winnower...Ras thought. *At least he isn't trying to kill me first thing.* "They...couldn't stay," he said. The situation warranted enough confusion that he wished he could have been quicker on his feet.

"Are we friends?" Foster asked.

Ras paused. Having the most powerful man in Atmo muddled and believing he was Ras' ally could be a great asset, as long as he wasn't playing a part to catch Ras off guard. "We can be."

Foster smiled an innocent looking smile, then began to walk toward Ras. His eyes focused on something other than Ras, taking in the wreckage around him. "I feel like I missed out on so much," he said. "How did this happen?"

As Foster turned to survey the broken machinery, Ras noticed no dried blood or scarring on Foster's neck or head. The uniform had been marred heavily, but the man seemed fine. "I don't know," Ras said. "This was before my time."

"That's not possible," Foster said, now looking directly ahead at Ras. "Maybe you just don't remember."

"Do you remember who you are?" Ras asked as Foster finally cleared the distance. He felt his legs tense as though his body were ready to run without his permission. It was everything he could do to stand his ground.

"I am your friend," Foster said, then threw his arms around Ras in a hug.

"Uh, ah..." Ras squirmed in Foster's unnaturally strong embrace, expecting a quick dagger to the back.

Foster pushed Ras back to arm's length, searching deeply into the younger man's confused expression. "Yes, I do know you." He continued his wide smile, then laughed. "How could I forget the man who saved me?"

Ras squinted, looking at Foster. New Foster—whatever he remembered, which apparently wasn't much—was even more unsettling than Old Foster. At least with his old adversary he'd know what to expect.

"Is she a friend too?" Foster asked.

"Ras? What's happening?" Callie asked, cradling her head as she stepped out from the shuttle.

"Yes! Yes, she's a friend," Ras said too quickly as though he were imploring Foster not too shoot her again. He patted one of Foster's hands, pivoting to escape the muddled man's grasp.

Foster cocked his head to the side, narrowed his eyes, then slowly turned his head to look directly at Callie. His dark expression vanished. "Oh, yes, I remember you as well," he said. "We can't have one without the other, now can we?" He left Ras, then walked toward Callie with arms outstretched.

Ras dashed to intercept Foster's route to Callie. "She's had a… long day."

"I just want to properly greet her," Foster said, an edge of irritation snapping into his voice.

Ras nodded slightly. The first hug was harmless, but would this man stay friendly if resisted? He looked back to Callie. "The man… wants a hug?"

Callie's eyebrows drew together, then searched Ras' eyes. He stepped out of the way with a shrug, and she allowed Foster to give her the embrace.

Foster stepped back. "You are different," he said to Callie, then looked back at Ras. "Why is she different?"

"Do you know my name?" Callie asked.

Foster turned back and stared at her. "I'm so sorry. For all that you've done for me, I haven't caught it. Will you give your name to me?"

She hesitated. "It's Calista."

"Calisssssta," Foster said, closing his eyes.

"So, how's the old jetcycle treating you?" Ras asked quickly.

Foster opened his eyes, cocked his head, and furrowed his brow.

Ras pointed behind them. "You know, the jetcycle," he said. "The thing you rode here on."

"Yes," Foster said. "A wonderful machine. It has been a valuable asset on my tour."

"What tour is that?" Callie asked.

"To find…" Foster snapped his fingers. "I believe you just called them *Convergencessss*."

"They seem to want to come to you," Ras said slowly.

Foster nodded. "They did today, didn't they?" he said, then angled his face, once more looking from the corners of his eyes. "But you put a stop to that." He placed his hand on his hip, dangerously close to the Energy pistol. "That's something you can do, isn't it?"

Ras quickly stepped in front of Callie. The quick motion snapped Foster's attention toward Ras, and he narrowed his eyes.

"Why did you want to find them?" Callie asked.

"Did? I think you mean do," Foster said, looking directly ahead again. "I want to find them because there will be peace once they're all gone."

How am I on the same page as crazy Foster? Ras wondered. "Are there more of them?" he asked on a whim. Insane men might not give reliable answers, but any information he could derive about Foster's newfound mentality might end up being useful. If nothing else, India Bravo might cut him some slack if he was able to inform her of the...unwell state of her son before returning him to her.

Foster gave the question consideration. "Some of their brothers have been trapped underground," he said.

"Buried by The Collective?" Ras asked.

"The collective of what?" Foster replied quizzically.

"Did you see those Convergences?" Callie asked.

Foster nodded. "On the way here, yes." He sniffed the air. "So you made the Convergences go away?"

"We destroyed them," Ras said. Giving Foster information seemed risky, but anything that could make Ras seem like someone to avoid crossing would hopefully work in his favor.

"How?" Foster asked.

"We just do," Ras said. He wasn't entirely certain of the math behind it. Something about him being a Lack because of his mother, whose grandparents were blessed by a Caretaker...*or something*.

"You didn't destroy those," Foster said, waving a hand in the air. "They've just gone to be with their brothers and sisters."

"And where are their...siblings?" Callie asked. "What do you mean?"

"Energy cannot be destroyed," Foster said. He held his hands in front of him, forming a ball with his fingers. "Maybe contained. Maybe shifted, but not destroyed." He paused, closed his eyes, and swayed with the wind. "They've gone to be with the others underground." He pointed back behind him.

An idea occurred to Ras. It could delay his mission for India Bravo and lead to the death of everyone in Atmo, and there was no guarantee that this was anything more than an insane and elaborate trap, but if crazy Foster really did know as much about the Convergences as he appeared to, it could short-circuit their quest to save Atmo. Well, what harm was there in asking? "Could you show us?"

Foster opened his eyes. "That would be counterproductive. I have more to see on my tour."

"If you come with us, our ship could get there much faster," Ras said. "It would save you time."

"Nothing could save time," Foster mused. "Not now." He looked thoughtful. "When we find another Convergence, what will you do to it?"

Ras paused. "The same thing we did here."

"You are after peace as well, then," Foster said. "I will travel with my friends."

"WHY IS HE NOT DEAD?" Dixie hissed at Ras while pacing Hal's library.

Ras sat on the large desk, palms up. "I don't know. It makes no sense—"

"No, I mean why didn't you kill him as soon as you realized who it was?" Dixie asked. "And why did you let him onboard?" She stopped pacing. "I need something sharp."

"There are more Convergences out there that we can't get to, and Foster says he knows where they are," Callie said, resting on a recliner. "He doesn't even remember what The Collective is."

"Dayus," Ras said. "What do you make of this?"

Dayus stared out of the large window out onto the horizon. "You said you saw him die."

"I *assumed* he died," Ras corrected, although the assumption had been an absolute in his mind merely an hour earlier. Now the man sat in the hold under the watch of Old Harley, Shane, and Caedmon under the pretext of quarantine after exposure to the Convergences. Finn was volunteered to do a checkup on Foster; Ras was more interested in the medical report than in actually seeing the symptoms treated.

"No, he *was* dead," Dixie said emphatically. "Your jetcycle had crushed him and his eyes were all open and nightmare inducing." She made a mock face, sticking out her tongue. "Kind of like that, but with a lot more blood."

"I see," Dayus said, placing a hand on his chin. "And you're certain that's your jetcycle in our hold."

"Definitely," Ras said. Despite being generally banged up, it had the telltale marker of the missing paneling lost during Dixie's plummet over *Solaria* when she tried to drop weight from *The Brass Fox*. "Have you ever heard of something like this?"

Dayus paused for a moment, looking lost in thought. "Where did he say the underground Convergence is located?"

"Tefka," Ras said. "I guess it's a Burrow back east."

Dayus nodded, then began walking toward the bridge.

"Wait," Dixie said. "If that is Foster, how did he escape the Time Origin? Wouldn't it take him years and years to make it out without Ras and Callie overloading next to it? I thought it slowed everything down around it."

"How close were you two to the Origin when you overloaded?" Dayus asked, pausing at the door.

Callie shrugged. "Maybe ten feet away, why?"

Dayus closed his eyes slowly. "I'll put out a message to Halcyon and see if he might be able to ascertain the truth from what you have just told me."

"If you know something, Dayus, tell us," Ras said. "That's an order."

Rapping his fingers against the door's threshold, Dayus sighed. "The Elders were established to protect the Time Origin against anything. At all costs. If something were to happen to it, something that might disrupt its natural functions, then suffice it to say…odd things might occur to this world." He turned away, then quickly said, "I can't say what, specifically, until I contact what remain of the Elders. In the meanwhile," he said, pausing for a moment as if searching for a word, "Foster should be handled cautiously." With that, Dayus exited, and in short order, *The Kingfisher* once more went airborne.

"If Foster doesn't remember who The Collective is," Dixie said, "then maybe we could give him back to mommy dearest and let her deal with him."

"She'd brainwash him," Callie said, leaning forward.

"Not if we did it first," Dixie said with a smile. "Tell him the truth of what Bravo Company does. Tell him he has an opportunity to put a stop to it."

"You want him to kill his own mother?" Ras asked.

"You say that like I could possibly have sympathy for either of those two," Dixie said.

"Right now we need him." Ras said. "Well, at least he could make things easier for us. Somehow he's a Convergence magnet, which is far more valuable to us at the moment. Besides, if this doesn't work out we can at least save all three cities by handing him over."

"Assuming India will keep her end of the deal," Dixie said. "You're way too trusting."

Ras pursed his lips. "You would know."

"Ras…" Callie interjected.

Dixie opened her mouth to retort, but instead gave him a half-chagrined look.

Finn entered the library. "He's a medical marvel," he said. "Obviously I don't have all the equipment I'd like to run tests, but aside from the odd conversational habits, I'd give him a clean bill of health."

"Did you give him the explanation why he had to stay in the brig?" Ras asked.

"Yeah, yeah, Energy quarantine," Finn said, waving a hand dismissively. "He seemed to think it was all right. He also liked to hug, which I'm assuming is a new habit."

"He was more into shooting people than hugging, last I saw," Dixie said.

"I know it's not my place to ask," Finn said, "but why are we giving him a ride?"

"Because," Ras said, "for once, we have the same goals."

Assuming Foster—resurrected, amnesiac, huggy Foster—really wasn't playing them after all.

CALLIE LOOKED THROUGH the porthole into *The Kingfisher*'s bay. She couldn't see all of Foster clearly due to Old Harley's makeshift tarpaulin quarantine.

It was impossible for Foster to be here. Technically, it was really just improbable, but the key bit of knowledge needed to cross that gap was eluding her, and staring into a porthole would do little to help ascertain what she was missing.

She knew she shouldn't go inside to talk to Foster for fear of shattering the quarantine illusion, so she decided seeking out the ship's expert on elusiveness would be the next best course of action.

As per usual, Dayus was the sole inhabitant of the bridge. Callie stood at the threshold, then rapped her knuckles on the bulkhead.

"Come in, Callie," Dayus said without turning his head.

"How did you know?" Callie asked.

"*The Kingfisher* told me," Dayus said, nodding to the glass in front of him. "Erasmus unknowingly installed such measures when he didn't make cleaning this vessel a priority."

Aided by the waning light and the coat of grime covering the curved windshield, Callie saw Dayus' reflection and realized he could see her where she stood.

"He's been busy," Callie said, stepping onto the bridge.

"Can I help you with something?" Dayus asked.

"I thought we could talk," Callie said. "One Illorian to another."

Dayus turned to look directly at Callie. His features softened. "If we're being honest with ourselves, I don't believe either of us truly identifies with that distinction."

"I think you're being withholding," Callie said quickly. "I don't know what it's about, but you're acting stranger than usual and with everything going on..."

"Have you read any of the books in the library recently?" Dayus asked.

"See?" Callie asked. "That right there! Indirect."

"I may take my time," Dayus said, "but I do make points in the long run."

Callie let out a slow breath through her nose. "No, I haven't," she said. "Hal said they're all written in Illorian."

"I've taken the liberty of translating some of the volumes over the years," Dayus said. He stepped over to the navigation station and picked up a blue, cloth-bound tome from the chair, then offered it to Callie. "There's a book I feel might put you at ease to see."

"Which book did you translate?" Callie asked as she accepted the book.

"It is more of an anthology," Dayus said. "A collection of relevant writings on a singular topic along with my notes on the subject."

Callie cracked open the book. Flowing script in faded ink adorned the title page: *The Thromus Solution*. "You pulled from *The Demons of Bogues*?"

Dayus scoffed, returning to the bridge controls. "Only in an effort to be thorough."

She flipped through the book, noting the writing looking less faded as she skimmed through pages of text and illustrations. "How long have you been working on this?"

"Far longer than I should have," Dayus said.

"Why?" Callie asked. "What's in here that's worth putting this much effort into it?" She continued to flip through the latter pages and came to detailed schematics of a structure that looked familiar. "What does *The Winnower* have to do with the bogeyman?"

"The Thromus is not a bogeyman," Dayus said sharply.

"Then what is it?" Callie asked. She flipped the page to see an example of how *The Winnower* was designed to encapsulate a crystal spire next to a series of complex looking formulas titled '*serums.*'

"It is the reason we are all here," Dayus said with a finality that caused Callie to not question the broad statement in the least. "Convergences, The Great Overload, The Clockwork War…it all begins with this."

Callie's mouth went dry. She looked down at the book, taking in all of the loving detail it possessed. Turning a page revealed an intricate illustration of someone overloading with the word "Bogues" as the title. "Were you at Bogues when…"

"When The Great Overload happened, yes." Dayus said. He held up a hand to stifle comments. "I still cannot offer an understanding of why it occurred, but there are stories, old stories, which have lent me something akin to insight into the state of things."

Callie lifted an eyebrow. "Why wait to tell me now?"

"Because events are escalating in ways we all may find…challenging," Dayus said softly. "And if something were to happen to me, I'd rather such information not be lost."

"I have to tell Ras," Callie said.

"You cannot," Dayus said. "If there is to be any hope of deliverance for us all, Erasmus cannot know."

"Then why tell me?" Callie asked. She glanced back to see if anyone were standing in the doorway to the bridge. Thankfully it remained empty. "Why is it my responsibility to know something and not be able to tell the person who can do something about it?"

"If The Reclaimer were to know what was required of him, he might not fulfill his duty," Dayus said. "Knowledge can be a liability sometimes, especially on the front lines. You are more than fit to be his...what does he call you, again?"

"His navi."

"Yes, you are his navi," Dayus said. "You are to guide him. Ras has so many tethers pulling at him, trying to alter his path. He needs direction from someone he trusts."

"How am I supposed to guide him if I don't even know where I'm going?" Callie said.

"He needs to know he is not alone," Dayus said. "That will suffice... for now."

"Can I at least get a high level overview about this Thromus thing?" Callie asked.

"I would advise you not to say the name out loud," Dayus said.

"But you did earlier," Callie said. "Don't tell me the whole 'you can't say his name three times' thing is real."

Dayus shrugged. "We tread in dangerous waters. It is best to be cautious," he said. "As far as a 'high level overview'...Are you familiar with any of the lore behind the Origins?"

"Some say the Energy Origin was a gift," Callie said. "The more mystic beliefs think it's where life comes from and returns. I don't know about Time's Origin. Are there more than two?"

"Thankfully, no," Dayus said. "I would wager, then, that the Illorian account of their beginnings has not made it across the mountains."

Callie sat, positioning herself carefully in the navigation chair.

"Some say the story is pure myth," Dayus said. "Some take it quite literally, while others find bits they like and call the rest poetic embellishment passed on through the years."

"Which camp do you fall into?" Callie asked.

"I'd rather this story stand on its own without it being tainted by my filter, if at all possible." Dayus fixed his gaze on the horizon, taking a deep breath. "It begins many, many years ago," he said. "I won't go back so far as to what Illorians argue over the beginnings of this world, but far enough back that man made his way, limited in understanding of his surroundings.

"Death came for all, personally," Dayus said. "A man's time was established, and there was nothing he could do to add a day to his life. You didn't leave this world until Death ferried you away, right on schedule.

"Until one day, a young woman had run out of time. Her name was Aura. At least every version of this story agrees on that detail. She had run afoul of a man with murder in his heart. So, as Death arrived on schedule to claim her, he did something he had never done before."

"Which was?" Callie asked.

"He made a judgment," Dayus said. "He knew Aura was kind and helpful to others. He had a love for her. Not in a romantic sense. The love from the one assigned the role of Death could never allow himself such carnal attachment.

"His choice was to claim the murderer instead, sparing Aura's life. But that wasn't how it worked. Her time was still running out, and Death would need to ferry her across to her afterlife, regardless of what was to end her time in Imago.

"However, the murderer still had a month of time left to his name before he was to run afoul of an impatient moneylender. Death transferred the balance of time to Aura, giving her another month to live.

"The rules were broken. Death didn't know what would happen to Aura's body or soul as she lived beyond her time. She was grateful to the 'man' who saved her from certain death, yet completely unaware of the illegal transaction made to extend her days."

"So she died one month later?" Callie asked.

"It took less than a month for Death to assign himself a new role: judge," Dayus said. "And executioner. At first he began small. Finding a day to shave off of a life spent selfishly to give to Aura. There were many to harvest from, and Death stayed one step ahead of Aura's deadline.

"Soon it became difficult for a man to appease Death, as he idolized Aura, holding her on one side of the scales, the constant standard for men and women to live up to. Nobody could match her goodness in the eyes of Death, and thus Death taxed their time.

"The system had fallen apart. Men who were to cause the deaths of others were no longer there to commit the crime, and those potential victims had to be claimed, lest their bodies go on without their souls in some grotesque manner. None received the treatment that Aura did," Dayus said.

"Did she age?" Callie asked. "Aura, I mean."

"Versions of the account vary," Dayus said. "She married, had children, but those souls shouldn't have been able to exist. They had no start or expiration date, and thus Death had to steal time for her children as well."

"Hold on," Callie said. "How did one person cover the whole world and manage when people would die?"

"As the story goes, he lived outside of Time," Dayus said. "Most called his realm Elsewhere."

"And how does this relate to the creation of the Origins?"

Dayus sighed. "I'm not one to let my mind wander and fail to resolve a point I'm trying to make."

"Sorry," Callie said.

"The creation of Aura's line continued to the third generation before one of Death's contemporaries took notice and challenged him on overstepping his bounds. By that point, Death had learned that transferring time was not a one to one transaction. In order to give Aura, her children, and their children more time, Death had to cause plagues, disasters, and other tragedies to claim lives to cover up his actions.

"Soon Aura's children were hunted down and their souls were banished to Elsewhere, never to cross over to Imago again. Death was placed on trial, and Aura was informed of the great cost that her continued survival, unbeknownst to her, had enacted on the world.

"Death was sentenced to banishment, and forced to see Aura informed of what he had done. He had stored up so much life in her through wholesale slaughter that she possessed a near incalculable amount of time left."

"Did they, whoever *they* are, kill her?" Callie asked.

"No, she asked to return that life back to the world," Dayus said. "And her wish was granted. On the other hand, Death could no longer be trusted, so structures were built to disseminate new essences throughout Imago."

"Energy to sustain life, and Time to wear everything down to its natural conclusion," Callie said, leaning back into her chair. "That's a sad story."

"I can appreciate your empathy," Dayus said, then reached over and collected the book from Callie, "but the point is that for centuries, there has been a struggle over the control of Life and Death. Strategies implemented, wars forged, losses incurred."

"So why is this called *The...You-know-what Solution?*"

"In Illorian, that name translates to Death, or the time keeper," Dayus said. "The Clockwork War was ultimately a struggle over this power, and although great losses were incurred by both sides, it remained protected."

"Until *The Winnower* came along and messed up the balance of things?" Callie asked.

"Much of The Collective's goals were centered on this pursuit, but...no," Dayus said. "The Time Origin remained protected until you and Erasmus overloaded next to it. At least that is my leading theory."

"Whoa, whoa," Callie said, standing up. Her heart pounded in her chest. "What are you saying?"

"I want to receive word from Illoria before I jump to any further conclusions," Dayus said. "But if the Thromus has been freed from the prison that nobody could enter nor leave, then we must make haste to destroy the Convergences."

"Or what?" Callie asked. She felt her hands tremble, so she closed the book and clutched it to her chest.

"Weapons will be created that could threaten all life in Imago," Dayus said. "The Great Overload would only have been a precursor of what could be coming." He pointed to the book, then left his hand outstretched until Callie returned it to him. "This is a matter most complicated. The more that is known about it, the more difficult it shall ultimately be to overcome."

"Which is why I can't tell Ras?"

"That, and he isn't ready," Dayus said.

"What am I not ready for?" Ras asked as he walked into the room.

"Tefka," Dayus said casually, nodding toward the windshield. "We're approaching what remains of the city." Ahead, the horizon burned a deep red. A spot in the distance glowed green, and several sets of dark, thick smoke pillars rose high into the clouds.

Chapter Twelve
The Refugees

"Put the ship down!" Ras shouted as *The Kingfisher* roared toward the burning city. A Convergence lumbered across the sky, easily five times larger than any of its predecessors.

Dayus hauled back on the controls, lifting the ship as the massive Convergence turned and moved back toward them. "I don't think that would be wise," he said.

As the ship rose, Ras caught a glimpse of Tefka. People ran about frantically. At first he thought he spotted the Burrow, but realized the gaping maw was actually next to the damaged city.

"Foster said some Convergences were trapped underground," Callie said, holding tightly to her chair as *The Kingfisher* continued to climb. "Why would it leave now?"

"It grew," Ras said, leaning forward to stare at the giant green orb. "Foster was right. Energy doesn't get destroyed…It just goes to be absorbed by other Convergences."

The ship leveled off, and within moments a voice came from the back of the bridge. "Could someone warn the crew next time we want to play '*pin the Dixie to the floor?*'"

"The time required to announce an evasive maneuver would defeat said maneuver's effectiveness," Dayus said calmly.

"Point goes to Stretch," Dixie said, plopping down on the armrest of Callie's chair. "I didn't think we had anything to evade down here."

"We made something to evade," Callie said.

"You know, I wouldn't talk half as much if you just explained everything instead of—"

"There's a really, really big Convergence, Dixie," Ras said.

"Can we call it a Super Convergence? It would save on words," Dixie said.

"Sure."

"Okay, then why don't you two just pop it? Isn't that what we do?"

"It is," Callie said. "But if there are more Convergences buried next to cities like this, the Energy from this Convergence would just grow those, and then we'd just be destroying cities one at a time."

"So, we lost already?" Dixie asked.

"Not yet," Ras said, rising from his chair. He watched the Super Convergence hover in place, wondering where it would go next. They would just have to revisit it later. There was no restraining something like that, as the wreckage of Tefka could attest. "Dayus, try to contact anyone from Tefka over the radio. See what you can find out." He began walking to the back of the bridge. "I'm going to see what Foster knows."

"Be careful," Callie called after him. "Please."

Once Ras reached the corridor, he took a deep breath, then doubled over, clenching his fists. Mr. Tourbillon's words of warning echoed in the back of his head. *You mean well, but you wreck things.* The city of Tefka was destroyed. Who knew how many had died? Who would take care of them? *Does saving Atmo mean destroying Imago?*

He couldn't indulge in letting yet another failure delay him. He had to be the strong captain everyone deserved. Slowly standing upright, he took another breath before someone could happen upon him. He had to believe in the course of action he chose, even if tragedy chipped away at his resolve, didn't he?

Foster sat on a stool in the corner of the hangar. The tarpaulin obscured the man, who remained perfectly still. Old Harley stood at the door while Shane and Caedmon inspected the jetcycle, doing a terrible job of pretending not to be keeping an eye on their prisoner.

"Rassssss," Foster said upon the captain's arrival.

Ras held a hand up to Old Harley, passing by the older man, then stepped underneath the crinkly sheet. "We have a problem."

Foster's smile vanished, but at least he looked at Ras directly. "Can you not destroy this Convergence?" he asked, pointing downward.

How does he know where that thing is? Ras shook his head. "We can. But we need to know more before we do."

"You seem angry, friend," Foster said, cocking his head slightly.

"You said there were Convergences underground."

"I did."

"How did they get there?" Ras asked.

Foster looked at Ras, then slowly turned his head, maintaining eye contact until he looked through the corners of his eyes. He paused, narrowed his eyes slightly, then an amused smirk played across his lips. He snapped his head to face forward once more; Ras jumped at the motion. "They provide power for the cities."

"So if we burst this Super Convergence, its Energy will just make another buried Convergence grow and destroy that city?" Ras asked, doing his best not to sound unnerved. *Or fly up to an Atmo city.*

Foster shrugged casually. "It does appear to be the way of things." He eyed his surroundings. "I have been meaning to ask when my quarantine will have concluded."

"Soon," Ras said dismissively. "Do you know where the other Convergences have been buried?"

"I do," Foster said. "All eight."

Ras' heart sank. Traveling to eight cities, plus solving the Atmo equation, was going to take too much time for *Nalon* to be saved. Maybe it was time to deliver this broken man to India Bravo after all. They had all the information they could get out of him, didn't they? He might as well see what else he could glean while they still had Foster. "Which eight cities? I'll have Callie get the map."

"One city," Foster said. "The city of Mason holds all of its Convergences in a structure they call The Heart of Mason."

Ras stood at the head of the dining room table, surveying his crew. Everyone looked expectantly toward him.

"When we set out to save Atmo, we didn't—I didn't know the scope of this undertaking," Ras said, gripping the back of the head chair firmly with both hands. "But we've gone too far to turn back now." He looked to Callie, who offered an encouraging smile. He made sure to gravely nod an acknowledgement instead of smiling in front of everyone.

"Tefka has been destroyed by a Convergence. A Convergence that grew because we destroyed all the airborne ones," Ras said. "Turns out we've been condensing them, and the pieces of a broken Convergence just find their way to the next closest one."

"Why don't you keep popping them until there aren't any left?" Finn asked, hand raised.

"One, popping the one that destroyed Tefka would send its Energy to Mason, blowing up the city. Two, if the Super Convergence wasn't attracted to Mason, it might find an Atmo fueling station—"

"With kids on it," Dixie amended.

"Right," Ras said, "with kids on it. Then instead of a city on fire, we'd have a localized Great Overload, and *then* a plummeting city on fire. And we have five days to pop all of the Convergences, sending the combined Energy into the Super Convergence."

"And when you pop that one," Dixie said, "the world will finally be safe?"

Ras gave a long pause. "I hope so. This is the closest thing I've managed to a solution. It's going to take three teams, and all need to be successful." He motioned to Callie.

"Like Ras said, our two main objectives are to knock out The Heart of Mason's eight Convergences," Callie said. "And then aside from the Super Convergence, all that remain are the twelve left in Atmo. If Ras and I can infiltrate Mason, we can knock out all eight at once, but we'll need Foster, Ace, and Tink to get us there."

"*The Kingfisher* won't be able to land anywhere near that city," Dayus said. "Mason was the Imago stronghold of The Clockwork War. It is where the Helios family set up their main defenses. *Derailleur* was modeled after the city, if that helps you grasp its scope." He held up a hand. "Fortunately for us, Tefka was destroyed."

"How is that fortunate in any way?" Ras asked, incredulous.

"From the chatter I could pick up on the radio, the survivors of the city are evacuating onto a train tomorrow morning," Dayus said. "A train I assume is heading for Mason."

"Then we'll have to intercept that train and find a way in," Ras said.

"Why not board it right now?" Finn asked.

"We can't be sure that's where they'll be sent," Ras said. "Plus, there may be checkpoints along the way. We'll get as a good a night's rest as we can, and then use *The Kingfisher* to track the train. Once we're sure it's going to Mason, we'll board," he said. "Ace, Tink, we'll need your glider expertise if we're going to hit a moving target, as well as your knowledge of how to fit in on the ground."

"We've never been to Mason," Ace said.

"It's likely most of the Tefkans haven't either," Dayus replied.

"The second team will focus on the twelve remaining Atmo fueling stations," Ras said.

"I'm on it," Dixie said, leaning in toward the table and tapping her fingers anxiously.

"I was hoping you'd say that," Ras said. "Because you're the only one who can call in the help we need."

Dixie furrowed her brow in thought. "Please tell me you're not planning what I think you're planning."

"Last I recall, Dr. O had a wonderful little device that knocks out engines," Ras said. "If we had that as a tool to knock out the fueling station engines, we could lower the stations, grab the kids, and then let out the Convergences to the ground where they wouldn't hurt anyone."

"Grandfather or not," Dixie said, "I hope you remember he's a madman."

"If he won't help," Ras said, "then maybe he'd be willing to trade for one of the Elder suits we have left onboard."

"There's only one," Dayus said, "and it's mine."

"We'll get you another one," Ras said without any knowledge how he could swing it. "Dayus, you'll be heading up the third team—"

"Wait, is it just me?" Dixie asked. "I might need some backup or else I'm going to get stuck wearing a slinky black dress, eating dinner with a rabbit, and sleeping in the pink palace again."

"I'm in," Guy said, raising his hand and Dixie's eyebrow.

"Yeah, me too," Finn said. "Might as well be the third wheel somewhere."

"Great," Ras said. "The three of you can take the shuttle to *Solaria* and work out a deal." He looked back to Dayus. "The rest of you will take *The Kingfisher* and fly back to Illoria. Talk with Hal and see if we can't get some Elder muscle to back Dr. O's play."

"I'm not sure Halcyon has had enough time to rally who remain of the Elders," Dayus said. "But I'll do my best."

"Thank you, everyone," Ras said, looking over the faces of his crew. "We have five days left until *Nalon* sinks. I know this is a lot to ask, but we all know what's at stake. So, let's save the world." Ras did his best to conceal how much the words coming out of his mouth terrified him.

THE SUN ROSE over the horizon as a silver line snaked through the hills and forests, carrying Tefkan refugees to Mason. High above, *The Kingfisher* kept an even pace with the train as it raced toward the sprawling metropolis.

Mason reminded Ras of Illoria's capital, the preserved, time-frozen sections of it, mixed with the grandiosity of *Derailleur*. The city was still small on the horizon, but loomed heavy in Ras' mind.

"How far do we have before their defenses notice us?" Ras asked into the comm unit on the hangar's wall.

"I wouldn't dawdle," Dayus responded.

Tink connected his harness to a cable attached at the back wall of the hangar bay. He secured the winch and gave a big thumbs up before slipping his feet into the glider.

Ace stepped over to Tink, holding a retractable glider out to Ras. "Here," Tink said.

Ras looked down and saw Tink was wearing the original glider and started to wonder which part of *The Kingfisher* Tink had disassembled, but opted to accept the gift instead. "Thanks," Ras said, replying in Tink's terse vernacular.

"He stayed up all night making that for you," Ace said. She took the piece of metal from Ras and quickly positioned it against his grapple gun forearm so that something clicked into place. She pointed at a spot between the two leather straps. "Here's the quick release mechanism."

Tink beamed at his handiwork with what came off as more of an awkward, lopsided grin.

Ras offered a thumbs up, then looked back at his crew. "All right—"

"If you're starting another speech," Dixie interrupted, "I'm going to push you out of this hangar, okay?" She smiled. "You do what you gotta do, and we'll do the same."

"Stay safe," Ras said.

"Where's the fun in that?" Dixie asked, then stepped forward and gave him a tight hug. "I'll tell Dr. O that Rastiban sends his love." She released, then reached up and tussled Ras' hair. "Go on, you crazy kids."

Ras looked over to Foster, who stood completely still, staring out at the world below. "Hey, you with us?" he asked.

Without breaking his gaze, Foster nodded.

"So, once Tink establishes the lock, we'll—" The hiss of unspooling cable cut Ras short.

Tink let out a joyful shout as he dove out of the hangar and let the wind catch his glider. Ras leaned over to watch the youth spin in a controlled corkscrew maneuver, righting himself.

The Kingfisher descended to give Tink less of a distance to drop, and before too long, he had expertly managed a safe landing onto the train, spooling the cable to its full extension. Dayus would need to be cautious so as not to put too much strain on the cable by picking up altitude.

Ace wasted no time hooking on her winch, then lifted her legs to let gravity guide her downward toward the train, bobbing the entire hundred yards until she stuck the landing.

A groan from the cable's anchor reverberated throughout the hangar. "Dayus, they're picking up speed," Ras said into the comm unit. "All right, Foster. Your turn."

Without a word, Foster winched up his harness and dropped out of the hangar, zipping along toward the train.

"Any pointers?" Callie asked, taking a deep breath as she adjusted the straps of her harness.

"Just pretend you're in one of your adventure books," Ras said.

"So, the usual," she said, the beginnings of a smile playing at the corners of her mouth.

"Yeah."

Dayus' voice crackled in over the hangar's intercom. "We're nearing the outer defensive perimeter of the city."

"Got it," Callie said, then leapt into the wind.

Ras heart skipped a beat as the cable mount protested further with Callie still on the line. "Keep up with the train!" He knew if they stuck too close to the train they risked alerting everyone aboard of the airship's presence, but he'd rather deal with that than lose Callie.

Looking down, Ras watched her reach the roof of the train. As the train chugged into a sharp curve, her footing failed, and she fell into a slide toward the edge of it. Before Ras could even cry out in useless despair, Foster was lunging toward her; he caught her by the arm and swept her gracefully back up to her feet.

Ras took a deep breath. He'd need to thank Foster later. Giving a quick glance back to his crew, he said, "Be good." With the harness secure, he let his weight take him down the cabling. The wind welcomed him with a rush as he exited the hangar, its sound competing with the whir of the grinding metal.

Ras watched *The Kingfisher* shrink, then turned his attention to the train. The line grew taut, then slack, causing him to fall for a moment. Two deafening booms erupted from behind. He twisted his body to see the approaching checkpoint, complete with rows of cannons and massive Energy pylons.

The Kingfisher took evasive action, snapping the magnetized cable connector away from the train. Ras worked the harness brake before he could drop much further than halfway down the cable.

The tail end of the cable swung wildly, causing Ace, Tink, Foster, and Callie to fall prone to avoid it striking their heads.

More cannon shots fired from the city's defenses, and *The Kingfisher* dropped low. Ras suddenly found himself lower than the train, mere feet away from the blur of ground beneath him. Instinctively he reached up and fired his grapple gun at the underbelly of his ship.

He felt the clank through the line as the magnet fell into place, and then Ras swung alongside the train, bumping into the speeding vehicle and spinning away from it just as violently. He released his harness from the winch as the cable caught itself up in the chugging locomotive wheels. Ras worked the cable respooling mechanism on his grapple gun, lifting himself level with the top of the train.

Callie stood to her feet, reaching out for Ras' outstretched hand. If only he could steady himself for a second, he could detach his cable and land safely on the relatively narrow roof. Their hands grasped one another's.

For a moment.

Before Ras could stabilize, *The Kingfisher* picked up altitude in an evasive maneuver, breaking his hand free from Callie's and flying him upward.

The city was fast approaching, and they had drawn far too much attention to themselves.

Another cannon blast ripped up at *The Kingfisher*, this time striking a direct hit. Ras couldn't let the ship continue in harm's way. He pulled the glider free and the wind almost ripped it free from his hand. Bobbling in midair, he slid his feet through the leather straps, and shot upward like a kite.

He had one chance to time this right. Digging in his heels to the wind, he took up on a lift, then as he ascended, he disconnected the grapple cable from *The Kingfisher*.

Having set the ship free to escape, he locked in another magnet charge, aimed his left arm down at the train, then fired. The cable went taut with a satisfying thunk.

Ras suddenly found himself surfing the wind behind a train.

He laughed madly and waved at *The Kingfisher* before realizing it was trailing smoke. Losing his balance sent him wildly to port, and he quickly readjusted before his time as a kite could be tragically cut short. Focusing on the task at hand, he began reeling in the cabling.

The train was entering the outskirts of the city. Buildings unravaged by Convergences whizzed past Ras. The city itself wasn't perfect, but after having seen Acerbis and Tefka, Mason looked absolutely pristine.

Even the stone tunnel the train was entering seemed well maintained.

Ras eyes went wide. He dove the glider down behind the train just in time for everything to go dark.

He narrowly avoided the wall, and soon found himself in a dark, hot world where the air spurted irregularly, making it incredibly difficult to keep the glider within the relatively small margin of error the tunnel allowed.

Above and on the sides, lights strobed by quickly. He was wondering how much longer he could maneuver when the deafening roar of flying through the tunnel subsided, and he once again felt the cool breeze of the open air. He could see Callie, Foster, Ace, and Tink all sprawled out on their stomachs three railcars ahead. Once more Ras began pulling himself back in toward them.

The train began to pass through an industrial section of the city. Large and medium-sized constructions were well underway. It took Ras a moment to realize what was being manufactured, since the new constructions were lacking airbags inflated above them.

Airships.

As Ras trailed behind the train, he began to garner stares from shipyard workers. Some seemed amused, but most looked confused at the flying man attached to the train.

Ahead, Ras could see the full opulence of the city's skyline. Something tugged at Ras' heart, telling him that this was the level of civilization humanity would now exist in all over Imago had it not been for The Great Overload. While Atmo was a piece of engineering marvel, the city of Mason was a work of art.

Its towers all had smooth lines, lacked hard edges, and were often embellished with a swoop or some other sort of flair. Even the sleek, streamlined train matched the style of the city.

With only a few moments left to reel in the last of the cable, Callie and Tink helped Ras land the glider, which alit with a thud atop the train.

"I thought we weren't going to see you after that tunnel," Ace said as she unstrapped Ras' feet.

"Ras has an uncanny ability to survive," Callie said, keeping her distance from Ras. He tried not to take it personally, even though he often enjoyed her celebratory hugs upon his survival.

"I know this place," Foster said, his voice barely cutting through the wind and train noises.

"Did you go here on your tour?" Ras asked.

Foster shook his head. "Before that. Before I fell."

Ras froze, the memory of their plummeting battle from *The Winnower* flashing to mind. He braced himself for an act of aggression from Foster. "How much do you remember, Foster?"

Foster looked back at Ras with an icy stare. "Everything, Ras," he said. "There is nothing I forget." The docile tone gave Ras chills. "But we are friends now. That fear in your eyes is unwarranted."

Sirens filled the air with an increasing intensity as the train slowly approached a gargantuan domed train station made of glass framed in metal circles.

"Let's try to blend in with the Tefkans," Ras said, cautiously pacing his way to the front of the passenger car, then climbing down the rungs to hide between two railcars. He looked through the window of the car behind him. Huddled refugees with nothing more than the clothes on their backs filled the car to its brim. It looked unlikely that he would be able to squeeze inside without earning the ire of the already desperate passengers.

Callie hopped down next to Ras, bobbling as she landed. He reached out to steady her, but she jerked back quickly, righting herself. "Sorry," she said.

"It's all right," Ras said as Ace and Tink hopped down next to Callie.

Foster joined last. "Where is the device that scatters the Convergences?"

"There's no device," Ras said. "Callie and I just have to touch each other." He wasn't sure how comfortable he felt giving Foster information now knowing how much the man could recall.

"Ah," Foster said simply. "Then you two must not be separated."

"That's a rule I try to stick to," Ras said.

The surroundings darkened above them as the train entered the station, where the sunlight filtered through the tinted glass in the domed roof.

"So, where are we going?" Ace asked.

Ras donned his KnackVisions. *Nothing.* "Foster, I don't see any Convergences."

"Look down," Foster replied, prompting Ras to once more glance at the black silhouette that was Foster.

Tilting his head, Ras saw one of the green spheres deep below. A line of Energy streaked away from it, running off in the distance. *Wonder what that is powering.* He looked around and saw the other seven a decent distance away, comprising a circle. *The Heart of Mason.* "If we can get down there, I think we can hit all eight at once."

"Kind of like *The Winnower*?" Callie asked.

Ras nodded as he took off the KnackVisions. "It looks like the Convergences are sending out Energy through pipes away from the city."

"They are," Foster said. "They power eight other surrounding Burrows."

"So, destroying them all…" Ace began.

"Blackout," Tink concluded.

"Wait, Mason controls the Energy flow to other cities, but not Tefka," Ras said, mulling over the equation. "Tefka had their own Convergence." He braced himself as the train brought itself to a halt. "Why?"

"Cities like Tefka and Acerbis were too far away to run a pipe," Ace said. "When you all arrived, everybody thought you were bringing a new source of Energy to power Acerbis."

"Sorry to disappoint," Ras said, scanning the open terminal for signs of Mason authorities milling about the crowd.

"Hey, we would have only had that Energy for a few days before you took it away," Ace said.

Men in uniform began filtering through the sparse crowd, just as the Tefkan train doors hissed open.

"Now's our chance," Callie said, hopping onto the platform. Before she could get lost among the crowd of refugees, Ras followed.

Ras tugged awkwardly at his grapple gun, which he considered a dead giveaway he didn't belong on the ground.

"Just act like it's some fancy arm brace," Ace said, picking up on Ras' reservations. "Nobody down here is going to know what it is. I sure didn't."

As they shuffled along with the huddled masses of Tefkan refugees, a sympathetic voice broke over the loudspeaker.

"Citizens of Tefka, the city of Mason welcomes you with open arms," the man's voice resounded throughout the plaza. "Please make your way out of the terminal, and we invite you to a very special orientation in the city square by our capitol building, where our Governor will address you directly. Please deposit any Energy using items or devices in the properly marked containers before leaving the station. We apologize for any inconvenience this may cause, but we'd like to remind you that Mason is the only non-Blessed city in the Burrow Alliance, and we ask you to be sensitive to our sensitivities."

"Non-Blessed?" Ras asked.

"I guess they didn't have a Caretaker," Ace said, prompting Foster to lift an eyebrow.

"So we're in a city full of Energy Knacks," Ras said. "No wonder they buried the Convergences so deep." He wondered if they fed people to the Convergences as well or if the eight stations just funneled raw Energy to power the Burrows around Mason.

The crowd marched toward the gates and Ras instantly became mindful of the goggles atop his head. He immediately pulled them off and stuffed them in a pocket as best he could. He looked above the heads in the crowd to see officers standing on platforms, surveying the refugees. He had never realized that standing just above six feet tall would be enough to make him stick out so much.

He made sure to hunch down slightly.

It wasn't lost on Ras how he had caused the plight of everyone surrounding him. It wasn't an unfamiliar feeling, but one he had hoped to never again experience.

As they reached the exit of the concourse, Ras locked eyes with one of the officers, then quickly broke away.

"Hey, you!" a guard shouted.

Ras slowly turned his head to see the guard making eye-contact not with him, but with the person directly beside him: Foster.

Panic swept Ras. He didn't know how someone in Mason could so easily spot Foster. Perhaps The Collective had secret dealings with Mason. *Foster does seem to know a lot about how the city operates.*

"I know," Foster said, addressing the guard. "I get it all the time. I just look a lot like him."

This seemed to deter the man, who cocked his head and exchanged a perplexed look with the guard standing next to him. At least it didn't *seem* plausible that Foster Helios III would have fallen in with Tefkan refugees.

"Well played," Ras muttered to Foster, who remained silent.

Exiting the terminal took longer than Ras had anticipated. The checkpoint funneled into a long corridor completely covered with mosaics across both walls. The art exhibit seemed to tell a story, starting with people farming, then leading to a renaissance depicted in terms of painters, sculptors, and smiling architects at work constructing more sophisticated buildings.

The artwork was intricately detailed in small tiles that glinted off the lights aimed at them from the ceiling. Ras couldn't imagine how long it must have taken to create. The story on the wall continued to more familiar sorts of buildings and more modernly dressed men and women.

Then the Elders appeared in their ships and mechanical suits, denoting what Ras assumed was the advent of The Clockwork War. A dashing figure with features resembling Foster's and dressed in a white long coat struck a heroic pose, pointing at the robots. An airship battle came next, with Illorian vessels on one side and the wooden craft on the other.

One white craft flew with the wooden airships. Ras assumed it represented *The Kingfisher*.

"Oh, my," Callie said, bringing Ras' attention to the following mosaic. A small city with Mason's skyline stood while the rest of the world erupted in green. People were depicted running away in terror while others were shown mid-overload.

The dashing Helios figure now looked more devious, shaking hands with a white-haired man resembling Hal Napier. *The Kingfisher* and Elders stood behind Hal. It almost looked like the mosaic was implying some sort of betrayal pact between the two factions.

Next was the launch of Atmo from the perspective of crying and angry Masonites, fists clenched above them.

A wide view of Imago's map showed the placement of The Burrows, and a somber person in gray stood next to every city but Mason. *Caretakers?* The next panel illustrated the growth of the city, trains going forth, and ended on a work in progress of the bottom half of an individual. Someone who wore knee-high boots was important enough to be immortalized into Mason's murals.

"Maybe that's the Governor," Ras said.

"Governor Bartleby?" an elderly woman next to Ras said, looking up at him. "It was right fine of the Governor to take us in like this. Right fine."

Ras offered her a half-hearted smile, then looked back to Callie. "Do you know how to get us underground?"

She shook her head.

"All right, let's cut through the crowd and see if we can't make our way down there," Ras said. He looked around for Ace, Tink, and Foster to fill them in on their plans, but the trio had been separated and were at least a dozen people behind him.

Ras attempted to turn back around as they entered the open city square, but the push of the crowd made it difficult. He sighed, then waved at Ace to move toward him.

"Excuse me!" Ace shouted, drawing the attention of a large number of refugees around her as she attempted to move through the crowd. Nobody budged.

This wasn't the time to draw attention to themselves. Ras held out a palm, indicating she should stay back. It would be just as well they snuck down later, after the crowd had dispersed. It wouldn't be as conspicuous as five people breaking away simultaneously.

Once the mass had filtered out of the mosaic hall and into a circular arena, Ras took note of the architecture. Large columns stood a good fifty feet tall, hedging them in and reminding him of the library columns on *Derailleur*. The structures made an almost complete circle, except for the gap where a stage had been erected. It seemed drastically out of place, built from wood in an otherwise marbled vestibule.

"Are you thinking what I'm thinking?" Callie asked.

"That you're about eighty years too late to return your books?" Ras asked.

Callie smiled.

The crowd filled the open square. Ras and Callie stood closer to the front than he liked by the time they stopped their slow shuffle forward.

A small blond man walked up the set of steps from behind the stage and approached the podium. He looked out over the crowd for a moment, placed a pair of spectacles on the bridge of his nose, then bowed his head in respect.

"Citizens of Tefka," he began. "As I understand it, the train we provided for you was woefully inadequate to ferry all of the poor souls devastated by your tragedy. The Governor will be here shortly, but has asked me to go over some of the more rudimentary house-keeping beforehand. First, if you are waiting on other family members to arrive, another train is on its way back to Tefka to collect more survivors. We will have registration tables set up after this so they will know where to find you," he said, sweeping an arm toward the left side of the area.

"Secondly, we have a policy in Mason that we feel is fair. You may enter the free market if you wish, but we are in great need of airshipmen and women. Those who go this route will be provided for with lodging, food, and training.

"Lastly, as best we understand, the reason your city fell was due to the Convergence we supplied. While we had not been aware of a Convergence's capability to grow since The Great Overload, we will look into this grave matter and reach our conclusions post haste."

Something caught the man's attention, and he turned back to look behind himself, then addressed the crowd once more. "It appears our esteemed Governor Bartleby has arrived. Governor?" the man asked, stepping aside while clapping his hands in an effort to garner a smattering of applause from the beleaguered group.

Several men stepped up before the Governor. One bald man with a slight paunch looked surprisingly familiar to Ras, but he couldn't place the man off the top of his head.

Then, as the Governor ascended the back steps, Ras could first see the long, red hair, then the eyepatch, and finally the whole of India Bravo as she stood in front of the microphone to address the crowd.

CHAPTER THIRTEEN
The Governor

RAS' EYES WENT WIDE. HE WHIPPED AROUND AND QUICKLY motioned for Foster to crouch before doing so himself. Looking to his side, he saw Callie had already decided not being seen by the dread sky pirate was a favorable tactic. Her expression mirrored Ras' confusion. "What in Atmo!" Ras whispered.

"What in Imago!" Callie whispered back.

"Good citizens of Tefka," India Bravo began in her sonorous tone. "It has been my dream since I was a small child that Imago be reunited, but this is not how I dreamed it would happen. Not like this."

"How long has she been down here?" Ras whispered, half to himself.

"Maybe it's *'how long has she been in Atmo?'*" Callie posited.

A crowd member looked down and shushed them both.

"What you have witnessed was a direct attack from the Skyfolk," India said, her voice growing cold. "It wasn't enough that they left us here to rot. It wasn't enough that they stole *The Winnower* from us in our time of need."

"Wait, what?" Ras asked to nobody in particular. *The Winnower* belonged to The Collective, didn't it?

"No, they had to kick us at our lowest after abandoning us." She paused for effect. "But Mason stands strong, fighting back against our oppressors. Just two days ago we struck the death blow to one of their cities, cutting off their fuel supply. This same city launched the attack that destroyed the Burrow of Einaud, just like yours was attacked."

Ras' mind spun. Tefka was his fault, but the other city she mentioned he had nothing to do with. *How are they the same? Why is she blaming Atmo?*

"Many from Einaud have since joined our ranks in the battle to overtake Atmo," India said. "And I intend to see this mission through. But we need men for our ships. Men who are willing to drive those vultures away, so they may never hurt us again!" A loud thud, the sound of a fist on wood, cracked the air. "Once the vultures have been cleared from their nest, I promise you here and now, you will have a new city. A *New Tefka*, free from the constraints of this world, high above the clouds, the way we should have been before The Great Exclusion."

This elicited cheers from the crowd for the first time. Everything in Ras wanted to stand up and fight the lies. Innocent men were going to take to the skies against people who were generations removed from whatever slights Foster Helios had committed against the rest of the world when he launched Atmo.

"Are you with me?" India Bravo asked. "Are you with us?"

The crowd erupted in cheers just as a man approached Ras' side. A sour face Ras now remembered from Bravo Company's flagship. Graham.

"You two are an awfully long way from home," he said, raising a cudgel to swing down upon Ras.

Instinctively, Ras lifted his left arm to protect his head. With a loud clang, the glider took the brunt of the strike, throwing Ras back into Callie and both of them to the ground.

The crowd around him scrambled as far as they could from the fight, which only resulted in a five-foot gap between the two men.

"You couldn't do what she asks, so you come down here to assassinate her, eh?" Graham said, looking back to the two men falling in behind him. He turned toward India Bravo and began to shout, "Your Ladyship! I'm—"

The snap of Ras' grapple magnet cut Graham off as the sky pirate's head jerked to the side. He crumpled to the ground, falling back onto the other guards.

"Man down!" one of the guards shouted.

"He's trying to kill the Governor!" a man from the crowd shouted.

"He's got a gun!" another yelled.

Before the crowd could further react, Ras grabbed Callie's hand and began bowling through people in an effort to escape. Sirens blared through the arena, and several steam-powered police skiffs launched above the crowd, their criss-crossing spotlights quickly finding their mark. Ras threw his hand up to block the bright light from blinding him. *Where did they get those?* The only place he had seen skiffs that could fly before was *Derailleur*.

Ahead, more guards stood at the perimeter of the crowd, cutting off Ras and Callie's exit.

"Here," Ras said, detaching the glider and handing it to Callie. "Smack anybody that comes close." He worked the cable release mechanism and popped in another magnet. He brought his right arm around Callie's waist. "Hold tight."

As the skiffs continued their circling pattern, Ras fired the magnet at one of the passing vessels. The body strap jerked hard against his ribs, lifting him as he struggled to hold onto Callie, who grimaced noticeably, either from the sudden flight or the beginnings of an overload.

Their feet quickly rose above the heads in the crowd as the entire square erupted into chaos. From his left, Ras felt a constant pressure on his body, the way he did when he faced Convergences with Callie. Without a free hand to extract his KnackVisions, he couldn't check on what might be causing it.

The skiff took a hard turn to the right, jerking Ras and causing him to almost lose his grip on Callie. They lifted up above the marble columns and away from the crowd. Flying among the tallest buildings would have been breathtaking if it weren't for the imminent danger. Ras found himself mesmerized by the grandness of the city's design.

"Where are we going?" Callie shouted, obviously pained. The overload was wearing on her.

"Wherever they want us," Ras said. They needed a new game-plan, one involving less flailing. He had to act quickly.

Flying wildly made it difficult to find a path to safety, but he spotted a couple of routes as they flew through a canyon comprised of incredibly tall buildings. The skiff looked to be heading over a water reservoir. Landing there would soften their fall, but growing up on Atmo had limited the number of times he had been submerged. It was likely Callie couldn't swim either.

Just in front of the reservoir, however, Ras found what he was looking for. A sky bridge ran between two tall buildings a couple hundred feet above the street.

"Can you put the glider on my feet?" Ras asked, lifting his left leg. Callie fumbled with the glider, but managed to slip his foot into the leather straps. He squirmed to maneuver his right foot in, then shouted in pain as the wind created drag, placing pressure on his shoulder.

As they approached the sky bridge, Ras angled his feet upward, lifting the two of them and allowing some slack in the line. He shifted his weight to compensate for his second rider.

At the apex of their ascent, Ras twisted the cable release knob. The glider ascended under what little power it had left as the skiff flew away, unaware it had lost its prey. He utilized the brief moment of weightlessness to load a spike charge. As they began their free fall, he targeted the nearby sky bridge.

At a squeeze of the palm trigger, the spike flew, striking the structure and sending Ras and Callie into a long pendulum swing. Ras angled the glider to begin flying them in smaller and smaller circles, slowing their momentum, all while gradually spooling out more cable to lower them closer to the safety of the ground.

After a descent of fifty feet, they landed on a rough, gray surface. Callie collapsed out of Ras' arms and lay on her back as bystanders gathered on the sidewalk.

"Get out of the road!" a woman shouted.

Ras looked up to see a four-wheeled skiff-like vehicle bearing down the pavement. A horn blared, and in one fluid movement, Ras dashed toward Callie, scooped her up, and dragged her to the sidewalk.

He detached the cable, noting he was running dangerously low. *That's going to make things difficult.* He had maybe one more shot if the target wasn't too far away.

He looked back to Callie. A small crowd had already formed around her prone figure.

"Is she all right?" an elderly man asked, leaning over her.

"Thank you," Ras said, gently moving the man away. "I've got this." He leaned over Callie. There were no obvious bruises or scrapes.

Callie moaned unintelligibly, then placed her palms on her temples. "I think that's the longest I've ever overloaded," she said.

"Are you going to be all right?" Ras asked.

"My head feels like it's about to split open," she said, opening her eyes barely. "I think it might be getting worse."

"I'm so sorry," Ras said. "Can you get up? I think if I carried you I'd be doing more harm than good."

"Yeah," she said breathlessly, lifting herself on her elbows. She blinked several times and shook her head.

"See, everyone? She's fine," Ras said, attempting to disperse the crowd.

"But you flew," the elderly man said.

"Yeah," Ras said, flexing his left shoulder. "It's something Governor Bravo—I mean, Bartleby, has had us working on in the lab. The kids are going to love it when it launches."

Callie got to her feet slowly. "Where are we going now?" she asked, steadying herself.

Ras pulled the KnackVisions from his pocket, then put them up to his eyes without strapping them on. As he suspected from the pressure he felt earlier, a half dozen Convergences were lined up not too far away at surface level. He took off the goggles and caught the elderly man as he was leaving. "Sir, what's off in that direction?"

"The train yard," he said. "Why?"

"No reason," Ras said with a dismissive smile. He handed the KnackVisions to Callie. "See? Looks like they've got other cities to power, like Tefka." He motioned to an alley and they began walking away from the crowd.

"I don't think I'm ready to overload again," Callie said.

"We'll just have to do it the old fashioned way," Ras said. "Seems like I remember a time once when I could ruin a perfectly good Convergence all by myself."

Loudspeakers across the city blared to life with the voice of India Bravo. "Citizens of Mason! It has come to our attention that two agents of Atmo have infiltrated our city's perimeter and are loose, armed, and considered highly dangerous. I offer a year's wages to the man or woman able to bring them in alive."

"At least she doesn't want us dead yet," Ras said.

"One is a young man of above average height, dark hair, and has a metal structure wrapped around his left arm. The other is a young woman, slight build, and has red hair," India said.

"She forgot your blue eyes," Ras said. "I don't know how anyone could forget those."

"You pick odd times to sweet talk a girl," Callie said.

It was true, but it was mostly an attempt to put her mind at ease. They had been fugitives in a metropolis before, but never one where every citizen was properly motivated for a little vigilante justice. The occasional bit of levity and flirtation helped lighten the mood.

With each step the plan felt like it was slowly falling apart, growing more complex until Ras might eventually wind up trapped inside the knot of destruction he was working so hard to unravel.

He looked over his shoulder. The coast was clear for the moment, but moving away from the crowd had instantly become a high priority.

"Do you think Dr. Lupava's Lack...Void...stuff is wearing off completely?" Ras asked.

"I think he overestimated his ability to perfect the serum," Callie said, stopping and leaning against an alley wall. "We should...we should keep going. Staying here and talking about my problems is just going to get us caught."

Due to taking back alleys and keeping a watchful eye for any authorities on the prowl, the jaunt to the train yard remained thankfully uneventful.

Ras hoped Foster hadn't been noticed in the crowd. It was possible he had, though. "Ace and Tink should be fine, right?" he asked quietly as they came to the end of the alley neighboring the trains. "It's not like anyone would associate them with us."

"I'm more concerned for *Nalon*," Callie said. "Now that India Bravo, or whatever her name is now, has seen us, she probably thinks we stopped looking." She shrugged. "Maybe it wouldn't be the worst thing in the world if she found Foster."

It wasn't a bad point, but one Ras didn't have much time to think through. The train yard in front of them provided a new mystery. A dozen brand-new trains sat in a row, similar to the one they rode from Tefka.

"I guess they're in the business of shipping Convergences now," Callie mused.

"Not after today," Ras said. He looked the front of the train over. Each had the word "EXPRESS" written in big, bold letters across a snub nosed front, but each had a different name above the word.

"Acerbis," Callie said, pointing to one of the trains next to the end of the group. "They're sending a train to Acerbis."

"Just like they sent one to Tefka, and that other city she mentioned."

"Einaud," Callie reminded. "But if both of those cities were destroyed…"

"It's a good thing Acerbis got us instead of their train, huh?" Ras asked, scanning the train yard for any other signs of life. They seemed to be in the clear for the moment. "Well, now we know how she rebuilt Bravo Company so fast."

"And why she wasn't afraid of *Nalon*'s Convergence," Callie said. "If she's using people immune to Energy for her fleet."

Satisfied they could make it to the first train without being spotted, Ras led Callie across a short gravel field, their footsteps crunching underneath them. Arriving at the first train, Ras donned his KnackVisions and found the Convergence two cars back. "What I don't get is why India is trying to sink Atmo when she's promising it to everyone down here."

Callie followed a few paces behind. "Maybe she's just threatening *Nalon* so you'll find Foster," she said, finding rest against the train's wheels. "Maybe she's bluffing about the rest."

"I hope so," Ras said, stepping up to a blocky looking vehicle which looked more like a piece of machinery ready to be installed than it did a proper train car. He pulled himself up a set of rungs on the side, and the Convergence inside protested his presence by beginning to destabilize and warp. "What I don't get even more is her saying *The Winnower* was stolen from them."

"I don't know," Callie said. "The whole mother-son thing is just making everything confusing. For all we know, sky pirates have always been from Imago."

"But then why did The Collective fight a war with sky pirates if India is really Foster's mother?" Ras asked. "I mean, I know Bravo Company got a pass in the war, but what about the Red Band pirates?"

"Maybe that's why India wants to reunite Imago," Callie mused.

Ras watched the Energy destabilize inside the train car, then tracked it through the crevasses in the container. Once the Energy caught on the wind, it headed straight toward the city. Eventually it took a turn downward, deep underground. "I think I found our path."

Ras destabilized the other five Convergences in fifteen minute intervals so as not to overwhelm Mason with enough Energy to kickstart another Great Overload. He watched the trails as they made their way through the city, plotting his course.

As he suspected, the Convergences deep below had grown with the influx of material, but thankfully didn't pull their stunt from Tefka and grow so large they would rip free from the ground.

Ras glanced back at the train depot and wondered why something so important to India Bravo's plans was so sparsely guarded. *Who would want to risk overloading on guard duty?* Nobody would mess with something that would kill anyone who ventured too close.

"How are we going to find Ace and Tink?" Callie asked.

"Secondary objective, I'm afraid," Ras said. "Maybe we could find a way to smuggle them out on that train to Acerbis."

"Then they could warn your parents about who Governor Bartleby really is," Callie said.

Ras nodded. Foster was still a wild card, but one he would allow himself to think about after they destroyed the Convergences deep below. "C'mon, let's go," he said.

Through another series of depopulated alleys, they managed to sneak half a dozen city blocks into the city before approaching the door where the Energy had traveled through earlier. The door was locked, and Ras kicked himself for thinking the most direct route would be the easiest. He released the glider from his grapple gun, then quickly struck the door handle with it three times before the knob broke off.

The commotion gathered too much attention from people in the area. At least thirty people had stopped what they were doing and stared at Ras. They all looked at each other hesitantly until a large man began the charge.

Ras threw his shoulder into the door to no avail, then switched his tactic to kicking. Two strikes, and the door swung inward as the crowd closed within twenty feet.

Callie had already entered the doorway by the time Ras turned his attention away from the growing mob to the dimly lit stairwell. He descended as quickly as his body would allow. The old wound in his leg started to flare up, causing his stride to catch and shoot pain up his spine.

He could hear the echoes back above him of the crowd bursting into the stairwell, but he didn't dare look.

The stairwell stopped at another door marked, "WATERWORKS," and as Callie approached it, Ras sincerely hoped it wasn't locked. He reached forward, turned the knob, and pushed, thrusting his shoulder into the door.

It didn't budge.

The crowd grew closer.

"Pull!" Callie shouted, wrapping her hands around his and throwing her weight back. The door easily opened and the pair quickly snaked through, then slammed the door firmly shut behind them.

He quickly loaded up a magnet, attaching it to the door, then spooled out enough cable to attach to the opposite wall. He turned only to realize there was no opposite wall. They were in an open cavern. He looked down, spotted the metal grating floor, and immediately linked the other magnet to it, securing the door.

Once more, the only way was down. The rickety metal stairs were bolted into a dark cliff face. Emergency construction lights offered a dim illumination, but not enough to show just how deeply the cave continued downward.

"See anything?" Callie asked, continuing to descend.

Once more, the eight Convergences glowed brightly to Ras. He couldn't tell how much the extra Energy from the train Convergences had caused them to grow as they neared, but now he was able to see that all eight were connected by an Energy-powered structure that began to look very familiar by its outline.

"I've got a riddle," Ras said, walking down the stairs.

"Right now?"

"Sure. What's got eight Convergences and should be hanging over the Time Origin?"

Callie sighed. "*The Winnower*. Are you saying *The Winnower* is down there?"

"No, but I'm guessing the Heart of Mason is its very shy, cave-dwelling little brother," Ras said.

"This doesn't make any sense, Ras," Callie said. "I get that Mason survived the war and Great Overload, but where would they get the resources to build something like *The Winnower*, or even be able to capture Convergences..."

"Which once again is Collective technology," Ras said. "Maybe The Collective stole all of their innovations from Imago?"

"Or maybe the Helios family is in charge of everything."

The dull yellow glow of the construction lights all shut off at once, dropping the cave into pitch black.

"I guess word spread that we're down here," Callie said. "How much grapple cable do you have left?"

"I'm about out," Ras said. "Why do you ask?"

"I figured we could speed this up if we just rappelled over the edge of the walkway so we could overload as close to The Heart of Mason as possible to get this over with."

"We could try from up here if you want," Ras said.

"I'm not sure I'm good for more than one more overload today," Callie said softly.

Something nagged at the back of his mind. He couldn't know Callie's threshold, so communication was important now more than ever. "If I ask you a question, would you be honest with me?" Ras asked, barely a whisper. "Completely honest."

"Of course."

Ras paused. He had been bothered ever since he learned of the pain overloading caused her. "You would tell me if you thought over-loading might kill you, right?" he asked. "Because I couldn't live with myself—"

"I would tell you, Ras," Callie said, giving a pained smile that Ras didn't know if he could trust. "But I wouldn't mind if knocking out these eight was my last big overload," she said. "I mean, once the Atmo fueling stations drop, you could handle those like you did the trains, right?"

"Definitely," Ras said, fighting a nagging suspicion that Callie would put him first even if such loyalty were to get her killed. "I wouldn't put you through pain if there was any other option at all."

A loud whirring noise began from deep below. It sounded pro-peller-like, and continued to grow. Nothing registered on the Knack-Visions. He couldn't see forward, and knew the path back up to the surface wasn't an option.

The emergency lights came back on in an orange hue, flickering in a pattern, making it difficult for Ras to gain his bearings for more than a second at a time. Looking below, the thing producing the noise looked almost like a gigantic insect, but three flashes of orange light later Ras could make out that it was a small, propeller driven flying machine with several men inside a bubble-like cockpit.

"Stay where you are!" an amplified voice barely made it out from underneath the propeller noise.

A small explosion and expulsion of smoke quickly resulted in sparks flying off of the metal stairs in front of them.

Ras reached out, grabbing Callie's shoulder and halting her momentum as the first shot from the flying machine turned into dozens. Soon, the metal grated walkway was riddled with bullets. He had never seen a weapon that could fire off that many rounds so quickly.

With a groan and a lurch, the walkway began to separate from the cave wall where it had sustained the most damage. In front of them, the grating fell away, cutting off the path.

Callie bolted up the stairs past Ras as the machine gained altitude. The walkway continued to shake, threatening to fall and take them with it.

A rope ladder dropped directly ahead. "Grab it!" Ras called to Callie, who wrapped an arm around it without hesitance and was immediately lifted from the walkway.

"Can you glide down there?" Callie shouted.

The distance down to the Heart of Mason would kill him if he fell. There was a chance he could build enough speed that he could grapple with what cable he had left and work the glider so that the last bit of the fall wouldn't kill him.

He couldn't do it.

Not only would he have to successfully knock out all eight Convergences by himself while unarmed, Callie would be alone with India Bravo, which he wouldn't allow.

Ras shook his head, then grasped the rope ladder a few rungs beneath Callie, placing his weight on the rope. After a moment, they began to ascend. Before he could think too much about where they were going, a light shone from above as a circular iris flexed open above them.

Light filtered down through the spinning propeller blades, and Ras' eyes struggled to compensate. In moments, the vehicle lifted back above the surface and into broad daylight.

Surrounding the circular opening were dozens upon dozens of armed soldiers with weapons trained on Ras and Callie. The owner of a shock of red hair stood front and center with the group. India Bravo didn't need words to make herself clear; her self-satisfied grin communicated that she would always hold the upper hand.

CHAPTER FOURTEEN
The Conflagration

THE ROPES ATTACHED TO EACH OF RAS' LIMBS SUSPENDED HIM several feet off of the ground within a wheeled wooden framework. The residual pain in his right shoulder had flared up, and his left arm tingled, a remnant of the dislocation he had suffered on the day he met Hal in Framer's Valley.

Graham pushed the framework along a high-ceilinged corridor within the Governor's mansion. He had a large, purple welt on his forehead where the grapple magnet had struck him earlier. The echoing creak of the wooden wheels and the hard claps of boots against the tile resounded throughout the room.

Callie was gone, taken elsewhere. Ras couldn't let himself think too much about what she might be going through. If they were going to be separated anyway, he might as well have tried taking out the Heart of Mason on his own. *Idiot.* His grapple gun, goggles, and glider had all been confiscated as well.

Uniformed guards holding long poles with blades attached to their ends opened the large double doors at the end of the hallway.

"Presenting Erasmus Veir," one guard announced loudly, "coward and traitor to Imago and the Burrow Alliance."

Ras pursed his lips, refraining from any sort of quip as the wooden structure bumped over the threshold and rolled into the expansive throne room on a long strip of red carpet. Stained glass windows adorned both walls leading to the dais, flooding it with colored light. Above, the domed ceiling was almost completely covered in small shields with various patterns of colors and designs. Crude white Xs had been painted over the majority of what Ras assumed to be family crests. *Families who left for Atmo?*

A slow clapping brought Ras' attention away from the ceiling and to the eventual end of the red carpet. Seated on her raised throne, India Bravo applauded her approaching captive until the wooden contraption creaked to a halt at the end of the carpet.

Graham stepped to the side of the frame, then gave a small spoked wheel half of a turn clockwise. The four ropes tightened, straining Ras' limbs.

A streak of pain shot through Ras' body, and he made no pretense of strength. "Why?" he demanded.

"That's a very large question," India said, resting her chin on a gloved hand. "Care to be more specific?"

"Why are you attacking Atmo, India?" Ras said, shifting his shoulders to ease the pain, but no positioning offered relief.

She motioned to Graham, who turned the wheel again, straining Ras' limbs further. "I have but one name, Veir. Uttering any other is punishable by death."

Ras groaned behind gritted teeth. "Maybe I need an introduction."

"Happily," India said. "My name is Governor Iridessa Bartleby. I take it you have failed at my task?"

"No," Ras said, unable to take a full breath. "Found him."

India burst from her throne, waving a hand to dismiss the guards at the door. Graham remained at the wheel. "Where is he?" she asked.

"Let Callie go," Ras said softly. "Please."

"I can appreciate your attempt at extracting sympathy from me," India said, slowly descending the steps to the main floor. "After all, don't we go to lengths for those we care about?" She held up a palm toward Graham. "But there are lessons you must learn, Erasmus, about who holds the power in a negotiation." At a flick of her fingers, the wheel began its spin and he felt his left shoulder socket begin to dislocate.

"I destroyed Tefka!" Ras shouted, momentarily halting the torture. He wasn't sure why those three words were the ones to escape his lips under duress. Perhaps it had something to do with wanting to stop the assault on Atmo. Perhaps it was an admission of guilt he needed to express before India killed him.

"Come again?" India asked.

"I found Foster," Ras said, panting. "In Treding. He's different, now. Talks to Convergences. Brought them there. I destroyed them. That…that grew the Tefka Convergence. Destroyed the city."

"And so The Reclaimer brought death to Mason?"

"I'm trying to save everyone," Ras strained out. "Atmo didn't attack Tefka. It was my fault."

"You're from Atmo," India said. "Same difference. Where's my son?"

Graham's grip on the wooden spoke slipped at the admission of parentage. The ropes relaxed, granting Ras momentary relief.

"Go," India ordered to Graham. "I know how to work this device."

Graham gave an apologetic look, then walked back down the long hallway. The sound of the double doors closing reverberated throughout the chamber.

Ras wrapped his hands around the slack in his rope, pulling himself up to relieve the tension on his shoulders. "I brought him here, *Governor*. Foster is in your city."

"Where?" India asked, her eyes dancing.

"We got separated when Graham attacked me," Ras said. "I doubt he's going to remember you, though. He doesn't even remember what The Collective is…was."

"Why?"

That's a very large question. "He fell from *The Winnower* and landed next to the Time Origin. He's just…*different* now."

"*Lupava*," India cursed under her breath. "I told him not to let that madman get too close."

What does Lupava have to do with this? With the limited opportunity he had, the rabbit-trail seemed like a secondary objective. "I did what you asked," Ras said. "Now as a respectable Governor, I expect you to keep up your end of the bargain."

India chuckled softly. "Certainly. Why not? You've likely killed us all anyway. *Nalon* may as well enjoy the final fireworks with everyone else."

"How in At—Imago did I kill everyone?" Ras asked. "Yes, Tefka was my fault, but—"

"You destroyed *The Winnower*, Veir," India said. "We had one shot at saving this world, and you destroyed it because Halcyon Napier promised to keep your city running, as though the turncoat could hold such sway."

"Turncoat? He stopped the Illorians during—"

"The Clockwork War, yes, I see they still teach that version in Atmo," India said, beginning to pace around Ras. "But we've been down here long enough, living with Convergences. Living with Caretakers. And now you come swooping in on Halcyon's ship and try to sell everyone on some savior story. We are beyond saving, Veir."

"Then why do you want Foster?"

India stopped at the wheel, idly pulling it one way, then another, bobbing her captive up and down slightly. "If our last hope is extinguished, I'd like to spend my final days with my family." She shot a chilling look up at Ras.

"We were told The Collective built *The Winrower*."

"Of course you were," India said, scoffing. "My father-in-law designed it when he built Atmo and the Burrows. He knew one day we would run out of Energy, and the only way we could survive was if we blocked off Time." She pulled on a lever, dropping Ras to the floor. "And we came so very close."

Ras lay sprawled on the red carpet, still tethered loosely at each limb to the wooden frame like a puppet. He watched India step back up to her dais and take her seat. "What if I told you I stopped the Time Origin?" he asked, sitting up and massaging his wrists where the rope cut in.

"Then The Reclaimer has gone one step further and *ensured* the destruction of this world."

"But you just said you wanted to block it—"

"Yes, so it couldn't be broken by you!" India snapped.

"Where is all of this coming from?" Ras demanded. "Where did the idea of The Reclaimer even start?"

"The Caretakers," India said, a strain in her voice. Ras looked up and saw the last thing he would have expected: India's shoulders were slumped and she held her head in her hand. "Not that Mason ever got one. Halcyon saw to that."

India looked defeated. The fight had temporarily left her. Ras surveyed the room for anything he could use to free himself from the ropes, but the sparsely decorated room gave no options. He would need to talk his way out of this one.

"You're a Masonite, born and raised?" Ras asked.

"Masonian," India corrected.

"My mother is Acerbian," Ras said. "She didn't much care for living on *Verdant*."

"Why are you still speaking?" India sighed.

"Because Foster and I both had fathers who thought they were saving the world," Ras said, "and we both still have mothers who would move all of Imago to keep their sons safe." He paused. India hadn't stopped him from speaking yet, which was a good sign. "My mother was twenty when my father—"

"Veir, I have no pity for you," India said. She stood to her full height, then gracefully descended the few stairs down to Ras. "There is no common ground to find. You want to compare your romanticized story of how your parents met? Fine. I met my late husband after hijacking my first dozen wind merchant ships to build Bravo Company. By the time *I* was twenty, I supplied him with a son in exchange for permission to down my first two Atmo cities to build *The Winnower* out of their parts. Of course it took a couple more than that, all sanctioned by The Collective to save the world…which you so deftly made moot." She gritted her teeth. "I may have taken on the role of the villain, but at least my destruction served a purpose. You've just made it all pointless. Those lives lost…" She pulled a knife from her boot, then tossed it down to the floor in front of Ras. "Perhaps you destroying us all will be an act of mercy."

Ras looked at the crude blade, notched and resharpened countless times. Was she setting him free? It felt like some sort of trick. He leaned forward, picking it up and began cutting his restraints. The idea of Bravo Company downing Atmo cities for just wanton destruction had never made sense to Ras. Building *The Winnower* to somehow save the world didn't exactly exonerate her sky pirate ways, but at least she appeared to have a rational side, however small it might be.

A set of shadows played behind the stained glass windows, stealing his attention. "So, why attack *Verdant* after *The Winnower* was built?" he asked. "Spare parts?"

India scoffed. "Bravo Company was placed under my son's control after he became old enough," she said. "After I lost my eye, I focused on being Governor. I only leave this city when the fleet needs a figurehead."

A smash of glass came from Ras' left, followed by a horrible shriek. Smatterings of popping explosions, blue smoke, and multi-colored sparks filled the chamber.

Fireworks.

One of the spiraling projectiles struck India in the face, causing her to recoil and tumble to the ground. The ember fell to the red carpet, and more smoke began to fill the room.

"Ras!" Ace's voice called from above. "Heads up!"

Ras couldn't see his cousin through all of the smoke, but the series of tied bedsheets dangling from the broken window was enough of a cue. He scrambled over to it as the double doors opened and guards flooded the room.

With his limbs so strained, he didn't know how effective of a climber he would be, but before he could make an attempt to lift himself, the bedsheets rose.

Musket fire struck the wall beside him as he ascended into the smoke. Quickly he passed the haze, rising into daylight as two sets of arms hauled him through the broken window and onto the roof. A pair of smiling faces looked down at Ras.

"You're lucky Tink is such a crack shot with a whirlygig," Ace said, helping Ras to his feet with Tink's aid.

"Where's Callie?" Ras asked, struggling to his feet on the slick tile roofing.

"I'm right here," Callie said.

Ras spun and saw her directly behind him. She looked unharmed. It took everything in him not to throw his arms around her. "Are you all right?"

"Guards," Tink said, pointing at the men struggling to ascend the base of the roof.

The four of them turned and began scrambling in the opposite direction along the mansion's long structure.

"What's the getaway plan?" Ras asked.

Ahead, one of the flying skiffs descended, cutting off their path. The guards gained ground behind them. They were trapped.

The skiff's door opened, and Foster stepped out, his eyes narrowed.

"See?" Ace said. "We got you covered."

"Oh, thank Atmo," Callie said. "I think."

"Stop!" Foster commanded, holding his hand up. The guards obeyed, standing down. He stepped up to Ras. "You aren't finished here, friend." His voice held a darker tone to it. "You two." He pointed to Ace and Tink. "Can either of you operate this thing?" he asked, nodding back toward the flying skiff.

"Tink can figure it out," Ace said. "Right?"

"Yeah," Tink confirmed.

"Good," Foster said. "Leave."

"What?" Ace asked. "What about Ras and Callie?"

"They still have work to do here," Foster reiterated.

"Ace," Ras said. "I need you and Tink to take that thing to the train yard and find the train heading for Acerbis. It's labeled, you can't miss it. Tell my parents that Governor Bartleby is India Bravo, that Mason built *The Winnower* out of downed Atmo cities, and destroying Convergences just makes one Convergence bigger." He paused. "And tell them I love them, all right?"

"Bravo. *Winnower*. Convergence. Love. Check," Tink said.

"But how—" Ace began.

"You'll figure it out as you go," Ras said. "You can do this. You're a Corin."

Ace wrapped her arms around Ras. "Did we do good? Rescuing you and all?"

"I couldn't be any prouder to call you cousin," Ras said, releasing the hug. He nodded toward the skiff. "Go."

Ace and Tink said their goodbyes to Callie while Ras slipped India's knife into his boot.

Once the skiff launched, Foster called the guards over. "Men, incarcerate these two in the sub-basement prison. They are dangerous. Keep them separated."

Ras shot a glance to Foster, hoping for a wink or anything to include him on the play. Nothing but a hard look reminding him of the man he fought to the death with on *The Winnower*. "What are you doing?" he asked.

"Bringing peace."

RAS STOOD ALONE in the empty cell, looking through metal bars across the hallway at Callie, who sagged, defeated, against the gray wall.

"Hey, it's all right," Ras said. Considering his surroundings, he felt oddly upbeat. He had confronted India Bravo face to face twice now and survived somehow.

"No, it's not, Ras," she said. "Just saying it doesn't make this any better." She waved a hand around, roughly pointing at her cell. "Did you see the look Foster gave us? He's back. We trusted him and now we've failed."

"Hey, remember when I used to be the moody one who thought everything was falling to pieces?" Ras asked with a half smirk. "Those were the days." He absentmindedly scraped his fingernails against a metal bar. "Besides, if we're down here too long, I'm sure Hal will come swooping in with an Elder fleet since we're kind of the linchpin of this whole plan working."

Callie gave him a sad look, then leaned back on the cot, resting her head against the cell wall. "I don't know, but somewhere along the way I was kind of hoping I'd get a chance to meet my birth parents. And I know we wouldn't speak the same language, and they probably wouldn't believe I was their daughter—"

"I'm sure having a family resemblance would help," Ras said.

"But still, I just want to know they're okay, and for them to know I'm okay," she paused. "Well, mostly okay."

"It's not like they abandoned you," Ras said. "They were just trying to keep you safe."

"Which is why I want them to know they succeeded," Callie said. "That through two wars and the whole world falling apart, that they kept their daughter safe because they made the right decision...and maybe even saved their entire country because of it."

"Who says that won't still happen?" Ras asked. "We've gotten out of scrapes like this before."

Callie tapped her temple. "I don't exactly get to free everyone if it's going to kill me."

"We don't know that," Ras said. "Maybe there's more serum where the last batch came from."

"But Dixie killed that creepy scientist," Callie said.

"I know," Ras said. "But who knows what's possible anymore. I've kind of resigned myself to the fact that I don't know what I don't know, so I just kind of have to roll with the surprises."

Minutes passed, then hours. Nobody came to speak with them. Night came, at least according to Ras' watch. Sleep was difficult to come by. Ras wondered how Hal and Dr. O were doing, and suddenly felt that while this was his mission, he had put too much of the weight onto other people's shoulders.

Capable people. People Ras trusted implicitly, but it still was a lot of weight. Of course, he didn't know how he could be successful without their help, and they probably didn't wish all of the responsibility to land squarely on his shoulders.

"Ras?" Callie asked from her cell, sitting up.

"Yeah?"

"Where is everybody?" she asked. "Not that I want to be interrogated again, mind you."

Ras shrugged. "Maybe this is their version of solitary confinement, or they don't know what to do with us," he said. "Or, maybe with Foster back, they just forgot about us."

Something rumbled a deep, bass roar. It was difficult to tell what was going on or from which direction the sound originated. Another roar began in a different pitch, joining the first. Ras placed a hand against the wall, feeling the vibration in the thick concrete.

The shaking cot was uncomfortable to sit on, so he stood. More rumbles joined in, growing in intensity, then tempering back down to a bearable level. The door at the end of the hallway opened, and a figure, difficult to see due to the now-flickering lights, walked in carrying a brown box.

"Foster!" Callie shouted. "What's going on?"

Foster strode up to the space between the two cells, then placed the open box on the floor. The container held Ras and Callie's confiscated effects. The outside of the box was stained with red handprints. Foster's handprints.

The formerly gray suit now was dotted and splattered with red. He had left bootprints down the hall in a track of blood.

"I am sorry I took so long to return," Foster said. "I had to ensure your safety before returning to my primary goal."

The blinking lights and flecks of blood on Foster's face starkly contrasted with the friendly smile.

"Ah…what about Ace and Tink?" Ras asked. "Did they make it out?"

Foster nodded, reaching into the box and extracting a heavy looking set of keys. He eyed Ras' lock and then selected a key seemingly at random. He inserted it, and the cell door ratcheted open.

He went through the same process with Callie's cell as Ras began reequipping himself from the box.

More than ever, Foster felt like a feral pet, ready to pounce at the first misstep.

"So I see you…found some resistance," Callie said carefully.

Foster stopped to consider Callie for a moment. "They tried admirably. I'll give them that."

Ras stepped out into the cellblock hallway. "What have you been up to, then?"

"I've been helping you, of course," Foster said, patting Ras' shoulder. "My friends."

A chill, no less frightening for the fact that Ras might have been imagining it, spread from his shoulder throughout his body. Ras forced his misgivings to the back of his mind and nodded for Callie to follow him, letting Foster take the lead. As they reached the end of the cell block, the smell of burning caught his nostrils.

Callie sniffed at the air. "Is something on fire?"

"Yes," Foster said. "This building, among other things." He opened the door to a horrible scene. The guard room, which formerly had held a dozen guards, now contained the remains of a dozen guards, the aftermath of the battle evidenced on the walls and floor, and in the dank scent in the air.

"You did this?" Ras asked, fighting a gag reflex. "By yourself?" He looked down at Foster's thigh. The Energy pistol remained holstered. This massacre had been perpetrated in a far more brutal, blunt fashion.

"A senseless waste. One I regret," Foster said. "Attrition was inevitable."

The rest of the walk out of the mansion's basement revealed no living soul, just the remains of those who used to work there. Each new turn out of the building horrified Ras more. The temperature had already begun to rise, and he was about to comment when they reached the top of the stairs leading into the foyer.

"I did my part," Foster said, opening one of the double doors to the outside world. Shouts of terror and explosions filtered into the mansion. "Now it's time for you to do yours."

Ras ran to the door and saw Convergences flying about. Men and women screamed in terror as they did everything within their power to escape their assailants. Those unfortunate enough to find themselves in the path of one of the swooping orbs immediately over-loaded, their Energy being sucked up into the green spheres of death.

It was the Second Great Overload, and Ras had to stop it.

The chaos was almost too much to bear. A block away, a giant skyscraper buckled in the middle as a Convergence exited it with a shattering of glass and a groaning of metal. The one hundred story skyscraper bent like a tree in the wind, then snapped, its top half careening into a dozen other buildings. Glass rained down as the iron giant smashed into the street.

"Callie," Ras shouted. He spun on his heel and extended his hand.

Callie reached out for him, but Foster stepped between them, grabbing Ras' wrist with an unnaturally strong grip.

"What are you doing?" Ras demanded, trying to wrest his arm free. "I have to stop this."

Foster pressed his lips into a line. "Once it's begun, it must run its course."

"This," Ras gestured with his free arm, "is not what I wanted. This is the opposite of helping me."

"But you failed to reach the Convergences," Foster said in a passive tone almost lost to the sound of the calamity. "So I brought them up to you."

Ras knew every second more he spent arguing with Foster would results in hundreds of lives lost. The screams and explosions made it difficult to think. "All right, fine." He lifted his free arm up in a motion of surrender. "Will you at least let me go grab a skiff so I can drive us somewhere we won't get crushed?"

Foster seemed to consider this for a moment. "I shall watch over Calista until you return." He released Ras.

"I'll be back," Ras said to Callie, then broke out into a run toward a row of parked jetcycles and skiffs. The door was locked, so he smashed the driver window with his grapple gun, then unlocked the door from the inside.

He considered for a moment hunting down and destabilizing each of the eight Convergences, but by the time he could have reached them, Mason would be completely lost.

He feared that it might be beyond saving already.

Hot-wiring the skiff was similar to getting *The Brass Fox* started. Sparking two wires together brought the skiff to life, lifting it a foot from the ground. Kicking it into drive, Ras spun the wheel hard to the left and slammed on the accelerator.

The skiff spun wildly; its engine roared as it picked up speed, tearing back in the direction from which Ras had come.

Callie was struggling to escape Foster's grip, which only solidified Ras' plan in his mind. He buckled his seatbelt and gripped the steering wheel so hard his knuckles turned white.

Pushing the pedal to the floor, Ras reached Foster just as the monster looked up. For the first time since Ras had found him in the middle of the Convergence, he looked surprised.

The left headlight smashed into Foster, sending the man flying up onto the hood, then onto the windshield, cracking it. Ras slammed on the brakes, and Foster tumbled forward onto the ground.

Without hesitation, Callie opened the back door on the driver's side and dove in.

Ras threw the skiff into reverse as soon as she closed the door and looked behind to ensure he didn't hit anyone else. When he looked forward again, Foster was standing with fists clenched and not a scratch on him.

Foster reached up to the sky, and then brought his arm down quickly. As Ras began to launch forward, one of the Convergences slammed down into the ground ahead of him, sending chunks of road flying. The skiff began to burn as it neared the large ball of Energy.

Callie placed her hand on his shoulder from the back seat, beginning the overload process.

The skiff lost power, diving the short distance to the ground, nose first. The concussive shock shattered the windshield and Ras slammed into the steering wheel. Callie flew forward from the backseat, her head striking the dashboard. She crumpled as the skiff skidded toward the sea of destabilizing green Energy.

The Convergence ahead erupted in a chorus of screams. The skiff's engine caught on fire. Ras fought to stay coherent, shaking his head. Callie lay unconscious, blood seeping from her forehead.

"Callie!" Ras shouted. "Callie! Wake up!" He struggled to unbuckle his seatbelt and forced open the door as the flames rose higher in front of them. Grasping Callie's limp form, Ras dragged her out onto the pavement. He struggled to his feet and began pulling Callie away from the wreckage.

Mason was burning all around them, and there were still seven more Convergences ripping through the city.

He felt helpless.

Without Callie's range, Ras couldn't pilot a skiff close enough to disperse them himself, and under Foster's control, the Convergences could play keep away, which brought up so many more questions he couldn't even begin to process at the moment.

"She will be fine," Foster said calmly from behind.

Ras gently lowered Callie's head to the ground, then stood to face Foster. "What about everyone else, Foster?"

"The Convergences need this," Foster said, backlit by the flames licking up a burning building.

"They need to be destroyed," Ras said. "And you're controlling them."

"They…listen to me," Foster said. "But I don't control them." A pause. "You struck me, Rassss." He turned his head to the side, once more looking at Ras from the corners of his eyes. "But you've done this before, haven't you?"

It was only a matter of time before Foster would remember their proper roles relating to one another, it seemed.

"You were going to stop the Time Origin," Ras said. "We would have all died."

"Then thankfully you did that for me, Ras," Foster said, a grin growing. "We want the same things."

"I don't want destroyed cities!" Ras protested. "That's a big difference."

"Not in the long run," Foster said, then gestured with a palm upward, lifting his hand. Above, the remaining seven Convergences lifted high above the city. The sounds of overloading people subsided, leaving the city with the eerie calm of crackling fire. "Do you wish to spare them?"

Ras looked around at the broken city. Some citizens had made their way out to the streets, watching the seven Convergences slowly rotating. Ras wondered if those people were blessed Tefkans and if any Masonians were even left. "What's to spare?"

Foster paused. "This is needed for peace to come."

"Then I don't want your peace if it means everybody has to die," Ras said, gesturing emphatically. "These people don't deserve this."

A low chuckle caught in Foster's throat. "I will grant you this: I will stop these Convergences. You may disperse them, but another city will feel their heat. And at that time, I want you to remember this moment and the price which mercy requires."

Foster turned his back and began walking away. He lifted an arm, then threw it down.

A Convergence flung itself from high above Mason down toward Ras. He dove over Callie instinctively to protect her. If she couldn't overload while unconscious, he didn't know if she was resistant to Energy as well.

The green orb hurtled down, slamming into Ras with a physical force he hadn't expected. The second Convergence took its turn, knocking his breath out of him, followed by the third through seventh in rapid succession. He fought to remain conscious as he watched Foster's form, wavy and distorted, disappear into the flames of the city.

Then blackness came.

CHAPTER FIFTEEN
The Defenestration

AN ETERNAL MOMENT FALLING; THEN THE ILLUSION OF WEIGHTLESSNESS, as though his upper back and the crooks of his knees were bearing him up and away from the ground. He felt like a small child as the world flowed slowly back into his consciousness. He could still hear the faint crackle of fire, but beneath that constant sound, lower and more fundamental to his ears, were rhythmic clomps, which reverberated through the supports holding him.

"Where's Callie?" Ras muttered, cracking open his eyes and letting in a bit of waning red daylight filtered through the haze of dark smoke. Blurry, jagged lines shot upward; the broken spires of the city.

"She is near," a mechanical voice said.

Ras opened his eyes wide in an attempt to sober himself. Only a foot away from his face was the molded helmet of an Elder suit, and he realized it was carrying him. With his left arm, he reached up and patted the top of the helmet. Something pricked the palm of his hand and he winced.

"What's on your head?" Ras asked groggily.

"You should know," the Elder said. "You put it there."

Confused, Ras arched his back to see the nub of grapple gun cable attached to a magnet, a makeshift cylindrical hat. "Carter?"

"My wife says keeping it up there will scramble my brain," Carter said. "Which is the only thing that can explain why I'm here right now."

Ras flopped his head over to see Callie draped over the shoulder of Guy.

"Oh, good, you're up," Guy said.

"You can let me down," Ras said. "I think I can walk." Carter had been one of the people he hadn't actually expected to ever see again after his trip to Illoria. Rescuing Carter from Dr. O's dungeon of a city had been an incredibly fortunate happenstance, but after his focus shifted to saving Atmo, he assumed Carter would live out his days behind the Illorian mountains. Nevertheless, the feeling of relief at seeing his old friend did manage to place a small dent in the hopelessness surrounding him.

With a whir of servos and the ratcheting of powered machinery, Carter let Ras down.

Ras' feet found the ground but failed to support him. Carter quickly grabbed him by the back of the vest, keeping him from falling entirely.

"Well, at least you *think* you can stand," Finn said, walking up to Ras and shining a light in either eye, one at a time. "Something to be said for optimism."

"Care to explain what in Atmo happened here?" Guy asked, offering Callie to Carter, who gently cradled her small frame in his free arm.

"Foster," Ras said as he tried to lift himself to his feet, moderately more successful this time. He coughed as a thick billow of smoke from a nearby burning building wafted through the ruined street. "He can control Convergences. Ripped them straight out of the ground. Overloaded the city."

"I thought the cities down here were immune to that," Finn said.

Ras shook his head. "All but Mason were." Aside from the carnage, the streets were empty. The depopulated city remained eerily quiet except for the crackle of fire and the intermittent screech of wrecked buildings settling into place. Checking his watch, he saw that it was early in the afternoon.

He stepped carefully to Callie. Usually when asleep she looked carefree, but now she appeared pained with her brow ever so slightly furrowed; like the waking nightmare she had just lived through was being replayed. "We need to get her back on *The Kingfisher*." He swept a bit of hair from her forehead to see a bandage had already been applied.

"Actually," Carter said, "we need to be gone before *The Kingfisher* arrives."

"Wait, what?" Ras asked.

"Let's get back to my ship," Carter said. "I'll explain while we move."

Ras took a deep breath, then shambled forward alone until Finn came along and offered a supportive shoulder. "All right, we're moving. Let's talk."

"Well," Carter began, "when Dayus sent a message to Colonel Napier—"

"Colonel?" Ras asked.

"Yes, Halcyon has regained full control of the Illorian military," Carter said. "But when we received Dayus' message regarding Foster's reappearance as well as you overloading next to the Time Origin, an order was sent to bring you and your crew in for further questioning. When I, among others, was sent out to find you, I recognized the signature of *The Kingfisher's* shuttle just outside of *Solaria*...

"I admit I was curious as to how far along Dr. O had gotten on rebuilding his city," Carter continued, "and I ran into Dixie and these two gentlemen, who were on their way back to Mason. They told me of your plan, and I realized how that plan didn't exactly mesh with Colonel Napier's plan."

Ras' head spun. Suddenly he was an ex-Captain with a crew. Did he actually have a crew now? Foster was loose, and if that monster could escape up to Atmo, then everything would fall to pieces.

"Why are you going against Hal?" Ras asked.

"I'm not, officially," Carter said. "But, if by chance I apprehend you and you manage to slip away when my back is turned, then a stern reprimand is a small price to pay for not being responsible for stopping the man trying to save Atmo."

Ras walked on silently for a few steps. "Thank you, Carter. But I think if Atmo falls, then everyone would still know who to point to."

"Then hopefully if it succeeds, everyone will point the same direction," Carter said. "Just because someone needs a little help, it doesn't mean you abandon them."

"So, where am I going to get a ship?" Ras asked.

"I'm very glad you asked, Erasmus Veir," a chipper voice from behind said. "I think you mean, '*Where am I going to borrow a ship from a friend to whom I will find myself incredibly indebted?*'" Dixie walked up to Ras, resting a large metal wrench on her shoulder, then reached up to ruffle his hair. "Sorry, I noticed your wrench holster was empty. Figured since you lost the last one I gave you..." From behind her back she produced a wrench bigger than her forearm.

"This isn't a moment I want to commemorate."

"There's more than one reason to remember something," Dixie said. "Sometimes we carry things to remember who needs to be stopped. And why." She slotted the wrench into Ras' holster, then looked at Callie. "How did Red get hurt?"

"Skiff crash that Foster caused," Ras said. "How did Dr. O's meeting go?"

"Oh, well, he sends his love," Dixie said.

"That doesn't sound like him," Ras said.

Dixie shrugged. "I read between the lines most of the time. It's faster that way."

"Is he going to help us?" Ras asked as the group turned the corner and arrived at Carter's ship.

Dixie hummed speculatively. "Not so much, directly."

"Then why are you so happy?" Ras asked.

"He didn't let us leave without a parting gift," Dixie said. "Actually, he didn't *let* us leave at all. I had to mount an escape attempt, so I borrowed something of value on our way out."

"He doesn't care that Atmo is sinking?" Ras asked.

"Oh, he very much liked the idea of being the only one piloting a city," Dixie said. "But I think I got myself written out of his will."

"He's not leaving his wheelchair and rabbit to you?" Ras asked.

Finn laughed. "Sorry, I forgot about the rabbit. Weird looking thing."

"Yeah, Bartholomew says hello too," Dixie said. "Actually, I managed to borrow his Forcible Engine Rebooter. He wouldn't help us against the sky pirates, so I took an early inheritance." She kicked a bit of rubble, watching it skid forward. "I figure we still need the Elders to get the kids out of the fueling stations, but at least now we can drop anybody who comes out to fight us before they can attack."

"Nice," Ras said. "One more thing you all should know...India Bravo is the Governor of Mason."

Dixie jumped ahead of Ras, pacing backwards. She took in the burning surroundings with a new look of wonder. "And you helped Foster blow up her city? I could kiss you!"

"No, Dixie," Ras said. "A lot of innocent people died here. She was tied in closer to The Collective than I thought. Foster, the version of him before he went insane and could control Convergences, ran Bravo Company most of the time. She was just responsible for downing enough Atmo cities so she could build *The Winnower*."

"Just?" Guy asked.

"You know what I mean," Ras said. "I don't know if she's even alive now. Foster had a lot of blood on his hands last time I saw him."

"He better not have killed her," Dixie said. "Because there's a waiting list and I'm at the top."

Carter's ship was dented and twisty in all the wrong places—Ras wondered for a moment how it managed to even stay up on its landing struts. The vessel looked even worse for wear than it had outside of *Solaria*.

"What happened to your ship?" Ras asked.

"I've been going to uncharted territories," Carter said. The ramp lowered as they approached, stopping a good foot off the ground. He stomped on the platform, forcing it to descend fully. "You'll have to forgive its quirks. Acid rain really does a number on the joints."

Ras saw the off-white of *The Kingfisher*'s shuttle gleaming against the dirty grey of the rest of Carter's ship. "What happened to your shuttle?"

"That's a long story," Carter said, ascending the ramp. "Well, no, it's not. I left my dear, sweet daughter alone on the bridge for a moment and she managed to eject it over an ocean. We've learned to go without."

"We?" Ras asked.

"Yes, you'll finally get to meet the missus," Carter said, ensuring everyone ascended the ramp before closing the hangar. He carefully set Callie down, then reached up to grab his helmet and dislodged it. "Honey, it's safe to come in now. We have new company!" he called out. He paused, then spoke in a lyrical sounding Illorian dialect, prompting a fair-headed woman carrying a curly haired infant with a joyous smile into the hangar.

"Seraphina," Carter said, motioning to his wife, then said something in Illorian, finishing with "Ras Veir."

Ras nodded an introduction and moved to shake her hand. She took a quick step back.

"Sorry, Ras, that's not customary in Illoria," Carter said. He clomped over to another, smaller Elder suit nestled against the far wall of the hangar, presumably Seraphina's.

"Your daughter is beautiful," Ras said to Seraphina.

Carter translated, Seraphina responded and gave a slight smile. "She says thank you. I'm sorry, she's just nervous to meet The Reclaimer, is all." He extracted himself from the back of the suit and walked up to Ras, towering over him still. "Let's move Callie into a bed until she comes to."

"She should be fine," Finn said. "She'll have a terrible headache when she wakes up. All of my supplies are still on *The Kingfisher*, but she'll be fine."

"I'll see what Seraphina has for her," Carter said, walking over to Callie and collecting her while conversing with his wife. As they all walked out of the bay, Carter leaned in to kiss his daughter on the head. "Can you say 'Ras?', Alba?"

The infant sputtered out a "Rasss," then squealed in a peal of delight, kicking her legs wildly.

"I also tried to teach her 'Astrid,' but it never took," Carter said, shooting a glance toward Dixie.

"She's a smart little girl," Dixie said.

Ras noticed a large conical device sitting in the back corner of the hangar. Its design didn't fit with the rest of the machinery surrounding it. "Is that the non-pistol version of the Forcible…engine killer thing?"

"That it is! Industrial sized," Dixie said, striding over and placing a hand proudly on its side next to a series of levers and pipes.

The discrepancy of size between the machinery and Dixie was comical. "How did you get it out of *Solaria*?"

"Well, after the three of us escaped and found Carter waiting by the shuttle, he let me wear his wife's Elder suit," Dixie said. "I still think being tall is overrated, but he and I stomped our way back in and made off with it." She beamed. "Ta da! Dixie Piper wins again." She gave herself a polite round of applause, then bowed as though receiving the adoration of a throng.

"Good work, Dix," Ras said. "That should really even the odds."

"If we figure out how to work it," Guy said.

"One step at a time," Dixie said, giving Guy a wide smile.

After Carter settled Callie into one of the largest beds Ras had ever seen, Finn stayed with her while everyone else made their way to the bridge, which looked much repaired with wires trailing everywhere between consoles. Ras had to remind himself that *The Kingfisher* hadn't seen regular use in almost a century, while this ship was probably a third-generation hand-me-down without a ready supply of unfrozen spare parts.

"What's the ship called?" Ras asked.

"*Caerberinth*," Carter said, then looked like he was trying to remember something. "In your language it means…Firefinch. It's my favorite type of bird. Birdwatching is one of my hobbies."

"Who names their ship after a bird?" Guy asked.

"You mean like *The Kingfisher*?" Carter asked. "That's a bird."

Ras lifted an eyebrow. He had always taken the name far more literally, assuming it had to do with finding royalty. He had never thought to ask Callie.

"Like I would know that," Guy said, crossing his arms.

"So, boss," Dixie said, walking over to Ras and leaning her shoulder into his arm. "What's the game plan?"

"Primarily, we can't let Foster reach an Atmo city," Ras said, looking down to Dixie. Her wide violet eyes stared back up at him, hopeful. *How did I never notice that before?* He had always thought they were a bluish gray. "If Foster can get close enough to a Convergence, he can control it, and he has no issues with burning cities to the ground, like Einaud, Tefka, and now Mason."

The fact that Ras wasn't completely responsible for the destruction of the cities was only a slight salve to what would otherwise be a complete spiral into depression. Then again, he still was somehow responsible for Foster's escaping away from the Time Origin.

"Overall, he wants what we want, which is all of the Convergences gone," Ras said. "I don't know why, but he does, and we can't let him go about it his way."

"How are we going to win?" Guy asked.

Ras sighed. "I don't know, which is as honest of an answer as I can give right now. We can't stay here for long—"

"I have a ship," Dixie said. "It's back on *Nalon*, and won't be easy to get to, but it's something."

"I'll take something," Ras said. "Where'd you get it?"

"Swiped it off a Red Band pirate after the rust bucket Old Harley gave me for my delegation run kept falling apart. I named her *The Pretty Princess Petunia*."

"Of course you did," Ras said.

"Mostly I named her that so I could laugh when other people said it," Dixie said. "Go on, say it. It might cheer you up." She smiled her winning smile. "I call her '*Three-P*' for short."

"Ras? It appears we weren't the only ones to launch from Mason," Carter said from the helm. He tapped the radar screen, then pointed out at the main windshield as *The Firefinch* rose above the smoke-tinted cloud cover. "Capital ship, looks like."

Ras recognized the flagship from landing on it back by *Nalon*. "It's India's, all right."

"Hey, maybe we can end this right here," Dixie said. "If we board with old robosuit here," she said, jutting a thumb at Carter, "maybe we can get her to release all of the fueling stations and free the children onboard. I mean, it's a long shot, but we have to take it, right?"

"Dixie, a handful of us aren't going to be able to storm a fully functioning capital ship," Ras said.

"I doubt it's fully-functional," Dixie said. "They aren't even shooting at us, and if what happened on the ground is any indication, I seriously doubt there's more than a skeleton crew. Besides, what if Foster is onboard? Huh? Then that's his ticket to destroying Atmo. We have to at least check."

Ras closed his eyes, weighing his options. Ever since Mason, his natural resting state included gritting his teeth or fighting tremors from adrenaline. The whole world had gone mad, it seemed. Was this his place, to facilitate further destruction? Wherever Foster was, the monster needed to be stopped, somehow. *Maybe a powered Elder suit could help make a stand against him.*

"Carter, would you be willing to play wrecking ball one more time?" Ras asked. He looked over to Seraphina and baby Alba. It was a lot to ask. He watched Carter and Seraphina break into an argument in Illorian until she left the bridge. "I guess that's a no?"

"She's going to go prep my suit," Carter said softly. "If this can save Atmo, then how can I not?"

"Great," Dixie said, running over and hugging the man. It was a comical sight, considering that he was a foot and a half taller than she. "I knew we could count on you!" She looked back at Ras. "I'll go prep my gear."

"Dixie, wait," Ras said. "I can't let you go."

Dixie's eyes narrowed. "Say what now?"

"We're going to attempt hostile negotiations—"

"And what's more hostile than me when it comes to India Bravo?" Dixie asked, pointing toward the flagship emphatically.

"That's my point," Ras said. "She gets under your skin, and if you kill her before we can force her to release all of the children, then who knows what Bravo Company is going to do to Atmo." He sighed. "I promise, if this doesn't work out, and we have an opportunity to kill her, you'll be the first person I think of."

Dixie pointed at Guy. "Is he going?"

Ras considered him for a moment. "Can you keep a level head?"

Guy nodded.

"I can completely keep a level head!" Dixie said, visibly shaking. "You can't do this without me. You can't." Despite her set jaw and narrowed eyes, tears began welling up.

"Dixie, last time you had a chance to hurt India, you went against orders and started the clock on *Nalon* falling, not to mention trying to destroy the ship Callie and I were currently on," Ras said. "We need India alive, and that's a condition I have a very hard time imagining if you came along."

"You're not my Captain," Dixie said. "This isn't your ship—"

"I'm going to have to stand with Ras on this one," Carter said. "I'm sorry, Dixie."

Dixie stormed off the bridge and out into the hallway. Ras considered following for a moment, but knew little good would come of it.

THE *FIREFINCH* LANDED SAFELY on board the deck of India Bravo's flagship. Nobody came out to greet Carter, Ras, and Guy, which Ras took as a positive sign. Beneath, the smoke from Mason hung heavy in the sky, darkening their surroundings.

Carter exited *The Firefinch* first, as planned, followed by Ras, then Guy. The ship lifted off as soon as they were clear, both as a precaution for Carter's family and to keep Dixie from sneaking out. The drop from high above left Ras particularly disoriented, as Carter's flying style wasn't quite as conservative as Dayus'.

"At least nobody's shot at us yet," Guy said, shouldering an elegant looking Illorian rifle.

Carter pounded toward the door leading inside the ship and kicked it open without trying to unlock it. Shouts of surprise came from inside the hallway, and as the light from outside poured into the dark interior, huddled figures pressed themselves tightly against the walls.

Children, mothers, refugees. Not sky pirates.

Ras stepped in front of Carter and knelt in front of a middle-aged man. "Where are they taking you?"

"I don't know," he said. "The Governor promised us somewhere safe is all. Who are you?"

"I'm here to make sure there are still safe places to land," Ras said.

Carter continued on past the crooked works of art on the wall. Ras issued directions to the bridge, past more refugees.

"I don't like this," Guy said. "Where is the crew?"

The stench of death wafted down the stairwell, foreshadowing the scene that greeted them when they emerged into the bridge. A solitary, shell-shocked young man stood at the helm of the expansive room littered with what remained of the other members of the crew. Foster had obviously been here. The young man looked green enough barely to be out of school.

"Where's India Bravo?" Ras said.

"H-he-he took her to the hold," the young crewman said, vaguely pointing to his side as he kept his eyes locked forward.

Ras took the lead and began running through the halls toward the side decks. "Foster is probably trying to hijack a smaller ship to see Atmo." The path took them down several corridors and multiple sets of stairs.

A trail of expired crew members led them to the sealed door to the bay. Through the porthole, Ras could see several smaller airships aimed out at the sky from the open hold. India Bravo stood by one of the vessels, a vision in red. Foster was behind her, fervently working on the bridge of a trade vessel.

Ras pulled at the door, but it wouldn't open. He slammed his hand on the comm button. "Bravo, we had a deal!"

She turned and looked at Ras, fear in her eyes, then shook her head and turned back to face her son.

"Your turn," Ras said, patting the shoulder of the mechanical beast and stepped out of Carter's way.

Carter slammed into the door, barely making a dent on the heavy bulkhead.

Ras tried the comm again. "He destroyed Mason. He's going to rip apart Atmo. Stop him. He'll listen to you." He didn't fully believe the last assertion, but he was running out of things to say.

India's shoulders dropped, and she approached the door. She reached over, engaging the comm unit. "I must admit, I didn't expect you to find him," she said.

"That monster is not your son, and he's going to rip through every Atmo city the way he did Mason."

India stared at him. "And how would you stop him?" she asked. The question seemed to be half sarcastic and half a veiled plea for advice.

"I wouldn't give him a ship," Ras said, pointedly shifting his gaze to Foster onboard the vessel. "What happened to him?"

"I don't know!" India snapped back, an unusual crack in her composure. "He's his father's child, always tinkering with medicine. Who knows what he's gotten himself into?" India shook her head, the faint tinkle of jewelry emanating from her earrings through the comm.

"Open the door. We can try to stop him," Ras said.

"He'll kill me, then you," she replied.

"Mother," Foster called out, his voice barely reaching the comm unit. "It's time."

India released the button on the wall, cutting off the conversation, then began to walk away. That ship's leaving meant the death of Atmo.

"Carter, we have to tear this door down," Ras said.

The Elder began to repeatedly throw his shoulder into the reinforced door, only managing to cause a slight bulge with each punishing strike. Between lunges, Ras could see India standing at the ramp of the airship as Foster lowered the gangplank.

The monster unholstered the Energy beam pistol from his thigh and walked to the bottom of the walkway. He gave no indication of acknowledgement of the pounding door but merely leveled the gun at India, uttering something that didn't reach the comm unit.

Ras could barely stomach the scene. He looked away, but a raucous crash brought his attention back to the porthole. The Kingfisher's shuttle skidded to a halt against the primed airship, crashing in at an awkward angle. Foster was nowhere to be seen, possibly pinned between the two vessels.

India Bravo stood in shock, backing up as the door to the shuttle opened, revealing an Elder.

"Seraphina!" Carter called out. "What are you doing?"

"That's not Seraphina," Ras said, watching the Elder blow a kiss his way. "That's Dixie."

The shuttle lurched away, revealing an undamaged Foster. Dixie instinctively sidestepped the Illorian vessel as it skidded past her, then pivoted and threw her shoulder into Foster, pinning him once more to the airship and forcing him to drop the Energy pistol.

India made a dash for the gun, but with a free arm, Dixie swatted her, knocking her to the deck five feet away.

Dixie reached back to punch, but Foster was quicker, already free from her grasp and scrambling toward a row of jetcycles in the back of the bay. Dixie stood her ground as Foster revved up a jetcycle and sped toward the open air.

She raised both fists high in the air, then brought the double-hammer down on the zooming jetcycle's engine, which squealed and coughed as it imploded. Sparks flew, and the sudden change in momentum threw Foster over the handlebars of the vehicle. He landed next to India, who had busied herself with attempting to collect the Energy pistol.

Dixie leveraged the powered suit to heft the ruined jetcycle to throw it at Foster, whose back was to the open sky. If only she could push him out, he would be stuck. She flung the machine toward him, but a couple blasts from the Energy pistol, which Foster had wrested away from his mother, ripped through the jetcycle, breaking it into two halves. Dixie was a blur, sliding under the wreckage and throwing a shoulder into Foster, almost knocking him off the edge of the hangar.

Carter finally burst through the bay door, and Dixie used the opportunity of surprise to grasp India Bravo by the throat, holding both her and Foster out of the hangar and over the open air.

"People used to tell me that I should forgive and let go," Dixie's mechanical voice came through the suit. "One out of two ain't bad."

A blast from Foster's Energy pistol evaporated the right forearm of the Elder suit. Dixie screamed as Foster's only point of contact with the ship disappeared and he plummeted out of the bay and into the sky.

"Dixie!" Ras shouted. His mind immediately went to the moment his father lost his leg to that pistol and began to overload. He couldn't save his father until he had Callie's help.

"Easy," Dixie said, fidgeting to reveal her arm, fully there, poking through the burned off Elder limb. "They make these suits for much bigger people than me." She used her free hand to disengage the helmet. It clanked to the floor behind her, revealing her beaming face.

"Dixie," Ras said, his smile disappearing. "Your eyes." A pit formed in his stomach as he saw the tinge of a green glow begin to form around the edges of her usually-violet eyes.

"What?" she asked shakily.

Ras ran up to her, looking for a place to undo the back of the suit. He saw the exit wound of the Energy beam on the side of her midsection.

She looked down at her suit. "Must have got me when he shot the bike," she said. She gritted her teeth and focused on India. "Oh, this would have been such a glorious day otherwise." Swallowing hard, she forced a smile. "Do you know why I'm smiling?"

India gurgled a response, still clawing at the vise-like grip surrounding her throat.

"I smile because I know that out of every city you dropped, every life you've ruined, and every ship you destroyed, you couldn't sink Dixie Piper," she said. "Yeah, remember that name."

"Dixie," Ras said softly. "If I step away, you're going to overload."

Dixie looked over to Ras, eyes glowing green. A tear rolled down her cheek, then evaporated as her smile faded. She looked back at India. "This is for my parents," she said, squeezing her grip tighter. "For all of *Solaria*, and for all of Atmo." She stared at India for a moment. "Goodbye."

With that, she released India into the abyss below.

After the scream faded into the howling wind, Dixie collapsed backwards onto the deck with a loud clang. She began breathing quickly. "Ras? I can't see anything. Why can't I see anything?" She shut her eyes tight, but the glow of the light illuminated her eyelids. Energy began to coalesce over her skin. "Ras, please don't forget me. Promise me you won't forget me."

Something caught in Ras' throat. "How could I?" he asked with a bittersweet chuckle. "How could anyone? Just don't go causing too much trouble wherever you're going next, yeah?"

"I make no promises," Dixie said, then curled her lip into a brave smile. "You better put those goggles on, boy. It's time for me to shine like the stars."

Ras lowered his KnackVisions to see the Energy from outside coming in to swirl around her, dancing over her body. He slowly stood, taking a step back.

With a blast of wind, Dixie Piper was no more.

CHAPTER SIXTEEN
The Return

RAS FOCUSED ON THE CLOUDS. NUMB. EVERYTHING WAS FALLING apart. The allies he needed were either imprisoned or dead or had turned against him. *Would it be such a bad thing to submit myself to Hal?* It had been the Elders' duty to guard the Time Origin: certainly they would know what to do if things went wrong with it.

"It always ends this way, doesn't it?" Guy asked, snapping Ras back into the present on the bridge of the flagship. "The good ones leave you."

Ras looked over at Guy, who didn't bother to wipe away the tear streak from under his good eye.

"I should have let her come," Ras said.

"No," Carter said from behind. "She would have been on the same side of that barrier as us. Atmo would have been lost."

Guy looked at Ras, eye bloodshot. "I'd like to think, in a world without people like Foster, or India, that someone like her and maybe someone like me…"

"I know," Ras said quietly. The sad fact was that both Dixie and Guy were byproducts of the wake of destruction from the Helios family. They had been survivors, and survivors needed each other. They needed hope, which was something Ras didn't know if he could provide anymore.

"Do you think we could rename this ship?" Guy asked.

"Don't see why not," Ras said. "Have something picked out?"

"*The Piper.*"

Ras nodded. "She would have liked that."

"I'm taking the refugees to *Verdant*," Guy said. "Can't leave them here."

"You're going to need Finn to look after the injured."

"Yeah," Guy said, briefly diverting his eye to Ras.

Two more crew members gone. "Guy, can you make sure all of the refugees are in one place? I want to talk to them."

"Maybe the comm system still works," Guy said.

"No, I need to see them," Ras said. "In person."

Guy nodded, then for a reached for the comm. "Everyone aboard, head to the mess hall," he said, his voice broadcasting throughout the ship. "The Captain has something he'd like to say."

"Ras, we've already spent too much time here," Carter protested. "The Illorians aren't going to be much longer, and after they arrive, I can't protect you."

Ras looked up at the large machine man. Despite the weariness that threatened a physical and emotional collapse, he managed a sad smile. "I'm done running, Carter. Especially from friends. Even if we can fly all the way back to *Nalon* and find Dixie's ship, it gives Foster a longer opportunity to find a way up to Atmo to wreck it." He paused. "If you want to get out of here, I'll understand."

"No," Carter said. "I'll stand by my actions." He paused. "Are you sure Foster is still alive?" Carter asked. "People don't survive falls like that."

"He somehow survived one like that before, so I can't take chances," Ras said. "Why don't you go see if Finn can wake up Callie while I think about what needs to be said?"

THE DINING HALL WAS CRAMPED, standing room only. Ras stepped atop the centermost table, surveying the hundreds of Masonians. He could see people huddled in the hallways outside, peering in. That was all right. His message would carry.

It had to.

"Citizens of Mason," Ras began. "In the face of loss, we find ourselves empty-handed. We wonder how things will go on. And they won't. At least not how they used to. I'm sure one hundred years ago that same conclusion was reached. But you have to ask yourself how you're still standing here today, even after this tragedy. And it's because one hundred years ago they didn't give up, even when it felt like the end. Even when it felt like their friends and family were gone forever, and even when they didn't know if they had it in themselves to take one more step. Because what's the alternative? Death?"

He shook his head. "Death may win this round, but it won't win this war. Not if we have hope.

"I know you have brothers and sisters scattered across the sky right now, doing the best they know how in the fight against Atmo. Up there, Governor Bartleby was known by the name India Bravo. She made decisions that have drastically affected so many throughout this world, but as of half an hour ago, she's not able to make those decisions. You're going to have to look elsewhere for a safe harbor, which is why I'm putting you in the capable hands of…" He trailed off, looking to Guy. "What's your last name?" he whispered.

"Masterson," Guy said.

"Captain Guy Masterson." Ras motioned for Guy to join him atop the table. "Captain Masterson will fly this ship to the last safe haven in this world," Ras said. "A floating city named *Verdant*." This drew muttering from the crowd. "The city is used to taking in people who need a place to stay. This doesn't have to be permanent, but until the monster responsible for the destruction of Mason, Tefka, and Einaud is brought down, *Verdant* is the only option left."

"Why?" an elderly man from the crowd shouted out.

"Because every other city above the clouds is fueled by Convergences, and those can be controlled like they were in Mason. *Verdant* has no Convergences near it so it can't run out of fuel as long as there's the Origin putting Energy on the wind. The other cities make fuel from Convergences by connecting children to them," Ras said, eliciting gasps and murmurs from the crowd. "This process must be stopped before those Convergences can be destroyed, or the atrocities like what happened today will continue. Humanity can't keep suffering like this. Not when we choose to stand up against evil."

A long pause reigned over the crowd, but then, Ras didn't expect applause.

"You're getting better at the speech thing," Guy whispered.

"It helps when you have the truth at your back," Ras said. "You're going to need to do a lot of reconvincing along the way."

"Maybe they'll be used to following someone with an eyepatch."

Ras suppressed a chuckle at the rare humor from Guy. Such levity didn't feel called for yet so soon after the loss of Dixie. "Guy, thanks for being part of my crew."

"Can't say it wasn't interesting," Guy said.

"You going to be all right with this?"

"I'd rather they see what *Verdant* is like than become sky pirates," Guy said, looking over the crowd. He paused. "Good luck, Ras. You're going to need it."

Ras cocked his head at the honest well-wishing. "I'll take it." He stepped down from the table to walk among the refugees. They parted as he approached. The men, women, and children reminded him of the ones from *Verdant*, just looking for a place to continue life.

One man smiled at Ras, nodding slightly. *Is that a look of hope?* he wondered, nodding back to the man. It was what these people needed, and if Ras was being honest, he needed it more than the rest of them.

They just want to believe someone is working for their best interest, Ras mused. If he chose to listen to India Bravo, hope was dead and gone. He couldn't believe that. There were still Convergences to take care of, and until they were dealt with, he couldn't rest.

THE FAINT ROCKING MOTION of Callie's bed gently transitioned her from a dream about riding on a raft into the waking world. The room looked like the one she slept in on *The Kingfisher*, but dingier. The sounds of a baby's laughing filtered softly through the walls.

Light came in through the lone porthole, shining directly onto one of her legs, warming it more than the other. She shifted, startling someone sitting in the corner.

"Miss Calista," a familiar voice said. "It's good to have you still with us. I was afraid we might have lost you."

Callie blinked twice, focusing her eyes on the man sitting, leaning forward. He brushed his hand over his buzzed hair, then looked expectantly at her. "Carter?"

Carter smiled. "How are you feeling?"

Understanding returned to Callie, and she whipped her head to the side. "Where are we? What happened to Mason?" The sudden jerk flared up the pain in her forehead. She slowly reached up and felt a bandage had been applied. "What happened to me?"

"To answer your questions in turn," Carter said. "You are on my ship, *The Firefinch*. Mason is lost, but your Ras is taking care of the survivors."

"And this?" Callie asked, pointing to her head as she slowly sat up.

"The more recent wound was from a skiff accident, I'm told," he said. "The longer term effect is one that I'm honestly surprised you've survived with for this long."

"I know I'm a Time Knack," Callie said. "Or a Conduit, I think Illorians call it—"

"No, Calista," Carter said softly, seemingly sensitive to her headache. "Do you remember when the Elders used you as a weapon against The Collective three months back?"

Callie furrowed her brow. How could she forget being strapped into that sphere, pain wracking her body with each Time-stopping shot the Elders fired in that short-lived war? "What about it?"

"You were injected with something," Carter said. "Under Fleet Commander Archer's orders. I heard him say you couldn't be used as a weapon without it."

"I definitely remember the needle," Callie said. "What did it do?"

"It expanded your capacity to overload," Carter said. "He assumed it would kill you. That's why I went off to find Ras like I did. When it turned out that you had survived, I assumed that the Fleet Commander had simply been mistaken. But seeing you like this…" Carter spread his hands apologetically. "He may have been right after all. I'm sorry. If I had thought it still posed a danger to you, I would have told you."

Callie took a deep breath. "Do you know where the thing they injected me with came from?"

"They found it with the Outsider weapon when they took it from The Collective," Carter said.

It explained why she was suddenly able to reach out so far with her overloads. Adding Dr. Lupava's Lack serum into the mix may have altered her overload orientation from Time to Lack, but not her range. "What am I supposed to do?"

"Not overload anymore, would be my guess."

"But Ras needs me to stop the Convergences."

"He's The Reclaimer," Carter said. "I'm sure he'll figure something out." He paused. "I just wanted to let you know all of this before it was too late."

"How did you find us?" Callie asked.

The sound of a shuttle's docking with *The Firefinch* drew Carter's attention. "I had some help," he said. The sound of heavy footfalls accompanied the shaking of the room as two men in Elder suits stood outside Callie's doorway.

"What's going on?" Callie asked.

"These men are with Halcyon," Carter said. "They will take you to him."

"What about Ras?" Callie asked. "Atmo isn't safe yet."

Carter moved to sit beside Callie on the bed, weighing it down considerably. "Hal is taking over the mission." He leaned in and hugged her. "I didn't have a choice," he whispered. "Trust Ras over Hal."

Callie nodded. "I understand."

FROM THE SHUTTLE'S WINDOW, Callie watched *The Firefinch* fly alongside as they ascended above the Illorian fleet and into the field of puffy, white clouds. The sky looked clean, devoid of the atrocities perpetrated below. She wondered if anyone would even have a good reason to travel up this way again if the ground became home once more.

A solitary Elder vessel hung high above the clouds. The shuttle made its way to the flagship. The Elder pilot said something in Illorian, received a reply, then altered course to dock with the larger vessel. Callie was trying to see if she could spot *The Kingfisher* anywhere when the enveloping ship eclipsed her view.

The pilot acted as an escort, leading Callie through the immaculate white hallways to a large, circular door. "Callie!" a familiar voice shouted.

Old Harley hobbled up from the side hallway. Without another word, he threw his arms around Callie. "I thought we lost you."

"I'm still around," Callie said. She noticed his wet eyes as he released his embrace. "What's wrong?"

"Oh, nothing to bother you with, Miss Calista," Old Harley said. "I...I just wish that I could still help Ras. The boys and I put up a fight to keep *The Kingfisher*—"

"What happened to the ship?"

"Hal said he needed it," Old Harley said, "and he's running things now. If you see Ras before I do, will you tell him he's been a fine captain?"

The circular door slid open, revealing a large chamber that reminded Callie a little of the courthouse back on *Verdant*. "I will," she said. "I think he'd be very glad to hear that."

Old Harley bowed low with a formal sweep.

The escort ushered Callie into the auditorium. Inside, Hal Napier leaned against a circular table in the middle of the room. His dark brown smoking jacket had been replaced with a stark white military uniform, decorated heavily over his heart in a variety of colors. He still kept his hair and beard trimmed short, and the color of them almost matched the white of his outfit.

The stern expression etched across his face softened slightly as he noticed Callie enter. He gave a dismissive gesture, and the Elder clomped back and closed the door behind him.

"Calista," Hal said, standing and motioning to one of the empty chairs of the tall wooden table. She obediently approached.

"Where is Ras?" she demanded.

"His shuttle should be along shortly," Hal said. He looked older than she remembered. Almost unhealthy, but still great for someone born one hundred sixty-four years ago.

"Why am I here?" Callie asked, slipping into a chair. "We have to stop the rest of the Convergences before it's too late."

"I'm afraid we have more pressing matters at hand," Hal said, making his way to the other side of the table and sitting down across from her.

"More important than saving Atmo?"

"Currently the Illorian fleet is busy shooting down any launching airship over Mason in an effort to keep Foster Helios grounded," Hal said. "What happened?"

Callie opened her mouth to respond, then pictured anyone who might have survived the Convergences in Mason only to be shot down when they finally had an opportunity to escape. "Foster was controlling the Convergences that used to be buried beneath the city…Ras did his best to stop everything—"

"I'm certain he did," Hal said. "The boy is tenacious, I'll give him that." He paused for a moment, then placed a fist to his mouth, coughing hard several times.

"Are you all right?"

"I'm fine. Old age," Hal said, waving a hand dismissively.

From behind, a scuffle of Elder suits could be heard. One of the double doors slammed open. "Let me go!" Ras shouted. "Do you not understand what voluntary means?"

"Ras!" Callie said, turning to stand. She wanted to run up and hug him, to let him know that she was all right, but all she could do was stand.

"Callie!" Ras said, wresting his arm free from the Elder's grasp and skidding into the room only feet away from her. He stood, arms tense at his sides. "I wish there was some other way than hugging to show you that I miss you right now."

"Your eyes say it," Callie said. "And your mouth kind of did too." The tension in her shoulders relaxed slightly as she imagined a painless embrace from him. "Did you stop Foster?"

"Yes, Erasmus," Hal said, "I would very much like to hear your account."

Ras pursed his lips. "We delayed him after he left Mason."

"We?" Callie asked. "You and Carter did?"

"Carter, Guy, myself," Ras said, then paused, "and Dixie."

Callie looked around. "Did they come on the shuttle with you here?"

Ras shook his head solemnly. "Guy is taking the survivors from Mason to *Verdant*. Dixie...she stopped Foster from escaping, but..." He cut himself off the way he normally did when trying to deliver tough news.

"No," Callie said, a pit developing in her stomach.

"Foster had his Energy pistol," Ras said. "I couldn't stop him." He sat down in one of the open chairs across from Hal. "She bought Atmo some more time, but we have to destroy the rest of the Convergences before Foster can use them to overload every Atmo city."

Tears began forming in Callie's eyes. She had seen so much senseless death in the past few days. So many lives had been lost, and the fullness of the tragedy hadn't solidified until now. She had lost a friend, and the pain made it difficult to breathe. The agony felt by those who had lost entire families would have to be immeasurable.

She didn't know whether those who had overloaded or those left behind were the more fortunate ones.

"Hal, I need *The Kingfisher* back," Ras said. "We have to save the children from the fueling platforms, then drop the Convergences to the ground safely, then—"

"*The Kingfisher* is needed in the Illorian fleet for now," Hal said.

Callie knew what that grinding of Ras' jaw meant; she'd seen it many times before, always as he was in the process of losing the final scrap of his patience. "How do you expect me to stop Foster?" he shouted. "If I can't do that, then everything that's gone wrong was for nothing."

Hal stared at Ras. "May I ask you to be mindful of where you are and with whom you are speaking?" His voice took a hard edge. "Why didn't you tell us you had overloaded next to the Time Origin after *The Winnower* began to fall?"

"Why does that matter?" Ras asked.

Hal half closed his eyes, taking a deep breath. "The Elder Council was formed one thousand years ago to protect...to *guard* the Time Origin," he said. "We were tasked as the jail keepers of something very powerful."

"What kind of *something*?" Ras asked.

"Death, if you like literal translations," Hal said.

"Well, that makes sense," Ras said, standing and placing his palms on the table.

"What do you mean?" Callie asked, wondering if Ras had somehow found Dayus' translated book about the Thromus.

"How many times have we heard that '*The Reclaimer brings Death*' now?" Ras asked. "I can't seem to avoid it."

Hal gave a deep sigh, then coughed violently. "If you're basing your decisions off of folklore, then we're all doomed."

"Are you saying Ras isn't The Reclaimer?" Callie asked.

"I'm saying whether or not there is even such a thing as a Reclaimer is neither here nor there," Hal said, waving a hand dismissively. "We have a direct issue, and you two are the only ones who can solve it."

"We've already tried fighting Foster," Ras said. "The man doesn't die. I've run him over with a skiff, Dixie choked him with an Elder suit and dropped him from who knows how high..."

"And he's currently running around Mason, trying to find a way out," Hal said. "We've already lost a few of our suited men on the ground to him."

"I guess it's hard to die when you have Death on your side," Callie said.

"Dayus mentioned Foster was near the Time Origin when you overloaded," Hal said.

"But if that has made Foster invincible," Callie said, looking to Ras, "then wouldn't we have the same kind of ability?"

"Dixie was close too," Ras said quietly, "and that didn't save her."

"Wait," Callie said. Her mind reeled. Something had to make sense. She closed her eyes, trying to remember the images from Dayus' book. The intricate equations came to mind. *Serums.* If she couldn't tell Ras, for whatever reason, she would lead him in that direction like a good navi. "What if something made him this way before we overloaded?"

Ras pointed at her. "India Bravo mentioned something about how Foster tinkered with medicine..."

"Lupava?" Callie asked.

"Lupava," Ras said.

"What about him?" Hal asked.

"Do we know much about his serums?" Ras asked, looking to Callie.

Callie knew the calculations were just translations of Napier's materials. She lifted an eyebrow at Hal. "You tell us."

"He...did work with some of the more fringe elements of science," Hal said, scratching at his beard. "We don't know everything he was capable of."

"He could expand someone's overload radius and turn a Time Knack into a...you know," Callie said, grimacing an apology to Ras.

"A Lack," Ras said. "If he could change the basic elements about a person, why couldn't he make someone incredibly strong?"

"Well, you were able to defeat him before he fell off *The Winnower*," Callie said, then quickly amended, "I'm not saying that you weren't strong, it's just that he—"

"I know, I know," Ras said. "Trust me, he's much more powerful now. And he's much more confused now."

"It's possible Lupava did something to him," Hal said, "but we cannot rely solely on this theory."

"We could go to *The Winnower* and see what Lupava has left in his lab," Ras said. "Callie and I are the only ones who can get in that frozen fortress—"

"*Sideways* frozen fortress," Hal amended.

"Yeah, it would be tricky to navigate, but nobody else would bother us. Do you have a better plan?" Ras asked.

"A safer plan," Hal said. "Not necessarily better. Before The Clockwork War, Illoria had developed a weapon designed as a second line of defense in case we needed to suspend something indefinitely." He placed his elbows on the table, making a dome with his hands. "A...

Time bomb, if you will. It had a freezing blast radius that could cover a large city. Some in Illoria advocated its use against Mason during the war, but thankfully it never came to that."

"So where is it?" Callie asked, feeling she already knew the answer. She wondered if this was the weapon Dayus had warned her about.

"A place best suited for exploration by people with your unique attributes," Hal said, crossing his arms. "Caelum."

"You want us to go into the Illorian capitol?" Ras asked.

The ghost city full of frozen men, women, and children still haunted Callie. "How would we even get this weapon free?" she asked.

"The heavy lifting can be done by the powered suits once the city has been reclaimed," Hal said.

"Hold on," Callie said. "Are you suggesting we unfreeze the Elders? All of them?"

"I am," Hal said.

The assertion gave Callie a phantom pang of pain, imagining having to overload yet again. Something felt off about the plan.

"Are they ready for that?" Ras asked. "Won't they rip Atmo apart?"

"They can be reasoned with," Hal said. "Unlike Foster. If he can indeed control Convergences, then we are running out of options."

"So what happens to the place that gets frozen?" Ras asked. "Everybody around Foster gets stuck forever too?"

Hal pursed his lips. "It's better than having this world go up in flames," he said. "Sometimes sacrifices have to be made. If there was a perfect solution, we wouldn't have had the Clockwork War in the first place."

"How long would they live?" Callie asked. "The Illorians, I mean."

"What do you mean?" Hal asked.

"When Dayus found me and the other children on the train," Callie said. "I was the only one who lived because I moved next door to Ras." She took a deep breath. "If we unfroze Caelum, how long would it take until everyone got sick like the rest of the children?" *How long would my parents live* was the more pressing question on her mind.

Hal pursed his lips, nodding. "They should have years, maybe a decade until they start to feel the effects."

"Why don't we just have the people from the Burrows annex with them?" Ras asked. "Tefka, Einaud, and whoever else is Blessed could keep them alive as long as they don't mind living with Imagoites."

"I'm afraid some of them might choose death over that," Hal said.

"Then it's their fault if they do," Ras said.

"How long would the Time bomb effect last?" Callie asked.

"Fifty years? A hundred?" Hal asked. "I'm not sure."

"What would keep the Elders from finishing a subjugation of Atmo after they stop Foster?" Ras asked. "Assuming they would live long enough to try."

"Erasmus, your plan requires there to not even be an Atmo in less than a week," Hal said.

"Except for *Verdant*," Ras said. "Still, assuming the device works, what would the Illorians do after all of this?"

"I suppose that depends on whether or not they have a country to come back to," Hal said. "These are things we can figure out later after this situation—"

"'*Figure out later*' is the reason I've had to keep unraveling this problem one layer at a time just to find another stopgap *solution* ready to blow up in my face," Ras said, ramping into a full shout. "If I don't find the right fix, the next generation will have to deal with this mess, and I'm not putting this on them. Not when they have so much going against them already." Ras stood, slamming his palms on the table.

"Erasmus, you broke the Time Origin," Hal said, carefully enunciating. "Who knows what ramifications that will ultimately bring to this world? Will we age after Time runs out? Will we simply keel over? We don't know. There might not be a next generation."

"Then let's stop Foster first," Ras said. "I can only try to save the world from one existential threat at a time."

"By going to Lupava's lab on *The Winnower*," Callie asserted, giving Hal as stern of a look as she could muster.

"Fine," Hal said. "But immediately afterward you must go to Caelum. Even if you find something of use in that laboratory, we need the Time bomb."

"Are you wishing you had picked someone else to collect wind from The Wild now?" Ras asked.

Hal looked up, the deep lines around his eyes making him look weary. "What's done is done," he said. "I do not have the luxury to form regrets."

CALLIE BUCKLED IN THE RESTRAINT on the back bench of the shuttle as Ras started the ignition sequence. She looked out the porthole at Hal, flanked by two men in Elder suits. The shuttle broke away from the Illorian capital ship and she watched the men shrink away as they launched.

Next to her sat a box of supplies Hal had left for them. It was mostly grapple gun cabling and charges along with a few rations. "If you want, I can reload your—"

"I can't do this, Callie," Ras said. "I can't give up, but every choice I make leads to more people dying. The world is falling apart because—"

"Because there is a madman running around killing people," Callie said. She knew that, if left unchecked, Ras could spiral into despondency.

Ras looked back at Callie from the front seat, pain in his eyes. "I can't lose you too."

Callie unbuckled her restraint and moved forward to sit beside Ras. "Don't worry, I'll be careful not to touch you."

Ras shifted over, allowing space for her to sit.

Silence prevailed for a couple of moments before Callie spoke. "I'm sorry I wasn't there to save Dixie," she said. "I mean, I know I couldn't have been, but…I miss her."

"Me too," Ras said, unable to choke out more without breaking his composure.

"I'll miss her spunkiness, her bossy attitude, and even the way she'd make me jealous for you," Callie said, stifling a sniff with a short laugh. "What about you?"

Ras sighed. "Do we have to do this?"

"I think we owe it to her," Callie said. "She deserves at least some sort of remembrance…even if it's just us. I just wish I had gotten a proper goodbye with her."

Ras nodded, setting the ship to autopilot. "All right," he said, staring down at the shuttle console. "She was annoying, insubordinate, infuriating…but one of my best friends, and I wouldn't have changed a thing about her." He sighed, looking over to Callie. "I'm glad she found closure with India Bravo."

"They reconciled?" Callie asked.

Ras smirked. "More to Dixie's liking than India's, I'm sure." He held out his arm in a choking motion, then opened his hand, miming India's fate. "It was a bit gruesome, now that I think back on it."

"But Dixie made sure India couldn't hurt anybody else ever again."

"Yeah," Ras agreed. "We renamed the Bravo Company flagship *The Piper*."

"I think she would have liked that."

Ras shrugged. "Then again, she probably would have preferred we named it *The Pretty Princess Petunia 2*."

"She did have a sense of humor," Callie said.

"I just wish it hadn't developed as a coping mechanism for everything she'd been through," Ras said. "She used to cross her eyes at me when she thought I was taking myself too seriously as Captain."

"You did take the role pretty seriously," Callie said, then lifted her eyebrows. "Not to say you shouldn't have. You just kept so much of the weight on your shoulders, and I think most of us wished you had shared it more."

"Well, next time I assemble a crew to save the world, I'll do that."

Callie gave a soft smile. "I like to think we're back down to a crew of two, like old times." She wondered how long it would last.

"You want me to share my burdens?" Ras said. "My deep, dark, super serious Captain's problems?"

Giving a mock salute, Callie smiled. "First Mate and Navi Calista Tourbillon, reporting for duty."

Ras apparently wasn't in the mood for levity. "I'm afraid I'm never going to get to hold you again," he said somberly. "I know the world's at stake, and I might have unleashed Death itself, but I can't imagine having to spend the rest of my life at arm's length from you so soon after things were finally taking a turn for the better." He let his eyes settle on the windshield. "I can't go to Caelum."

"But what about the Time bomb and refreezing Foster—"

"If setting Caelum free means losing you when we overload, I'm not willing to risk that," Ras said. "I couldn't live with myself if I let that happen."

"Do you ever feel like we're pawns in someone's big game?"

Ras looked over to her. "A little bit."

Silence fell as the shuttle rocketed toward the cliffs that formed the barrier between Imago and Illoria. Flying in had been such an ordeal before. Memories of not too long back flooded Callie. The white train, Dixie's betrayal, the Elders, the Second Clockwork War. Her eyes immediately shot open and she lunged for the ship's controls, pulling the shuttle out of autopilot, jerking them hard to the side.

Ras grabbed at the controls. "What are you doing?"

"Look. We almost flew into my invisible Time minefield," Callie said, pointing to the remains of Bravo Company and The Collective's fleet. "If we had hit it one of those frozen Time pockets, the two of us would have been smashed against the windshield."

"Thanks for remembering that," Ras said. He scanned the horizon. "I keep looking for purple light from the Time Origin. I guess it's not there anymore." He piloted the shuttle upward to gain a better vantage point. "It should be just past those mountains."

Ahead, the topmost part of *The Winnower* could barely be seen. The giant fuel creation station that formerly trapped all the Energy from the Energy Origin had been wrecked when it lost its fuel source upon Callie's very first Lack overload with Ras. Foundering in thick Time, it stayed exactly where Callie last remembered it.

As the shuttle moved forward, more of the sideways vessel crested over the top of the mountain range, looking like a large metallic ring.

A ring with the bottom quarter missing.

"What in Atmo?" Callie muttered. The shuttle cleared the mountain range, revealing the dark purple spire of the Time Origin, no longer pulsing like a living creature. Shards and chunks of *The Winnower* lay strewn around it.

"Hey, I can see half of my house from here," Ras said, pointing to the wreckage of *The Brass Fox*.

The ship lurched forward, as though speeding up, although no changes were evident on the control panel.

"What's going on?" Callie asked.

"As best I can tell, the Time Origin stopped sending out...Time."

It had been explained to Callie that the Time Origin actually ebbed out friction, and the thicker that friction was, the harder it was to move through it. She guessed it was easier to just consider it as Time, especially with the Thromus connotation. "Maybe it projects the Time out from itself," she said, "and since we broke it, the Origin stopped doing that."

"Yeah, I think we just entered the bubble where there's no thick Time," Ras said.

Callie pointed up. "So, the part where *The Winnower* is missing…"

"…is where Time is literally running out."

CHAPTER SEVENTEEN
The Derelict

RAS SHIVERED ONCE AS HE LANDED THE SHUTTLE AT THE TOP OF *The Winnower*. He took a moment to reload his grapple gun, then spent a good five minutes coercing the door to open in the thick Time. Disembarking from the shuttle, he walked to the edge of the sideways disc and looked over the side.

"What are you doing?" Callie asked.

"Seeing how far I fell," Ras said, eyeing the distance. Small pangs of vertigo played at him, which felt a far cry better than the abject terror that heights used to cause him. He checked his new grapple gun cabling out of habit, then tapped his glider and wrench as a reminder they were still on his person.

"I forgot how eerie things sound in thick Time," Callie said, clapping her hands in front of her experimentally.

Ras almost asked her to stop, worried it would alert someone. But the sound wouldn't travel quickly, so anyone still onboard couldn't hear them anyway. He walked over to a broken window, which looked to be their most likely entrance. The interior was somewhat dark, but the opposite wall was only a ten-foot drop.

Retrieving a long coil of rope from the shuttle, Ras returned to the makeshift entrance, then took the end of the rope and tossed it as high as he could. The rope froze about a foot above where he let go. Giving it a tug only moved it a slight amount, and he noted that the further down he climbed, the more of the rope would be anchored in Time.

Placing all of his weight on the rope, Ras quickly descended into the darkness, letting go of the rope when his toes touched the surface of the far wall. "Your turn," he called up.

Callie wrapped her legs around the rope, shimmying down until her feet reached the wall next to where Ras stood. "I guess we need to be extra careful not to touch right now, huh?" she asked.

"What, aside from maybe killing you, all it would do is create a Time-free pocket big enough for this monstrosity to crash to the ground with us in it..." Ras shrugged. "Right. No touching." He looked throughout the disheveled room. No frozen people, just a lot of upended tables and chairs. He pulled India Bravo's knife from his boot, then cut the rope. Picking up the rest of the coil, he slung it over his shoulder. "This trick might come in handy again."

They exited through a sideways door and found the hallway was only a small drop down to the opposite wall. Ras looked at the structure with a new level of disgust, knowing the machine had been cobbled together by downed Atmo cities. *I wonder if I'm walking on part of* Merron *right now.*

"Now we just need to find Dr. Lupava's lab," Callie said.

"We'll just have to ask someone," Ras said. "If we can find our way to one of the elevator shafts, we can have a bit more mobility." He continued to walk forward down the corridor that now eerily resembled a sideways version of *Verdant's* Engine. A beautiful curtain of sparks hung in the air around them. When Ras stepped too closely to one, it would shoot across the room until it left his sphere of influence.

Eventually, due to the circular nature of *The Winnower*, walking along the wall meant their path quickly began to slope downward. Ras halted just before the hallway dropped out entirely from beneath their feet.

"At least there aren't any green-eyed men this time," Callie said.

"If they show up, I'm blaming you for saying that," Ras said, unstrapping the rope from his shoulder and anchoring its edge in Time above himself. "Wait here for a second while I check for any elevator doors down there." He climbed down the rope, which almost ran out by the time he reached a bank of elevators nestled inward, allowing him a ledge to land on.

If he had to guess, they had probably traveled one-third of the way down *The Winnower*. Somewhere beneath him, the sideways amalgamation of cities was falling apart, and he hoped Lupava's lab wasn't among the pieces already scattered around the Time Origin.

Ahead, three figures were frozen in various states of escape from the elevator doors. The ceiling lights lit everything from his left, occasionally flickering on and off.

"Found someone! You can come down!" Ras shouted up the hallway. He watched Callie test the rope, then slowly descend toward him. Getting back up would be a challenge, but thankfully not an impossible one. As Callie continued to slide down, he turned to inspect the men.

Something caught Ras' eye, jolting him. But when he looked, it was just his own shadow on the floor to his right. He chuckled nervously, then looked back to see Callie reach the elevator bank, concluding her descent.

"They don't look like they're ready to hand out information," Callie said.

They walked toward the men stuck mid-scramble, faces masked in terror. The one still in the elevator shaft was looking back behind him into the dark.

"Maybe we should ask this one," Callie said, pointing to the man who had already cleared his way into the alcove.

"Sounds good," Ras said, then stepped over and placed a hand on the man's shoulder.

The officer jumped, then spun quickly to face Ras. "Wh-what? Who are you? How are you doing this?"

Ras didn't quite feel like explaining, but oddly felt he owed it to the man. "Since we're near the Time Origin, there's this—"

"Magic," Callie said quickly. "It's magic."

"Can you get me out of here?" the officer whispered, panic crinkling the edges of his words.

"We have to get to the lab level," Ras said. "Do you know which one it is?"

"Can you get me out of here?" the officer repeated, grabbing fistfuls of Ras' shirt.

Ras stepped back, freeing himself from the man's grasp. The officer froze in place once more. "Why do I get the feeling they're all going to react this way?"

"Let me try," Callie said, stepping to the youngest looking of the trio. "Why don't you stand back, maybe out of his sight?"

Ras obliged. "What are you going to do?"

"Just watch," she said, smiling. She knelt down to the young man half out of the elevator shaft and took a deep breath. Placing a finger on the young man's lips, she said, "Shhh. This is a special moment in the midst of chaos—"

"I know you!" the young officer said. "You were on the bridge! What's going on?" He finished scrambling to his feet, then grabbed Callie by the shoulders, shaking her.

Ras sprang into action, clamping down a hand on each of the young man's shoulders, then threw him away from Callie and into the bulkhead, where he froze.

"Wasn't expecting that," Callie said, smoothing out her shirt.

"What were you trying to do?" Ras asked, lifting an eyebrow.

"Make him think he was dreaming or something," she said. "I don't know, I read something like it in a book once."

"I'd appreciate it if you stuck to being just my dream girl," Ras said. "Wait, that came out wr—no, no that's what I meant," he said with a smile, then looked beyond the last officer. "If he recognized you from the bridge, we know—"

"Shh!" Callie said, holding a hand out. "Did you hear that?"

Ras' perpetually wind-whipped ears from being an airship pilot had slightly recovered since he began spending more time in an enclosed ship, but Callie's ears would be far keener. He shook his head.

"Tap-tap-tap-tap…Listen," Callie said, holding out a finger, tapping in the air.

Watching her hand, Ras could spot the rhythm among the slow roar of the crashing machine's being slowed down. "Where is it coming from?" Ras stood, looking down the dark elevator shaft. He pointed, raising his eyebrows to Callie as a question. She nodded.

Ras climbed down into the shaft, eventually finding his footing. *Why am I walking toward a creepy sound in the dark?* He dropped his KnackVisions over his eyes and the lines of Energy in the structure lit up around him.

Tap-tap-tap-tap. Pause. *Tap-tap-tap-tap.*

The fact that anything could make noise or even move that quickly in the current environment was off-putting. Instinctively, Ras pulled his wrench free from his thigh-holster. He didn't figure Foster's old guard of the Lack Squad soldiers could have somehow survived their imperfect serum, and even if they had, they should have starved months ago.

Taking cautious steps forward, Ras heard the tapping grow louder. Nothing registered on the KnackVisions. *Must be something outside of the shaft.* He turned back to see Callie still standing at the lighted entrance. "It's okay, I think the sound—"

"Look out!" Callie shouted.

"Ah-hah!" a voice exclaimed directly behind Ras.

Out of shock, Ras swung his wrench, solidly connecting with something, which caused him to scream, which in turn caused Callie to scream.

The tapping stopped.

"What did you do?" Callie cried, descending into the elevator shaft.

"It said, '*Ah-hah!*'" Ras shouted, pointing the wrench at the dark form crumpled before him. "What idiot shouts that and doesn't expect a wrench to the head?"

Callie jogged over, stopping at the body. She prodded it with her foot. "I think you killed him—"

"Ah-hah!" came the voice as the body sprang up from the ground.

Ras held the wrench directly in front of him, keeping the dark form away. "Who are you?"

The bit of light from the elevator bay allowed Ras to make out that the person in front of him was a balding man with a large, bushy beard wearing a faded white frock stained mostly red.

"Ras, it's Dr. Lupava," Callie cried out.

Lupava had already turned around and began running away down the shaft, four steps at a time, then a pause, then four more paces in short steps.

"But Dixie shot him," Ras said. "We both saw that. I mean, right?" He holstered his wrench. "Why can't people just stay dead? Everything would be a lot simpler if everybody just stuck to the rules."

"Where are you going?" Callie called, starting to chase after Lupava.

"Here and there," Lupava said. "Everywhere!" He stopped, then turned back to Ras and Callie. "Do I know you?" He paused, then smiled wide, lifting his beard. "Yes, yes, I do. You must have knocked loose my memory and good sense. Have you come back to pay me a visit?" he asked, wringing his hands.

"Strangely enough, yes, that's exactly why we're here," Ras said. *At least it is now.*

"Good! Good!" Lupava said, clapping his hands like a child. "Follow me. You'll have to excuse my sideways laboratory. It has, shall we say, made scientific breakthroughs far more interesting."

Callie gave Ras a worried look. He shrugged. "Why is he here?" she whispered.

"Doctor?" Ras asked, trailing behind. "Mind if I ask what you're still doing here? On a crashing ship. Frozen in Time."

"Frozen in Time?" Lupava asked, then threw his head back in an inappropriately long laugh. "There's no such thing as being frozen in Time. Quagmired by entropy. Slowed by friction, perhaps, but Time stops for no man!" He threw an outstretched finger into the air and practically skipped forward.

Ras decided to wait until they reached the floor containing Lupava's lab before he dared ask any further questions in case the mad scientist decided to suddenly become difficult. The wrench incident seemed to be forgotten or forgiven already. There was a little blood on the scientist's temple, but no wound seemed to be present.

They finally made it to the hallway, having to complete a small leap over a potentially lethal chasm and onto Lupava's doorframe.

"Ah, here we are," Lupava said, thrusting his arms forward. "Lab, sweet lab. I'm so glad it didn't go anywhere."

Ras looked at the disheveled room. Large glass jars contained men in various states of decomposition, all strapped down to gurneys similar to the ones he and Callie had endured onboard *The Halifax*. At the end of the line, two men appeared still to be alive. One was frozen mid-scream while the other struggled against his restraints, somehow immune to the thick Time.

"Do you know any of these men?" Lupava asked.

"I can't say I do," Ras said, eyes furtively searching for serum vials.

"Oh, they were very generously donated to the noble pursuit of science!" Lupava exclaimed.

"How are you still alive?" Callie blurted out. "We watched you get shot three months ago."

"Science!" Lupava said.

"What did you eat for the last three months?" Callie asked.

"Science!" Lupava repeated. "Well, there's a mess hall with non-perishables enough for the entire crew, which I now represent a much larger percentage of, so I justify stockpiling."

A loud rumbling emanated through the ship, followed by a slow groaning noise. More of *The Winnower* was struggling to break free, it seemed.

"Do you remember injecting Callie here with something the last time you saw her?" Ras asked, stepping over toward her.

Lupava squinted his eyes, then adjusted his thick glasses. "Yes. Talarpassus Q, I believe it was," he said. "The Lack Serum, as Foster so lovingly named it. I preferred the name *Void*." He held out a sweeping hand as though he imagined the word floating in front of him, then cocked his head. "Have you noticed any side effects?"

Callie nodded, which sent Lupava into a fit of squealing delight. "Marvelous!" He opened a drawer of a sideways desk, dumping papers on the wall. He picked up a pile, then discarded all but one. He fished a pen out from his white coat. "Please, describe them in full detail. I do love new data," he said. "They're so hard to come across as of late."

"Well, anytime I would touch Ras," Callie said, "I would overload, Time would regulate, and Convergences would dissipate."

Lupava's eyes went wide. "Those *are* quite the side effects..." He jotted something down furiously on the piece of paper. "Yes, yes, this would be due to the Lack serum being derived from our friend here," he said. "You are reaching the source of your serum, the way a Knack would react to Energy or a Conduit to Time."

"It's in a two mile radius," Ras said. "Give or take."

A low hum resounded from Lupava. "Sounds like someone has been mixing my serums," he said. "I gather there have been *other* side effects, then?"

"Headaches," Ras said.

"Hmm, well, yes, death is a side-effect of mixing and overuse," Lupava said casually. "If subjects One through Four could talk, they would confirm this themselves." He waved a hand as if greeting the dead men in the large glass domes. "But, for now you'll have to take my word."

"For now?" Callie asked.

"If subject number Six is any indicator..." Lupava paused, then turned his attention to the screaming at the end of the line. "Six! Sometimes you make it so difficult to think! Such inconsideration.

You'd think he would be more grateful for another shot at life." He sighed. "Then again, I might as well enjoy the relative peace until the rest of them come back and join the chorus."

"Did you test this *'come-back-from-the-dead'* serum on yourself?" Ras asked. "Out of curiosity."

Lupava gave a wide grin. "Yes. How did you know? Oh, yes, you were there when I was shot." He narrowed his eyes. "You weren't the one who shot me, were you?"

"No," Callie said, looking to Ras. "We were just as surprised as you."

Ras had a hunch forming, and so he slid his KnackVisions back over his eyes.

"Do you see a lab experiment about to blow up that I don't know about?" Lupava asked.

The KnackVisions showed Ras what he expected. Lupava was a dark silhouette, as were the two reanimated men. The decomposing subjects each had a small black blob within them, but it wasn't fully formed yet. "You gave this serum to Foster, didn't you?"

Lupava took a breath to say something, then held it. He furrowed his brow and cocked his head to the side. "Foster doesn't even know that. I thought it might be a wise insurance policy, as he's yet to produce an heir, and we can't have the world fall into complete disarray, now can we?"

"So, he's never going to die?" Callie asked.

"Oh, eventually his body will deteriorate. The Thromus serum isn't perfect," Lupava said, waving his hand dismissively.

"Thromus?" Ras asked, turning to Callie. "Wasn't that from—"

"My library book," she said quickly. Too quickly. "*Demons of Bogues*. He was the bogeyman."

"Oh, he was far more than that," Lupava said. "Foster was so enamored with the folklore of Thromus and Aura. So obsessed with Death himself. He always denied this was why we came to the Time Origin, but I had my suspicions." He sighed with a contented grin. "Such idiocy, believing a myth like that. Otherwise he was so brilliant."

Callie stood with jaw dropped, trying to form words. She looked over to Ras, then shut her mouth.

"What?" Ras asked.

Lupava continued. "I planned to give him the sister serum to put him out of his misery if things worsened to unacceptable levels. But in the beginning stages of the process, I dare say you could survive just about anything. Even death." He laughed heartily. "I named it ironically."

Callie shot Ras a look. "So, does this Thromus serum allow one to...communicate with Convergences?"

Lupava stood, walked over to a cabinet filled with syringes, and selected one filled with a gray liquid. "Oh, there are definitely voices." He looked about the room. "But they haven't been around since everything went...sideways."

The scientist stepped over to the container holding the sixth test subject. The glass had already been broken and Lupava stepped through. "Now, let's make room for fresh data!" He plunged the syringe into the screaming man's neck, silencing him.

Ras looked through the goggles, watching the black silhouette dissipate and break down. Lupava unstrapped the man from the gurney, then flipped him unceremoniously to the floor. The room fell silent.

"There, peace," Lupava said. "Now, Ras, you wouldn't mind climbing on the gurney for me? I'd hate to have to carry you." He made a muscle with his bicep and slapped it twice. "Although I could. This serum really does wonders. I just find physical labor distasteful."

"What about Callie?" Ras asked quickly.

"Excuse me?" Callie said, spinning to face Ras with eyes wide.

Ras gave her a slight wink. "I mean, you'll lose a valuable test subject if you don't nullify the...mixture of serums. After that we can test the anti-Thromus serum on me."

"Or I could just test that on her," Lupava said. "Excellent idea!"

"Ah, but in order for her to die, she'd need to overload, which would send this entire structure falling," Ras said. "You'd lose all of your data..."

Lupava stroked his beard. "There are many ways to induce death, but they wouldn't give me such clear test results...What do you propose?"

Ras thought for a moment. "Can you nullify the two serums in Callie?"

The scientist laughed. "Child's play."

"Ras," Callie whispered. "If we do that, we can't unfreeze Illoria."

"Trust me," Ras whispered back. "All right, Lupava. After she returns to normal, can she have the Talarpassy...?"

"Talarpassus Q," Lupava corrected. "You want her to become a Lack again?"

"We can't do science if she's frozen in Time, can we?" Ras asked.

"No, of course not."

Ras walked over to the cabinet of syringes filled with different colors. He spotted the gray liquid, noting two doses of them remained. Underneath them was the label Cholantankus Y. *Might as well have named it 'the Foster killer.'* He grabbed both, tucking one quickly underneath a strap on his grapple gun for later. "So, first we need the nullifier. Cholan..." he trailed off to allow Lupava to confirm he had grabbed the right serum.

"Yes..." Lupava said, warily. "It would nullify both the Talarpassus Q as well as the Epeendir B."

"Which gave her the overload range, yes?" Ras asked, walking the nullifying serum back to Lupava.

"That is correct," Lupava said. "I didn't know you took an interest in such things."

Ras offered the serum to Lupava as he caught Callie's eye, offering her a pitying look. "It's for science."

Lupava took the syringe, flicking it while expelling air bubbles. Some of the liquid trickled out. "Now, before I do this," Lupava said to Callie. "Are you willing to join Ras in my test for immortality?" He looked up, then bobbed his head to amend himself. "Well, relative immortality."

Callie took a deep breath, then held it and nodded.

"Great!" Lupava said, quickly plunging the nullifying syringe into her neck, eliciting a cry of pain.

Ras stepped forward to catch her as she collapsed backward. The floor beneath them groaned mightily for a moment, then a tremor shook the room. She was finally back to her old, Time Knack self. *No overload.* "Now, the Lack serum?" he asked, holding a barely conscious Callie.

"I think, to act as insurance, you should take the Thromus serum now," Lupava said. "To get yourself warmed up."

Though he had no intention of taking the death serum, Ras nodded. Then he considered for a moment. The concept of being on the same level as Foster was tempting. If he could plunge the nulli-fier into Foster, he'd even have the advantage and possibly be able to control Convergences. *But does the heartlessness come with the Thromus, or does it just amplify evil tendencies?* he wondered.

Ras put Callie on a wheeled chair and rolled her along with him. "If she doesn't stick by me, she'll Time overload," he explained as he looked through the cabinet once more. "It might be difficult to get a syringe in her." Several black syringes named Thromus lined the bottom row beneath the Lack serum. "Out of curiosity," Ras said,"what was the serum that expanded her range? Expander B?"

"Epeendir B, why?" Lupava asked.

Ras spotted it. "Just curious." He gave himself a moment for a quick mental calculation, then took action. In a swift motion, he grabbed the Lack serum in his right hand and the expander serum in his left. He plunged the former into Callie and the latter into himself. A rush of tingling caused him to suddenly become woozy and filled with pain as his Lack ability became amplified.

He swung his grapple gun covered arm into the row of Thromus serum syringes, shattering them and spilling black liquid onto the ground.

"You traitor to science!" Lupava howled and lunged forward at Ras with a surprising ferocity. Within seconds, Lupava was on top of Ras, throwing punch after punch.

Ras reached over for Callie's leg. Suddenly, the world become clearer as the expanding serum took effect and the rush of the over-load surged through him.

The Winnower lurched, and all of the halted sparks flared into motion as the world caught back up to speed. Ras kicked at Lupava, landing a square shot to the scientist's chest as the floor dropped away beneath them. Lupava went flying back into one of the glass containers. The wall underneath Ras shuddered, and he immediately let go of Callie's leg.

"Hold onto your chair!" Ras shouted as he lifted his grapple gun and aimed it at the wall high above them.

Lupava picked his way out of the glass shards and began his manic charge toward Ras and Callie.

Until the floor gave out.

Attached to the ceiling by cable, Ras used his free hand to hold on tight to the arm of Callie's chair. Lupava's scream was all that remained of him in the room as the Time-free zone sheared off the lab—and the rest of that layer of *The Winnower*.

Looking down at Callie gave Ras a terrifying view of how far he had to drop. With all that he had in him, Ras lifted Callie's chair high enough that he could activate the cable respooling. Callie tried to shift her weight by placing a foot on one of the cabinets bolted to the floor, only to have it snap free and dump out with the rest of the debris.

The cable retracted, allowing Ras to swing Callie in her chair to the doorway where she perched precariously. The view into the hallway was filled with daylight, indicating there was no floor out there either.

"Are you all right?" Ras called out over the deafening groan of metal all around.

"I'm definitely wide awake, if that's what you're worried about," Callie replied, sitting on the sideways door frame.

Ras swung his cable back and forth by pumping his legs until he reached the doorway, then released the cable. He sat down next to Callie, careful not to touch her. "The Lack serum treating you all right this time?" he asked.

"I think so," Callie said. She smiled. "No headache...I just feel tingly again."

Ras aimed his grapple gun high and fired it up the vertical hallway as far as he could. The magnet flew thirty feet, then froze in the air. "I think we found the bubble."

He began the cable's retraction, then took a death grip on one of the chair's arms. "Here, hold onto the other arm. Whatever you do, don't touch me."

Callie looped an arm around the chair, and Ras swung them into the hallway.

The corridor around them shook, then sheared free all around them as the next layer of *The Winnower* departed. They hung out in the open air thirty feet below the newest low point of the machine.

"I don't know how much longer I can hold onto this thing," Callie said, a look of pain playing across her features.

He didn't have the heart to tell her they were going to need to continue climbing for at least another half hour.

"Just hold on a little longer," Ras said. The strain of having Callie dangling and being pulled up by the grapple was beginning to wear on him. Something familiar played to his ears, but he couldn't quite place it.

"Ras, I—" Callie said, then broke into a scream as the arm of the chair snapped off and she fell beyond his grasp.

Without thinking, Ras released the cable, dropping into a free fall. He pulled his limbs into himself to pick up as much speed as possible to catch up with Callie, who had flattened herself out.

With the ground still a good half of a mile away, he sped over to her, grabbing hold of her calf and wrapping himself around her. The distance-boosted overload sent a wave of tingles throughout his body.

The overload began.

Above, the sound of *The Winnower* loosing itself from Time assailed his ears as the city-sized structure resumed toppling at full speed.

"What are you doing?" Callie cried.

"I'm not leaving you," Ras shouted. "Not now, not ever!"

The plan was idiotic. He loaded up a spike cartridge into the grapple gun and angled himself so they fell in the direction of the Time Origin. He could possibly grapple the spire, then wrap the cable around the tall structure until they reached the ground.

At least until *The Winnower* could come down and crush them.

The familiar sound buzzed louder, and Ras looked behind him to see a ship flying in their direction. "*The Kingfisher!*" he shouted, instantly changing his plan. Precious seconds were lost as he struggled to undo the body strap of the grapple gun, eke out some slack, and extend it around Callie's torso.

Changing the grapple from spike to magnet, Ras realized he wouldn't be able to make a shot for how long it would take *The Kingfisher* to reach them. He had to give the ship a target.

Angling his arm up toward *The Kingfisher*, Ras fired.

They continued to plummet. *The Kingfisher* fell under the shadow of *The Winnower*, diving to adjust for the lumbering behemoth. The magnet flew slack, then pulled the line taut as it reached out for a metal source to connect with.

Clink. The line connected with *The Kingfisher*, but they continued to fall as the ship roared by overhead.

Ras kicked in the cable retraction mechanism as he and Callie kept plummeting. *The Kingfisher* passed at top speed above them, immediately jerking Ras and Callie along in a trajectory that took them dangerously close to the tip of the Time Origin's spire.

Ras tightened his grip on Callie as shards of *The Winnower* started tumbling down around them. The groan of metal ripping apart reverberated throughout Ras as hunks of *The Winnower* fell on either side of him. The bulk of the massive machine hurtled downward.

The Kingfisher darted about through the debris, narrowly avoiding clipping one of the plummeting engines. A piece of hull crashed into the wire, jerking Ras forward and down until his line snapped.

Once more in free fall, Ras dislodged the glider and strained to work his feet into the straps. His momentum swung hard to the left as Callie threw her weight on his shoulders. A deafening explosion roared just to his right.

Spinning in the chaos of the wreckage, Ras felt the glider catch on the wind. He did his best to curb his descent as the remainder of *The Winnower* toppled around them. *The Kingfisher* had begun a loop around to starboard, and Ras threw his weight to his right leg, peeling away before the large glass dome of *The Winnower* could come crashing down on them.

The momentum of the dive allowed Ras to glide low enough to narrowly avoid the behemoth as it shot dust into the air upon its final collapse.

Finally clear from the falling debris, Ras craned his neck to see the Time Origin still standing amidst the heaping wreckage, and he wondered if Lupava had somehow survived.

His heart pounded. All of the chaos had been heightened by the extended overload. He checked the inside of his grapple gun strap, and a wave of relief rushed over him as he spotted his Foster-nullification serum.

As *The Kingfisher* neared, Ras fired off a magnet to reattach to the vessel. The ship began its slow descent, allowing Ras and Callie time to reel in the cable so they could reunite with the magnet in order to avoid being dragged along the barren, craggy ground.

After landing, Ras detached himself and Callie from the ship and each other. The prolonged overload left him feeling invigorated, but as the ship landed next to him, he checked on Callie. "How are you feeling? Headache?"

Callie sat up, wide-eyed. "My heart…is going to explode."

"Literally?"

"No," Callie said, smacking his arm. "I just fell to what I assumed was going to be my death."

"Well, it's still a valid question."

Callie wiped her red hair back out of her forehead. "I think…I think all I'm feeling is the tingly after effect of the Lack serum," she said. "No headache, at least not right now."

It would have to do.

The hangar ramp of *The Kingfisher* lowered, revealing Dayus once more in his wide-brimmed hat. He squinted, looking back in the direction of the wreck.

"You're thorough," Dayus said. "I'll give you that."

Coming down from the tingling sensation of overloading, Ras struggled to find his footing. "Where have you been?" he exclaimed. "You gave away my ship!"

Dayus sighed. "Might I remind you that I flew to Hal under my Captain's orders?"

"I…" Ras began. Dayus had a point. "Is it mine again?"

"I'm certain you could make a case for it after you unfroze Caelum," Dayus said. "Which, I believe you overshot."

"True, but Caelum didn't have this," Ras said, pulling the nullifying serum from underneath the strap. He had a smile he couldn't lose. For once, he had an understanding of what needed to be done, and the means to accomplish it.

"And what might that be?" Dayus asked.

"The end of Foster Helios III."

CHAPTER EIGHTEEN
The Time Bomb

THE KINGFISHER REJOINED WITH SEVERAL OTHER ELDER SHIPS JUST outside the half-frozen metropolis of Caelum. The airships stuck in the sky above the city still unnerved Ras. *A militia waiting to be reawakened.* Despite the recent win, something about Hal's plan put a pit in his stomach.

"Hey, are you all right?" Callie asked, interrupting his reverie. He turned from the windshield and smiled wanly at her.

"Yeah, I just can't help but feel like we're setting up the third Clockwork War because Foster just has some chemicals running through his body," Ras said.

Callie nodded slightly. "Dayus, before we overload, do you mind if Ras and I—"

"Go find your parents?" Dayus asked.

She seemed taken aback for a moment, then sighed and nodded. "It's just that I don't know if I'm going to have an opportunity later."

"I know where they are," Dayus said. "I'll come with you."

"You'll be frozen unless you stay close to us," Callie said.

Ras didn't entirely enjoy the idea of Dayus' hand on his shoulder for an afternoon. "Any word on Foster?"

Dayus brought *The Kingfisher* into a soft landing near some cracked pavement outside of the city, then turned his attention to Ras. "He's left Mason on foot, heading west."

"Can you tell Hal that I have the anti-Thromus serum?" Ras asked, tapping the vial in his grapple-gun strap.

"I…" Dayus said, looking over to Callie for a moment and cocking his head. "I'll pass this along." He transmitted something across the comm in Illorian.

"What's the closest Atmo city?" Callie asked.

"*Worick*," Dayus said. "It's a little further north than what remained of *New Crispin*, which I understand you're familiar with."

Ras nodded at the reminder of yet another city to which he had brought ruin. But he couldn't focus on such things.

Though they were walking, they quickly reached the perimeter of the frozen half of the city. The sun beat down on them, reminding Ras that this part of Illoria was one of the only places he had ever seen where the clouds didn't cover the land. "All right, Dayus," he said, "if you don't want to be frozen, you'll have to..." He trailed off as Dayus simply strode forward into the frozen area, gave a glance back, and nodded for them to follow him.

"But how?" Callie asked, quickening her pace.

"Suffice it to say there are certain restrictions which do not apply to me," Dayus said as they walked underneath a gigantic marble archway leading into the city.

"I don't think leaving it at that suffices anything," Ras said. The golden-hued street was sparsely populated with frozen citizens of Caelum, and he had to be cautious not to bump into any of them. "Why didn't you tell me you were a Lack?"

Dayus stopped and turned to address Ras. "I am *not* a Lack," he said forcefully enough to take Ras by surprise.

"Then why doesn't Time effect you?" Callie asked.

"Because I am Blessed," Dayus said, turning and continuing to walk down the street toward an open market square.

"Hold on," Ras said. "If Time doesn't affect you, then how are you still alive? I mean, all of those years Hal pumped *The King-fisher* with Time thick air so he could live longer. Time would have passed normally for you, so you should have died a long time ago, right?"

"I am Blessed," Dayus said. "And as such, there are certain longevity...perks."

"So you just pretended to move slowly around Hal?" Callie asked.

That brought a rare chuckle from Dayus. "No, Miss Calista. Halcyon knows of my unique traits. I spent much of my time off of *The Kingfisher* searching for solutions and doing research for when the time was appropriate to set things right."

"And you think that time is now?" Callie asked.

"I certainly hope so," Dayus said. "Or else I fear my life has been lived in vain and I caused more damage than I did administer hope."

"So, did a Caretaker bless you?" Ras asked.

"You ask many questions," Dayus replied.

"Well, it's kind of how I figure things out," Ras said. "I'd like to know if everyone on Acerbis is going to live as long as you." He looked at Callie. "Or if those of us with a Blessed parent are going to live longer than those without them."

Dayus sighed and stopped walking. "Your Blessing is diluted, Erasmus. You needn't fear outliving Calista, not with the way you behave." He paused. "How is your shoulder doing?"

"After dislocating it, being shot, or strung up?" Ras asked.

"You've been a surprisingly quick healer, have you not?" Dayus asked.

"You do tend to take a lot of abuse and keep going," Callie said.

"That is a part of your Blessing," Dayus said, "passed down from Emma."

"So, why is it that Ras can destroy Convergences when everyone in Imago is Blessed too?" Callie asked. "Shouldn't they have weeded the Convergences out a long time ago?"

"But my parents were able to destroy a Convergence once," Ras said. "It was before I was born. That's why my mom could never go on Energy collecting trips with my dad."

Dayus pursed his lips. "It seems that a mixture of Energy Knack and Blessed appears to be the unraveling agent, and you hold both pieces."

"Then someone from Imago and someone from Atmo together should be able to destroy a Convergence," Callie said. "Blessed and non-Blessed."

Dayus turned and continued to walk. "It would appear as such, wouldn't it?"

Ras stepped up in front of Dayus and began pacing backwards as they entered a town square. "So, where did you get your Blessing? I'm not the only one who can tap dance around the concept of being indirect, you know."

"Ras," Callie said, "if he doesn't want to talk about it—"

"I am a Caretaker," Dayus said, stopping Ras instantly. He didn't break stride. "The last to roam Imago. The only one who refused to die and offer my diluted Blessing to a city because I thought I could do more good alive than dead." His fierce gaze softened and his eyes fell to the ground. "But it is more difficult now to be so certain of such things."

"You were Mason's Caretaker…" Ras said. *That's why they weren't immune to Energy.*

"I would have been if I had accepted the role," Dayus said. "It was my assignment to protect them upon my arrival and then pass on my Blessing after I died. I thought they would be safe with the overbuilt defenses Foster Helios had erected, and that a solution for the Convergences would be discovered before…" Dayus paused, taking a deep breath. "I was there when Bogues erupted. I saw The Great Overload firsthand, the sparks that ignited the world."

Ras stepped up in front of Dayus. "Do you know where the Convergences came from, then?"

Dayus stopped walking. "Halcyon led an assault with the First Airborne to push back the Illorians using Energy concentrated from the Origin. The tactic first worked over Treding. The men and women inside the suits would overload."

Callie's jaw dropped. "So it was Hal's plan?"

A shake of Dayus' head dismissed the blame. "As a Caretaker, there are certain things we understand. Certain possibilities we know to explore, and certain tenets we may ignore at our own peril. I thought I saw a path to peace once, but now I better understand the role of a pawn."

"Using Energy as a weapon was your idea?" Ras asked.

"The initial concept was mine, yes," Dayus said. "A prolonged war risked the lives of too many, ignorantly fighting for something larger and older than themselves. What resulted was an unintended permutation. Once begun, the shattered pieces were impossible to reconstruct. However direct it might have been, I am responsible for The Great Overload."

Silence hung in the air. Ras struggled to speak, unsure of how to even begin to field such a bombshell. Things began clicking. "And that's why you didn't go to Mason," he said. "You wanted to fix things?"

"I had to," Dayus said, gritting his teeth. "Guarding a well defended city felt too small of an atonement for what I had created."

"Who else knows?" Callie asked.

"Only Halcyon has been aware of my role in this world before now."

"If I can ask," Ras said, "where do we stand on the whole *'putting things right,'* front?"

Dayus cocked an eyebrow. "Hope remains," he said, fiddling with a chain around his neck that Ras hadn't noticed previously. "But there are many moving pieces, and it would be very unwise of me to say more at the moment."

"Well, at least we're on the same side, if not the same page," Ras said.

"I must say I expected a different reaction, Erasmus," Dayus said.

"What? Your good intentions caused something bad to happen, you're doing your best to set it right," Ras said. "I think I can relate. We're all just doing the best we can with what we know."

Dayus nodded slightly. "It's very much a relief to hear you say such things, Erasmus," he said. "Very much indeed."

"Why did we stop here?" Callie said, looking about the square. "Do my parents live in this area?"

"Decades ago I tracked down the parents of every child sent away on that white train," Dayus said. "It took me three years."

"And?" Callie asked. "Are they all right?"

Dayus merely pointed a long finger toward the center of the city square.

A woman with tied back red hair hugged herself as a man leaned over her protectively, his arm over her shoulders. They both looked pained. The woman's eyes were puffy and bloodshot.

"Look at them," Callie said, her voice cracking slightly. "They're never going to see their little girl again."

Ras stepped up beside her. "You're always going to be their little girl," he said, offering his hand.

"She can't be more than twenty-five," Callie said. "She looks more like an older sister than my mother."

"I know how that feels," Ras said, hand still extended.

"I want to tell her I'm okay," Callie said, wiping a tear away on her sleeve. "Tell her she doesn't have to be afraid for her baby anymore."

"We can arrange all of that," Ras said.

"I don't think I'm ready," she said, looking up to him with her watery blue eyes. "I don't know if I'll ever be ready...my adoptive parents—"

"They'll always be there for you," Ras said. "But right now we have a rare opportunity to ease two people who love you into some very big news."

Callie nodded. "Dayus?"

Without a word, Dayus strode forward to the young couple, then gently placed a hand on each of them. He whispered something in Illorian, and the red-haired woman stirred, tugging her head out from against her husband's chest. She looked about her with confusion as the man loosened his embrace of her; their eyes looked to Dayus at the same time and they both began to speak, but he quieted them with a gentle shush. They fell silent, glancing with bewilderment at one another, then back at Dayus.

"Calista?" Dayus called with arm outstretched to her. The couple looked her way. Dayus continued to speak softly, then turned his attention back to Callie. "I'd like you to meet Piotr and Isla. They—"

In a rush of red and white, Callie moved forward and threw her arms around her parents, breaking into heavy sobs. Her parents paused for a moment, then immediately returned the embrace as Dayus stepped back.

Piotr said something to Dayus, who translated. "He says you've grown more beautiful than he could have imagined, and asks if the one with the shaggy hair is your husband."

Callie released the hug, then looked back at Ras. "No, but I do love him," she said. "He's saved my life so many times now." Dayus relayed in flowing Illorian speech.

Hearing her speak those words served as a reminder for Ras. He hadn't ruined everything. The woman he loved reciprocated, and knowing she didn't see him as a failure made it difficult to see himself that way.

Isla gave Callie a squeeze, then moved to Ras, but froze in place between them.

Ras stepped forward, gently reaching out a hand and placing it on her forearm. Isla jumped back with a confused look, then said something in a similar sounding voice to Callie's.

"She's asking if you're The Reclaimer," Dayus said.

"How do I say 'yes' in Illorian?" Ras asked.

"Ie," Dayus said.

Ras looked to Isla, nodded, and said, "Ie."

Isla threw her arms around Ras, crying and speaking quickly.

"I'm not catching all of that," Dayus said. "But she thanks you and asks where you're from, and how you know Calista. I'll tell her these are pressing times."

"Right, yes," Ras said, patting Isla comfortingly on the shoulder. "I'm sorry, Callie, we're going to have to catch up after we stop Foster."

Callie nodded, then reached an arm out while still holding her father's hand. Ras touched her shoulder and began the overload process. The sphere of Lack influence burst out from around them, bringing back everyone in the square back to life. With an almost electric charge, the frozen city snapped back into a semblance of its former vitality—for a moment.

Above, several airships that had been half-preserved and half-decayed along the border of the Time bubble simply fell from the sky. Gasps came through the city as crashed ships slammed into buildings. In the chaos, nobody seemed to notice the three new people in the city square.

Ras looked at the people in the square. He didn't know how he would manage a peace between the Time-sick Illorians and the Blessed Burrow-dwellers, but at least he had years to figure such things out.

The weathered remains of the Illorian military zoomed over the city, heading for the capitol building in the distance as the clouds rolled into Caelum for the first time in almost a century.

"I do hate to cut this short, but we're going to need to as leave as soon as we can," Dayus said, then repeated the sentence for Piotr and Isla.

"Tell them that I'll come back, please," Callie said, wiping away a tear. "Tell them I grew up happy." She looked at Ras. "And that I think they chose the best option."

BACK ONBOARD *THE KINGFISHER*, Dayus initiated the launch sequence as Ras settled into the co-pilot chair, unsure if he was still the captain of the vessel.

"How long do you think it'll be before we find out if Hal convinced the rest of the Illorian Council to help rescue Atmo?" Ras asked.

Dayus pulled a lever and the ship quickly gained altitude. The field of view above Caelum revealed a launching fleet. "I'd say not too long."

The comm crackled to life. "Dayus," came Hal's voice. "Bring *The Kingfisher* into formation. Our first target is the Atmo city of *Worick*."

"You mean the fueling station on *Worick*," Ras corrected.

"Yes, Ras," Hal replied. "They understand the mission."

"And that there are children onboard those fueling stations?" Callie asked. "Did you tell them about that?"

"I was not aware of this detail," Hal said. "I'll make note of this."

"Please do more than that," Callie said. "You're still fighting for Atmo, you're just using the other side now."

"A side which I'm not certain I can retain full control over for long," Hal said.

"You're Halcyon Napier," Callie said. "You'll think of something."

Ras muted the comm. "Did Hal know about Energy being used as a weapon for The Clockwork War?"

"He wouldn't have joined a side so outgunned and outnumbered if there hadn't been an edge involved," Dayus said.

"Why did it start?" Callie asked. "The whole war, I mean."

Dayus piloted *The Kingfisher* into formation with the rest of the Illorian fleet, confirming his position over the comm. "The Illorians were tasked by the Caretakers—"

"What do you call them...I mean, yourselves?" Ras asked.

"We are...were from a place called Aether, which is far more than I care to explain at the moment," Dayus said. "But, back to your explanation, a side effect of Illoria being so close to Time was that they developed slowly. Even the most advanced ships begin to look obsolete when your neighbors learn how to finally fly."

"So they were afraid the Outsiders would advance, overtake them, and get greedy for the Time Origin?" Ras asked.

"After the debacle with *The Winnower*, I'd say those fears were not entirely unfounded," Dayus said. "But yes, they wished to expand their borders beyond the mountains, giving them a larger perimeter to advance their civilization at the same rate as their neighbors."

"Well," Ras said, turning back to Callie. "There you go."

With the Illorian fleet operating at full speed, the voyage to *Worick* was relatively short. Far below, Ras could see the floating city surrounded by hundreds of ragtag airships. "Word must have gotten out."

"We ain't giving up the city without a fight," a gruff voice said over the comm.

"It doesn't have to come to that," Hal responded. "We just need to relieve you of a weapon that can be used to destroy your city. It's for your own good."

"Yeah, sure," the sky pirate said. "We'll just hand something like that over all nice-like. We got you outnumbered at least five to one. I wouldn't try anything."

"Ras," Hal said, "I'm switching to a private channel. Can you see the platform and Convergence with your KnackVisions?"

Sliding his goggles into place, Ras looked down to survey the many specks of green light. Most were created by sky pirate ship engines. Eight larger signatures were from *Worick*'s city engines, but just to its side, the solid green orb of Energy hung in the sky, unmoving. "The Convergence is just to the west of the city."

"Excellent," Hal said. "Then we're not too late. Stay up here until we've freed the children and sunk the fueling station. We can't afford to lose you."

Orders came across in Illorian, and the thirty Elder warships dove, clearing a path of bombardment. Ras watched with his Knack-Visions as a few of the green specks of Energy engines blossomed, then winked out. The Time engines of the Illorians were invisible to him, and aside from overhearing the sounds of the war in the background over the battlefield chatter on the comm, he had no way of knowing how the Illorians were faring.

A bolt of green Energy shot upward, coming dangerously close to *The Kingfisher*, and the comm came to life with shouts of confusion.

"They have Collective tech!" Ras shouted. "The Elders are going to take heavy losses if we don't get down there!"

"We don't have weapons." Dayus said.

"No," Ras countered. "But maybe those beams won't work if they're in our field of overload." He unbuckled himself and stood quickly. "Is the jetcycle still in the hold?"

"Yes, but—" Dayus began.

"Ras!" Hal barked over the comm. "We're not seeing a fueling station. Can you reconfirm the Convergence?"

Ras looked through the KnackVisions once more. The Convergence moved slightly, slowly edging toward one of *Worick*'s engines.

"The Convergence is down there, but it's loose. Must be below the city. Callie and I are on it."

"Why is it free?" Callie asked.

"Don't know," Ras said. "Dayus, we'll take the jetcycle. We can't afford *The Kingfisher* going down."

"I wholeheartedly concur," Dayus said.

Ras reached for Callie's hand. "Can't do this without you."

Grabbing his hand, Callie sprang up from her seat, and together they ran to the hold to find the jetcycle waiting for them. Ras opened the bay door and then straddled the jetcycle. He turned the key in the ignition; the machine roared to life, and his heart leapt at the shuddering sound of his old friend. Ras adjusted his goggles, then looked back to Callie. "Hold on tight."

"I will—"

Ras gunned the throttle on the handlebar, shooting them out of the hold of *The Kingfisher* and into the stark brightness of day. The engine caught, then rocketed them forward as a white contrail shot out behind.

Dropping the jetcycle's nose, Ras took in the full view of the battlefield. A green Energy beam shot up toward an Elder vessel, but the overload cut it off before it could reach its target.

The green glow of the Convergence overlaid itself atop the KnackVisions' view as it burst through the clouds beneath *Worick*.

"How did it get below the clouds?" Callie shouted, holding Ras tighter. The jetcycle continued the dive to avoid a pair of sky pirate biplanes strafing an Elder gunship.

"I don't know!" Ras said. He flicked on his comm. "Dayus! Keep a watch for any ships coming through the clouds."

A sky pirate airship just above them took the brunt of a mini-cannonball barrage as Ras leveled the jetcycle off. With the Collective Energy weapons disabled, the Illorians appeared to hold the advantage.

"If we kill the Convergence, we can just end the battle!" Callie said.

"We can't let it reach the city!" Ras shouted back, throwing the jetcycle into a full dive to intercept the sphere, which looked to be well on its way toward *Worick*.

From beneath the clouds a lone jetcycle broke through, a white contrail streaking behind it.

Foster.

"Why is he doing this?" Callie asked. "He said he wanted all of the Convergences gone."

"I think he wants to grow them first," Ras said. "I'm still trying to figure out why." The pressure of the Convergence's presence pushed hard against Ras' Lack bubble. The Convergence stopped its ascent as Ras and Callie dropped beneath *Worick*'s surface.

Foster jerked his jetcycle to port, and the Convergence followed suit.

"I can see Foster," Ras called out to his comm. "He's playing keep away."

"Try and get him to land on the city," Hal said. "We'll deploy the Time bomb and trap him."

"What about the citizens?" Ras asked.

"You can pull them out one at a time if you have to," Hal said. "But hurry, we're taking far too many losses to do this eleven more times."

"He's not going to try to hit the city if I keep chasing him," Ras said. He had an idea. "I'm going to the surface of *Werick*. I'll make a stand there." He pulled up on the controls, gaining altitude until they leveled off with the city's docks.

With a jolt, the wheels of the jetcycle hit pavement. Men and women in the marketplace quickly parted to avoid being run over. Callie reached one of her hands forward, pressing on the center of the dash between the handlebars. A horn blared a warning to the pedestrians.

"I didn't know it could do that," Ras said with a laugh.

"It came with the owner's manual. I got bored once," Callie said.

Ras drove the jetcycle up the avenue toward the central capitol building. After only a few minutes, Ras brought the jetcycle to a halt at the steps of *Worick*'s University. He hopped off, ending the overload.

"If we stop overloading, the city will be in danger," Callie protested.

Ras looked around beneath him with the KnackVisions. "That's what Foster needs to think." The Convergence was flying far away from the battle, then began to pick up altitude. "That's right. Come on back."

"Uh, Ras?" Callie asked.

"Yeah, what's up?" he asked, watching the massive Energy signature through the capitol building.

"Sky pir—er, Masonians," she said.

Ras turned around to see a mob of fifty men and women, their number growing quickly as they approached the steps of the capitol. He took off the KnackVisions and handed them back to Callie. "Let me know when Foster gets close, then grab my hand."

"What are you going to do?"

"Convince them not to kill us?"

"I like that plan," Callie said. "That's a good plan."

He turned to face the mob, then backed up onto the steps a few paces. "What seems to be the matter?"

"Reclaimer!" a middle-aged man shouted.

"You know who I am?" Ras asked, genuinely surprised.

"Of course, you gave us the speech on Governor Bartleby's ship," the man said.

"Some of us," the man said. "We agreed with Captain Masterson that we couldn't let what happened to Mason happen everywhere else, so some of us stopped here and convinced the city to save the kids and drop its fuel supply."

"That's amazing!" Ras said. It suddenly made sense why Foster was able to gain control of a Convergence. With the best of intentions, the crew of *The Piper* had unwittingly supplied ammunition for Foster. "And that's happening everywhere?"

"Yeah, and we're supposed to wait for someone to save us," the man said. "And I guess that's supposed to be you."

Ras watched the Convergence climb higher on the horizon and then looked down at the Masonians. "Any chance you can convince your friends in the sky to stop fighting? The Elders aren't trying to kill us."

"Ras?" Callie asked. "He's diving!"

He looked back at Callie to see her looking directly up, pointing. The Convergence was dropping straight down toward them. He grabbed Callie and held her tight. The pressure from above immediately forced him down to his knees as the overload took hold.

Ships above collided with the Convergence, shearing them in half. Others erupted in explosions as their crew overloaded when they flew too close. Debris began showering down across *Worick*.

The crowd screamed and dispersed as half of a sky pirate ship plummeted, smashing into the dome of the capital, then began rolling down the steps toward Ras and Callie.

Moving felt near impossible with the Convergence's downward pressure, but above the green orb had nearly stopped. Ras only had moments to decide before the wreckage would crush them.

He shoved Callie away from himself and dove backwards as the half ship tumbled over where they had just been standing. The Convergence made another dash toward *Worick*.

Ras scrambled to his feet and dove toward a prone Callie. His fingers reached her ankle and he suddenly felt the pressure of the Convergence slamming down on his back. He looked over the city to see if any of the people were overloading, but aside from the chaos caused by the airship battle, *Worick* itself seemed safe.

Ras crawled forward, pulling closer to Callie. "Are you all right?"

"I will be when that thing goes away!" she shouted.

The Convergence pressure began to let up as the orb destabilized until the Energy dispersed. The city was in the clear.

"Ras!" Hal's voice called out from the jetcycle's comm.

Ras pulled himself to his feet and ran down the steps to his vehicle. "I did it—"

"That's great, but we still need to freeze Foster and we just lost the ship with the Time bomb on it," Hal said.

"Did the Convergence hit it?" Ras asked.

"No, we lost contact with the pilot, and—"

A loud crash erupted two blocks away as an Elder vessel careened into the city. Another white ship began flying erratically, with no smoke or obvious damage until it also smashed into *Worick*.

"Hal! What's going on?" Ras shouted into the comm.

"Crew members are passing out here on our ship. I—" the comm cut off.

"Is there anyone not passing out that was just unfrozen?" Callie asked. "Ask him!"

"I thought they'd have years," Dayus said, cutting into the conversation. "Time is catching up to them."

"No!" Callie screamed. "My parents!"

Another Elder vessel smashed into the city by the docks in the distance. "We have to stop that Time bomb from going off!" Ras shouted. "We have to refreeze Caelum before it's too late." Had he really just doomed yet another metropolis to mass genocide by good intentions? "The first ship that crashed had the bomb, right?" He saw the trail of smoke a couple blocks down, then heaved up the jetcycle and straddled it.

"Dayus, can you retrieve the Time bomb?" Ras asked into the comm.

"Let me take care of that," a familiar voice said as a shabby looking Elder vessel flew into the fray.

"Carter!" Ras shouted. "Be careful! With all of the other Elders dropping, you're going to be the only target."

"Not if they can't fly," Carter said. *The Firefinch* buzzed by, approaching two sky pirate ships. They swung about to assault the Elder vessel, murderous intentions plain, and then with a series of loud blasts their engines backfired as one, leaving them drifting aimlessly. Dr. O's engine killer would provide Carter a clear path to the Time bomb.

Ahead, another jetcycle circled around for a landing on the lawn of the University.

Foster.

"Carter, don't let that thing go off here. Caelum needs you," Ras said into the comm. "I'll take care of Foster."

"Won't let you down, boss," Carter said. "Just promise me you'll pull us out after this thing goes off, all right?"

Ras hadn't thought of that. Carter had just signed himself and his family up for a deep freeze. He looked up at Foster. He just needed to get close enough to utilize the nullifying serum. Running Foster over with a jetcycle seemed like it would disrupt the monster for long enough to get the needle in. "What do you want?"

"Just you, *friend*," Foster said with a sidelong stare. "I am the craftsman, and you are my tool."

"Not today, I'm not," Ras said, letting the wheels of the jetcycle peel out. As he approached Foster, he lifted on the controls and became airborne.

The Energy blast from Foster's pistol struck the underside of the jetcycle, severing it and sending Ras tumbling atop only half of the destroyed vehicle. The handlebars jerked him down until the machine crashed out from underneath him. Landing hard on the road, he tumbled and skidded until momentum left him.

Ras could feel the sticky warmth of blood from a cut on his forehead. He looked at Callie, who stared at him with wide eyes.

"Ras, he's coming!" she said quickly.

Ras held a shaky hand to keep Callie from approaching, then forced his protesting body to stand. "All right," he said, holding his arms wide. "You have my attention. What do you want?"

Foster's eyes flicked to Callie, then back to Ras as he disembarked his own jetcycle and began a slow walk forward. "We still have so much work to do, you and I."

"So you can have your so-called peace?" Ras asked. Foster closed the distance. *Good, come closer.* He crossed his arms for better access to the syringe. "The Convergences are free. Why don't you just call them all together, and I'll pop them all at once? We won't have to worry about this whole '*destroy every city we see*' tour, huh?"

Foster halted merely a foot away from Ras' face. He sniffed the air. "Would you like to know how much time you have left?" he asked, eyes wild like a feral animal. "I don't usually tell, but I have always found it entertaining when I do." His voice had taken on an entirely different cadence from that of Foster's. The monster smiled. "Or how about the girl? She has even less time."

"You don't determine how much time I have," Ras said, inching his hand to the syringe tucked in the grapple gun's strap. Foster didn't track the movement with his eyes, but his unnaturally fast arms grabbed Ras' left arm by the wrist, holding it high.

"What have we here?" Foster asked, looking the grapple gun up and down. "You rely on this so much...yet, like all things, it will betray you." He clamped down on Ras' hand, forcing it to move as directed until the grapple gun pointed at Foster's jetcycle. Foster crushed Ras' hand in his own, deploying the magnet and cable.

The last thing Ras saw was Foster's elbow approaching his face.

Chapter Nineteen
The Thromus

Flying rarely featured in Ras' dreams, at least without an airship. And a good thing, too, since he associated equipmentless free-fall with terror rather than freedom.

The first thing he noticed was the ache in his left shoulder, followed closely by the deafening and constant rush of wind pressing against the top of his head. His back was hot, but his front felt chilled.

Where am I? He blearily opened his eyes to see the ground far beneath him, and nothing else. He jerked awake and stifled a scream of surprise. His left arm pointed level with the horizon. He struggled to raise his head, until at last his begoggled eyes could follow the cable running from his grapple gun to the jetcycle, which was piloted by a black silhouette.

To release the cable meant death, even if Ras put on the glider. *The glider.* Regardless of whether it would save his life in the event of a fall, it would spare his shoulder the constant torment.

Moving his aching body, he pulled himself into a ball, then used his free arm to detach the glider and maneuver it onto his feet ever so carefully so the wind wouldn't rip it away from his grasp.

With a twist and an awkward lurch, the glider caught the wind, lifting Ras into the burning contrail of steam, then through its top. He grabbed the cable with his right hand to give the point of tension in his left shoulder a respite. *How long have I been out?* he wondered.

Once under relative control again, Ras took stock of the sky around him. The clouds were still above, which he found disorienting. The ground below was mostly arid, but patches of green sprouted up here and there. He spun to check if anything was following him.

Ras' eyes went wide when he saw the eleven regular sized Convergences, with one almost city-sized Convergence trailing last of all. He didn't know whether to be elated that Guy, Finn, and the refugees had successfully freed the children while releasing the remaining Convergences, or devastated that without Callie nearby, he couldn't pop them at this range and complete his mission once and for all.

For a moment he considered cutting his cable and gliding, so the Convergences would run into him, but the latter half of that plan involved falling to his death, which ultimately lacked appeal.

On the horizon, a faint green glow emanated from the ground in the form of a spire, tiny against the vast and distant backdrop of Imago. Ras remembered watching the Convergence strike the Origin only a couple days ago and he wondered if this was going to be an encore, with twelve times the cast—one of which was utterly enormous.

If he squinted, Ras could spot the break in the clouds where *Derailleur's* engines pushed through. *That must have been a hard sell to get them to release their fuel source,* he thought. Then it dawned on him.

Every person in Atmo had just staked his life on trusting him.

Granted, they were motivated primarily by not wanting their city ripped apart by their fuel creator, but Ras decided a win was a win, and he'd see this through to the end.

The jetcycle descended as they approached the Energy Origin. He had never really given much thought to why the spire existed, other than that it just was a part of the way the world worked. But he had to admit the concept of a structure providing Energy for the whole world was a little bit odd.

As they dropped altitude, Ras had to swing the glider to the side to avoid being caught in the jetcycle's hot contrail. Foster turned his head and noticed Ras, then pushed the jetcycle into an accelerated dive.

Within a minute, the vehicle had forgone flight for utilizing its wheels, and Ras worked hard to keep the glider afloat so as not to be dragged along the craggy ground.

The contrail stopped and the jetcycle skidded to a halt. Ras quickly moved to disconnect the cable lest he be flung across the stopped vehicle and his arm pop out of socket.

With a satisfying snap, Ras was free from the cable. He glided onward toward the Origin, which was nearly a mile away.

How did Tink expect anyone to land this thing? Ras wondered as he lost speed. The glider dropped, then skidded on the parched dirt, bouncing him back up into the air a few times. He dug his heels into the ground and thought that he'd be able to brake the glider to a full halt until the front edge of the metal wing caught a rock, hurtling him face forward into the dirt and then spinning him out of control. The world whipped around him, disorienting him as he rolled until the momentum wore itself out.

Coming to a stop, he stared up at the dark clouds swirling above him. Blinking twice, he immediately checked first for the syringe. Thankfully it hadn't been damaged or lost. Second, his pocket still contained the engagement ring. He wasn't quite certain why that was second on the list over bodily harm, but he reasoned it had more to do with recent habit than anything else.

With his mental checklist complete, he felt the scrapes and bruises blossom into pain throughout his body. He slowly rolled over, noting the scar he had made along the ground on the parched land. Foster still sat silently on the jetcycle as though allowing his opponent a moment to collect himself.

Ras unceremoniously detached himself from the glider straps by kicking the ruined device against the ground, then slowly made his way to his feet. "All right, now what?" he asked, taking a few slow, experimental steps toward Foster. If he could only get close enough to plunge the syringe into the man, his goal could be accomplished.

Foster lifted a hand, then motioned two of his fingers toward Ras. One of the eleven smaller Convergences launched forward.

Bracing himself for impact, Ras leaned forward for the strike, but nothing came. Ahead twenty feet, the Convergence destabilized in front of him and the Energy dissipated, flying to join with the Super Convergence, adding to its circumference. The wind picked up, shoving Ras back as the chorus of Energy wails blew past his ears.

Thank you for the increased range, Dr. Lupava, he thought. The second Convergence came screaming in at him. This time it took slightly longer to destabilize, breaking up fifteen feet ahead of him.

Once more the Super Convergence's mass increased.

"Why are we here?" Ras shouted over the cacophony.

"Because this is where it all began," Foster replied, motioning for Convergences three and four to fly forward. Each broke up ten feet away.

The serum was appearing to have a lessening return with each application, and Ras still had a hundred feet left to close before he reached Foster. If it wore off before the Super Convergence was flying at him, he didn't know how well he would be able to weather such a force considering that seven Convergences in Mason had laid him out flat earlier.

"She didn't deserve this," Foster said, shouting over the wind. "She deserved so much more."

"Who are you talking about?" Ras asked.

Foster brought his arms in a sweeping motion in front of him, and the remaining seven smaller Convergences moved in a coordinated effort, circling around Ras. They continuing to spin at a safe distance, kicking up even more dirt and dust into a whirlwind. "How little you know, Rassss. And how could you? How could anyone in this world? You have so little time," Foster said, entering the spinning circle of Convergences. "In the grand scheme of things, this is just a waiting room for you." He stopped five feet away from Ras.

"A waiting room for what?" Ras asked, stepping toward Foster.

"For what really matters," Foster said. "I tried to grant such wisdom that comes with the perspective of longevity, but I was punished."

"I'm starting to miss the old Foster," Ras said. "He at least made sense—" Before he could take another breath, Foster moved forward inhumanly fast, clenching a hand around Ras' throat and lifting him.

"You are but a tool. The hardened spike with which I will shatter this world and bring peace."

Ras gasped for air, clutching fruitlessly at Foster's wrist. The spinning circles of Convergences closed in tighter. He could feel himself imploding underneath their pressure as the seven orbs constricted. Maybe the sensation was enhanced by Foster's grip, but consciousness began to slip away from him. He needed to make his move.

Releasing Foster's wrist, Ras aimed the grapple gun into the monster's midsection. He squeezed the hand trigger as he pulled the syringe from the strap with his right hand.

Foster swatted away Ras' arm before the shot landed. The decoy worked. The Convergences all spun into a frenzy, then coalesced together with a jolt.

Fingers gripped tightly around the syringe, Ras swung his right hand down at Foster's neck.

The syringe found its home.

Foster let out an inhuman roar, dropping Ras as he stumbled to the side. He shakily felt for the depressed syringe protruding from the side of his neck as Ras struggled to catch his breath.

The Convergences dissipated, all feeding their Energy into the Super Convergence, which expanded beyond the size of *Verdant*. Ras choked on the dusty air that filled his lungs.

Foster steadied himself, slowly removing the long needle from his neck as the wind around them died down. He let out a wet cough, which transitioned into a gurgling chuckle. "Did you think this could stop me?" He looked at the syringe, then threw it to the dirt.

Ras looked through the KnackVisions. The black silhouette had dissipated into a murky shadow of its former self. "Well, Foster, that was kind of the hope."

"That's not my name," he said. "Thromus will suffice for your tongue." He gave a wicked grin, turning his head to the side, then frowned. "It appears as though Foster is completely gone now." He shrugged. "Pity. His memories were of value. Oh well. Perhaps you can be my lone witness to the beginning of a new peace."

Thromus? Didn't Lupava say he was Death himself? Ras' mind spun. Maybe Foster really was dead, and what remained of Lupava's machination was all that was left. Maybe The Reclaimer literally did bring Death, and all of the destruction the being in Foster's body had caused was directly his fault.

Wherever reality stood, his only plan didn't work, and the backup had been spent on saving Caelum. He felt utterly out of his depths against an enemy who was far beyond him.

The man who was no longer Foster raised his hand, and the Super Convergence slowly rose. "The children do ever so miss their mother. What say we reunite them?" He flung his arm forward.

A deep rumble shook the ground as the Super Convergence slowly picked up speed, racing past Ras and Thromus toward the Origin.

Ras scrambled to his feet, running toward the jetcycle, but only made it two steps before Thromus tripped him, then pounced on his back like a predator on fallen prey.

Thromus grabbed Ras by the scalp and pulled back hard. "I want you to see this, Ras. One thousand years of oppression end today, and I couldn't have done this without you. I truly do wish we had been able to stay friends," he said in a cadence so erratic that it caused Ras to want to get as far away from the monster as possible. "Not that you would have lived much longer than anyone else."

Ras struggled against Thromus, and found himself better able to resist the no-longer serum enhanced body. At least part of his plan worked toward leveling the playing field. "I won't let you win," he said, unsure how he could make good on such a statement.

"Let me?" Thromus laughed with a shrill, piercing tone as he struggled to keep Ras pinned. "You enabled this. *All* of this. If history were to continue to be chronicled, you would be deemed its bringer of destruction."

Ras couldn't give up. Not now. He screamed in frustration, throwing an elbow into one of Thromus' thighs repeatedly. Seeing no result, he reached into his pocket, grabbing the metal ring box case, and swung it above his head. The box connected solidly with Thromus' temple, giving him a split second opportunity to scramble free. Grabbing a handful of lose dirt in his escape, he threw it in Thromus' face, then dashed toward the jetcycle.

Running was physically problematic, but he was properly motivated to work through the pain. As he made it to the vehicle, the Super Convergence reached the Energy Origin. A flash of brilliant green light blinded him, followed moments later by a deafening crack that reverberated through the ground with a shockwave, bowling him over.

Flat on his back, Ras felt a somewhat familiar sensation as small droplets of water began to cascade down around him. He shook his head to clear his senses as he sat up slowly. The Energy Origin still stood, having successfully repelled the attack.

The Super Convergence screamed away, flying toward the mountain range behind Ras. He let loose a triumphant laugh he didn't expect, then crawled over to the jetcycle as Thromus raced toward him at an inhuman speed.

"Got another plan or is it going to take you another thousand years?" Ras shouted over the deafening roar of the deluge from above.

He climbed on the vehicle and gunned the throttle. Rocketing forward, the jetcycle launched into the sky.

Thromus became a speck on the parched ground, and Ras turned his attention to the city-sized Convergence. It wasn't difficult.

The behemoth had already begun toppling every mountain in its path. The jetcycle could barely keep up, and Ras opted to follow at a safe distance. He hoped that the Convergence was traveling far enough away so as to be out of Thromus' control range.

The orb began to slow. As Ras neared the Convergence, it began to take up his full field of view. He realized the scope of it, and wondered if the essence of every person who had ever overloaded was comprising the single sphere.

He didn't know if his Lack ability would be enough to dissipate the monstrosity without Callie's aid, but he still had to try. At least if he died in a fiery jetcycle wreck, Atmo could land safely.

Gunning the throttle, he raced toward the small green sun.

The air warmed him to an uncomfortable temperature as he neared, evaporating the rain and making it difficult to take a breath. The Super Convergence put off so much Energy that the heat of it was making the jetcycle handlebars painful to hold.

A faint resistance pressed against him. "C'mon!" he shouted. "Just die!"

The Super Convergence slowed its momentum, then shot straight upward toward the clouds and away from Ras' small sphere of Lack influence. It hadn't destabilized in the least, and was obviously under Thromus' control once more.

Ras pulled back to gain altitude and pursue the Super Convergence. His heart sank as he traced its trajectory.

It was heading straight for *Derailleur*.

If the mass of Energy wasn't large enough to overcome the Origin, Thromus would add to it by overloading every citizen on Atmo's most populated city.

Ras opened the throttle as far as it would go, and the jetcycle began to gain on the Super Convergence. If he couldn't stop the monstrosity, he could at least try to warn the citizens. The Super Convergence began climbing into the clouds, punching a hole in them as they withered away at the Energy orb's presence.

Changing his angle, Ras opted to head toward *Derailleur* underneath the clouds instead of wasting time trying to pick up altitude. As he leveled off, the torrential rains soaked him, the droplets acting as tiny needles over his body.

The jetcycle picked up more speed, approaching the glowing green spot in the dark clouds. He was winning in the race to *Derailleur* against the slow moving behemoth. He turned his knob on the jetcycle's comm unit to the standard wind merchant emergency channel.

"Mayday! Mayday! Convergence is inbound!" Ras shouted. He figured *Derailleur*'s citizens were already plenty aware of the danger, but he needed to do everything he could. Anyone already in an airship might have a better shot of avoiding overloading, and the more he could warn, the better. "I repeat, Convergence is above the clouds and is inbound for *Derailleur*. Evacuate the city, immediately!"

Shouts of panic returned on the comm. He switched channels and repeated the message. There was only a minute until he would reach the city. He traded speed for altitude, beginning to enter the cloud cover as he started repeating his message on every channel he could.

Suddenly, the air heated up around him, burning away the clouds. The jetcycle lurched as the Super Convergence sped up behind him, flew above Ras' altitude, and blazed a trail through the clouds on its way to the largest city of Atmo.

Ships launched from the city in all directions. Those unfortunate enough to be leaving from the eastern docks were the first to explode.

Ras could only look on in horror as the Super Convergence collided with *Derailleur*, knocking the structure off-kilter. The first pops of explosion echoed like fireworks, each life lost contributing to the mass of the Super Convergence.

The ripple effect had begun, and there was nothing Ras could do.

The lights on the dash of the jetcycle flickered, then winked off as the controls began to go haywire and the engine sputtered.

The tipping city lost a large chunk as the Super Convergence struck it again. Ras had to tear his eyes away from the horrible display in front of him and focus on not crashing the jetcycle, as it had locked in its course directly for the crumbling city.

Ahead, pieces of airship and city rained down from the sky. With minimal control over the jetcycle's trajectory, Ras ran through his options. Several gasbag wind merchant ships drifted by in various states of disrepair, their crews having exploded while on board.

Ras loaded up a grapple spike, readying himself to transfer off of the doomed missile of a jetcycle. Of the three potential targets approaching, he selected the leftmost airship and aimed his grapple gun. A city block of *Derailleur* fell on the vessel, crushing it as they plummeted. Ras looked up to see if any other major debris might strike either of the remaining ships, then selected the one on the right.

As the jetcycle rocketed forward, Ras fired off his grapple, which connected solidly with the wooden hull. The jetcycle continued as the cable went taut, leaving Ras as it fell from between his legs.

He was pulled free in an upswing, his momentum carrying him underneath the ship and wrapping around the hull. He struck the balloon and bounced down to the deck of the ship, landing squarely on his back; the impact knocked the wind out of him.

Pain filled his chest as he sucked in as much breath as possible until air once more filled his lungs. The sounds of more explosions erupted above, filling his imagination with thoughts of horrors inflicted across the city, from the great library to Orville's clock shop.

Survive. He had to focus on surviving. Survive so he could kill Thromus and stop the Super Convergence so the rest of Atmo could land. But what then? He couldn't live with himself, knowing he had caused the death of tens of thousands of men, women, and children.

If he could live beyond this rain of debris and somehow stop the Energy Origin from being destroyed, then he would give thought to the future. He scrambled to his feet.

The wind merchant ship reminded him of *The Brass Fox*. As he ran toward the bridge, he avoided the large hole in the deck leading down to the engines below where someone had overloaded.

The ship's controls still responded even though the port side of the bridge had been blown away. Ras took the ship's spoked wheel in his hands and threw it hard to starboard, punching the throttle forward.

The engines below sputtered. They were likely Helios-made, and not designed to bathe in a flood of Energy. The airship limped away from the wreckage, steadily losing altitude at a marginally safe rate for a crash landing.

Ras took the opportunity to run down to the captain's quarters to search for anything he could use as a weapon against Thromus. He had to assume the worst about whatever Thromus was. He couldn't underestimate his enemy. Whether or not Death himself could die, he would have to be satisfied with damaging the Foster-entrapment.

He hobbled down the stairs, then ripped open the door to find an upended room with its back wall missing. Wind whipped the contents about, and Ras immediately began rummaging through personal effects. Clothing, books, and silverware. Nothing useful unless a dull bread knife could do the trick.

Turning, he saw a picture frame dancing on the wall. A family of three had posed for a photo. A loving father had his arm around his young bride, who held a baby.

Ras looked away from the photo, and his eyes fell on a pink cradle in the corner of the room. His heart broke, and he ran out of the quarters as tears burned his eyes.

"Ras! Ras!" Callie's voice squawked over the comm back on the bridge. "Are you there? Are you okay? Please respond, over!" She sounded so frightened. He ran up the bridge and grabbed the comm.

"I'm here! I'm here!" Ras shouted back. "Where are you?"

On the distant horizon, he could see a rusted ship. He adjusted his heading away from the cascading wreckage of *Derailleur* toward *The Kingfisher*. "I'm in a wind merchant ship, heading toward you!"

"Ras, is Foster down there?" Dayus asked.

"Foster's gone. He says he's Thromus now," Ras said. "He's trying to destroy the Energy Origin. Why would he want to do that?"

"He's trying to end all life in Imago," Dayus said. "We're on our way."

"I couldn't pop the Super Convergence on my own," Ras said. "I couldn't get close without it destroying whatever ship I was on."

"Then we'll overload," Callie said. "Together."

The glow of the expanded Super Convergence bathed the world in green light as it descended beneath what remained of the cloud layer.

Ras could once more feel the oppressive heat at his back. He glanced over his shoulder, then back to *The Kingfisher* as the Illorian ship did the majority of the work in closing in.

The Super Convergence sank back to the ground, destroying every wrecked piece of *Derailleur* it came into contact with.

The Kingfisher picked up with a burst of speed, and Ras ran down to the deck, ready to reunite with Callie before the Energy Origin could suffer a second attack. The Elder ship approached with its bay door open. Ras spotted Callie's red hair blowing in the wind as she held onto the railing to steady herself.

"C'mon," Ras said to himself, ready to make the leap into Callie's arms. He glanced back at the Super Convergence just sitting there. *Are you taunting us?* He couldn't spot Thromus among the wreckage. It felt like too much to ask that a chunk of the city might have fallen on him.

The Kingfisher came in hot. Dayus evidently didn't mind a collision with the wind merchant vessel if it meant shaving seconds. Before Ras was fully ready, he made the awkward leap from the wooden ship and was swallowed into *The Kingfisher*'s bay.

As he landed, the Super Convergence shot toward the Energy Origin. Ras collapsed into Callie's arms, feeling the world around him shift as the overload took hold. *The Kingfisher* collided with the wind merchant vessel, shaking both ships violently.

A blinding light caused Ras to flinch. A moment of silence passed, then a deafening explosion clapped throughout the landscape with a shockwave, shaking *The Kingfisher*.

"Did we destroy it?" Ras asked, numb. He didn't dare ask if the Super Convergence had just destroyed the Energy Origin. At that point most questions were moot.

Callie pulled herself up, crowding forward to look. "It's still there," she said, shaking her head.

"The Origin or the Convergence?" Ras asked.

"Both!" Callie said.

The Kingfisher climbed steadily, avoiding the Super Convergence, which had once more been successfully repelled by the Energy Origin.

"Ras! Callie! Get up here!" Dayus shouted as the bay door closed.

Ras scrambled to his feet, Callie's hand still in his. "I tried to stop it. I tried to save *Derailleur*."

"I know," Callie said. "You did what you could."

"It wasn't enough," Ras said. The oppressive feeling from the Super Convergence continued as they kept up the overload on their way to the bridge.

Dayus' eyes didn't leave the Super Convergence below. He spun the ship and began to head west.

"Why are we going toward The Bowl?"

"Because he's going to the next closest source to grow the Convergence," Dayus said, throwing the throttle wide open.

Callie's eyes went wide. "No! He can't."

The Super Convergence began moving again.

Toward *Verdant*.

CHAPTER TWENTY
The Homecoming

"WE'LL JUST CUT IT OFF AT THE PASS," RAS SAID, HOLDING TIGHT TO Callie's hand. "That way it won't even get into The Bowl."

Dayus shook his head, continuing toward the main pass at a higher altitude to avoid having to thread through the canyon. "If it flies higher than your overload, then it might reach *Verdant* before we can. I think we need to make our last stand on the city itself."

"I could overload for two miles before," Callie said. "Shouldn't that make it easy?"

"Dayus is right," Ras said. "It seemed like that last batch of Convergences burned through some of the serum I stole from Lupava. I don't know how long this is going to hold for me." He watched the world blur by underneath him as *The Kingfisher*'s engines churned smoothly along at max capacity.

"What have we done?" Ras asked.

"Everything he wanted us to do," Dayus said.

"How do we stop him?" Callie asked. An anger played on her face unlike anything Ras had seen from her before. "He's taken so much."

"He has," Dayus agreed. "But once his Convergence has been destroyed, he'll be considerably less dangerous. Thankfully, the role given of regulating time was stripped from him before he was banished inside the Time Origin."

"So that's really Death?" Ras asked.

"I cannot say," Dayus replied.

"You seem to have a pretty good idea!" Ras shouted. "Better than the rest of us, anyway."

"Did you accomplish your goal with the syringe?" Dayus asked.

"I managed to get the nullifier in him. The reanimated Foster part of him is gone, so he's not as strong anymore," Ras said. "If we kill the body, shouldn't that end him?"

"We are more than just our physical forms, Erasmus," Dayus said. "Foster's body is now a limitation for Thromus. I think it more preferable to know what he looks like than to have his essence floating about."

Ahead, *Verdant* gleamed on the horizon as the sun set behind it over the mountain range. A large ship almost a quarter in length of the city hung nearby. *The Piper*.

Ras jumped on the comm. "This is Ras Veir, calling for Captain Guy Masterson. Over."

A pause, then Guy's voice crackled over the speakers. "Ras? What are you doing back—"

"The last Convergence is on its way," Ras said. "You've got to put as many people on your ship from *Verdant* as you can."

"I thought destroying Convergences was kind of your thing," Guy said.

"It just took down *Derailleur*," Ras said, his voice shaky. "I don't want to take any chances."

"On it," Guy said, and then the frequency went quiet.

With KnackVisions on, Ras looked aft. The Super Convergence had begun its run on *Verdant*, picking up speed. With a rippling series of explosive cracks, the giant orb laid waste to the canyon, creating a new, wider opening.

Ras shook his head. The prolonged overload had given him heightened senses. Without them, he felt numb to the world. "Are you still okay?" he asked, looking at Callie.

"I can't think too hard about that question right now," Callie said. "It feels like there's no future left."

Ras wanted to disagree, but had little ammunition for an argument.

The Kingfisher pulled up to *Verdant* at a reckless pace. "You two keep guard at the docks," Dayus said. "If you have to, move to the center. I'm going to find reinforcements."

"Against *that*?" Ras asked.

"Yes," Dayus said, pulling the ship into a full stop. "Now go!"

Ras dashed out of the cockpit with Callie in tow and didn't stop running until they made it outside. The ship had slightly overshot the docks, and they found themselves at the edge of the marketplace. As soon as they disembarked, *The Kingfisher* launched once more, and Ras watched it until it dove out of sight.

A familiar groan from *Verdant's* engines filled the air, and the city began to lean, sloping toward the edge of the city where they had been dropped off.

"Ras, we're causing the city to sink," Callie said. "The engines can't find Energy if we're overloading around them."

The earlier escape attempt from Sheriff Pauling came to mind, and he looked back at the nearing Super Convergence. "Then we sink *Verdant*," Ras said. Thankfully the city had backup Energy reserves that would prevent an outright plummet, but even those would be stressed with the overload.

"What?" Callie protested.

"Callie, if *Verdant* can land safely and stay within our bubble and we pop the Super Convergence, it doesn't matter if the city lands," Ras said. "All of the Energy will go back to the Origin and people can live on the ground again."

Chaos ensued in the marketplace as vendors split their time between packing up their wares and running for their lives. A deep rumble punctured the city as the Super Convergence neared.

The city continued to slowly sink, and Ras could feel the presence of the Super Convergence pushing hard against his body, making it difficult to walk toward it.

"What happens if we can't stop this?" Callie asked quietly, staring straight forward.

"We don't give up," Ras said. "We don't ever give up."

Ships launched from the docks while Verdantians ran in the direction of *The Piper*. Amidst the chaos, Ras felt like a pawn in Thromus' plan, step by step enabling the madman to end the world when all he wanted to do was save it.

In the distance, the Super Convergence came to a complete stop, but still pressed hard on Ras. "Are you feeling this too?" he asked.

"No. I used to before you reset me," she said. "Look!"

The Super Convergence began moving laterally to the side, as though it might find success from another angle.

"Let's move toward the University," Ras said. "We need to even out this city."

Running against the flow of the panicking populace proved troublesome at first, and the jostling from the crowd caused Ras to lose Callie's hand twice. Both times he felt the pressure pushing harder against his body as the Super Convergence took the opportunity to rush forward, but the returning overload successfully repelled it back.

"So, I couldn't help but notice we're not destroying the Convergence," Callie said.

"Yeah," Ras said, starting to feel a bit winded after their extended run. "Either it knows it'll get destroyed if it comes too close, or it can't move closer while we overload."

"We can't keep this up forever," Callie said. "Right?"

He squeezed her hand. "This is the only tool we've got right now. I'd love to see what Dayus has in mind for reinforcements."

They continued to run toward the center of *Verdant* when deep booms reverberated from below.

"They're firing the cannons," Ras said with an amused laugh. The shots would do absolutely nothing to the Super Convergence, but it signified something more important. Not everyone had given up on the city yet, and people in The Engine weren't going down without a fight.

Ras and Callie cleared the residential zone and entered the outskirts of *Verdant* Park. Ahead, people stood on the steps of the University to watch the coming of their end. Dark clouds began spilling over the edges of the city, sparking further panic from the citizens.

"They're going to think the clouds will kill them,' Callie said.

"They'll calm down in a minute when they figure out they're still alive," Ras said.

Upon clearing the park, Ras and Callie wound up at the base of the steps, out of breath. The rain from the clouds soaked the faltering city for what was likely the first time ever. The tops of

Verdant's tallest buildings disappeared into the clouds, and the glow of the Super Convergence cast the sky in a bright green hue.

"Okay, I don't think it can reach any part of the city now," Ras said.

"Callie!" a voice exclaimed from behind them. Mr. Tourbillon ran down the steps of the Capitol. Upon reaching his daughter, he threw his arms around her. "I thought I lost you," he said, squeezing her tightly. His eyes traced her arm to her hand, which was still firmly connected to Ras. "I'm just going to assume this is all his fault."

Callie pulled herself out of the embrace, backing up toward Ras. "Daddy, I love you, but you have got to start showing Ras the respect he deserves. He has risked his life time and time again to save Atmo, and we are one step away from doing that. So, please, for me, understand that I love him, and that there isn't a man in Atmo, Illoria, or Imago that is better for me than Erasmus Veir."

Ras looked at Callie, her fierceness a new beauty blossoming. His heart quickened, and he felt a push from the Super Convergence. He looked above as the rainclouds began to burn away at the sphere's influence. The orb wasn't doing the pushing, but his overload sphere was growing. "Uh, Callie? Can you say something nice about me? It's…for science."

Callie shrugged. "Your eyes are the color of a misty forest I love getting lost in?"

"I'm not sure what that means, but I'll take it," Ras said, feeling the pressure from the Convergence once more. Whether it was *Verdant* falling or the Super Convergence being pushed further away, he wasn't entirely certain, but if he could knock the monstrosity out with a better emotional connection to Callie, there was one thing he could do.

He felt the ring box in his pocket.

The moment wasn't ideal, but the world wasn't currently populated with perfect opportunities. Everything had grown so dark, and experiencing firsthand the loss of Dixie, Mason, and *Derailleur* still hung heavy on his heart. If there was any way he could bring a bit of light into the world, he would take it. And if this was truly the end, Callie deserved to know exactly how much she meant to him.

"Callie," he said, stealing a glance at her father. "I love you more than anything. If I could save Atmo by myself to protect you from the danger, I would. But, I can't. You're my Navi, my best friend, and the woman I want to grow old with. I want to tell our grandchildren stories they won't ever believe, even though we'll know they're true. And all of those stories will be just that much better because it's you and me like it's always been. I don't know what the future holds, but I will do everything in my power to make sure you're in it." He began fishing in his pocket, the Super Convergence being pushed back by his expanding radius.

"Yes," Callie said.

Ras took a knee, smiling. "Calista Tourbillon—"

"Yes," she said again.

"Will you do me the honor—"

"Yes."

"—of letting me finish telling you that no matter what adventures await us, I will be here for you, and that you would make me the luckiest man alive if you would consider spending the rest of your life with me." He cracked open the box, revealing the clockwork ring.

Callie's lips pressed into a thin line and tears formed in her eyes. "Can I answer a fourth time now?" She shifted her left hand free, replacing it with her right hand in Ras' grasp.

Ras beamed, pulling the makeshift ring free and slipping it onto her finger.

The city shook with a mighty rumble, and everyone fought to catch their bearings as *Verdant* landed. At the edges of the city, Ras could barely see the tips of Energy-blocking pylons sticking up over the lip of the docks. *The Piper* had followed the city down, wisely staying within the overload sphere.

"I think we just annexed Acerbis," Ras said. He thought for a moment about *Verdant's* structure. The bottommost part of the city was circular, and could feasibly socket into the Burrow. Maybe it had been Helios, Sr.'s intention all along for Atmo to return.

Ras stood to embrace Callie, then looked over to Mr. Tourbillon, whose gaze was fixed not on his newly engaged daughter, but on the park in the distance.

"Is that Foster Helios?" Mr. Tourbillon asked.

Closing his eyes and taking a deep breath, Ras gritted his teeth and said, "It is most certainly not." He leaned in and kissed Callie on her soft, sweet lips. "Celebration is going to have to wait." He took Callie's hand, releasing the embrace, and began walking toward Thromus.

Thromus stepped clear of a banged up flying skiff he had likely salvaged from the wreckage of *Derailleur*. He looked haggard and wind-whipped, now that Lupava's serum no longer bolstered the body.

"You can't have this city," Ras said, walking out to Thromus. "She isn't yours, and she never will be."

Thromus pulled out his Energy pistol and aimed it at Callie, who flinched. He pulled the trigger. The gun clicked, but nothing emitted from the barrel.

"Don't you hate it when that happens?" Ras said, holding up Callie's hand. "Do you know what this means, Thromus? It means you, your Convergence, your gun…nothing pertaining to you is welcome here." He lifted his left arm and fired the magnetic grapple charge at Thromus.

The magnet latched onto the gun. Ras jerked back his arm, yanking the Energy pistol from Thromus' grasp.

Thromus leapt to the ground after the gun, breaking into a crawl before the cable fully retracted and pulled it out of his reach.

Ras stooped and collected the weapon from the ground. "I get that you want Callie and me to let go of each other so you can destroy *Verdant*." Ras wiggled the gun. "And it's going to work, because I can't wait to see you go."

"They stole her from me," Thromus said, swallowing hard. "My Aura." His voice cracked. "Aether didn't know what they asked of me when they wanted someone to ferry the souls after they died. You have to understand."

"Who is Aura?" Ras asked. "Someone worth slaughtering hundreds of thousands for?"

"You would do the same for your Calisssssta," Thromus said. "The liars, murderers, and thieves, all thinking they deserve more than the innocent. If you had a choice, you would do anything for her."

"You know what the problem with selling yourself the same lie over and over is?" Ras asked. "You start to believe it until it's the whole truth to you…and it's sad."

"Don't insult me with your pity," Thromus said. "You deserve it more than I."

Ras shook his head, aiming the Energy pistol at Thromus.

"Don't listen to him," Callie said.

"You wouldn't shoot an unarmed man," Thromus said.

"You're not a man," Ras replied. "You're a monster in another monster's suit." He motioned to the Super Convergence high above them. "And I have seen that thing wreck too many lives to ever call you unarmed."

Thromus gave a wicked grin, then leaped forward in a mad dash toward Callie.

In the span of a breath, Ras released Callie's hand, felt the overload cease, then fired a shot with the pistol.

The beam emitted, striking Thromus in the midsection, halting him. After a few staggering steps, he dropped, clutching his stomach where the Energy beam had burned a hole clean through.

The Convergence dove toward *Verdant*.

Ras reached back for Callie. Once more the rush of overload staved off the Super Convergence's advance, and pushed it away before a ripple wave of overloads could begin. Acerbis' pylons seemed to be doing the work of keeping *Verdant* within an Energy-free zone, but if the Super Convergence could destroy mountains, then taking out the pylons would be no problem.

"Thank you," Thromus said, falling to his knees. "Now I get to see her again. My Aura. The Reclaimer has freed me, my Aura, and soon it will be just us. Alone. Until the end of all things."

The hole in Thromus' stomach burned as he collapsed to his back. His eyes began to glow green, turned crimson, then finally black. Thromus let out a throaty laugh. "Erasmus. I want to thank you." He paused, struggling to speak. "I want to thank you for playing your part flawlessly. I couldn't have asked for more." His dark eyes narrowed. "If you see the one called Dayus, tell him he was wrong. Tell him that hope dies with you." He took a short breath, then the body burst into a black expanse of overload.

A single, black ember flitted up and away on the wind.

Ras put his arm around Callie, pulling her in close. "Let's kill this thing and call it a day."

She looked up from her ring. "We're still going to have to help the rest of Atmo land safely."

"And figure out a way to make Illoria understand they have to live with Imagoites to survive," he said. "I just hope the world can rebuild. We've already lost so much."

He tried not to let his mind wander to Mason or *Derailleur*. The pressure of the Super Convergence lightened up without Thromus to push it around.

The wind picked up, and from the city's docks, *The Kingfisher* buzzed over the Capitol before circling around into a soft landing on the lawn of *Verdant* Park. The ramp lowered, and Dayus ran down to meet Ras and Callie.

"Are we too late?" Dayus asked, looking around.

"We?" Ras asked.

Ace bolted down the ramp, almost tackling Ras in a hug, forcing him to focus on not losing Callie's grasp.

"I survived!" Ace shouted.

"I see that," Ras said. "Looks like you got the train figured out."

"Yeah, bunch of levers," Ace said. "Once Tink worked out what the coal shovel was for, we were good to go."

At the top of the ramp, Elias Veir stood on two legs, one of them mechanical, with the support of his wife. Behind them, the rest of the Corin family peeked their heads out to take in their first view of the formerly flying city.

"Dayus said you needed some reinforcements," Elias said, cautiously making his way down the ramp with the new appendage and help from Emma. "But it looks like you have everything under control here." He clapped a firm hand on Ras' shoulder. "Good work."

"What about Acerbis?" Ras asked. "Prentiss told me there was going to be a civil war if we landed."

"It took some fancy talk," Elias said. "But I think I got them to give us a shot, for now."

Callie lifted her left hand for Emma to see, beaming proudly.

Emma grabbed the hand, and her eyes shot wide open at Ras. "Now? You picked now?"

"I wasn't sure there was going to be a later," Ras said.

"Can we omit that romantic tidbit when we tell the story later?" Callie asked.

"Where is Thromus?" Dayus asked.

Ras swung the Energy pistol around on the cable. "He overloaded. We're safe now."

Dayus shook his head empathetically. "Ras, we needed him imprisoned in Foster's body. Without that, he can—"

A low rumble emanated from the Super Convergence in the distance. Its bright green hue shifted, turning a dark crimson, then shimmered into a pure black, darkening the sky.

"Dayus, what's it doing?" Callie asked.

"Becoming Thromus' new body," Dayus said. "I think."

"You think?" Ras asked, incredulous.

Dayus looked over to Ras, uncertainty played in his eyes. "This is new territory."

The black Convergence shot upward until it hung high, well above *Verdant* and Ras' overload bubble.

"Should we take *The Kingfisher* up to meet it?" Ras asked. "See if we can stop him?"

"I...I don't know," Dayus said.

Ras gritted his teeth. This was what Thromus wanted all along. He wasn't lying when he said Ras was his tool every step of the way. "Mom, dad, maybe you can help boost my overload range, but we have to let him think he's getting close without resistance." He let Callie go and the overload ebbed away, leaving him numb. He blinked his eyes, waiting on Thromus to make the first move.

With a deafening cry and screech, the Thromus Convergence began speeding down toward *Verdant*.

"Now?" Callie asked.

"In a moment," Ras said, watching the black sphere grow larger.

"Ras, what are you waiting for?" Elias asked.

"I want him to see us and know he can't win," Ras said. The air took on a distinct chill. It was time. "Now!"

Callie grabbed Ras' right arm, clinging to it.

The fight began.

Pressure from the Thromus Convergence nearly buckled Ras' knees out from underneath him. Pain ripped through him in a new way. Instead of the usual pressure, he felt like needles were being pushed into him from above. Elias moved in to hold him straight. Looking up, the momentum of the Thromus Convergence slowed to a crawl, but it continued its descent.

Dayus stepped up, gently placing Emma's hand on her son's shoulder.

The addition of both parents bolstered Ras, but he didn't know whether it was real or just perceived.

"Here," Dayus said, stepping up and lowering the KnackVisions over Ras' eyes.

The view of the world shifted, and he could see the border of his overload battling against inky black tendrils whipping around the Thromus Convergence. Their every strike against the barrier was a strike to Ras, beating back the sphere of protection.

"I don't know if I can stop this thing," Ras said, watching his radius continue to shrink.

"Look," Elias said, nodding toward the hundreds of men and women in fine black clothing filtering onto the streets of *Verdant*. "I told them what happens when a Knack and a Blessed person join together. Hopefully that should protect the city...both cities."

Ras could see small pockets of resistance form as Verdantians and Acerbians joined hands. The pressure from the Thromus Convergence lessened significantly.

This was what the world needed to fight back. It needed a once-in-a-century reunion.

The orb began to warp ever so slightly, spinning wildly as a storm erupted inside it. Lightning flared out from its core and struck *Verdant*. Sparks flew from buildings, setting structures on fire.

Black tendrils continued to flail wildly, then began moving in a pattern. The lightning subsided, but the tendrils lashed out, targeting the couplings of Skyfolk and Imagoites.

Explosions erupted around the city.

Searching out the source of the explosions, Ras was horrified when the answer came in currents of Energy flying up to join the Thromus Convergence. Lone Acerbians lay scattered about—their Verdantian counterparts had been struck by the tendrils and overloaded.

The pressure from above doubled on Ras as he once more bore the brunt of the attack on his shoulders.

The world around Ras chilled to an almost unbearable level as the Thromus Convergence crushed down, blackening out the sky with its girth. He could feel Callie shaking from the cold, and he held her tightly. "Just hold on."

The Kingfisher zoomed away. It wasn't like Dayus to run. He had to have something up his sleeve.

A headache began forming behind Ras' eyes, and the Thromus Convergence pushed itself against the radius so much that Ras' sphere of influence barely held up.

An explosion reverberated outside of the city as *The Piper* went up in a hail of explosions. Green currents of Energy swept their way to Thromus. His protection no longer covered all of *Verdant*.

Guy, Finn, and the Mason refugees were gone.

"No!" Ras screamed, pushing back with everything he had in him to little effect. His right leg buckled and he stumbled. "Thromus!"

The radius of safety continued to shrink. Starting with the outside docks, ships began erupting, and the sounds of distant pops of overloading Verdantians broke Ras' heart.

"I believe in you, Ras," Callie said, turning his face toward her. "Focus on me."

"What have I done?" Ras asked. "I thought I could fix things."

"It's not over," she said.

Thromus gained ground as the ripple effect of overloads reached the markets and vendors.

A ring of deafening explosions engulfed them as the residential zone of *Verdant* crescendoed into an upheaval of destruction. Homes in the residential zone exploded. The glut of Energy fed the Thromus Convergence, adding to its strength as it bore down on the city.

Ras shook uncontrollably from the cold. The range of overload continued to shrink. Men and women on the Capitol steps began overloading around them. The heat from their Energy provided a sickening respite from the cold as Ras looked up to see the empty spot where Mr. Tourbillon had stood.

"Daddy!" Callie cried, then buried her head in Ras' shoulder. "Tell me this is a dream. Tell me this is a dream."

It was a nightmare.

Ras looked behind him. Elias clung to his Blessed wife, but even that wasn't enough to stop his eyes from beginning to glow.

"No!" Ras shouted, reaching out a hand for his father, who reached back only to have his body erupt in a wash of green and fly upward.

The force of Elias' overloading threw Emma backward into a sobbing heap. Her parents and brother pulled her away to care for her. Ras, through the strength of rage, was able to stand.

"Ras," Callie said softly.

He looked up, letting loose an animalistic cry, sending the heat of his breath onto the air.

"Ras…"

"What is it?" he asked, looking back down to Callie. Her eyes were closed. Dread filled him. "Why won't you look at me?"

Tears streamed from her tightly shut eyes and she shook her head. "I'm so sorry."

"Callie, look at me."

She opened her eyes. Instead of blue, or even black, they held the faintest glow of green.

Ras looked up and shouted at the sky. "You can't have her!"

"Don't quit, Ras," she said. "The world isn't over. It's going to need you."

"But I need you."

"I love you," she said, wrapping her arms around Ras, clinging tight.

Ras held her so tightly he was afraid he was hurting her. "I can't do this."

"You have to, Ras," she said. "I believe in you. No matter what happens, I love you."

"I love you t—"

Callie shook in his arms. The whole of her glowed with a green fire until the force of her Energy overload threw Ras back into the burning wreckage of *Verdant*.

Epilogue

RAS VEIR WISHED THE EXPLOSION HAD TAKEN HIM FROM CONSCIOUSNESS, but such would be too sweet a mercy for someone who had failed to save Atmo, doomed the world, and freed the monster who had killed countless thousands, among them his close friends, father, and fiancée.

The concussive force deadened his hearing. As far as he could tell, there was no screaming, for there were few left to scream. The Acerbians who had attempted to help looked appropriate in their mourning garb.

The crackle of fire mixed with the deep hum of Thromus' Convergence was all that remained.

A soft sobbing ebbed into Ras' periphery. He rolled over to see his mother crying into her hands as she knelt. Blood matted the side of her face and her shoulders heaved as she nestled in her father's arms.

Ace looked over to Ras, mouthing something he couldn't make out. He had no words to reply with anyway.

Ras' head swam as he rose. His city was laid to waste. The Thromus Convergence still hung in the sky, chilling the air, but he had spent so long overloading that his senses felt permanently dulled. Only twenty feet ahead of him, Thromus' battered skiff sat.

An idea came to him. A dark idea, selfish and selfless at the same time. If he could pilot the skiff above the Convergence, if it would even reach such heights, he could drop himself into the Convergence in hopes of somehow destroying the monster.

It would be difficult for Emma to lose both her son and husband in the same day, but if Thromus destroyed the Energy Origin, who knew if there would even be a world left to save.

Ras ambled over to the skiff, getting it running. "Mom," he said softly. She continued to sob.

"Mom," he said louder, prompting her to look up. He nodded behind himself. "I only have one shot left at killing the thing that killed dad."

Emma rubbed her eyes, not focused on anything in particular. She stood and shakily made her way over to Ras and wrapped her arms tightly around her son's midsection. He didn't know if this was her attempt at saying goodbye or not letting him leave.

The Thromus Convergence began to move, and quickly.

"I have to go," Ras said. "I'm so sorry." He slowly pulled himself free from his mother's embrace and sat down behind the wheel of the skiff.

"Ras!" Ace shouted as she ran toward him with her arm outstretched. She offered Tink's glider in her hand. "If you're going to do what I think you're going to do…you might need this."

Ras silently accepted the device, then gunned the accelerator to begin his pursuit.

As soon as the Convergence left, he had to slam on the skiff's brakes in order to not collide with a ship landing right in front of him.

The Kingfisher's bay opened and Ras drove the small skiff inside. If anything could fly him high enough to drop in, the Illorian vessel would be it.

The Corin family followed him into the hangar, but before Ras could ask why, the bay door shut and The Kingfisher launched. He exited the skiff, steadied himself, then began walking toward the hallway entrance. His mother just leaned against the skiff, hugging herself and staring at the wall as her family attempted to comfort her.

It wasn't ideal for the last image he'd have of his mother, but there was no such thing as ideal anymore.

He entered the bridge. Dayus stood at the helm, stoic with his jaw set, staring intently at the black Convergence ahead.

"Why did you leave us?" Ras shouted.

"I told you not to kill Foster's body," Dayus said quickly. "And look what happened."

"Just drop me into the Convergence and I'll—"

"You want to commit suicide, Erasmus?" Dayus snapped, turning to address Ras. "No. Too much is at stake for The Reclaimer to be selfish now."

"How else am I going to stop him from destroying the Energy Origin?" Ras asked, gesturing wildly as he moved up to the co-pilot chair.

"You can't," Dayus said. "Nobody can stop that now."

"Then what's the point?" Ras asked. "Why are we arguing? Everybody's dead anyway, they just don't know it yet." He slumped into the chair, rubbing his eyes. "How long will the world have left after that happens?"

"Long enough to make a difference," Dayus said. He took a deep breath, then looked back at the Convergence. "There is always hope, Erasmus," he said. "As long as there is Aether, there is hope."

"Callie is dead," Ras said, slowly enunciating the painful words. "My father is dead. Fathers everywhere are dead."

"That depends on your definition of the word dead," Dayus said.

Ras lifted his head. His mouth was suddenly dry. "Explain. Now."

"We are more than our bodies," Dayus said. "There is more to Imago than we can see."

The numbness clouding Ras' mind disallowed him any interpretation involving hope. "Can you be just...a little less cryptic?" he asked. "Are you trying to say that Callie isn't dead?"

"Ras, there is a path before you," Dayus said. "It is not easy; neither were you made for it, nor were you designed to traverse it." He sighed, gripping the controls again. "But you are the only one who can."

"What are you talking about?"

"Elsewhere," Dayus said. "It is the space between Imago and Aether. It was Thromus' realm until he was locked away. But if you go through its gate and find the path to Aether, you will find your Calista."

Ras eyes went wide. "Are you saying I can bring her back?"

"I'm saying that if Imago stands a chance of surviving, you'll need to bring every single soul that has been trapped in a Convergence from The Great Overload until today. You can reclaim them," Dayus said with a hint of a smirk. "You can reclaim them all. That is the hope. That has been the hope all along, ever since Thromus fell and the Origins were created."

An unexpected laugh escaped from his lips. He wasn't amused in the least, but the idea of hope remaining was almost too much. "Why...why didn't you tell me *any* of this before?"

"If Thromus knew he was using you for his own demise," Dayus said with a rare smile, "he wouldn't have broken the world to the point where he would be the most vulnerable. I hope you take no offense, but I needed to keep this to myself lest you accidentally say anything."

"I'm supposed to kill Death?" Ras' heart pounded. "But why me?"

"Many reasons," Dayus said. "I discovered you long ago when I was searching for a suitable home for Miss Calista. I knew she would be safe next to you and your mother. There was no mistake when I selected your father for Halcyon's mission, nor was there one when I trapped the Convergence in Framer's Valley and watched you disperse its Energy." He smiled faintly. "Sometimes one has to play the long odds."

Ahead, a blur of black motion caught Ras' attention. The Thromus Convergence screamed toward the Energy Origin on the horizon. As the orb struck the spire the world fell utterly silent. Ras began to say something to Dayus, but no noise came out.

A blinding light erupted from the Energy Origin, robbing Ras of his sight as well as his hearing.

The Kingfisher violently swung underneath Ras' feet, sending him falling backwards and tumbling into nothingness until he landed on something hard.

The light faded. Ras could see the bridge return to his vision and Dayus struggling to right *The Kingfisher* as he held onto the sideways controls.

A singular sound grew from outside the ship: Screams joining in with a beautiful counterpoint melody. Ras hauled himself up to see the Energy Origin shattered into thousands of shards. The Thromus Convergence's Energy leaked out, its essence flowing into the broken base of the Origin. A ticking clock now hung over all of Imago.

As *The Kingfisher* flew by, a lone figure stood at the center of the wreckage.

STANDING NEXT TO THE DARK PURPLE SPIRE of the Time Origin, Ras stared up at the tall structure amidst the scattered remains of *The Winnower*. He had prepared as best he could, outfitting himself with everything he might need for a place called Elsewhere.

Even with his KnackVisions, grapple gun, wrench, and Tink's glider, he still felt woefully unprepared. He patted his satchel with the provisions his mother had packed, wondering how long they would last.

Emma had run out of tears long ago. She looked up at the dead Origin, then down to her son. "Where did Dayus go?"

"He said he had to find something in the wreckage," Ras said, looking through the large pieces of *The Winnower*, hoping he wouldn't spot Dr. Lupava.

"So, what's on the other side?" Emma asked.

"Eventually, Dad. Callie too…and *Dixie!*" Ras exclaimed. "She overloaded too!" He ran a hand through his hair. "Millions of people, counting on me to bring them home."

"You might run into your grandfather," Emma said. "He overloaded well before you were born."

Ras looked at his mother. She was worn down. Even though her family was nearby, she looked so alone. "Are you going to be all right?"

"I guess my hope is that we'll all be, before this is over," Emma said, placing a hand on Ras' shoulder. "I want you to know I'd go with you if I could."

"I know you would, mom. But you, Grandpa Cornelius, and whoever else is willing have to oversee Atmo landing safely, and eventually the people from the Burrows will have to free Illoria from Time."

"It's going to take a while to mend those fences," Emma said. "It was a miracle your father persuaded Acerbis to help *Verdant*. He figured that would have been more helpful than being with you on your trip." She gave a sad smile. "Although I could tell where he really wanted to be."

Dayus came traipsing out of the wreckage with a sphere held high.

"What's this?" Ras asked, eyeing the familiar item as Dayus entered the clearing.

"The compass of *The Brass Fox*," Dayus said. "Let's just say it'll come in handy in Elsewhere."

Ras took the familiar piece of his old dashboard and clutched it in his right hand. Callie's typewriter bracelet clanked against it, urging him not to give up. He walked toward the Origin. "After you, I guess."

"That's not how this works, Erasmus." Dayus said, pulling out a small brass container at the end of a chain around his neck.

"You're not coming with me?" Ras asked, eyebrows lifting.

"Not like this," Dayus said. "This vessel has served me well for too long."

"Vessel?" Emma asked.

"This body," Dayus said, looking at his hands. "But you can't go into Elsewhere without my Blessing, and it is not meant for me to go in on my own. I don't know if an Imagoite has ever received a full Blessing. Please be wise with it."

Dayus turned to Emma. "Madam Veir, I do sincerely apologize for any frustration or trouble I may have caused you through the years."

"It's all right, Dayus," Emma said, nodding.

"I would recommend making our goodbyes quick," Dayus said. "Time is of the essence, and The Reclaimer must fulfill his true purpose: to bring the world back to its natural state, without Origins or stopgap solutions of the like."

"How am I supposed to know how to do that?" Ras asked. "If you're not coming with me—"

"I'll be there," Dayus said, pointing to the Time Origin. "Things are...*different* in Elsewhere. You will see me again."

That much was a comfort to Ras. However, the load of responsibility nearly overwhelmed him. Why did so much have to come down to the decisions he made? "Just, before I go. .where did the idea of The Reclaimer even come from?" he asked. "Please, just tell me that."

Dayus nodded. "I came up with it," he said. "I perpetuated the hope that someday things would be put straight, Erasmus. A hope that reached beyond me. Beyond the Caretakers. I never imagined the extent of the role you would have played, but you have done a magnificent job. But your work isn't finished."

"How did you know things would happen like this?" Ras asked.

"I knew Thromus well before he ferried the souls from Imago," Dayus said. "He is too prideful to imagine our defeat meaning anything other than victory for himself."

"So this all was some sort of match between you two?" Ras asked. "And both of you think of me as your pawn?"

"You are more than that," Dayus said, placing a hand on Ras' shoulder. "So much more. You have been given an opportunity to set things right, but we must hurry to make good on it. More will be explained once you are in Elsewhere." He gave a tired smile. "I would recommend saying farewell to your mother now."

Ras nodded, unsure of how he felt about the fabricated role of The Reclaimer. The title had to originate from somewhere, so it might as well have been from someone he knew, he supposed. He turned and gave his mother a prolonged hug. "I won't come back without Dad."

"Don't say that," Emma said, squeezing him tight until she trembled slightly. "You'll find your way home. You always do."

He released the embrace, giving his mother a kiss on the forehead. Not being able to bear looking at his mother putting on a brave face for more than a moment, he turned to Dayus. "What is Elsewhere going to be like?"

"It'll be easier to understand as you experience it," Dayus said. "Now, please do not be alarmed by what transpires, and for the love of Aether do not lose this." He held up a brass tube about the size of a thumb, smiled, then held it to his lips. "Erasmus Veir, I offer you my Blessing, fully and without lien or loan. My work in Imago is completed. May the wind be at your back." He took a deep breath, exhaled slowly, and his eyes rolled up. His lanky body began to collapse unceremoniously.

"Dayus!" Ras quickly moved to catch and ease Dayus down to the ground. He felt for a pulse. Nothing. The mysterious man was gone, giving his life to protect those around him, like the Caretaker of Acerbis had.

"Did he just die?" Emma asked.

"I don't know," Ras said, reaching down and collecting the brass tube. The container felt warm to the touch. The green glass end of it glowed, ebbing slowly in and out. *Dayus?* He had to trust that he would see his friend again, somehow.

Putting the chain around his neck, Ras tucked the Blessing under his shirt. With the tube against his chest, he felt an odd sense of peace amidst the calamity. He opened his arms for one last hug from his mother, then turned and faced the Time Origin.

There was so much he needed to know about what lay ahead. Rescuing everyone from The Great Overload was a daunting enough task, but how would he stop Thromus from choking the life out of Imago if he could even make it back? How could he fix the Energy Origin? Too many questions, not enough time.

At best, the plan felt ill-advised, hastily crafted, and short sighted. It had to work.

With arm outstretched, he took one step forward toward Callie and straight into Elsewhere.

Ras and Callie will return in
The Elsewhere Knight.